THE SHINING MOUNTAINS

THE SHINING MOUNTAINS

A NOVEL

ALIX CHRISTIE

High Road Books | Albuquerque

HIGH
ROAD

High Road Books is an imprint of the University of New Mexico Press.

Library of Congress Cataloging-in-Publication Data
Names: Christie, Alix, author.
Title: The Shining Mountains: a novel / Alix Christie.
Description: Albuquerque: University of New Mexico Press, 2023.
Identifiers: LCCN 2022019650 (print) | LCCN 2022019651 (e-book) |
ISBN 9780826364654 (cloth) | ISBN 9780826364661 (e-pub)
Subjects: LCSH: McDonald, Angus, 1816-1889—Fiction. | Nez Percé Indians—Wars, 1877—
Fiction. | LCGFT: Novels.
Classification: LCC PS3603.H7523 S55 2023 (print) | LCC PS3603.H7523 (e-book) | DDC
813/.6—dc23/eng/20220516
LC record available at https://lccn.loc.gov/2022019650
LC e-book record available at https://lccn.loc.gov/2022019651

Founded in 1889, the University of New Mexico sits on the traditional homelands of the Pueblo of Sandia. The original peoples of New Mexico—Pueblo, Navajo, and Apache—since time immemorial have deep connections to the land and have made significant contributions to the broader community statewide. We honor the land itself and those who remain stewards of this land throughout the generations and also acknowledge our committed relationship to Indigenous peoples. We gratefully recognize our history.

Cover photograph: courtesy of Jeff Finley on Unsplash
Maps by Morgan Hite, Hesperus Arts, Smithers, BC (www.hesperus-wild.org)
Designed by Felicia Cedillos
Composed in Chapparal Pro 10.5/14.25

for my mother

"I made enemies among the whites,
because I corrected them about their stories."

—DUNCAN MCDONALD, JANUARY 1928

Cast of Characters

In Strathconon and Dingwall, Ross-shire
    Donald and Christina McDonald, the parents
    Duncan McDonald, the elder brother, and his wife, Ann
    Maggie and Marion McDonald, the younger sisters

HUDSON'S BAY COMPANY FUR TRADERS

Heads of Columbia District, based at different times at Fort Vancouver
    Chief Factor John McLoughlin
    Chief Factor Peter Skene Ogden
    Chief Factor James Douglas (later first governor
       of British Columbia)

At Fort Colvile, 1838
    Archibald McDonald, Chief Factor, great-uncle of Angus McDonald
    Jane Klyne McDonald, his mixed-blood wife

At Fort Hall and environs, 1840–1846
    Richard Grant, Chief Trader
    Young George Simpson, mixed-blood son of
       HBC chief George Simpson

Fur trappers and mountain men
    Baptiste "Coquin" Rascale, HBC trapper,
       métis father of Catherine Baptiste
    Joe Meek, free trapper, later colonist and US marshal

At Fort Connah, 1847–1852

    Angus McDonald, Trader

    Catherine Baptiste, his Nez Perce-French-Iroquois wife,
        their four children

    François Finlay, employee and '49er miner

1852 onward

    Michel Ogden, mixed-blood son of Peter S. Ogden and Julia Rivet/
        Revais (Salish/French)

    Angelique Ogden, Michel's wife, half-sister of Catherine Baptiste

1867–1872

    Duncan McDonald, trader, son of Angus and Catherine

    Camille Dupree, clerk

At Fort Colvile, 1852–1870

    Angus McDonald, Chief Trader

    His wife, Catherine, and children, John, Christina, Duncan,
        Donald, Annie, Maggie

    James McKenzie, clerk

    Joseph Morelle, teamster

Other traders

    Andrew Pambrun (Fort Nez Perce)

    François Payette (Fort Boisé)

NATIVE AMERICANS

Nez Perce Tribe (Nimíipuu)

Tookpemah or Alpowai band (Kaix-kaix-Koose/Clean Water,
Clearwater in English)

    Chief Flint Necklace (Apash Wyakaikt), also known as
        Chief Looking Glass

    Margaret de Naie, his aunt or cousin

    Looking Glass the younger (Allalimya Takanin), his son, later chief

    Bird Alighting (Peopeo Tholekt), a warrior

    Catherine Baptiste, daughter of Margaret de Naie and
        Baptiste Rascale

Angelique Bonaparte, Catherine's half-sister

Elizabeth (Kyuka), Catherine's half-sister

Red Ox (Skulp-yu-e), Catherine's half-brother

Lam'tama band (Salmon River)

Chief Eagle from the Light (Tipyehlene Kaupu),
cousin of Catherine Baptiste

Chief White Bird (Peopeo Hihih), post-1861

Other chiefs

Chief Red Owl (Koolkool Snehee, Nez Perce/Salish),
Clearwater band

Chief Joseph (Heinmot Tooyalakekt, Thunder Traveling over
the Mountain), Wallowa band

Chief Lawyer (Hallalhotsoot, Shadow of the Mountain)
Christianized chief near Lapwai

Skúlepi Tribe (Kettle, Later Designated As Colville)

Chief Bighead (1838)

Chief Pierre Jerome (1850s)

Yakama Tribe

Chief Kamiakin

Chief Owhi

Qualchan, son of Owhi

Pend d'Oreille (Ql'ispé) Tribe

Chief Alexander (No Horses) until 1868

Chief Michelle (Many Grizzly Bears),
succeeded Chief Alexander

Antille, second chief

Red Horn, a hunter

Quil-see (Red Sleep), his sister

Bitterroot Salish Tribe

Chief Victor (Slem-cry-cre, Easy-to-get-a-herd-of-horses/
Many Horses), until 1870

Chief Charlo (Slem-Hak-kah, Claws of the Small Grizzly),
    his son and successor
Second chief Arlee (Henri/Red Night), Salish/Nez Perce

MISSIONARIES

Marcus Whitman, Presbyterian, Waiilatpu, Oregon Territory
Joseph Joset, Society of Jesus (Jesuit), various missions
Anthony Ravalli, Society of Jesus (Jesuit), various missions

MISSOULA RESIDENTS

Telesphore Jacques "Jack" DeMers, founder of Frenchtown
Robert McGregor Baird, clerk and teacher
Andrew Hammond, clerk and lumberman
Lydia Wood, schoolteacher

THE SHINING MOUNTAINS

BOOK 1

PRO PELLE CUTEM
(A SKIN FOR A SKIN)

The Oregon Country, 1838–1849

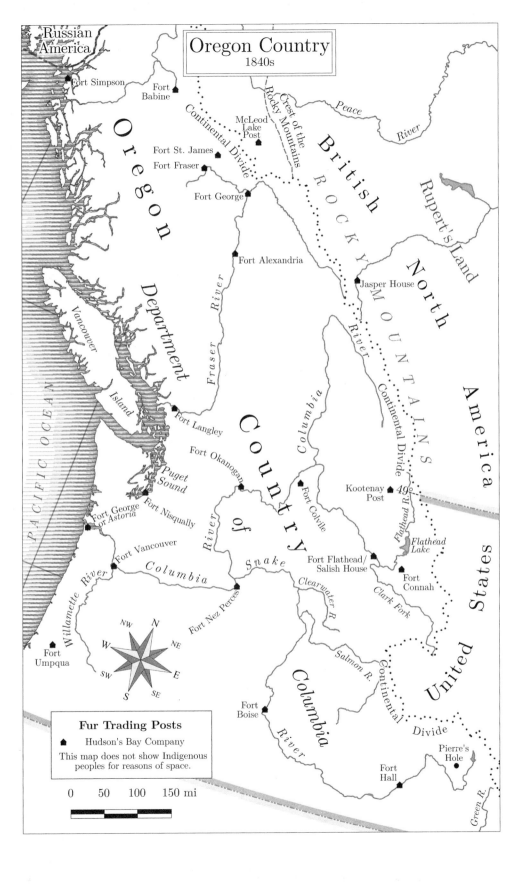

Oregon Country
1840s

Russian America

Fort Simpson

Fort Babine

Continental Divide

Crest of the Rocky Mountains

Peace River

McLeod Lake Post

British

Fort St. James

Fort Fraser

Fort George

North

Fort Alexandria

Jasper House

Rupert's Land

Oregon

ROCKY

Athabasca River

America

Fraser River

Columbia

Continental Divide

Department

Vancouver

Fort Langley

MOUNTAINS

Island

Fort Okanogan

Country

Puget Sound

Kootenay Post

49°

PACIFIC OCEAN

Fort George or Astoria

Fort Nisqually

Flathead R.

Flathead Lake

Fort Colvile

United

Fort Vancouver

of

Snake

Fort Flathead/ Salish House

Fort Connah

Willamette River

Columbia

River

Clearwater R.

Clark Fork

States

Fort Nez Perces

NW N

W   NE

Salmon R.

Continental Divide

Fort Umpqua

SW E

S   SE

Columbia

Fort Boise

River

Divide

Pierre's Hole

Fur Trading Posts

⬟ Hudson's Bay Company

This map does not show Indigenous peoples for reasons of space.

Fort Hall

Green R.

0   50   100   150 mi

"The American claim [to Oregon] is by the right of our manifest destiny to overspread and possess the whole of the continent which Providence has given us for the development of the great experiment of liberty and . . . self-government entrusted to us."

—JOHN L. O'SULLIVAN, *NEW YORK MORNING NEWS*, DECEMBER 27, 1845

CHAPTER 1

PIERRE'S HOLE (PRESENT-DAY IDAHO)

1840

SHE WATCHES THE men from the shadow of the lodge as they play for silver coins. They play not with sticks but little pictures—throwing them down then scooping them up again, roaring with joy or fury. One with sunflower hair fakes a cough and slips another picture out from underneath his shirt. The other *soyapo* trapper sees it too. He shouts and tries to stand but he's too full of drink. Grunts fly from his lips as he falls back; a man from her own village slaps his chest and falls down laughing.

Catherine Baptiste laughs, too, quietly to herself, at their stupidity. She grabs her little brother and moves, weaving through the tumult of the trading rendezvous. She can't even see the sky for smoke from all the campfires, thick as stars across the nighttime valley. Tipis and trappers' tents rise to the pines that edge the hills; the smells of roasting meat bring juices to her mouth. Alexander drags behind her, he, too, licking his small lips.

They look for their father from camp to camp, stopping to watch a chained wolf on its hind legs straining for a lump of heart and then a round of stamping dancers in their feather anklets. Each group has its own section of the valley: their father's Company in the middle; the Bostons to the south; their mother's people to the north beside the willow cover of the feeder streams. She expects to find Baptiste upright and prancing, recounting his tales to the half-starved men like him who've dropped out of the mountains desperate to see another living soul. But he's not with the white men. Here he squats in a *nimíipuu* camp, a battered stump of a man much shorter than the others. Even so he's always moving, grinning, showing his bad teeth, right hand wiggling like a snake. Catherine's cousin Eagle from the Light is here too, acting big, hollowing his cheeks to impress the white men hunkered in the firelit ring.

She knows better than to interrupt her father in the middle of a story. Suddenly Baptiste leaps. "Ai-yah!" He mimes the mountain lion, brown eyes shining in his rough chapped face. For all the lankness of his long dark hair, the scar along his jaw, she thinks him handsome. He's Iroquois and French and can sniff scat at a great distance. "I seen it *sur montagne*, so big!" His muscled arms fly out. His daughter glances at the men who watch, the traders from his Company: one old, one young, both hairy as the beaver. She gauges coolly how they see him. His speech is comical, a hash of French and Mohawk, Chinook-wawa. They call him "Coquin"—rascal—after all. But they are riveted, it seems, and she feels pride that he can hold their gaze so tightly.

She needs to ride up to the Salish camp. Baptiste won't mind, so long as he knows. Soon everyone will leave this place, each group upon its different path. Her stomach tightens with excitement and a touch of fear. She's old enough at last to help him trap, and not ride with her mother to the plains. Soon it will be time to say farewell. But that's not why she wants to ride up to that camp. The truth is she has never seen a Black Robe.

None of them have—which is why the Bitterroot Salish and Q̓lispé have come in such great numbers to the rendezvous this year. They'll take these new priests from the sunrise to their homes. It's said they'll bring the white god's power to their people. Catherine wants to see if they look powerful—if the strong medicine the Black Robes' god possesses can be seen on their faces, or touched, or felt. If she doesn't get up there soon, she'll miss it all.

"When," she finally darts in, pulling at her father's sleeve. "When do we leave?"

Baptiste blinks at his daughter. She's sixteen summers old, born in spring like a foal and, like a foal, for many years all limbs and awkward speed. Now, suddenly, she looks much older. "*Après demain*," he says, pulling her into the circle, Alexander dragging behind. "You know my girl," he says to Eagle from the Light, who leans toward her.

"I see *Lam'tama* eyes," her cousin says, approval in his voice. He names their grandmother's band, nimíipuu of the Salmon River canyon. Despite herself Catherine stands taller, though she can't see much resemblance. Her cousin's face is long while hers is rounder—still, they share the same square jaw and kinship with a chief is a great honor. She nods and glances sidelong at Baptiste. Now can she go?

But he's turning to the white men, hand still clamped upon her arm. "Gentlemen," he says: "My daughter and son."

The old trader is covered in gray fur, like moss. The younger one tries to stand, lips red as a boil in a nest of brown hair that covers his whole face and twitches as he pushes out some words—nimíipuu words. All Catherine can think is that it's like watching a dog talk. She covers her own mouth to hide her laughter.

"T'ac haláxp," he's saying, and the man beside her cousin points up at the crust of moon and grins.

"T'ac kuéewit," her cousin responds gravely. "Kuéewit is evening. Haláxp, afternoon."

"Ah. Many thanks." The trader takes a paper from his vest, a stick, and scratches for a moment. She stares frankly while his face turns down. Never has she seen such fur upon men's faces. This is the same one who watched them racing earlier, she on her roan against her cousin's buckskin and the Bostons' stocky horses. He yelled as they barreled past. Afterward she noticed how he looked at her. This is the first summer men look at her like that.

"Papa," she says, shaking his hand from her arm. If Alexander falls asleep, she'll have to tie him to her horse.

"Kitalah wants her mother," her cousin says mockingly. Catherine cuts him with her eyes. She's as powerful as he, more powerful perhaps. She has two names, two sides, two pieces to her being, while he has only one. She's Catherine from her father and the Black Robes from the eastern lands from which he comes. She's Tipyelenah Kitalah from the Clearwater village of the nimíipuu, who the Frenchmen call Nez Percé, though everyone knows they never pierced their noses. She doesn't know what Catherine means, but in her mother's tongue she is the Eagle Rising Up. Then Baptiste lets her go and she can breathe, shaking the white man's odor from her nose.

The three peaks they call the Three Teats rise like pillars of salt to the east; even in the dark she sees them glowing. It gives her a strange feeling, to see them for the first time and think that it could also be the last. There will be danger all along their journey, her father has warned. It'll be long and hot all down the Colorado. "Long time ago, beaver plugged up every stream here," Baptiste says, but now their mountains are trapped out. They'll trap a long way to the south, maybe even to the sea. Catherine can't picture what this means, the sea.

There are crowds around the little man who wears the Black Robe to his toes. He's a most ugly man: short and with a mean face like a hawk. His long nose hooks, his mouth draws down. He calls to them in French: He brings them Jesus, Son of God. The people cluster toward him, trying to touch his robe. "The Lord Jesus died for you," he calls.

Catherine feels the breath snort from her nose. It makes no sense. God isn't dead. The Father Spirit made this earth; it listens to him still. She doesn't need to listen to this Black Robe. She reins the roan away and with a kick rides back down toward the fires of her own people. She'll put the boy back in his mother's arms and ride into the world of fur: a thrilling, unknown world of flashing waters, thrashing beasts, her father's Company—and her.

ANGUS MCDONALD BARELY slept the night before, afraid he'd packed the horses wrong, forgot to clean his gun or shine his boots: a thousand other ways he might have failed. But now, at last, he's here. Two years— two years!—of drudgery before he wrangled free, escaped his uncle's farm. And finally he's trading with red Indians for fur. He squats among them, sucks their pipe and hands it round. He feels his face on fire and does his best to keep his eyes from shining. He knows he's here to work: these are the men he'll deal with. He'll have to learn to bargain hard. But even so it's hard to stay aloof, so brightly does this fire burn, and the brandy, and the song. And then it comes to him: why should I? For after everything that has gone wrong, this feels entirely right.

This afternoon when they arrived, like some medieval army—all banners and clatter and beasts—he and Captain Grant set out to meet the trappers who will swap their pelts for goods. A haze hung over the bowl of Pierre's Hole, but even so Angus counted hundreds, thousands of people. And speckling the far hills nearly black, the Natives' horse herds. He brushed his beard in the glass hung on a branch and his new Chief Trader laughed, though not unkindly.

"They'll not be looking at your teeth, lad, I assure you." Grant raised one hoary eyebrow. It won't be young Angus McDonald they see—eager, untested, brave, a trifle vain—but a representative of the Company of Adventurers Trading into Hudson's Bay. Angus thinks now it was that one word—*adventurers*—that cinched it, when in panic his father and brother cast about for a way to save his hide. He resisted, of course—he was no poacher, though the laird would see the thing that way. But they bundled him onto a ship, and he clung to that word through the Atlantic gales, the northern ice, the months of loneliness. As if he were only hibernating all that time, like the massive gray-backed bear he saw that first long winter. Now adventure is at hand; he, too, wears the trader's bright red waistband. As soon as their brigade arrived a roar went up among the waiting men, all of them trappers for the Hudson's Bay.

"Well, fellows," Grant hollered, "I've seen perkier mules, and that's the truth. It looks like you could use some sousing."

Amid the cheers Angus eyed the height and breadth of each man: some tall, some squat, most dark with long black hair, part Indian at least, all wearing stained fringed buckskin, shirts that hadn't seen a soap in years. He thought of Big Michel, the tall French Cree who steered his boat the whole way down the Columbia. Angus thought him magnificent, that mixed-blood voyageur: powerfully muscled, graceful, seemingly fearless. The whole summer it took to get from Hudson's Bay to his great-uncle's place at Fort Colvile in the Oregon Country, Angus was taken by the voyageurs' songs, throats beating out the time to flashing paddles, stories they told in the night in their strange mix of tongues. They were as wild and beautiful as this continent itself, the vast overpowering spread of peaks and forests rushing past on either side. And now here he finds the same strange crew, a riotous mix seemingly sprouted from this very ground, only these are trappers and not steersmen. He should have seen it sooner, he thinks: this whole Company is French and Indian across its base, with just a thin white scrape of icing at the top, which is the Scots.

Captain Grant is a Highlander, too, from Argyll, though he isn't captain of anything as far as Angus can see. It's just a mark of honor. What Grant is, is a widower, a veteran of more winters than Angus cares to imagine in the howling frozen north, before this posting to the arid southern desert of Fort Hall. Shipped to the very edge of Hell, the Chief Trader observed drily when they met on the boat from Fort Colvile to Fort Boisé. Their job, apparently, to hold the Company's southeastern flank against the damned Yankee trappers—not just the Missouri firms but the lousy freemen who have no allegiance to a body but themselves. These are the vermin they'll find at the rendezvous, competing for the diminishing beaver with their own men, the Chief Trader added when not a week later he gave the order to set out.

Now at the fire Angus drifts. He hears distant drumming and thinks hazily he should have brought his bagpipes. They'd match these reedy flutes, the rising, falling voices. If only Duncan and Maggie could see him now, and Father and Mother. What letters he will write, to light their Dingwall nights. He watches the faces and hands, the lean handsome bodies, shining in the heat of summer and the fire. He'll note their gestures, their habits, practice the words he's already learned. The little trapper called Baptiste barks and leaps. Buffalo steaks sizzle and Angus wolfs the steaming meat. His body and mind are still stunned by the wonder of it all. Such a country they traversed to get here: how these jagged peaks soar, scraping at the sky. The hills of Ross-shire can't hold a candle to this range that cleaves the continent in two. His heart hasn't stopped hammering the whole three days—and not just because they ran into Shoshone the first day out. He still smells the scorching needled understory where they waited to be murdered, hands slick on their pistols— only to marvel at how smoothly Captain Grant turned those warriors into buyers, eagerly fingering the knives and awls and copper pots. Angus McDonald got a bona fide master class in the fur business right there in a wide spot on the Snake River trail, the way he sees it.

Grant made a beeline for a Nez Perce camp, though, on this first night. This tribe are the greatest of hunters, he said, furnishers of the most valuable pelts: lynx and mink and cougar and elk. And buffalo. Angus has yet to chase that mighty beast but he, too, is a hunter and his fingers itch to try. The Company trapper Baptiste is cavorting like a Hogmanay acrobat until he stops as though his spring's wound down. Two youngsters hang at the edge of the light and he plucks at the older one, a girl. "My daughter and son," he says proudly. They shrink—both dark, but fine-featured, nothing like their cussed-looking father—like any child thrust into a ring of judging elder eyes. Something in the way the girl twists reminds Angus of his sister and it pierces him: how terribly he misses his gaggle of brothers and sisters, racing up the creeks and *braes*. Perhaps that's why he swelled all day with happiness, he thinks: the place is heaving with families. The gimlet-eyed mountain men don't draw him half as much as the Natives in their clans, their bands: their grannies, babes and mothers, and throngs of children screeching as they run around. He watched them gamble, wrestle, race their horses, laughing, tossing what were surely insults in the teasing way that families do. The only kin he's seen in two whole years are Uncle Archibald and Aunt Jenny's little brood. Instinctively he bends his long self forward, searching for some words. Archibald said he needed only a few phrases, but Angus, as always, begged to differ. All last winter he applied himself to the Salish tongue and the Sahaptin spoken by the Nez Perce and other plateau tribes.

When he stands and forms the words, he hears one laugh. If at first you don't succeed, his gram said: try, try again. The young Nez Perce who corrects him is courteous, at least. Captain Grant rouses himself to say he'll roll up now, though Angus ought to stick around. A fur-trading rendezvous is a young man's business. Proof comes a short while later, when three Yankee trappers stumble in, hollering hallo at Baptiste. They're drunk as hell, but one with a bullet for a head, big, pouched eyes, and a flaming red beard manages to plant his bowlegs and slur, "Well, here's a new pup," and seize his hand in a crunching grip.

"Angus McDonald."

"Jesus, can't they think of anything but Mac?" The fellow grins, hoping for applause, but the others are already cozying up to Baptiste's jug. "Joe Meek, free trapper," he goes on. "Care to join us in our great debauch?"

Debauch! The word brings a grin to Angus's lips. "Who could resist so elegant an invitation?" This mountain man might look thick, but clearly isn't. Over the next few hours Angus hears such a fountain of ha'penny locutions he feels compelled to ask, "Where on earth did you learn all that?" Meek pulls Angus to him by the scruff of the neck. "Same place you will, marooned as we are, hurled by the icy hand of fate into our isolated caves." He grins, looking pleased with himself. Trappers mostly work alone or in pairs, he explains, stashing their books dog-eared and waterlogged in winter shelters for the next poor slob to find. Not junk, of course, but the great authors: Byron, Cooper, Scott.

"After my own heart," Angus marvels. "*If I should meet thee, after years . . .*"

"Oh Lord." Meek turns toward his fellows. "A regular minstrel we have here." Only then does Angus notice that the fellow is missing his right ear, replaced by a bright ring of red scar like the wattle on a cock.

"No gawking, now." Meek whacks him gently. "You should have seen the bear."

Thus, in the way of these things, they're pledged to a shooting match before the night is out. The next morning, even with a wicked pain in his brain, Angus doesn't regret it. Marksmanship, after all, is his great skill. Sardine tins on a distant stump are all he needs, and Hoolahan, his rifle, more precious even than his pipes: thirty-two inches of gleaming Baker barrel, accurate to at least a hundred yards.

Meek goes first and knocks the thing to kingdom come. A new tin is procured. Angus squeezes off the shot, hitting with such clean propulsion that the tin spins once and wobbles, but stays standing. He re-primes the pan and blasts it clean away. Meek is staring down the distance, thick lips pursed. He shakes his head, announces deadpan: "Game's over, fellas. No contest here." When he turns to Angus, he grips him hard by either bicep. "Before you know it, he will have us all in skirts."

Angus laughs and slips Meek's grip. Slick as an otter he twists and pins one beefy arm behind the trapper's back. He hears the hiss of pain and eases off. "Ye needn't fear it, Joe," he breathes. "I much prefer them on a lass." Not since he shot that stag up on Ben Wyvis has he felt this good.

CHAPTER 2

IN THE BEGINNING, Hunyawat, the Creator, dropped a rope down from the sky world. All the strands as it unraveled were the different religions. Catherine's mother Margaret told that story when they first beheld the Black Robe. Now as the bands disperse, each leaving for a different land, this rope returns to Catherine's mind. Her mother, too, is straight and tall, a pole against the bright blue sky as the nimíipuu ride one way and she and Baptiste another. Her heart pounds in her throat to see them go.

Her sister Kyuka rides to buffalo with Margaret and her new man, their new baby in the cradleboard, and something inside Catherine burns. She tries to stamp it out. Her sister can sense any hint of envy. Kyuka, who some call Elizabeth the Witch. She entered the world first, with power. Catherine is blessed with other gifts, her mother assures her. The problem is she doesn't know yet what they are. She watches until they disappear, burning their figures in her mind. So many fall in battle on the plains. The thought buzzes inside like the song of the striped wild bees that hide in rents of mountain rock. It's a mournful sound, and suddenly she wonders whether she too will return. Each season friends do not come back: those who join the dead do not return.

Her father's watching as if he reads her thoughts. "A nice hat from the first biter you catch." Beneath his grin his eyes are shrewd. "Prettier than some *vieux bufle, non?*" She shakes herself and smiles her thanks. Only a few dozen families are heading south, mixed Native and French like her own, plus a few white trappers for the Company. Baptiste brings his new wife and baby and her half-brother Alexander, six years old. Together they're safer, he says; they'll join a larger group soon. At the first swift mountain river she strips to her undershift and moves the saddle high on the withers, ties Alexander on, and plunges in, keeping the roan downstream. She holds the rope loosely, gasping and stroking hard to keep clear of his hooves. The men build rafts but she knows her mother wouldn't trust the children to such flimsy things. When they scramble to the shore, she laughs with the other girls at their skin, the flaming color of wild rose, the wet fabric showing off every bump and contour. There aren't any young men here to peek at the new breasts that lift the sticky cloth, though there's one at home whose eyes she wouldn't mind.

After two more rivers they arrive at the gathering place to join the main expedition. Already this land is drier, hotter, nearly treeless. There are scores of horses and nearly a hundred white men congregated at the wooden house, their skin burnt where it's not covered with hair. Some are French but most are Bostons, watching the women as they arrive. Baptiste warns her to stay close to Dalpier, an old friend he's trapped with many times, if by some evil chance he isn't near. Her joking father is all business now: they must get meat for the long journey. He and his wife go off with a group to hunt, leaving her to mind her brother. It's not so bad: there's a river and many children and others her own age, nearly men and women now. She's to feed the children fish and camas, mend the ropes that hold her father's beaver traps. Before leaving he takes her by the chin and tells her firmly that he's only lived this long because he never stops his eyes from moving side to side. Catherine stands on a ridge above the bend of the small river, scanning as he instructs, but all she sees are antelope and looping creatures of the air.

Days pass and the shadows shift, and she thinks it must be the season of the salmon's return to the high rivers of her country. Here many weeks' ride south it's still hot, and they lie in the shallow water cooling their skin. Currant bushes graze the water, bent like fishing poles with their burdens of red and yellow and black. They're splashing and laughing when a boy spies shadows in the underbrush and they slither out and run back to camp. "Enemies!" the boy hisses and the children scatter to hide. She holds her breath, hand clamped on Alexander's mouth, until her chest is burning.

A thundering of hooves and yells breaks out across the water as the raiders whip the horses to stampede the herd. The horses are neighing and kicking up dust when the trappers' leader, a tall red-headed Boston, shouts and lunges for the trailing halter ropes. Catherine sees her father's moon-colored horse and without thinking pushes her brother down and darts across the stream. She swings up, clutching a hunk of mane, digging her heels in hard. "Take 'em!" the leader shouts, and she bends low, slipping to the far side of its flank where bullets won't find her. One finds the American, though: a bloom of red shreds his whole neck and he falls into the water just behind her. She's all nerve and sinew, clinging to the mane with both hands, leading what beasts will follow across the stream.

Then Dalpier's there, pulling her off and whisking her behind a log. "Head down," he hisses. The sudden silence is too sharp; it's a ruse. The enemy—who knows who they might be, how many—is creeping toward the camp, knives in teeth, to finish them off. Her skin prickles. She knows from stories Baptiste tells that they've planned it well, waiting for the hunters to move off. She sees their chief then, on all fours like a dog along the creek, warriors crouched and shuffling behind him. He's naked but for a headdress made of feathers, ermine, horns.

"See how they creep." A black-skinned trapper crouches beside her. Dalpier swings his gun to load it and it catches her above the eye. She wipes away the blood. The Negro whispers, "You're Indian, you know what he'll do. What do you think?"

The chief on all fours has a black heart drawn on his chest; he turns his head from side to side as if to sniff them out. She thinks as hard and fast as she can.

"The fight depends on his life. If you kill the chief, we still—"

The two men fire at the same time. The chief's head jerks back as two balls pierce it, one in the center of the forehead. And he sinks down, as if for a nap, his dark blood swirling in the stream. His warriors mutter among themselves and seemingly lose heart. They pull his legs, tugging him to them, crawl backward, and withdraw.

That night under an orange moon their whole camp flees. Their leaders are dead and half the livestock lie arrowed or hacked. Catherine takes her brother and some meat from the rack, looking back at the grasses stiff with blood. How heavy and silent the place now seems. She shudders. She's heard of such battles and now she, too, knows that life is a flickering thing. They turn their faces, their weary horses, into the night. Several miles away the enemy is camped and they can hear the loud wailing staining the clear air.

She can't sleep the next few days for fear Baptiste won't find them when he and the hunters return. They move steadily south and west and in her small French she tries to tell the black trapper. He takes a stick and draws a map in the dust that's in their eyes and throats all the time now they've left the river behind. Her father will come to this big wooden house, he says, where everybody knows to go. They arrive and wait, trading the fish they've dried for meal to mix with water. She sings to Alexander, a crooning tale about a man who strays too far and is returned home by his wife, both of them now turned to swallows. "I pray papa, too, will fly back, straight to our lodge," she whispers in her little brother's hair. On the fifth day they see the dust and their father's shape in that cloud is unmistakable: his hair tied in a knot, his sharp nose streaked either side with yellow. The relief makes Catherine dizzy, almost sick. She doesn't know this country—where to find roots, which plants will sour her stomach, which are good. All alone, she's feared the looks of the white trappers.

Baptiste's face is slicked with paint for war, but those who attacked them have long since disappeared. Dalpier tells him how bravely she fought, how she leapt to save the herd. "That's my girl." Her father squeezes her face and looks into her eyes, holding her tightly as Alexander runs to his mother. Baptiste, too, has felt fear—or perhaps he feels this new fear of hers. For the first time there's a sense in her of strangeness, of apartness: she isn't part of this land, she isn't cherished and nourished by it. It isn't the mother from which she comes.

This feeling only grows more powerful as they move further south. The world is paler, hotter. From far away they see the salty lake, a huge expanse of shining pan. They start to trap the streams that feed the Colorado, a huge brown flood. Catherine is not impressed. Beyond a fringe of green the land around is barren, dreary. She wants to be home again, though by now at home it's nearly winter, while here it's as warm as summer at Big Hole. Their guide is a one-eyed Spanish Indian who reads the starry skies the way her people read the rocks and grass. In the pathless waste above, he makes the silent lights his roads, the space between them valleys. He takes them up and then straight down a cliff, a sheer so rude a Bighorn would balk. Two horses break their legs on the way down but it's a gift. For they're shot and skinned and serve to make a dinner and a light canoe. And so they cross.

The next day they push deeper into the river and up its brush-filled streams. The beaver they start finding are immense, old and unmolested in their dams. With joy the trappers bait their metal jaws and wait. She's to work with her father now, pulling out the fat old things. The first time she grabs one's tail, it flails in her hands and she half-drops it, shrieking. Baptiste laughs. "I thought it was dead," she says.

"You have to club it sometimes." He sloshes toward her with a cudgel he's carried all this way. She looks at it and then the thrashing beaver in the trap. She's taken deer and elk, but never close enough to see the rolling of their eyes. This creature suffers now; it moans and twists and bites its leg. She raises the club and whispers, "Hush," and "thank you for this gift," and lets it fall. The power courses through her arms. Her father nods as the skull cracks and the animal expires. Its suffering is over now. Baptiste shows her how to release the trap and then they drag it out. He teaches her to cut the pelt from tail to vent beneath the chin and peel it back. She fleshes it and pegs it out to dry. Her fingers stroke the soft, slick golden fur and she breathes thanks, exultant.

THE HUDSON'S BAY Company covers this continent like the heather that blankets Strathconon in summer, Angus writes to his family. From that eponymous Bay clear across three thousand miles of Rupert's Land, then plunging south to where he is, in the last grinding molar of the Rockies, which the Native people call the Shining Mountains. The Oregon Country, his masters call this whole southwestern chunk, encompassing the drainages of the Columbia and Clearwater and Snake, west of the continental divide. He doesn't know for sure, but he thinks there are about two hundred forts and depots across North America where the Baymen meet the Natives and buy fur.

The operation is vast; it boggles his mind. Great-uncle Archibald has been with the Company since 1819, up and down the Pacific Coast; now Angus too has been promoted, from ordinary servant to postmaster, the next rung up. "They run it like the army," he writes, "which makes sense for a firm that covers one-tenth of the earth's surface." The fact startled him when he learned it. The Company he reluctantly signed onto is astonishingly powerful and ancient in its way. "HBC—'Here Before Christ', as the old wags say." If they spy the pride between the lines he doesn't mind. For the first time in his twenty-one years, he's part of something large and grand and endlessly exciting.

The business works like this, he goes on. Twice a year the traders buy, swapping English goods for furs. The men who trap the furs are mainly *métis*—mixed bloods—Indians, and some whites, who are freemen or employees of the HBC or rival Yankee firms. They bear these pelts down from the mountains to the Baymen in their lonely posts or meet them at the rowdy mountain rendezvous. Each trapper swaps them for a load of goods—flour, cloth, nails, blades, weapons, anything that man, not nature, can devise—and climbs back to the wild. And then the traders, Angus now among them, pack the furs out to the coast in long brigades. He and Captain Grant, for instance, take them overland each spring and fall along the Snake—a blasted, otherworldly territory pitted as the moon. He works with several others: Walker and a métis boy who Grant just calls Young George. Their string of laden mules follows the river to Fort Boisé then turns toward Fort Nez Perces, five hundred miles north on the Columbia. From there the bales are shipped downriver and across the sea to the hatters and haberdashers of London, who prize above all else the felted pelt of western beaver. Across this continent scores of other traders are doing just the same.

Think of it like rivers tumbling, he adds, warming to the play of language and imagination: starting as the tiniest watery wisps, trickling from the spine of these huge mountains, then merging, swelling, racing east and west. Along these waterways, hundreds of people are moving—men in red sashes, servants—horses, mules, canoes, and heavy boats, sliding up and down the lifeblood of this place. There are women and children, too, whole villages of Natives moving in the scene he sees in his mind's eye, though these he doesn't know about, not yet.

He's happy enough to have adventures to relate: his progress with their languages; his prowess at the hunt; the sight of piles of gleaming furs in shades from midnight black to tawny red, the golden skin of the big cats. But even so he must make haste. By the time they reach Fort Nez Perces it's nearly October and almost too late to get their post upon the boat. The pelts go downriver but the letters go up, racing to beat the winter ice to York Factory on the lip of Hudson's Bay. Every Bayman, from plain servant to the Chief Factors at the top, hustles to get his news on the York Express. That's how their hawkish, penny-pinching boss, George Simpson, travels too—on the Company's swiftest canoe.

Angus's first summer was spent at Archibald's at Fort Colvile on the Columbia, and his letters and his family's always seemed to cross en route. A year later it's no different: he receives one from his brother Duncan just after he's put his own in the waxed pouch. They're like figures calling indistinctly to each other across some mighty gorge. This time Duncan's words are loud enough, and clear: *Brother, do not think of coming back.*

He'll grace their door again when his five years are up, Angus has just written. *Even the factor cannae hold a grudge that long.*

He reads Duncan's on the wind-whipped bank, blood freezing. Their whole clan has been evicted from the farm. The crofters, aye, had long since been turned out, and now it was the tacksmen's turn—the McDonalds, too, who ran the sheep, but still were of no greater consequence to Hay-Mackenzie, laird of the estate. All are in the alms house now in Dingwall, Duncan says: mother and father and Maggie and the little boys, along with Duncan and Ann, his wife. *Worse, we lost wee Annie just before the New Year. How it grieves us, you may understand.* Angus lets his hand drop, stares across the mud-brown water.

Both Father and I now carry the daily post, his brother continues: *there's naught to employ us but charity or the Crown. I say this frankly so you see our situation clear. There are no prospects at home but dearth, and you've a hopeful situation there.*

He sees the pinched white face of his father Donald McDonald then, in the gloaming as he sent Angus away. The anger fills him anew: how merciless and grasping are these overlords, these men who run the Highlands now, treating human beings worse than sheep. He should go home, he thinks wildly, to stand their ground, to raise his Hoolahan once more—but this time in dead earnest. Then he remembers his mother's hand on his arm, her whispered prayers. "Go now. It can't but be a better place."

He'd not intended it. Who intends such a thing—the thing that irretrievably will shape one's life? All he'd hoped for was some small and meaty thing. But there it was, the stag. Its flank was the red of dogwood in winter, the same rosy flush he pictured coming to the cheek of Duncan's newborn bairn. Wee Annie would not die; her mother would make milk to give. They none of them would starve upon this land that still remembered all its proud and ancient clans.

He fancied the beast with its fine rack could hear his fevered thoughts: apologies and bitterness, and at the last, his simple thanks. *Mòran taing, Mòran taing.* Always give the animal your thanks. His heart was loud in his ears but not so loud as the shot would be when he took it. That was all he feared: the noise, the aftermath. The shot itself was easy.

He'd been roaming for hours, rising stealthily from the farm, leaving the glen by animal trails, rising and falling with the granite pleats toward Ben Wyvis, where the sheep tore at the summer pasture with their ceaseless maws. He'd shoot them all if he could, but it would change nothing: all of them would still be starving. Too late, his father said: the English stole the land and broke the clans and even turned their own chiefs into lairds who ran the Highlands now, the kind of men who'd sell their people out for sheep. Angus was thinking of Mackenzie and Alexander McDonald, fifteenth chief of the Glencoe McDonalds whose own spawn wouldn't even bail a kinsman from the tollbooth down at Inverness. They'd fetched his great-uncles from the glen to fail one by one with the chief's bloody sheep, and now his father, too, was failing though he wouldn't yet admit it. The wool was worthless and the potatoes had failed and famine gripped the land. Angus aimed at the lifted red chest, acknowledging its sacrifice. Here was the true native life of the Highlands: red deer, brown trout, the russet waxwings.

Above the falls of the Conon he was remote enough: no one would hear. He shot and watched it fall, and when he was satisfied the rifle's report had not been heard he climbed up and set to work. He slit the carcass from throat to tail along the belly, sliced perpendicular at neck and rear, and with both hands ripped up the hide. He'd have liked a pony to convey it, but all he had was unmarked sacks from his great-uncle's shop. He trusted Duncan and Angus to pack and ship the barley, mark the provenance and weight of every lot they sent to Edinburgh for brewing. But ye cannae live on barley-bere, nor tatties only, said their mother, knitting socks for sale.

He worked steadily slicing the warm meat from the ribs, pausing every few minutes to raise his head and turn it from side to side, as the stag unaccountably had failed to do. He'd smuggle the meat to town, avoiding the farm at Dalbreac. At eighteen he was too big to thrash—but more than this, his father must not know, so he could in all innocence deny the crime. The factor of Cromarty was a brute: he it was who booted both great-uncles out, poinding all their cattle when they could not make the rent. Angus must be quick about it—silent and quick.

He stopped to wipe his slick red hands upon the grass. Shame he couldn't take the half of it. He planned to tie a sack to each end of a stout branch and bear them down. He was casting about for one, amused at the thought of himself come a-milking like a maid, when high above him something sounded. A horn, or a dog. His stomach cramped. A longer, distant howling. Fear froze him until he shook himself, arms jerking, stuffing meat madly in the sacks beside the bloody and half-opened stag. Again he heard it—unmistakably a hound—and there was nothing for it but to grab a sack with either hand and start off running.

His track was as wide as a plow, a goddamned plow. Disgusted he looked back and knew they'd catch him. He was below the falls when the high strangled yelping of not one dog but several rose, and he heard cursing and dropped both bags and bolted with all the speed he had. His own skin was all he could save then as he leapt and twisted, beanpole that he was. Only once did he turn and look back and that was his last mistake, for as he did he saw the factor and his boy silhouetted against the sky and if he could see them, they could see him too. As if in confirmation, a ball whistled past. Ducking and weaving and running as fast as his lungs would let him, he tried to vanish into the riverbed, crossing back and forth downstream, muddying his scent, melting into the waters of the Conon as they flowed into the firth.

That night it all went so fast. He crept from the shed above the canal to hear them talking in low voices: Duncan and his father, just behind the wall in Duncan's house. So Father knew; he'd come to Dingwall from the farm. They stared at him when he entered and his father said with a clipped and mighty fury, "Did he ken ye? Did he ken ye, boy, I said?"

"Your wife needs meat," is all he remembers saying. And that he wasn't sorry. He wouldn't see them starve.

He'd rather see them all turned out, then, would he? rasped his father, and Duncan shook his head and said, "It needn't come to that." The two of them looked at one another and Angus knew already they'd discussed what was to be done. *He* was the problem now—he who'd only ever tried to help.

The factor knew, they said. He'd find a way to prove it. Angus remembers so little of it now. Archie would find a way, fix him up with the Hudson's Bay. The factor would find him, one day, if not here, then in Glasgow, Edinburgh—London, even. Duncan—oldest brother, oldest friend—spoke kindly, firmly though. Already they were strangers, those beloved men; they meant to put him on a boat and send him far away.

His father's face was crumpled. "There's naught here for any of us," he said, and it was true. How long had Angus plotted his escape from this bleak struggle, tatties rotting, threadbare trousers, want. He'd always known that he'd escape—to study, teach, use his mind. But not like this. They'd seen them go, whole villages sometimes, toward the ships that drained the people from the Highlands. But never in a thousand years had Angus thought he'd take one.

His sister Maggie was so angry she wouldn't speak to him. Only when he asked did she help him pack, weeping silently, wet ribbons either side of her long nose. They put his books in two saddlebags, his Tacitus and Shakespeare and Burns. Their mother and father could barely sign their names, but he and Duncan and Maggie were the blessed fruit of a Highland parish school—that great engine, their master constantly harped, of Scots enlightenment and progress. "Tell Annie," he whispered, then didn't know what else to say. Saucy Annie Fraser, with her wicked lips and jet-black hair—he'd lose her too, by his fool rashness. How he hated himself then, and the blasted deer. She'd think he ran away.

"You'll soon come back." Maggie gripped his arm and Angus couldn't tell if it was an order or a prayer. He gave her his volumes of Waverley, then folded two woolen trousers, his Glengarry vest and coat. On top of this his bagpipes. His father walked him to the gate and he was seized by sudden panic. "Will you come all the way?" he blurted, but his father shook his head. He'd better stay and show his face.

Angus remembers whistling the *Green Hills* to his bent, retreating back; his father raised a hand but did not turn. At the solicitors' in Stromness he signed a contract with the Company of Adventurers Trading into

Hudson's Bay. Their motto, *Pro pelle cutem*, a skin for a skin. He signed on for five years as General Servant at twenty-five pounds per year. Before the ink on his paper was even dry, he instructed the clerk to deposit half his first year's pay to the account of Donald McDonald of Dalbreac Farm. With the rest he bought a China trunk and two white shirts, arranged his few possessions inside it, except for his pipes.

These he took to the fore of the *Prince Rupert IV*. He blew into the chanter, inflated the bag, and piped a slow Highland lament. Though it was June, the sea was dark, the north wind fierce. That same chill wind that blows from Hudson's Bay all the way to him here on the bank of the Columbia, he thinks now. He remembers how cold his lips were on the reed. *Per mare per terra*, by sea and by land, the motto of Clan Donald.

Now, as then, he thinks of that little boy called John, age twelve, who escaped with his mam from the massacre of the clan. Angus's grandmother told the tale of the massacre of Glencoe every winter of his boyhood. That boy John was her own granddad, said Margaret McDonald: we must never forget. How he escaped by the skin of his teeth and survived—and only by that grace do we now walk this earth.

As he too has escaped, Angus thinks. Bolting to save his own skin—cleared off, displaced. Unaccountably, he too has been spared. He is surviving, even thriving so far, he thinks with some surprise, in this great and glorious place.

CHAPTER 3

CATHERINE AND BAPTISTE can't eat all the beaver they trap, so they leave the extra meat in the villages they pass through. You wouldn't even call them villages, she thinks, just clusters of huts every few miles down the broad brown river. This country is harsh; what roots she digs are thin and tough. Still, there is life: the birds, especially, are new to her, and accompany her along their route. One in particular she almost thinks has followed her all the way from Green River, though this can't possibly be. They must be numerous, identically tiny and bright, watching her all along the Colorado. A little bird no bigger than her palm with bright yellow cheeks, a white scalp, black beak, his black wings edged with yellow. Day after day he sings to her as she sets her traps and stakes the pelts out. She listens as she works, her arms growing harder and darker. *Little bird*, she whistles back. *What message do you bring?* She listens intently until she can tell each of his different songs. There are eighteen in all, each surely a story, a statement of joy or instruction or warning. He is sent to keep her safe on this long voyage, she is certain. How she misses her mother and sister then, her northern mountains. How happy is the little bird in its own home, she thinks, while men range the waste in eagerness and haste, anxious to be rich.

They travel with the white trappers for safety only. "Otherwise . . ." Baptiste rolls his eyes. He keeps his distance from these Boston white men: they have no regard for Indians, he says. And indeed, as the moons pass, they grow wilder, more coarse—as if the further they go from their wooden houses, the looser the reins that hold them. The week before, they came upon a hut with two children waiting for their father to return. The Americans' leader, a man called Black, grabbed each by the wrist and tied them to his saddle so that they were dragged along stumbling and weeping. Catherine started forward until Baptiste grabbed her sharply by the arm. "Leave it," he hissed. "That's a mean one, that Black."

The littlest one is the age of Alexander, her half-brother; his tears make a trail down his dirty face. But this is nothing compared to what happens a few days later. In a bend in the brush two Native women are digging roots when Black and his men come upon them. With a barbarous yell they swoop and haul them upright. The two women are nearly choking with fear, eyes huge in their faces, when Black leans from his horse and pulls the thinner one toward him by her long dark hair. She moans and points to her breasts, which are large, miming the baby she's left behind. It will die if she cannot suckle him, they understand, but Black just leers at his men, saying something disgusting that Catherine does not need to know the words to grasp. These women too are bound and forced to stumble after, weeping silently, and that night at the fire Catherine hears them keening until hard slaps stop their voices, only now and again crying out in pain as the man, or men, go into them again and again.

In the morning as she crouches at the stream to get water Catherine sees the young mother, tied to her fellow, being tugged roughly toward a bush where they can do their business. Milk streams from her breasts and her hands lift and try to ease their heavy bloating, but still the pale liquid drips. Her face is bruised and her sobs unrelenting, as she cries for her child. The sound makes Catherine's own heart surge in her chest, her own breasts ache, a tightness swell all up her throat and neck. The pity she feels swiftly turns to fury. From this moment on she watches and listens, trying to spy a way to help them escape.

Over the next few nights when the men are drinking Catherine creeps to the tent where they are tied.

"Don't worry," she whispers through the canvas. "You're not alone. You have friends here." Their language is not the same but the young mother's pleas are clear. Her baby, her child. Catherine sings so quietly no one else can hear. Songs of courage, of the new day sure to come. "I will find a way," she whispers fiercely. It will not be easy, though. Over the nights they stay camped at that place, there is no time when the soyapo does not lurch suddenly to his feet to check on his woman. He likes the taste of her milk, Black tells the other men, laughing coarsely. Now she knows why Baptiste won't let her go more than a dozen paces away from him.

On the third night they hear yelling from the white men's camp. Some traps have disappeared, it seems. She looks at her father and raises one eyebrow. *Their* traps are never stolen; sometimes the villagers even guard them, in return for their kindness with the meat. Black, though, is enraged and howling for revenge. "I'll show these stinking savages what a Yankee does to thieves," he roars, stomping around to the other fires, enlisting men to teach these "animals" their place.

"We come for fur. Not killing." Baptiste leaps to his feet. "You don't even know who took 'em."

"Filthy savages will get a lesson coming," growls the trapper, looking hard at Catherine.

It's barely light the next day when they wake to the sound of gunfire. She hears the shots in her dream and jumps, scuttling to where Baptiste is crouched behind a tree. Above them on a bluff six white men stand, firing, reloading, firing again and again; the smell of powder scorches the air. Catherine lurches out, screaming at them to stop, but Baptiste has her arm in a grip and is hissing at her to be silent. "Bostons shoot us too," he mutters grimly, and she twists away, covering her eyes and ears. Even so she can't help but hear the shots and screaming and smell the smoke as the trappers rush the camp and set it afire. She smells iron, the heavy smell of blood and death. There is splashing too, and she peeks out to see women and children trying to make their way up the stream but as she watches the trappers turn and start to pick them off. One by one they stumble and fall forward in the water like birds with broken wings. Her body shakes and then she knows. She whips to the tent where the captives are, bent low and running. Even her father's frantic whispers do not reach her ears. Catherine slices the rope with the knife at her belt and rubs the burning wrists. "Hurry!" she hisses, dragging the young mother up and pushing them both out the flap. She tugs them toward her section of the camp. The gunfire is slowing and she doesn't have much time. Frantically she rifles through their packs. She finds a parflèche of meat, a shawl, and presses them into their hands, then pushes them up toward the sandy slope. Bare feet flash as they scrabble away, a hand to a mouth in farewell and thanks.

The white men are very pleased with their fine business, joking as they return to the main camp with all they have pillaged. Even when Black discovers that his prize has fled and starts running around shouting, another white hits him on the shoulder and tells him to shut up. "Win some, lose some." The man shrugs, turning with an evil look toward the

Company men, who are silently packing their tents and lodges. Baptiste and Dalpier have already given the order to go. Her father has already pushed Catherine deep into the rear of their camp, and now he stands shoulder to shoulder with the other Company men to block the Bostons.

"Going so soon?" Black's voice drips venom. "What's ours is ours, you'd better remember—and you can be damn sure that I won't forget."

The quicker they leave, the safer they'll be, Baptiste breathes in her ear, and they swing up to lope away. Catherine leans forward, flattening her body against the horse's neck, expecting at any moment to feel the pounding of hoofbeats in her gut, hear the whistle and whine of bullets. "No longer safe from them devils," grunts her father beside her. He has told her many times how he fought them as a young man beside the British. Still, he can't help but be a little proud, she thinks. And indeed, he gives her a cock-eyed grin. "You are brave, my girl, but reckless."

"Wonder where I got that." She laughs and reaches across to pinch his arm.

She has seen so much on this long journey. It has opened her eyes to the brutality of men, and how the world continues on despite their tumult and their violence. She saw a man hit so hard his eyeball hung out; she saw her companions take a scalp with hair as long as hers. And yet beneath the bloody outer layer of the world, she has also seen things marvelous to contemplate. She saw the two tallest sisters alive holding hands among the Coyoteras, black hair to their hips, their breasts like unripe cherries. She saw uncountable birds on that mysterious thing, the sea, the unfathomable Deep that rises and breathes twice a day like a man.

They arrive home in the fifth moon of the year, the Camas moon. She has a scar on her forehead from where Dalpier's rifle struck her. There are more attacks on their way back. Their enemies pursue them for horses, territory, honor. The white men, too, attack for goods, but mainly out of hate. They crush the red man like so many bugs. She can't bear the sight of their white skin now. She's seventeen winters by the time she returns to her people—older, stronger, marked.

Angus tries to mask his distress on the long trail back to Fort Hall. Captain Grant is well pleased with the autumn returns, as is Dr. McLoughlin, their Chief Factor at Fort Vancouver who runs the Columbia District. Between the two of them, Grant tells Angus with a wink, they can afford to be generous with the brandy and tobacco. Yet even so, or perhaps on account of that grog, night after night Angus finds himself staring blankly into the fire. Since Duncan's letter his brain has churned so furiously it has all but exhausted itself. He no longer knows how to picture himself if that picture does not someday include brothers and sisters, nieces and nephews, and his own bairns, not to mention the rush of the Conon, the long arm of Cromarty Firth.

"Bad news?" Grant finally asks and he nods shortly. "The clan are hurting," is all he answers, embarrassed by their straitened state. He thinks of his own contribution in yearly installments, and something shifts. He meets his superior's eyes. "It would help if I knew my own prospects."

"A tad ahead of ourselves, aren't we?" Grant's tone is teasing.

"Not intentionally, sir. It's just—I'd like to send a little more."

Now the chief trader is shaking his head, not even trying to suppress his smile. "How long have you been with us, then?"

"Two and half years. I signed on for five."

"No rush, then. You've been raised once already, I gather."

Angus nods. "I'm twenty-one soon, that's all. I'd like to know the way the land lies."

Grant knocks the ash into the fire and puts a hand on his shoulder. "I'd say your prospects are excellent." His face is a chiseled map of his years in the wild. "You've shown initiative, you speak the languages, you get on with the men. I see no reason why you shouldn't rise."

"How far?"

At that Grant laughs out loud. "You'll want to show your haste a little less. No need to show you're angling for my job."

Angus feels his cheeks color. "Not at all!" Grant is the kindest of souls, fair in his dealings, secure enough in his own authority to be friendly to his men. The very opposite, in fact, of Archibald. "I'm fully aware I have much to learn."

He looks at the fort with new eyes when its white adobe hulk comes into view. Weighing his own future, the shape his life might take. At night he takes out his first and only communication from Dr. McLoughlin, informing Angus McDonald, general servant, of his rise to postmaster, now at fifty pounds per annum. He reads and rereads it until it is soft with refolding, picturing himself rising through the ranks: postmaster to Clerk to Chief Trader to Chief Factor even, Angus McDonald of the Hudson's Bay. His spirits rise—and then, as winter sets in, they sink once more. How is he to stick it out in this godforsaken place? For as miserable as Fort Hall is in the baking heat of summer, in winter it is worse. Ice storms roar down the canyon, burying the world in blocks of white. The biting snow blows horizontally; trees crack with a sound like rifle fire. Wind knifes between the clay blocks with such fierceness he might as well be at the North Pole, in huts of ice he's read about by Esquimaux. Most alarming of all, the Shoshone camped outside the wall simply vanish one day. They've moved to more sheltered foothills, according to Young George, who's half Indian and ought to know. Only hunger and the fear of death by dullness forces the Baymen out into the stinging air, hands wrapped in otter skins and bear fat smeared across their lips. And even so, Angus's skin splits and ice rimes his beard and he's afraid to brush it clean for fear that it might snap right off.

The cold is so brutal even the Yankee mountain men straggle in for a few days. Three days to be exact, jokes Joe Meek: one to get drunk and two to get sober. In such weather the only thing to do is find some fur in which to hide. "In other words," he cracks, "we're on our way to join our wives."

They decline the offer of a room and pitch their tents out in a corner of the yard, beside the tipis of the mixed-breed laborers. "No offense meant," says a fellow by the name of Russell, "but I don't cozy up to Brits."

"None taken," Angus answers with a smile. No point in instructing them on the difference between Scots and Englishmen. To Americans they're one and the same, those damned redcoats they revolted from, kicked out, and whupped in war, and yet—by Jove—the goddamned redcoats were still there. Nor does he mention how they rely on these same foreigners to trade their furs for supplies.

This visit Joe Meek is less jocular. "Something eating you?" Angus asks when they set in to drinking. Joe snorts. "Haven't made a friggin' dime. You bastards stripped the whole west side." He raises one eyebrow. Their own firm, American Fur, has packed the business in, no thanks to the

Hudson's Bay, the freemen growl. It's the first—but not the last—Angus will hear of his Company's infamous Snake Country brigades, which for a decade relentlessly trapped the beaver to near-extinction, mainly—and apparently, effectively—to drive the Yankees away.

"Don't see why Uncle Sam even lets you people stay," Russell mutters.

"Sounds like you could use some heating up," says Angus, liberally dispensing Grant's best claret. "So where, then, have you stashed these wives?"

In a Nez Perce village up the Salmon River, Joe Meek tells him. He raises his glass. "The only recompense for all this mayhem and starvation."

Archibald's wife flashes to Angus's mind. Jenny McDonald, born Klyne, a daughter of the fur trade, Scots and French and Cree. He sees her golden skin, her kind dark eyes. Archie's first wife, too, the full-blood daughter of a Chinook chief, who died while giving birth to their first child. Many, it seems, do take a Native wife.

"You all have one?" he asks. They nod.

"In point of fact, I'm on my third." Joe holds up three thick fingers. "My present wife, Virginie." He ticks one off. "The last one who ran off, the witch, and took my baby girl."

"For cause," his partner says. "Drunk as you were the whole damn time."

"You'd drink too if you'd lost a fine girl like my Mountain Lamb." Joe looks both woeful and indignant. He turns to Angus. "She was the first, my Uementucken, and the best. Lord, how I miss that girl."

He proceeds to tell the sorrowful tale. Mountain Lamb was a Nez Perce beauty, as he tells it, and a bobcat both. He bought her a horse, quality cloth for her skirts, her neckerchiefs, bright ribbons for her lustrous hair. Her moccasins were of the finest quality; she shone upon her dapple gray. Once she was surprised berry-picking by the Blackfeet, but she swam away amid a hail of bullets; once she tricked a trapper who tried to strike her, holding him at gunpoint till he begged for his own life. Many were the times they rode together to the hunt, Joe says, his eyes gone distant, a little smile upon his lips. Until the Bannock got her, put an arrow through her breast. He shakes his head. "I miss her still, and that's the truth. I'd have died a dozen times without her."

"Squaw men we are and that's a fact." Russell nods. "It's that or your own fist."

Angus laughs. "That part I grasp. What baffles me is why they'd even touch your ugly mugs."

"Greed."

"Avarice."

Two voices answer at once. "They're hooked now on the beads and lace, the guns and grub. And we're the ones who can procure them." Joe beats his chest. "Tat for tits, is how I see it." He flashes Angus a tight smile. "Haven't trapped the clap so far—you ought to try it."

A regular Falstaff, thinks Angus. Ever clowning, yet deceptively sharp. Joe Meek is wicked too, in his way: he sets the idea in Angus like a barb. It's not as if he hasn't thought of it before. Lust bubbles in him just like anybody else. But still he'd kept himself for Annie Fraser. Now that prospect's gone—just burned away—and things look different. The idea doesn't become a plan until that winter visit of the mountain men. But then he knows. Every step of his life so far has been reaction: school, then flight and exile—even now the fact he can't return to his own home. It's high time he set things in motion for himself—high time he made his own life happen.

CHAPTER 4

GREEN RIVER (PRESENT-DAY UTAH)

1841

THERE ARE HARDLY any white men at the rendezvous when Baptiste and his daughter arrive the following summer. They see nearly a hundred lodges of Shoshone, scores more of nimíipuu and Salish returned from the winter hunt. All these months a sharp fear of reprisal by those vicious albinos has traveled with her like a burr. But there are none of these Bostons at the rendezvous, and Catherine can finally exhale. Only Baymen to represent their white race, Baptiste exclaims, rubbing his hands in anticipation. "Plenty riches, my girl!" He grins. Even she, a novice, can tell their catch is magnificent.

Before anything her father winds his way up to the Salish to brag a bit. "Your daughter did *merveilleux*," he tells the woman who is no longer his wife. Margaret de Naie assesses her second child. Her daughter's body is fuller, harder, her eyes steadier than before. "I am not surprised." Her stern face softens ever so slightly and she holds out a hand. Catherine takes it and feels a new warmth, a kind of buzzing between their palms. When her sister arrives, she tilts her head to assess her. "All grown up," she murmurs, her black eyes combing her younger sister's face and lean muscled arms. "You too," Catherine laughs, daring to poke Kyuka's belly, which is wider, almost bulging, now. Her sister makes the slightest sour face, so swiftly no one else sees. So it isn't that, Catherine understands. Instead, the offerings the people keep bringing—the best back fat, the sweetest berries—in thanks for the medicine Kyuka brings to the hunt.

"You should have seen it," Baptiste begins and then he's off, telling how Catherine guided Dalpier's bullets, how she clubbed biters the whole length of that endless river. How her heart bled at the evil of those Bostons, burning brightly when she set the captives free. She even rescued the horses on their terrible parched return, he crows, digging in that waste to the depth of her own body for a trickle the creatures might lick. "Eagle High Up in the air now!" Their father grins before embracing both his daughters and bouncing away.

Catherine tries not to show how his words spread warmth all inside her. Their mother expects nothing less. They are descended from head men and medicine women and while Baptiste might brag, the Lam'tama don't. Even so she wishes she'd brought them a golden skin of the beaver of the Colorado—far lighter than those of the north, as if each hair held a piece of that southern sun.

Kyuka twines her fingers in hers. "See," she whispers. "Your turn came after all."

But now what, Catherine wonders. A little thought comes to her, a hot memory of a young man's eyes; perhaps it is time. Kyuka tightens her grip. "Yes, that, too," she grins, a little wicked. For once Catherine's glad that she can see inside her mind. *Then help me.* She sends it direct into Kyuka's eyes. Their mother, she means. Margaret has her own plans. She has risen, humming to herself; she's opening the flaps of the lodge and tying them back so all can see her pride. Her two strong daughters.

"If you stop being angry." Catherine isn't sure if Kyuka has said it out loud, or only inside. "Just stop being jealous. All right?"

"All right."

⋀

AS SOON AS they arrive in late June, Chief Trader Grant curls up like an old lion and dispatches Angus and Young George to trade. What pride Angus feels at running the show fades by noontime the first day. One by one the Natives lay their pelts out, painfully slowly, never pile by pile. Two made beaver for one Sheffield knife, six for a Smithfield rifle. For hours he stands, cheek muscles cramped from smiling, until finally dusk arrives.

He makes his way upriver to the Indian camps. Laughter and music rise as the bands reunite after winter on the plains. He roams and listens

33

and moves on, feeling his own strangeness. What is he doing, skulking about, he asks himself. He's about to slink away when he sees Baptiste Coquin, skinnier than last year but still a bundle of bouncing nerves.

"You haven't been to see me yet." They slap each other's hands. "I thought you might have drowned."

"Not me." The trapper grins. "No water where I was, not hardly."

"Plenty beaver?" Angus looks around him as he asks. Firelight plays on faces, battered, burnt, the brims of hats. He nods, and they nod back.

"Hoolah," Baptiste says. "A fat pack and some."

"Where's your clan?" There are only men at this fire, Angus can't help but notice.

"*Parlez, parlez.*" Baptiste flaps his jaw and gestures north. "Yakking all the time."

Angus laughs and walks out, circling up toward that last fire. And if he too should woo a Native wife, how would he even start? Boys are making birdcalls up where they watch the horses. He feels his blood beat in his throat as he comes near. In a clearing there is dancing, lines of women moving past, elders at their drums. He smoothes his beard. The girls and women jig in place, a sheen of sweat upon their faces. They move as if in trance to the warbling of an old man. They do not dance to be admired, he thinks: they close their eyes; they hold their arms stiff at their sides. The talk around him is Nez Perce. He feels the glances of the men and tenses until just as swiftly their eyes flick away. It comes to him that he is known and thus no threat: the tall soyapo trader with his splash of red.

The women circle, some round-faced, some narrow, older ladies thicker at the waist. Each time the circle moves new faces are presented. All wear their finest fringed regalia, tunics sewn with beads and quills. One or two he thinks he's seen before. Here's a broad strong woman with a necklace made of twisted bone and otter strips around her braids; she eyes him fiercely as she passes. A few girls down he sees another face that he recalls, with long black braids, a furrow in the brow. The lass he saw last time—Baptiste's daughter, racing her small roan. He thinks of Archie's Jenny once again: the softness of her voice, the kind way that she answered all his questions when his uncle never would. How smooth her hands were, how directly she looked at him through her slightly slanted eyes. By the time the vision passes the circle has moved on. He feels dazed and slightly ashamed, as if these women are just meat upon a rack. He slips away.

The next afternoon he's totting up his receipts when the flap parts and Baptiste pokes his long nose in.

"Good time?" he asks, and Angus nods. The trapper steps back out and hauls a sled in, piled with gorgeous tawny pelts. And just behind this comes the girl—the one he thinks he glimpsed last night, and certainly last year. Taller than her father, lips pressed hard together, aloof—whether haughty or shy, he can't tell which.

"My girl here trap with me. Much luck!"

"My pleasure." Angus steps out from behind the folding desk, holding out his hand. Baptiste takes it with both hands and pumps it. His daughter nods slightly, arms glued to her sides. Angus turns to the pile of pelts.

"Incredible. They're so much lighter, thicker."

"Big fat old men, yes. Down the Colorado."

"You caught these too?" he asks her in nimíipuu.

She has large bright eyes and shining hair, her father's thin, strong arms.

"Oui." She answers in French. Perhaps it's forward, addressing her in her own tongue.

"I'm impressed." He switches language readily and smiles.

She arches one eyebrow. That is your mistake, the eyebrow seems to say.

"My name is Angus. Angus McDonald."

"My daughter, Catherine."

He wishes Baptiste would shut up so he could hear her voice. But she is cool, removed.

"A pretty name. But not your only name, I think."

She frowns.

"We met last year—your cousin, I remember him. Or is that wrong?"

She glances at Baptiste and he recalls the way she strained, a filly yearning to escape.

"Well, let us count, then." Lightly he turns back to his ledger and makes a sign to George. Eighty-seven skins they count, father and daughter lifting each and smoothing it. Bigger, plusher than the Rocky Mountain biters, Baptiste argues; Angus nods and gives him more credit than he perhaps deserves. Mostly he's watching Catherine from the corner of his eye, admiring her poise, the long oval of her face, her fingers on the golden pelts she slips before him.

CAPTAIN GRANT HASN'T felt well since late winter. He's subject to bouts of black mood and inexplicable bursts of anger. Angus chalked it up to confinement and his advancing age. But that evening at the campfire, he learns something that puts it all in a different perspective.

He could get to like this life, he'd just observed, making conversation. So long as from time to time a fellow got a break. "Men get furloughs, I suppose?"

Grant grunts and lifts his eyes. "Many do, though I've not had that privilege."

"Of course," says Angus carefully. "If I were to stay, I'd want to marry. Find myself a wife."

Grant's face goes stiff. "Och," he says. He swivels to look him full in the eyes. "Now there's the rub." He sighs. "They've turned against it now." In the ensuing silence he seems to struggle with himself. "*Custom of the country*, as we called it. Once we could wed the girls we wished, but not so anymore."

"But surely it's within our rights!"

"Our rights." Grant snorts. "We all had rights, until the bastards changed their minds."

He stands and goes to his tent, returning with the jug of brandy. He fixes Angus with his light, sad eyes.

"You can still get out and live a normal life. I'd do it if I could."

A normal life. What would that be, in times like these, his homeland overrun with greed, the ceaseless grinding of the bloody sheep?

"But they've all done it." Subtly, that whole winter, he had probed the men. "McLoughlin, Ogden, Archie—even Simpson." The superintendent of the whole Company; one only had to scan the fort. Exhibit A: dark-skinned Young George . . . Simpson.

"He didn't marry her." Some deep emotion flickers in Grant's eyes. "Not one of them, the ones up top. Not Simpson, Collins, Hargrave."

"I don't quite follow."

The trader reaches for a stick and pokes the flames. "Time was, you took a wife and honored her. That was the rule here when I started. You married, had some pups, you kept your word. Course there were always those who sowed their seed and had their fun and turned them off when they went back to England. Still, most of us found our small comfort, kept our pledges."

"Yes." Angus, too, leans forward. "That's all I want."

"Too late. They'll bust you down as far as you can go if you so much as broach the subject now. Our notions are too primitive, that's what they say, to fit the world as it is now."

"Things haven't changed, though, on the ground. There's still not a woman of our own race for thousands of miles."

"Oh no?" The trader's laugh is bitter. "I had a wife, you know. She died a few years back. Then I found Mary and she brought some ease to Oxford House, to me and those poor children both."

Angus says nothing, waiting.

"Until that cockface Hargrave—let you pray you never meet that pompous, hypocritical prick—laid down his law. He would have none of it; custom of the country is a sin, the girls are sluts, never mind that every man who's been here twenty years or more is married *à la façon du pays*." He turns, lips working. "I blame the priests, I do, but more than that, it's the hypocrisy that makes me sick."

"He sent you here?"

"I sent myself. There wasn't any greater distance I could put between us."

"He would not recognize her, then?"

"Recognize! I was to cease, desist, abjure her and our child. I begged the man to leave me be, or at the very least allow my transfer with my son. But he refused it." Grant's eyes are burning. "I pass my time in pleas to governors and factors, writing damn near every post. I'll not let up until they let my boy come back."

It is despicable, if true. But Angus never knew the man to lie.

"That's why they shipped Young George down here."

"Out of sight is out of mind. They knighted the old goat for service to the Crown. Who plowed his way from fort to fort, quite glad to fuck and cast them off, then lecture us all piously on sin. Three poor unfortunates he's made, at the last count. Young George is just one by-blow."

Angus rocks backed, stunned. "What am I supposed to do then, in this godforsaken land?"

"Wait for the ship that brings the frail white rose of England, I suppose," Grant sneers.

As if a Highlander would want a wench so simpering and useless. A girl with fire, like Maggie his own sister, Annie Fraser—even, maybe, Catherine Baptiste.

"That's what they did," Grant growls. "Simpson brought his lady cousin over last year, Hargrave right after."

They stare at one another for a long while, lost for words.

Angus thinks of Duncan and their father, bent and crushed by English rule. Why should he now, in this new life, still bend to English law? The governors of the Company in London still lord it over Scots who risk their lives and break their backs with toil. As if they'd not fought proudly to control their destiny at Bannockburn, Culloden—at this last battle Archie's grandpa too. An ancient sense of grievance wakes in Angus, the old resentment he was born imbibing. McDonalds have been thwarted always: death and destitution, wholesale murder, clearance. He will not take it lying down.

"My dad would laugh," he says at last, "to know their rule reaches this far."

"Or else he'd cry."

"Aye."

CHAPTER 5

ONLY AFTERWARD DO they grasp that this will be the final mountain rendezvous. At the time, it just strikes Angus as different from the previous year. Without the American firms, the Indians are among themselves, doing what he imagines they've done for years uncounted. Racing and gambling and dancing and feasting, besting one another in foot sprints and shooting matches. Highlanders, too, carouse and compete at their clan gatherings. The main difference Angus sees is the horses.

If he'd been told three years earlier he'd spend his days in a saddle, he would have scoffed. Draft horses and nags were all he knew. Now he knows there's a different kind of creature on this earth, courageous and swift. And of all the steeds that flash across this continent, none are finer than the steeds of the Nez Perce. They've been breeding them since the Spanish first brought them here, apparently. Angus likes nothing better than to watch the herds lap the hills, piebald, dappled, blazed, pale as moonlight, gleaming black, cream and brown and rust and gray. Whenever he steps out to catch the air, he watches them shift and move, the way he watches clouds. Two days later, suddenly he knows. Horses are the way to the nimíipuu heart.

He feels his pulse speed as he tells Young George he can close up for the day. He's not defying Grant so much as refusing something patently unjust, is how he sees it. The Governors can't bar them from the few joys of this harsh and thankless life. Since David Thompson crossed the Rocky Mountains forty years before, every fur trader has settled with a Native wife. The tribes embrace the practice too. The chiefs, pragmatic, see the value in alliances that give them better access to white guns and goods. Or so one part of him reasons, while a more private part simply longs for the taste of love.

He walks briskly to the hillside, hoping she'll come to snare her roan.

An hour drags by as warriors lope up, shaking ropes, nickering, and collecting their mounts. He fills a pipe and smokes it. He is a hunter; he is patient. When that patience is at last rewarded, Angus straightens, raising slightly his right hand. Catherine tosses her head and says something to the other girl. They coil their ropes and whistle sharply. In no time they have caught their horses and he follows as they tether them beside some aspens.

She looks quickly at him before her eyes flick back.

"*Il est vite*." He'll speak to her in French. "You might just win."   .

Catherine lifts her chin. "He's only one of three. Who will ride is not decided." Her voice is low, as if she forces out the words.

"But you ride well, I know."

She steps around the roan, to put its bulk between them. Her friend whispers something and moves off with a spotted mare.

They stand there silently as he wills her to look up. Instead, she loops the hair rope on the horse's nose, looping once again to make a halter. He starts to come around to help her as she grasps the horse's mane to pull up and she *tsks* at him. A little hiss. And then she's mounted in the smoothest pull and looking down upon him. She settles and seems more at ease. She rather likes the vantage, he suspects, though he's still tall enough to nearly meet her eyes.

"You have no horse?" Her voice is rich, sarcastic.

"Of course." He strokes her pony's neck and looks directly in her eyes. Her iris is a lovely shade of brownish gray, not black as he first thought. "Though ours, it's true, are not as swift as yours."

She smiles at last, the swiftest flash of white.

"Nor quite so beautiful."

She reins the horse then sharply and leans forward, squeezing with her legs. He watches her ride off, so light and lithe, and like a fool, all weakness and desire, he follows.

The racecourse is a yellow meadow whose long grasses have long since been pounded down. The horses and riders mill on the far side. The whole camp has turned out, hundreds of people clamoring and hooting. He wedges his way in. The riders are striped with paint and covered in buckskin and the throng is so thick he can't pick her out. Only when the sprints start does he spy her with her cousin and some others on the far side of the track. The racers streak by, earth churning underneath their hooves. He sees red gaping nostrils and arms whipping at the shining flanks, and then they're past. He waits and waits but still she doesn't ride. From time to time he glimpses her in shift and leggings, then the crowd moves and she's swallowed up again. After the sprints another set begins.

Someone shouts and different groups begin to fill the oval: small clusters of people holding mincing horses. The groups are teams, he guesses; each group stands by a set of horses, three or four, he can't quite tell. He cranes but can't see past the first clump to the other teams, maybe six in all. Then there's a crack—of whip or gun—and they spring off, a rider on each back, and he perceives her as she flashes by. Her horse is chestnut, not the roan; she sits it like an arrow shooting forward, arms stretched out along the reins to just behind the horse's mouth. The other riders look like boys, but all are thin and light and whip their mounts as they slice past and take the first big turn. Catherine disappears and Angus ducks and weaves to get closer to the place the race should end.

They're coming back around now and he sees the flush upon her cheeks, the frown of concentration as she rounds the turn. Yet she doesn't stretch out to take the finish—instead veers toward her team in a great spray of flying dirt. He sees then it's a relay: her teammates hold a fresh horse ready. And she is flying, literally flying, as she leaps from the spent pony to the fresh, grabbing the mane as it bolts before she's really on, and then he's shouting with the others as the teams pound even more ferociously around.

The next time he is closer, ready, watching this girl he barely knows lunging from the bay onto her roan; she's saved the best for last, her own. He's struck with wonder at her strength, her will, the timing it requires to slide from one onto the other as it leaps from standstill to full gallop. He sees her cousin, fleetingly, and hears him shout "Kitalah, go!" and Angus too is cheering, calling "Go, lass, go!"

She comes in third. He sees her slip down, tight-lipped, shaking her fine head. She mutters something to her cousin. She reaches up to scratch the roan beneath its jaw and lays her face against its neck. And it is then he falls, for that one gesture. Not just her power, or her fearlessness, the flowing beauty of her limbs, but that soft moment of affection and forgiveness.

IF HE MUST, he must, Grant growls. Though it is frankly insubordination. He's always been a troublemaker, Angus cheerfully allows. But taking risks is what this trade is all about, is it not so? Grant frowns. He'll do it right at least; he'll get permission from her parents first. So on the last night of the rendezvous Angus seeks her father out.

Baptiste stands when Angus is done with his speech. He pats him on the shoulders with both hands, then down his arms, as if to measure his full worth. He looks him up and down, a gleam in his sharp eyes.

"I am a Bayman, many years. The Company is good." He stops and pulls at his chin. "But Catherine, she is not only mine." He frowns. "Her mother will decide."

His look is not encouraging. "She rules them there, that's why I stay down here. With my new wife." He makes a face. "I ask her for you."

"Wouldn't it be better if I asked myself?"

"Better not."

"At least—" he gropes, "I'd like to give her a sign of my intention."

Baptiste thinks this over. "You can do this. I will bring the gifts, explain."

Angus bites his tongue. He'd rather make his own case. No other girl he's seen burns quite so brightly. With luck he could show that behind this stranger stands a man with his own flame. "I'm a clerk, soon a trader—one day even chief of my own post. Our marriage would be good for all."

Baptiste sits him down, extracts a pipe. "We smoke to say it's good." His eyes are hooded, downward slanting, like his daughter's. If not for his brown teeth, his broken nose, he would not be bad looking. Still, Catherine has clearly inherited her high cheeks and fine nose, her firm square jaw, from her mother's side.

"I'll send a gift," says Angus.

"Your gift will speak for you." Her father smiles. "But Nez Perce women speak from their own mouths. I warn you!"

CATHERINE FLINGS THE pack at the lodge wall, heavy as it is and tied with bright red satin. She hears the crusted snow dislodge outside and slither down. Her mother's face is placid. At least Kyuka isn't here to laugh at her misfortune.

"You should have said no." She can barely speak for fury. "You know very well how hateful they are."

"I wanted to see you first." Her mother's calm infuriates her even more. "I hadn't seen you in such a long time—I didn't know how you had grown."

It's a bald-faced lie. Margaret sees everything, whether near or far. Catherine stands, her hands clenching and unclenching. "I'm grown now, as you see. I can decide for myself."

Her mother pats the rug beside her. "Come, Kitalah. Let us sit awhile."

She's up to her usual tricks. She'll act all soft and kind, and then as soon as you're disarmed, turn cold as metal. When Catherine was little she admired this. Now she understands that when her mother sets her mind, no one withstands her. She's the daughter of one chief and cousin to two others—a force not to be trifled with, like Kyuka. Already Catherine's sick of hearing how her sister called the weather on the hunt and drove their enemies away.

She sits coiled, arms tight around her knees.

"I too was once young." Now her mother's hair is streaked with silver like the hammered bands that flash around her neck. "My father never liked your father. But he could see that it was smart."

"I hate them all." She says it with all the venom she possesses. "Ask my father, he knows what we saw."

Her mother puts out a hand and lifts her chin and looks into her eyes and Catherine knows she can see exactly what Catherine herself cannot unsee, no matter how hard she tries: the screams and bodies, Black's snarling face, the blood and drowning babies, flames.

"I understand," her mother says. "But he is not like them."

"You don't know that." He smells as rancid as the rest; his skin is blotched and hairy.

"There are white men and white men," Margaret says.

No girl she knows has been forced to live with a soyapo. She shakes with anger, planning how she'll creep out, seek her uncle, tell him she refuses. Chief Flint Necklace has led their band as long as she's been alive, from the Clearwater to the plains to the rendezvous and now to the Smoky Ground. He would not force her.

"Even the council sees the sense," her mother says, and Catherine covers her face with her hands. Even inside her own mind, her thoughts are not safe.

"They'll keep on coming, these soyapo. As my grandfather warned when they first came." Margaret glances away, as if toward that past time, and Catherine can breathe more freely—until her mother looks back and holds her like a vise once more. "We have lost too many already."

Her mother's voice is hard. It's the voice she uses when she expects the men to listen to her counsel. This, more than anything, catches Catherine. Her mother has never spoken to her in this firm, relentless voice before.

"The trader wants you. Many men will. You're everything they'd want. But he is . . . useful, possibly." Her mother catches Catherine's hands and tugs her to sit down. "I'm not talking about small things, blankets, guns." Contemptuously, she shrugs. "He may be one of them, but he can speak our tongues. Not like the Bostons." Her eyes are distant, measuring. They latch back on Catherine's face. "With you, he could be useful, help us push off those soyapo who bring only death." She nods to herself and reaches out to touch Catherine's hair, combing it with her fingers, disentangling the knots. "The only way to deal with them is cunning."

Catherine holds herself entirely still, like some small, defenseless prey.

"The Baymen have been our friends a long time." Margaret smiles. "You more than anyone should know this." She slides a finger down Catherine's arm, as if to trace the French blood there. Catherine swallows. She cannot deny it: she has been nourished by these white men, brought into this very life by their endless appetite for fur.

"And father?" she asks, sobered by the touch, the tone.

"He thinks as I do. This man is a good one, he says, he'll keep you safe."

"I do not need to be kept safe," she growls. She's battled animals and enemies and hunger and thirst. A scar shines on her forehead from Dalpier's rifle. "Besides. He stinks like rotten meat."

Her mother smiles. "I can show you a way to make him sweeter." She juts her chin toward the wall where the package lies wedged. "You haven't even looked at what he sends."

Catherine sighs and pulls the gift toward her. Inside the folded hide are three thick Hudson's Bay blankets the shade of the summer sky. "For you, not me," she says, not even trying to disguise her disgust.

"Look deeper."

Between the blankets the trader has slipped a flat packet wrapped in the same pelt of beaver she sold him. She'd know its tawny slickness anywhere. At least he grasps that she can trap—and hunt and do the things he does—she thinks as she unwinds it. A flash of silver falls into her lap. She raises it and turns it in her hands and starts to laugh.

It's a large necklace made of hammered silver: a center piece in the shape of a clamshell, from which three smaller silver pieces hang. On each piece a shining river stone is mounted. But that's not why she laughs. Each hanging pendant is a little beaver, slightly rounded, attached to the shell by its snout.

"He prizes you, I think."

She looks up, her heart squeezing. "But—"

"The question is whether he is worth the prize." Her mother is regarding her thoughtfully.

And if she refuses to be a prize for any man—to choose herself a mate of their own people? For once her mother does not seem to hear—or deign to see—her inward pleas.

"We'll set him a test." Margaret speaks with finality. "I want to see this man myself, before we decide."

"And if I still don't like him?"

Her mother gives her a shrewd smile. "You put his shoes out."

Catherine feels instantly lighter. She thinks of Elk Springs, the woman with three kids who threw her man out just last summer. Or even Margaret herself, who shed Baptiste. There isn't any shame in changing mates. The band will still divide the meat and roots, the women keep the food and share it out.

"Think of it as a gift only you can give the nimíipuu." Margaret's look is sly. She knows full well the way that envy twists inside Kitalah. "You always asked where you would find your power." She tucks a lock of hair behind her daughter's ear. "Maybe it lies in this. Who knows? Only the seasons will reveal it."

CHAPTER 6

THE RIDERS APPEAR at the fort late one February day. Angus marvels at their hardiness. Captain Grant doesn't even bother posting sentries until May, so brutal is the weather on the Snake. But here are three mounted Indians banging on the gate. Ice drapes their fur-wrapped faces. Their horses look done in, fetlocks cut and bleeding. He keeps his hand on his gun until the first one speaks.

"I see you, Whiskers," says the fellow in Nez Perce.

"As I see you," he answers. It's a greeting; it's a memory of a prior meeting; in their language it can mean either thing.

A mittened hand unwinds the fur and he's looking in the face of Catherine's cousin, Eagle from the Light. A bolt of fear shoots through him. "Has something happened?"

The young man laughs. "Just hunting. The one you don't ask about is fine." All three are young and haggard and extremely hungry. Still, they take their time rubbing down their horses and bandaging their legs. Inside they fall upon the food that Grant sets out: a roasted grouse, some corn mush, and potatoes. It's rare to have visitors this deep in winter, the Chief Trader observes, his question clear.

"Trust me, I wouldn't have come if we weren't sent." Her cousin barely breathes between his slurps. "We slept two nights inside an elk in the last storm."

Angus is the only one who understands their words. It gives him immense satisfaction to convey them to the others. Even Eagle from the Light appears impressed. "Watch out, the trader knows," he joked right off to his companions. "No secrets here!" His face is long and narrow with gray eyes that kindle in an instant when he grins. "You work hard!" His friendly slap is just as hard. "Even if your mouth sounds full of rocks."

After the third helping he pushes his bowl away. "My uncle wants you to join us for the winter hunt." His face is flushed with the heat; his friends look amazed by the great wood beams in this house they find themselves.

"Which uncle?"

"My cousin's uncle—mine too. Chief Flint Necklace. You know him."

"If not by name, then face, most certainly," says Grant.

"Chief in my cousin's village and leader of the winter hunt," Eagle from the Light explains. "The Bostons call him Looking Glass."

"Is this an invitation, or an order?" Angus asks.

"Let's say he'd like to talk to you."

It's as he hoped. They want to check him out. By damn, he thinks, they're entertaining my proposal. Grant, too, is pleased to grab the chance to beat the Yankees hunkered in their winter holes. Only Native hunters are tough enough to hunt the bison when their robes are thickest and most prized.

They set out with three extra horses, enough dried venison to hold them for a week. It takes exactly half a breath to get Young George to join. The lad has never seen a buffalo. No more has Angus. In times long past they ranged the West, but not in his lifetime, says Eagle from the Light. Their route is north, five days. Angus is struck by how surely the nimíipuu horses find their footing on the rocks that edge ravines, the lighter crusts beneath the trees. The wind is so biting the humans barely speak. His fur-clad hands turn into claws glued to the brittle reins, the air a grinding blade that slices in his chest each time he breathes. The first night he's close to weeping when the flints ignite the moss, and he can hold his frozen mitts and feet toward the flames. He doesn't know which is worse: the pain of thawing or the new pain when they start again to freeze.

Eagle from the Light and his younger brother, Eagle Robe, look on him with a kind of pity. They build a shelter of pine boughs and bank the snow and line it with their robes and never did a hardened hunk of jerky taste so good.

"You know why there's no buffalo west of the mountains?" her cousin asks. Angus, gratified to see that he too shivers, mutely shakes his head.

"Coyote tried to take them west, to make food for the people there." He winks. "Before the human beings came, he lived on Snake River, they say. He decided to travel to buffalo country, where he found them grazing.

He rounded some up and took them to the western people, all the way through Nez Perce country to the big river going to the sea."

Che Wana. Big River. Even in his grogginess Angus grasps their name for the Columbia.

"Only!" Eagle from the Light widens his eyes, and Angus sees a story told a thousand times. "There were such forests! Miles and miles of trees and no plain on which the buffalo could graze. Coyote went all the way to the sea but there was nothing. He was mad. He was sad for the people because there wasn't anywhere for the buffalo to feed. He came back to the herd. 'It's too far to take you back now,' he said, and so he left them there. They're still there—they sat so long they turned to rocks beside Celilo Falls." He holds a burning twig to his pipe and sucks and hands it to Angus. "From that time there were no buffalo west of the great mountains."

Young George is tucked in so close he's practically sitting on Angus's lap. Angus whispers so as not to wake him. "We tell our stories in the winter nights as well."

"Tell my uncle some then." Catherine's cousin's look is wry. "Every night he drones on and on."

All he'll say of their destination is that it's a place of special power. They'll meet Catherine's band from the Clearwater as well as his own band from the Salmon River. Other buffalo hunters, Salish and Sheepeater Shoshone, will join them. They're awaiting them now on the Bannock trail leading to the plains.

The next morning they drop down the last ridge and Angus can only gape. Nothing makes sense: the world is upside down. In the depths of winter the distant marshes are a shocking yellow-green; clouds appear to rest right on a white plain at their feet. Thin plumes of smoke rise all across this pitted, flaky waste, giving off a putrid stench. Out of nowhere a jet bursts from the crust before them. His horse rears and nearly lands inside a blue-green pool, until it shies. Angus dismounts to test the water when he feels a hand restrain his arm.

"Take care," says Eagle Robe, dipping a branch to show how the leaves instantly curl. Only then does Angus perceive the belching bubbles in the steaming, muddy hole. "Hot, hot spring," the Nez Perce says. Their people call this place the Smoky Ground. Angus swipes off his cap to let the warm winds lap his blistered face. The whole valley is a single vast hot spring, he grasps at last, amazed. Everywhere there are pools rimmed in bright blue, deep red, violet, magenta: the earth itself is rainbow poxed.

Young George is throwing rock after rock into the hole that held the jet of water. Nothing occurs. As he turns, it spouts again and belches one rock straight back at him, clouting him above the ear. He howls and wipes away the blood.

"Serves you right." Their guide's look is severe. "You need to show respect."

The Celtic kingdoms too were underlain by legendary dragons, Angus thinks. These holes might be their nostrils flaring. They're dismounted, threading through a mist of vapors hanging in a milky band when suddenly these lift. Six feet away stand half a dozen beasts: great shaggy brown-black monsters with square heads, absurd small horns, enormous grinding jaws. "Buffalo," breathes Young George. The creatures raise their heads, return their stares en masse, and roll their eyes before they whirl and pound away. Angus is startled at the way the huge orbs spin inside their sockets till the pupil is near-vanished and they bulge entirely white. Truly it's as Eagle from the Light has said. This is a place of mist and mystery—an utterly different world.

THEY ARE LED to a spot near the chief's lodge, much larger than the rest. Angus faintly recalls the yellow-and-blue striped tipi he saw at his first rendezvous. How did he not know that Catherine was kin to a great chief? In a way, he thinks, pitching his own canvas tent nearby, he's glad he didn't. This ignorance makes his intention feel purer, somehow.

Chief Flint Necklace is relaxing, eyes closed, legs stretched out, when Eagle from the Light brings Angus in. He takes his time in opening them.

"Ah. The Bayman." He pulls himself to sitting. His hair is streaked with gray, spread loosely over strong, broad shoulders; his nose is prominent, his brown eyes shrewd but slightly twinkling.

"Angus McDonald, sir." He bows.

The chief looks him up and down and Angus holds his gaze; at least her uncle's face looks kind. After a minute that face grimaces and the chief bids him sit. "I'm getting a crick in my neck." Flint Necklace smiles as he bends forward and extends a hand, while the other stills the rattling objects hanging from his necklace. Quills, a sharp gray rock, a little convex mirror. Ah, yes, thinks Angus to himself: his Nez Perce name is Apash Wyakaikt—necklace made of flint—but Yankees call him Looking Glass.

Angus has brought a sharp new skinning knife sheathed in a beaver case. This he presents to the head man with both hands. Flint Necklace examines its handle, patterned with brass and steel nails, nods in thanks, and hands it to a boy beside him—his son, apparently. This young man will succeed his father and take his name when he is gone, Catherine's cousin has explained. A few more men trickle into the lodge.

"You have powder to sell?" Flint Necklace looks at him fiercely for a moment, then laughs. "I'm glad you answered, anyway. We heard about you, but I wanted to see you for myself."

"I'm glad to see you too." Suddenly Angus is extremely nervous.

"How is it you speak our language?"

"I wanted to learn it. For my work. To communicate."

"It's unusual," the head man says, one eyebrow raised, and Angus wonders if this is good or bad. But then her uncle speaks again. "You're not frozen? My nephew was good to you?"

"Very nice." He pauses, mind racing. He has to make a good impression. He hazards a small joke. "Of course, I let him take a deer or two," he smiles, "so he'd feel big."

"Hey!" Eagle from the Light protests; the others laugh.

"He'll hunt with you then, so we can see this skill."

"I've never hunted buffalo."

"Animals are animals, big or small, four feet or two. They're not hard to kill." The chief's tone is sardonic. "You soyapo have been killing them for quite some time." Suddenly his voice grows harder. "Your Company is guilty, like the Bostons—that's something we'll have to discuss."

"I wait with interest for that discussion." His heart shrinks. He'll be lectured on the Snake brigades that stripped the slopes. No matter that it started long before he came, the outcome was the same for all whose lives depended on the animals the Baymen killed. He had hoped he might see Catherine, meet her mother, lay out his proposal. Now he knows that he is being judged, and this will have to wait.

The whole camp moves the next day; still he hasn't seen her. Angus rides near the front, ever eastward through the iron-colored sky. At night he eats with her cousins, crushed meat and berry pemmican that tastes like mincemeat from pies he dimly recalls from a lifetime ago. His mind wanders to his family: it's so odd to think they're still going about their daily lives while clear across the globe he's setting out for buffalo.

The wind scours him clean in a way he finds strangely exhilarating, and in the last teeth of the great divide he understands that he has been liberated through some ineffable grace he can't begin to understand. It all stemmed from the stag, from his own hand—his rashness that perhaps was something else, a kind of daring. And sorry though he is for his poor family, scraping along in that depleted land, he feels no shame. Mountains are for proofs of endurance and for visions, he tells himself: this is the way of every native people he has met so far. It is the Nez Perce way, Catherine's way—perhaps one day even his way as well. His heart is large and the future is broad and he feels entirely blessed. And then, in a flurry of white flakes, they drop from the Rockies onto the plain.

What can he say of the buffalo? He is enamored, instantly, of this strange creature, the peculiar winter chase. In summer, Eagle from the Light tells him, they creep downwind toward the herd, crouched bareback. Cutting out this cow, that bull, riding on the creature's right so the arrow, or sometimes the ball, is delivered to the left, and plunges straight into its lungs and heart. It's fantastic, the warrior says: a pounding, swerving race. But when they seek their mammoth prey in winter, death comes in a different fashion.

The snow is too deep for horses. They set out on snowshoes, after praying for success. The hunt chief scans the white expanse, looking for ridges, hillsides, anywhere the wind might catch and scour. Bison will cluster in such places, where the wind lifts the snow and they can paw what frozen grass remains. It can take days to find a herd, Eagle from the Light has warned him. This hunt, though, the signs are propitious. By midafternoon they see droppings, then a trampled, icy highway. It runs over a rise; the hunters creep up and peer over. In the glare a dark splotch can be seen half a mile away. Scores of animals crowd together, rump to nose, pitifully snorting.

The hunters ready their clubs and knives, crouching behind the brim of the hill. At the chief's shout they rise en masse and barrel down the slope, and the heavy beasts lurch and try their best to flee. They turn and plunge into the deeper snow of the ravine, each flailing motion digging them in deeper, till their death is a lumbering dance, the hunters gliding toward them on their snowshoes like fell angels, towering above them on the crust of blinding ice and snow. The knives flash once, twice, deeply, silently: no need of ball or powder.

There's something sacrificial to it, Angus thinks. He grasps the horn with his left hand and looks the creature in the eye, and thanks it silently, and plunges with his right arm deep beneath the jaw. They're all stabbing and thrusting and breathing heavily, moving from one struggling monster to the next. They are a score of men with bloody blades and one by one the creatures crumple in the snow. Angus has killed five, six, maybe more. His arms and chest are wet with gore. He hears a shout of "Whiskers! Hey!" and looking up sees Eagle from the Light abreast of him across the river of black bodies, his narrow face slick with joy and sweat. He holds up nine, ten fingers, makes the sign for question. Angus shakes his head.

Then it's over and every last buffalo is dead, and the snow is a foamy pink with dark brown streaks. They strip the robes; it's a monumental task to dig each carcass out. Four men are needed just to flip it. The viscera yield screaming as they rip each heavy skin off. And then they simply leave the meat. They pull the hides to the side to be collected by the women. The butchered torsos they just leave, after cutting off the humps and eyes as special treats.

Angus is appalled. "You don't take any meat?" He doesn't even try to hide his horror. The hunters look at one another, then at him. A silence grows. Finally the leader—Red Heart, with his cowl thrown back—spits into the snow.

"Your people do the same. You know this, all of you do this." He looks with distaste at him. "After all, you buy our robes."

THAT NIGHT THEY feast. The women have butchered at least one of the bloody hulks, Angus is relieved to see. Soon the smell of roasting fat is smoky caramel in eyes and noses. Dogs wriggle toward the fire; his stomach growls. He sees her finally, across the hubbub at the fire, and feels his neck hairs lift. She's laughing in a ring of bright, lean faces, dark eyes snapping, white teeth flashing. Among these young nimíipuu of both sexes she stands out, he thinks: she is admired. She'll want one of her own kind, not a white man—a soyapo, he thinks, his spirits sinking. How he loathes the word: it's much too close to one that means "it stinks."

All evening he waits for a word from her uncle, any kind of sign. Watching, he sees that she speaks little, though others listen when she does. There's something grave about her, he thinks. They traveled and trapped for nearly a year, Baptiste told him. Even as hardy as his own sisters are, he can't quite see them doing that. Memories stir him then, the grand old stories of yore, and he leaps to his feet, decided. A peacock displays, he thinks, and so can I.

He slips to his tent, then into the trees, blowing softly into the bag. He pats the hard leather as it groans and stirs. By the time it's done bleating, the Natives have gone silent, faces turned toward the peculiar sound. He steps out of the shadow, fingers skirling, left arm pumping the inflated bag. He serenades her with *The Sweet Maid of Mull*. A lilting tune—though as he draws breath he has to smile. Half of them cover their ears; the rest shrink as he passes. The bagpipes are piercing, of course, but therein lies their beauty: the pageantry, the sheer peculiar blast of sound. It's not unlike their wailing cries above the drums. Young George is tapping his right hand on his crossed legs, by now familiar with this caterwauling. Then Eagle from the Light stands and starts to jig in place, a wicked grin across his face. Angus stops before Catherine Baptiste and shifts to the tune he loves best, *The Flower of Scotland*. Young George starts to clap, elbowing the men beside him, lifting his hands to show them how. Most look uncertainly around, then shrug and smile and start to clap as well. If only his kin could see him now, serenading all these dark and shining faces. The tune breaks off abruptly, as they do. In that stunned silence he gives her a slight bow.

Later that evening he's summoned to Flint Necklace's lodge. When he steps in, he sees that she's waiting between her uncle and a woman who can only be her mother. Catherine looks straight ahead; she has changed into a white skin dress with some blue decoration. As he comes closer, she rewards him with a glance. He's shocked to see a flatness in her eyes. Sweat chills his back. How will he ever reach her?

"Welcome, trader." Her mother's voice is soft, though her look is penetrating. She's beautiful and terrifying, a Columbian Valkyrie: tall for a woman, with a wide face and narrowed eyes, a fall of black and silver hair. It's the eyes, and the hard set of her mouth, that makes him slightly quake. "You've traveled a long way to see us."

To see her, he thinks, glancing again at Catherine. By the way her eyes dart away he can tell she's observing him. Without planning to, he smiles.

"It's a grand land. Every time I move across it, I'm impressed." She takes this in, her lips softening. There cannot be that many white men who speak their language. Angus stands taller, facing her.

"You haven't been here long."

"This is my third winter. I am postmaster at Fort Hall on the Snake." He feels her assessment like a hot wire running up one side of him and down the other.

"I hear you slaughtered some buffalo," Flint Necklace puts in. He nods and everyone sits.

"It was too easy." The poor things had no chance. "I'd prefer the summer chase, at least how Eagle from the Light describes it."

"Don't believe everything our nephew says." Her mother smiles dryly and Catherine looks up. She glances at them both, eyes crinkling slightly.

"He also says you shoot well. I think he's a little jealous." The head man's eyes smile for a moment. But his face remains cool. "That's good. There's always someone waiting to take what's yours or kill you for it. In the buffalo country especially, enemies lie in wait."

He pauses; his eyes pin Angus. "We welcomed your kind when they came. The first ones who came, long before your Company, in the time of Twisted Hair and Red Bear. Then your people came to hunt our mountains." He frowns. "You Baymen took the game."

Angus nods, trying to keep his eyes from the shining girl.

"I didn't ride to buffalo as a young man." Flint Necklace signals for a pipe. "Just now and then, for fun." He takes in a rush of air and sighs it out. "We had enough in our homelands. But now we trade our horses for your guns." His expression is strange—a mixture, Angus thinks, of frustration, anger, disgust. "We didn't need the guns either, before. But now we need the meat, the robes." He leans toward Angus. "So we can sell them back to you, and so it goes. Much as I regret it, our destinies are joined." He takes the pipe into his mouth and nods toward Catherine's mother.

"My brother doesn't say it easily, especially to his own people." She takes the pipe in turn. "Life is getting harder." She takes a deep draught, holding Angus with her gaze, then lets the smoke out. "Your Company has taken and taken. Now it's time to give."

He grasps their meaning. If he's to be admitted, Angus must pledge his arms to the defense of his new clan. But this is not it, not exactly.

"We welcomed this trade." Flint Necklace speaks meditatively. "We didn't see how it made us weak. Now we can't live without it." He laughs without mirth and points the pipe at Angus. "So you Baymen must stand with against the soyapo who follow."

But I'm only one man, thinks Angus—not the whole Company. For this is what the head man seems to mean.

"I understand our people have been close." He searches for the right words. "I'll do everything in my power to assist you. For it's my hope that we will be much closer, as you know."

"Yes." Her mother leans to scatter a dried herb into the fire. The odor is subtle, a memory of summer. "Kitalah and I have discussed this." When Catherine looks silently up and nods, Angus understands that she's not allowed to speak while the elders deliberate.

There's no further talking then for what seems a long while. Angus waits—eager, overwhelmed. He too shuts his eyes but does not pray. Instead, the image of his own sweet mother comes into his mind. He wishes she could see him now.

"We're of the Lam'tamah and Took'pemah." Her mother speaks at last. "I am Margaret de Naie. I married a man from the northeast, the father of my daughters. A trapper for your Company, Baptiste." She looks hard at him to see that he's attending. "Our people have lived in Lamotta and along the Winding Waters for many generations. By her blood Kitalah is partly of your kind, partly of mine. She comes from a great and ancient people."

He understands exactly this enumerating of their root and branch. The Gaels have always done it, too.

"I am Angus McDonald, son of Donald, of the MacDonalds of Glengarry and Glencoe. The ancestor of my clan is Young John, Iain Og, descendant of Angus of Islay, Lord of the Isles."

Speaking aloud his Gaelic *sloinneadh*, his lineage, he feels both proud and strange—as much an exotic on display as they to him. They're looking at him with interest and a certain bafflement. Just as he has no idea where Lamotta is, so Glencoe means nothing to them. "We're not unlike in ancestry. In my country, my clan is also strong and old."

The two elders exchange a glance.

"My brother and I," her mother says, "have given this much thought."

They don't look that much alike, fleetingly he thinks. The word for cousin is the same as that for brother. Angus waits, a tightness in his chest, as she looks toward her daughter. Catherine rises and approaches him, holding out a hand. He clambers to his feet. She dips her head and he takes her fingers in his. Her skin is cool; her hand is light and strong.

"You'll be one of us," her mother says.

He needs to know that she is willing.

"You choose this, too?" he enquires, so softly only she can hear.

She flushes, very faintly. "I'm here."

It's a start. Her fingers flex and he can feel the way her life force moves.

"As I will always be for you." He turns to the two elders. "You do me a great honor."

Then he lifts her hand to his lips and kisses it, his whiskers brushing the dark skin, and is delighted when she trembles and begins to laugh.

CHAPTER 7

SOME MISCHIEF MADE her laugh out loud when first she felt that hairy face. Only later could she tell him this. It took some time to teach her body not to shake whenever he came near.

At seventeen, standing in her uncle's lodge, her first thought was that she was just like the wife in the old stories. This man to be her husband changed his shape. Now he was a wolf, now a puma, now a badger. She would bear her children with this creature covered all in fur. Maybe they'd be furred as well. She suppressed a shudder.

The next morning it's clear and bright. According to custom they must speak, though they won't be wed until the summer. Catherine regards this Bayman frankly. Reddish-brown hair covers his face and springs from his sleeves and neck. When he sits he must fold the long sticks of his legs like a hopper. He holds his hand out, pale and speckled.

"You shake it," he says in her language. She seizes it with both hands and pumps it, like shaking water off a pelt.

"Ow! Not like that," he laughs.

She flushes. *I will do it however I please.*

He smooths the hair beneath his mouth and nods. "I'm sorry, I didn't mean to laugh. Our customs are very different."

She's trying to imagine how she can keep a line around herself. A skin, to hold herself apart, though she'll have to spend her nights with him.

"I'm so happy," he says, and she's surprised. Happiness has nothing to do with it. Alliance, the Company, her people. Happiness is her own horse and a man from her cousin's band who looked in that way at her last summer.

"Are you happy, Kitalah?"

She tries not to react as he reaches again for her hand. "I don't know yet," eventually she says. It makes her uncomfortable, the way he admires her, his eyes moving across her lips, her cheeks, her hand captured in his, ivory over bronze. These hands do not belong. Her father at least was also Mohawk, born from this same land.

"Of course." He lets it go. "I won't push you, I promise."

This surprises her. Is he soft or hard? She knows nothing about him but what Eagle from the Light says. A good warrior, her cousin tells her: fierce in the hunt, and fun at the fire.

"What does your name mean? Kitalah? Your mother calls you that."

He's trying, anyway. She smooths the skin of her skirt. "Tipyehlehne Kitalah," she enunciates clearly so he gets it right. "It means the Eagle Rising Up."

"So many eagles in your band." The way he pronounces the nimíipuu words, as if his tongue is swollen, makes her smile.

"Why do you smile?"

She shakes her head. She'll speak to him in French instead. French feels like a kind of skin. "Et Ayngoose? *C'est un animal aussi*?"

"Ayng-gus," he corrects. His eyes are a strange color, green and brown with little flecks of yellow. "No. It means nothing, that I know. But Mac means son of—McDonald is son of Donald. That is my band."

She can't think of anything to ask. Get to know each other, her mother said, learn the kind of man he is. Catherine has no idea how to go about this. She frowns.

"Is something wrong?" he asks.

Everything, she'd answer if she could. Hair sprouts from him all over, from ears and nose and neck. She blocks the thought of the rest. The bodies of her people are smooth and hairless and hard, and she shrinks from the thought of all that hair, the insects that must writhe within that nest. In desperation she racks her mind for a question to ask.

"How many have you killed?"

"How many what?" He looks startled.

"Men." Of course. "In battle."

He doesn't answer right away. "In my country we only kill in war," at last he says. "But I haven't been to war."

The nimíipuu too only kill when they must, she thinks with scorn. To protect and feed their people, they have no choice but to face the Blackfeet on the plains. "Bostons kill for fun," she says, leaning forward. "I've seen this myself."

"Not King George's men." The way he looks at her is a touch more respectful. "You'll see, when you come to my fort."

At this a hard knot forms inside her.

"It's not far from here," he says.

"But your home is."

"Yes, very far. Across the sea. You know the sea?"

"Of course." She bridles a bit and he looks sorry. Catherine hugs her knees. He's only trying to be nice. "There's a big sea to the south," she adds. "Where we went after the beaver. How it breathed and bit my feet!" She smiles to think of that vast water and the clouds of wings that rose above it like a thousand lodges flapping.

"I never saw it till I came here." His voice is far away. She sees suddenly that he's young, almost as young as her. "I'd never even set foot on a ship."

"What's a ship?"

"Like a canoe, but bigger, very big indeed. Someday we'll take one, would you like that?"

The knot inside grows harder. "I prefer to stay close to my people."

He nods and reaches again to touch her. She tells herself to breathe. This is the time in which they are to see if they fit together as they should. Touching is part of it, it's important. It can be wonderful or terrible, Kyuka says.

"I understand," he says softly. Despite herself she feels a flutter in her belly. "I want to know you, Kitalah."

"Catherine," she blurts. "I'd rather—you call me that." It's who she is in this French skin—like with Baptiste. The two men are similar, she suddenly sees. They share a certain giddiness. Last night at the feast after blowing his strange horn the trader took two sticks and asked the men to bang the drum and made a cross upon the ground. And then he held his arms up in the air and started hopping, kicking out his legs and beating them against each other, grinning as he spun.

"What are you thinking now?" he asks.

She has to laugh. No one has ever asked her that. "That you looked foolish in your dance. But I still liked it."

"Good." He moves his hand beneath her chin. "I want you to know me too."

She feels her breasts stiffen against the buckskin as he moves his finger all along her jaw, across her throat. This man will be her husband. She shifts; he drops his hand.

"I won't push you," he says again. "You choose the time."

She nods; she looks him fully in the eyes. His lips are red, much softer close up than they first appeared. She feels an urge to touch the hair but isn't ready—not just yet.

"I'd like to see your land too," Angus says.

"It's not like any other place." The very thought of it brings joy.

"You live along the Clearwater, I've been told."

She nods. It strikes her suddenly that she could take him there, that she could have them both, her people and this man. She rises abruptly and strides to the flap and returns with a stick. "I'll show you." She squats near the crusted snow at the entrance and starts to draw.

"Wait." He reaches in his pouch and pulls out a block and peels it apart. Inside are the blue skins on which he scratched his numbers in the trading tent. "Here," he says, putting a cool reed in her hand. "Use this. See, it draws, like this." Then he's holding her hand and guiding it across the sheet and from the reed comes a black line. She laughs and holds it to her eyes. "Show me your home," he urges.

She scrapes the metal tongue across the sheet. She makes two lines for rivers that meet and flow into another, bigger line. "Che Wana," she says. "Columbia," he answers back. The southern tributary is the river of Winding Waters—the Snake. She draws its undulating course. He bends closer, pointing to a spot with his finger. "Here is my house, where I'll take you."

She nods impatiently and returns the reed north to where the rivers join, pressing hard, drawing her own river eastward toward the peaks, then swooping in a southward arc. She knows its every turn by heart. Just where it turns, she marks a few dark squiggles, pointed arrows for the mountains, lodges. "*Kaix-kaix-Koose*," she says, undulating her hand like a muscled trout. "Clean Water." She touches the paper, then her heart.

Angus smiles. She's showing him her most precious thing, her homeland.

OFF TO THE hot dry place she goes with him early that next summer astride her roan. He seems surprised at how little she brings—only clothes and baskets and kettles. The horses and rifles he gave Flint Necklace at Big Hole stay with the band. The high plain the newlyweds ride through is brittle and hard. The river slashes the land like a knife and lies in the cleft of dark rock far below. From the plateau they hear water but cannot see it. In this unfamiliar land she is to make a home. Pitted boulders block their path, the only sign of life some small and thorny bushes. And then she hears a bird, the same one, she is certain, that she heard last year along the Colorado. Here above the Snake she looks for his yellow cheeks, his black striped tail, but does not see him. Still his song is a balm.

At last the cliffs drop away and here is the bottomland, wet and green, the tendrils of the river like a spreading plant. Skidding down she sees rice grass and arrow leaf and at the bottom a swaying lake of pale green cattails. There is food everywhere if you know how to look. Across the river Fort Hall shines whitely: they swim the ford and she sees the chalk upon the dried mud bricks. *Ah-do-bee*, Angus says. A gate swings open. How many times has she camped outside such walls and never been inside? Here too there are lodges, an encampment of Shoshone at the water's edge. Friend or enemy, it is hard to tell. Her parents have raised her to be wary.

The horse park is full, the yard bustling with men of the Company, French, and Iroquois, as well as big Kanakas from the distant islands, pale King George's men of whom her husband Angus is the tallest. There is the storehouse for the fur, there the trading room. Women are stirring big vats. Some few Boston trappers have just arrived. It's late to be fitting out, long past the season of first root. Her father's outfit has long since set its traps, she's sure, though she hasn't seen him since her marriage.

Entering the main house Catherine is surprised to see a fire burning. These mud walls hold the cold as well as the heat, she'll learn. An old man in a red coat stretches his hands toward her. This must be the chief, the fort's *bourgeois*, as Baptiste calls them. His stomach pushes out the buttons of his coat; his gray beard is thin as a rat's tail, but there is warmth in his face.

"You are most welcome here, my dear." Proudly, Angus introduces them. He is Chief Trader Richard Grant. "The captain," Angus smiles.

"Of a listing ship!" the bourgeois answers, laughing.

Momentarily she's confused. What ship? Angus seems to sense this; he's all tenderness as he shows her up the stairs. Gingerly she puts a foot on the first step. He smiles again, encouraging. When she's up in the room that will be theirs, she steps back from the window, startled. The people below look shrunken. She has a curious feeling that she has died and gone to the sky world. But then her husband wraps her in his long arms from behind and she feels her heartbeat settle.

A STRANGE THING happened at Big Hole, when the bands gathered to celebrate her marriage before the summer hunt. As soon as her hand was placed in the trader's, her people treated her with respect. It was little things, a duck of the head by certain women, an unaccustomed gravity in her cousin's tone, the looks the men gave her and Angus when they exited Flint Necklace's lodge. She was a girl no more: she was the trader's wife. She hadn't expected it would make a difference. But now people look at her as if she is someone important. Part of her still wants to flee, but another part rustles and swells.

It wasn't rough or hard, his hair. This at least put her mind at ease. She could barely breathe when they went to his tent the first time, she was so terrified. She, who's afraid of nothing under the sun. She spoke to herself sternly. Kyuka had told her what to do. Childbirth will be worse, she told herself. This was hot and uncomfortable, his hand so suddenly beneath her shift before she was prepared. He looked awful, sweaty and ashamed when she jerked away. Again they tried and she thought of the way a stallion mounts a mare, how horribly he crushes her, and tried to push this picture from her mind. Angus was fumbling at her as she touched his upright sex and suddenly he groaned and it jerked and sprayed. And that was it. Catherine found herself surprised. So much is made of this.

"I'm so sorry," he was saying, and she lay there wondering *What for?*

"I want to give you children," he said next, his cheeks flaming.

"Then you must put it inside." She remembers the look he gave her, mortified. And too, how swiftly that awkwardness faded. He confessed that he had never before lain with any woman. Nor had she lain with a man. She pulled his strange soyapo leggings down, worked bee's balm in the hair across his chest, then all the way down there. Already it was hard again, and waving. He smelled better and began to touch her as she spread the balm along her belly and her thighs. She smelled their scents together. She wouldn't touch it this time, she decided. He too was careful; he was determined, she thought—this time he'd do it right. He stroked her up and down from breast to thigh, between her legs, his fingers searching for the door. And then he was pushing into her, burning hard.

So it went for a moon, sometimes fast, sometimes long, each time slightly different. They were like newborn babes, he laughed, his manner with her constantly surprising. He could be gruff, proud, a bantam with her cousin, steely-eyed when shooting the deer that came at dusk to feed. But alone in their tent, he seemed younger and less assured. They would lie afterward curled, whispering. She told him about her village, the gardens above the rushing river. Corn and squash and more besides, sky water that fed the plants when they went off to buffalo. "And in the season when the *nacó'x* swim back, we too return." "Nacó'x?" he asked, and she mimed leaping salmon. While the fat gourd of moon poured light down on them, he'd show her things and name them. *Dentelle*, he'd say and wrap the lace around her arm. *Himtux*, she'd answer, tugging at the beard she'd made shiny with bear fat. She'd shown him the shape of her country, she whispered one night, but knew nothing of his but his whistling bag. Angus sat her on his lap and told her the stories he'd heard all his life. Of the McDonalds of Glencoe, that clever, scofflaw clan, warriors and herders who the English hated most, and thus decided to destroy. They set their soldiers on them on a winter's day, he told her, massacred the chief and people as they slept. He himself only walked this earth because his ancestor survived. We learned to flee to survive, he said—just like he'd been forced to a few years back. He shot a deer on another chief's land, which is why he had to leave his country. Catherine wound her arms around him. "But the deer offered itself," she said. He nodded. *Exactement.*

How glad he was now for that shot, he murmured, for it carried him to her. As she too was glad now she was some part French, she began to think. She liked how he spoke to her, even more how he listened. White men rarely listen to a woman in this way. He wanted to know everything about her, all at once. Day after day it warmed her to him. And, too, they learned the ins and out of every curve and crook and found a use for tongues and fingers—found that they could make each other gasp at last.

NOW THREE MOONS later she's in his world and the people look like ants below.

"You like it?" he's whispering, face rubbing against hers. "Tonight we'll bless this room. But first I want to show you off." He draws back and smooths his breeches, plants a small dry kiss upon her cheek. "Captain Grant is most insistent."

Their marriage must be made again, it seems, in the way of King George's people.

"For your own protection," says *le captaine* Grant, pursing his thin lips.

Catherine is relieved that he speaks French; she knows only a few words of English. *But we're married already*, she thinks but does not say. "We must do it by the book," the bourgeois goes on, turning and pulling a face at Angus. "The tide of great morality arising."

"Any excuse for a party."

"None of those either now, except at New Year."

When Angus says, "No, honestly?" the Chief Trader's face turns foxy. "Of course, one might argue it's a new year for you both here."

Once more she wears the white deerskin dress that's so soft it's like wearing clouds. The large *V* she worked in blue and green beads points straight to her womb—for luck she made it in the season of *Hauqu'oy*, when the doe is pregnant and may not be killed. She descends, holding to the railing, anchoring herself.

And then her husband appears below and she laughs out loud. He wears a blanket around his middle that barely reaches his knees; his legs are white and hairy. He looks a little like a digging stick. She covers her mouth, for he's looking at her severely.

"These are my family's colors," he says gravely. "This is my kilt."

It's the evening of her very first day and Grant asks Angus and her to face him, their backs to the surprisingly large group that comes to watch.

"By the authority of the Hudson's Bay Company, I hereby solemnize this rite." To her it sounds like mallards quacking. "You confirm that you, Angus McDonald, postmaster in the Company's employ, are united according to the custom of the country with Catherine Baptiste, daughter of Baptiste Coquin, a half-breed servant in the Company's employ." Angus nods, so she follows suit. "Today then, before these witnesses, we renew those vows which you have made already."

Because she doesn't speak this language, she observes closely the man who does. There's an intensity to this Captain Grant, a tautness in his jaw, as if he's blocked up like a river strangled by a dam. He's looking at her tenderly, almost mournfully, and yet he holds a fury in him also. Some men sign the paper he holds. When she hears glasses clinking, she knows why so many people are there. Everyone lines up to get their glass and kiss her on the lips. At first she finds it horrid, but she has a drink herself and then it's interesting, how each man and woman in the fort comes up to press their mouth to hers: lips thick and thin and dry and wet. The women stroke her dress and murmur praise at the fine work.

Never in her life has she seen what she sees next. They call it dancing but it looks like bolting from a biting swarm. One man has a box he drags a stick across, another a reed pipe. Angus has his bag that whistles and she smiles, remembering the way she shrieked when she first heard it. They all did, thinking some rabid creature was coming screaming from the forest. The wailing when he set it down reminded her of something dying. Now when he starts the guests leap to their feet, flinging out arms and legs, whirling and banging into one another. Angus is stomping back and forth, his cheeks puffed out, and she can only watch them with amazement. After a while they call for the bride and groom and Angus puts his pipes down. Time for our dance, he says.

She'd like a drum, that's all, a beat from several sticks. "Fiddle us a tune," her husband says, and the stringy thing obliges. It's sweet and slow and this she understands. She holds his hand and dances in the way she knows, lifting one foot and then the other, bending, bowing, gracefully, her form erect. Her husband mostly watches as he holds her lightly by the fingers, tapping his feet, now and then twirling her gently. Then they stop, and there are hoots and howls and the wild dance kicks up again.

CHAPTER 8

SUMMER 1843
Fort Hall

SHE CUPS HER breasts each morning to see if they are growing. She waits until her husband wakes and rolls out of the blanket. She hates the way they sleep so high: inside a lodge she would feel safe. Nor would she swelter so. In the blistering summer at Fort Hall, these clay walls bake her like a root.

After Angus descends, she moves to the glass set on his wooden chest. It's still hard to believe the image it returns is real. Catherine has only seen herself in water or her father's tiny metal square, which shows at most her eyes and nose. Now she's a woman of nearly nineteen winters, and her husband's glass is tall enough that if she stands upon their bed, she sees her neck down to her legs.

Her breasts are the same as the day before, the week before, the moon before. A year has passed and still no baby grows inside her. She'd know. He is attentive to her pleasure, he loves nothing more than to put his seed inside her. But still nothing has started to grow. She moves her hands over her belly, her hips; yes, she is thicker, but this is only from the traders' food, their fat and cream and eggs. She's thick and sleek now like an otter but it isn't pleasing. She catches him looking at her sideways sometimes and feels a stab of fear. She ought to be carrying a child by now.

If only she could ask her mother or her aunties or the girls she grew up with who are wives now too. Sometimes such matters require medicine. At least she could describe to them this shaky fright that comes at night, like a cold hand pressing at her side. They could find a way to send it away.

The fort women are cheeky as squirrels. If she were to tell one, all would talk. They're like endlessly chattering streams, the servants' wives—Shoshone and Cree and Salish, women of many tribes.

She dresses herself in the lightest cloth she can find, covering those parts of her that Angus says a lady does not show. The instant she steps into the yard the biting insects smell her. They're what she and everyone at the post hates most, what drives Captain Grant so mad he stomps around waving his arms, shouting "Bloody mosquitos!" Only to blush when he sees her and say, "Beg pardon, my dear." If only she could escape with the horses to the uplands across the river where they are free of these clouds of giant ravenous insects. The horses are luckier than the humans, she thinks. How her own people would roll their eyes, laughing at these people who don't have the sense to seek some kinder land. There must be some leaf, some oil, these biting creatures will not eat. She resolves to go to the Shoshone camp and inquire.

Almost as soon as she steps out, she hears a cry from a sentry above her. *Wagons!* he calls. Catherine freezes. Like last summer, she thinks with dread—when out of the east came a convoy unlike anything anyone had ever seen. At first she thought the clouds had come to rest upon the earth. Billows and billows of white, the tall, hooped cotton crawling slowly through the parching desert. Emaciated oxen, creaking wheels: a wave of white canvas and pinched white faces, crawling inexorably toward them.

THE YEAR WAS decent, in terms of fur. Some twelve hundred beaver, lynx, and fox, plus eight hundred buffalo Angus hunted in the winter with the Native bands. Dr. McLoughlin will be pleased, as Grant already is. Angus has shown initiative, his superior says, capturing the Nez Perce and Salish trade while the Americans slept in their winter dens. The snow seems a lifetime ago, but that's because of the heat and the goddamned mosquitos. Scots aren't made for these temperatures, Angus tells himself and Richard Grant.

"Ought to give the whole blasted hellhole to Mexico," the head man grumbles.

It's late August and in two weeks Angus will take the furs to Fort Nez Perces on the Columbia to be shipped to Fort Vancouver. Indeed, they're well pleased with themselves—until, one blazing day no different from any other, the dull buzzing air is disrupted by the sound of thousands of hooves approaching from the south.

They muster to the palisade. Grant sets sharpshooters at the slots. Already Angus has rounded up the fort residents, enclosing them securely in the compound, when he joins him in the corner bastion. Looking southeast they see a white column spooling far into the distance. It's longer by far than the wagon train that came through the summer before. The canvas covers judder and sway like sails above the jolting wagons. Exactly like the sails of an armada—like the Viking hordes in Gaelic tales, thinks Angus, pouring south across the sea. This western sea is baked to a light brown, but the feeling of invasion is the same.

Grant has the glass at his eye. "Good Lord in Heaven." He counts beneath his breath. The train is sheathed in dust; behind it, horns and hooves glint in a thick brown fog. Angus's heart sinks as he measures the extent of it. A mile of horses and mules at the back, at least a thousand head; four miles of oxen pulling wagons. Where will they pasture them, who will feed these hordes of people? The first lot of settlers was not one-tenth so large. Yet all were dropping with exhaustion, hunger, grief. Wrung with relief, certainly, to find Fort Hall, and yet offended too, to see the British flag.

The Chief Trader retracts his telescope to a flat disk and slips it in his pocket. "God Almighty," he says again. It's late in the day and their only hope is that the caravan will bivouac some distance away, giving them time to organize themselves.

"How many do you reckon?" Angus asks.

"Near a thousand." Grant pulls at his beard. Then his expression brightens. "A bundle in horses, though." Bone-tired emigrants are more than happy to part with cash for a mount that will make it to Oregon or California, they have learned. Several hours later they receive the emigrants' leaders: a tall Southern fellow and a retired soldier who serves as their guide, along with a missionary and a short balding fellow. Simultaneously, Grant and Angus exclaim.

"How d'you sneak back east without me hearing?" Grant pumps the hand of Marcus Whitman, a Presbyterian minister who runs a mission near Fort Nez Perces.

"For the love of Pete," is all Angus can summon at the sight of Joe Meek, all cleaned up in collar and braces. His russet beard is trimmed, but he still looks like a monkey in a suit.

Neither, however, beats the emigrants' leader—a Mr. Burnett from Virginia—to an answer. "Water first, Reverend Whitman, if you please," he barks.

Grant looks at him askance while Whitman murmurs, "Mr. Grant is well acquainted with our needs." At least the preacher has been in this country long enough to show some manners. "We'll not trouble you tonight," the missionary adds. "But our women and children would be grateful on the morrow of some kindness."

They spend most of the night hauling water and at first light building fires and heating stones. The heat barely abates and, in the morning, when Angus and Grant ride out to the convoy they recoil. The oxen are little more than hide and ribs; the equally emaciated horses and milk cows stand panting, tongues flecked with foam. Their misery is now compounded by the stinging insects; the flanks of every last beast stream with blood.

"Let them swim." Angus moves swiftly to show the drovers the low trail toward the ford. Otherwise, they won't survive the loss of blood. The families huddle inside their canvas hulls, the children's faces streaked with dirt, the same bites and blood. The women are trying to make breakfast, whirling their arms to clear the buzzing clouds. Over the whole camp reigns a pall. The message is passed that they are welcome to bathe and rest at the fort.

Every last hand is required to keep the big kettles boiling and even rawhide bags with heated stones; no receptacle is too small to serve. They send the men out past the western wall and give over the long bunkhouse to the women and the children. There are seven hundred thirteen settlers in all; Angus has Young George count them. The habit of counting runs deep in him now, though he wonders how many they were when they set out.

He watches Catherine at the bunkhouse door, her hair in one plait at the back, smiling and distributing berries. Her night was spent grinding sagebrush to an oily paste and adding fat, kneading the whole in a leather bag. Her new ointment brings surprising relief: the bugs can't stand the taste of it. Her only regret, she says, is that she can't work fast enough to coat the horses like she coats the people.

▰

CATHERINE HAS SEEN more white men than she cares to. Not so many white women. She glimpsed a few last summer but never close up. They were like startled deer, she thought then, dashing back to their wagons at the slightest approach. Now they're moving in a slow line past her. She holds her basket in her left arm and scoops the currants with her right, tipping them into the cupped hands. The children are eager, the women more guarded. They're covered in cloth from head to toe even though it's very hot. Maybe it's because of the bugs. But then again maybe not. These dresses all pinch them in the middle, cutting them in two like a wasp. The pinching pushes up their breasts; the cloth lies tight against their skin. Below the waist there is much bunched cloth swelling over their rumps and dropping to the ground. All she can think is that they must be boiling in all that cloth.

When the last one enters, she goes in and closes the door behind her. The beds and benches have been pushed to the walls and in the center are three giant tubs. The mothers are bathing the little ones first. Captain Grant ordered the clerks to give out cloth for drying and Catherine is shocked to see them rip the pretty bolts of red in strips. At first things are stiff and awkward, but at the feel of warm water the children laugh and whoop and the mothers and older sisters join in. Smiles and laughter bounce around. The fort wives like herself stand away, now and then offering a piece of soapweed, a comb, more water.

Mostly they watch. She tries to block the first picture that comes to her mind at the sight of their pale bodies. But it's hard to unsee: a litter of albino pups, all pink and squirming. Pink isn't a color she sees much. All of them try not to stare, but they can't help it.

Two women nearby have hair nearly the color of bone, a mother and daughter. It reaches only to their chins. Their skin is so transparent she can see blue traces like small rivers underneath. When the daughter looks shyly at her, holding out a mashed and useless stick, Catherine hurries over. Their breasts are globes, like hers, but milky white with bright pink tips. These rise from a ring of darker pink, like blossoms, she thinks, blushing as they catch her looking. The mother stares at her as if she is a ghost. Her eyes are not like any Catherine has seen: bright green like springtime clover. Her daughter too has eyes of green. One of the younger women is hugely pregnant and the others help her into the tub, and Catherine is pierced by such a longing.

What has this girl done that she has not?

All at once the most terrible thought comes into her mind. She shakes her head, but still it sticks. She sees his pale white legs, his hips, his sex, her own brown form beside him. Is it because he's white that her womb rejects his seed? Or did she call this blockage down upon herself, when she at first refused his suit? He'll leave her, she thinks suddenly, rooted with horror; he'll cast her off and find one who can give him the children he so desires. The soyapo women, pink, flushed, delighted, pin back their hair, pull on their undergarments. They emerge from the bunkhouse like butterflies, flapping their drying wings.

The enclosure is filled with their men, likewise clean and smiling, and everyone can feel the throb, the excitement, of their bodies, free now of the dust, loose with a kind of abandon. From the upper walkway the men of Fort Hall are watching. Catherine finds her husband bent over like the rest, his eyes roving over these women with skin so pink and white, women of his own kind.

THE LEADING EMIGRANTS dine at Fort Hall that night. Richard Grant sharpens his proverbial knife while servants place the partridge soup. He's good at extracting news from people passing through. Hardship and isolation make men loquacious when at last they meet their fellow man, he's often said.

Peter Burnett, elected the wagon train's leader in Missouri, brings his wife along. Whitman and Meek come too, with their guide and a Jesuit and several younger men. Angus pulls Joe aside, joking that he's dressed like an undertaker, but Joe just cocks an eyebrow and sits down.

Catherine turns out in her best finery, including a white shirt Angus has never seen before, while Burnett's wife, pinched and waspish, stares with hostility at both her and Young George. You'd think she'd never seen an Indian before. The Americans Angus has known till now have all been trappers, rough but honest. This group is not like that. A peculiar attitude lifts off them: swagger, he might term it.

It's a pleasure, therefore, to watch Captain Grant operate. He starts with a smile and a toast: "The day and all that honor it. Even the Reverend won't begrudge us that."

Whitman indeed wets his whistle; Grant employs the pause to hang out his first question. "To what, then, gentlemen—and madam—do we owe this expansive delegation? I do hope the United States are not collapsed?"

His little joke does not elicit a laugh. Burnett looks at Whitman and Meek as if weighing how much to say, then raises his own glass. "To the glorious territory of Oregon, newly joined to these great States." His twang is almost incomprehensible. "We're joining the new provisional government in the valley of the Willamette."

Whitman turns, explaining to Grant: "You may have heard that Senator Linn's bill has passed the Senate. Every American can now claim a section to farm."

"We hear many things." Grant's smile is thin. "It's often hard to separate rumor from fact."

The Oregon Country is vast—but not that vast. Angus feels a pressure in his throat. What territory do they mean, and what on earth is Meek doing among these people? "Quite a crowd to move across such a difficult distance," he observes. "How long have you been underway?"

The answer is three months, since the 22nd of May. They were eight hundred seventy-five souls when they set out from Independence, Missouri—now barely seven hundred.

"Savages at every turn," one of the young men heatedly bursts out. "We killed as good as we got, but still." Mrs. Burnett makes a choking sound. Angus glances at Catherine, focused intently on the inflections if not the words. Grant shoots him a warning look.

"I'm so sorry. It is indeed punishing country." The chief trader signals for the second course. He goes on to ask what conditions pushed them to emigrate and the men burst out with explanations: taxes, drought, flood, fever. And, too, the papers are full of the glories of Oregon, another young man says. Grant sagely nods, waving the servants to keep filling the wine. The famished travelers fall on the duck pie, a scramble of eggs, more chicken, bread, some cheese, more wine. Angus covers his glass as the servant moves around the table, pouring, pouring.

"Outstanding," the soldier calls, lifting his fork. "One bonus with squaws, they sure cook good." He grins and turns toward Angus, who feels his skin flash hot, then cold. Burnett's wife hoots loudly. "Honestly, Captain Blake! When all these savages can do is roast their bloody meat."

"Now, madam," Grant murmurs, but she pays no mind.

"Then how do these squaws eat?" Her face is ugly with the drink. "Half naked, without manners, I should think."

The blast of hate Angus feels is instantaneous. "That's not a word we use. Since you, madam, presume to speak of manners." He speaks coolly, though in his mind he's mashing her face into her plate.

"Hey, now." The husband bristles, half-rising from his seat.

Grant cuts in. "We've much to learn from one another, that is certain." He takes a breath. "What interests me is how you plan to govern that whole country. If I have got you right, each man will take a tract of land, and these you will defend?"

"Yessir," says Burnett, sinking back, directing a look of spleen at Angus. "Five hundred able bodied men should do it."

Clearly they know nothing of the local population. Their purported Paradise, which they call Willamette, is home to half a dozen tribes. Already there's trouble north and south of Fort Vancouver. Whitman's mission to the Walla Walla and Cayuse is said to rub the Natives like a blister. There have been altercations, they've heard—words and blows, ill feeling growing. The Company will certainly resist this attempt to seize the land. But as dinner drags on, Angus starts to understand. These people don't give a good goddamn about the Hudson's Bay Company, their hosts included.

Joe Meek, meanwhile, is lying low. Two can play at this, thinks Angus.

"What provision will be made for those whose land you take?" He drops it like a jack of spades, to flush him out. "Mr. Meek, I hear you know this region well." As if they've never met. "I cannot think you believe it will be easy."

Joe looks him coolly in the eye and speaks so the whole table hears him. "This country must be pacified." He shrugs. "It's much too rich to leave to a few bands of Natives."

Angus stares at him for long moments afterward, but Joe does not return the look. He chats with the young men, cleans his teeth, drops a comment now and then. All cleaned up and playing a role like some kind of politician. Angus can scarcely believe it. Joe Meek, widower of Uementucken, husband and father of Indian women—turned Yankee settler, prospective farmer, colonizer.

Grant's trying to worm out more details of this "provisional government" but Angus just feels sick. Who appointed them bloody king and cabinet? They seem to think they can march in and take over. Last he heard, the Oregon Country was territory of the British Crown. For as long as he's been here, Britain and America have been arguing over which parts of the continent each can claim. The Hudson's Bay Company has always assumed Her Majesty's government will assert its right to the Columbia watershed; its forts dot the whole region. Possession, after all, is nine-tenths of the law.

Talk turns to the Protestant missionaries who've arrived to try to convert the Indians. One is now Indian Agent west of the Rockies, Whitman informs them. Grant frowns; they'd only been told the fellow was missionary to the Cayuse and Nez Perce. Catherine stiffens to hear her tribe named. God only knows how Angus will explain this to her. What on earth, he wonders, is an "Indian Agent?"

"We wish him luck, in any case." Grant is no longer smiling. "And any help we can give—though the Company, of course, can't involve itself in political discussions."

"Damn right it can't." Burnett is lounging now, one hand playing with his empty glass. "For all we appreciate your hospitality, the fact is, you're out. A foreign company competing with our traders on American soil, we'll hear no more of it."

"American soil?" Grant frowns. "There's no treaty yet, to my knowledge."

"The whole Columbia will be ours, up to the 49th, to the west as to the east. There isn't any doubt." Burnett's nasal twang is more than grating. "No offense, but it's time y'all started packing."

"We'd welcome you in our new government, of course." Marcus Whitman, at least, appreciates their expertise. "Dr. McLoughlin is keen, I hear—he's claimed some property, and like the rest will need to join in its defense."

Only Angus sees the shock Grant swiftly covers. "Tell that to your settlers," he says coldly. "They got up a petition calling for our ejection, as I'm sure you know."

"Some people are not properly Christian in their outlook." The preacher waves a hand. "Your Company's generous support of our community has not gone unnoticed. The petition is not taken seriously, I assure you."

"How do you know?" Grant retorts. Things on the ground must be worse than they imagine. They hear almost nothing of the settlers and their politics. All they know is that Simpson and McLoughlin are at each other's throats for reasons of their own—and thus not keeping a close eye on the Americans.

"Well," sighs Whitman, with decidedly un-Christian pride, "I met with the President more than once. He assures me the United States will deal honorably with your government."

"With the President himself. My, my, Mr. Whitman."

"You know as well as I things can't continue as they are. Law and order are needed urgently. We've endured such abominations lately at the mission."

"What's wanted is an iron rod. That's all the red man understands." Their guide has dedicated the meal to sloshing red wine down his gullet. "Whip 'em, hold their feet to the fire."

"We live as neighbors." Grant stands. "I'd counsel you to think of that before you go in waving guns and confiscating land."

"Counsel all you like," mutters Burnett.

The meal is clearly over.

Yet Whitman will have the final word. "The situation is too hostile. We must deal with it, and soon—you know it. Once the Company pulls out."

"Getting a little ahead of ourselves, aren't we?" Angus can no longer restrain himself.

"Of course, you will be compensated."

"And you, I guess, will be a bishop."

The missionary doesn't blink. "They've already started building Fort Vancouver's replacement. It'll sit north of the boundary on an island in the Sound, I hear. They're calling it Fort Victoria."

Grant's eyes seek out Angus. There's no disguising his fury now. Even he, a Chief Trader, has been kept in the dark.

CHAPTER 9

HARD AS HE argued, he couldn't convince her not to go. She was beside herself, turning and turning in their room. "They spoke of the nimíipuu!" she said wildly. "Captain Grant was angry and so were you. Why do they come, these Bostons, with their women and children?"

Even now, when they've parted, Angus can see her, fists tight, eye-whites flashing. He hears her announce with no prospect of rebuttal: "I will go to my mother for some time."   .

He wishes he could ask Maggie how women work. In these matters he has no experience. Catherine isn't just angry and afraid—offended by these Yankees and their ugly mouths. They both know it goes deeper. "It's good to be with your own people sometimes, no?" she said with the strangest look that awful evening. "You, too, to speak your English?" He didn't want her to leave; he forbade her to go. She just looked at him with defiance. "You do not tell me what to do."

How he regrets it now. He'd hold her close and tell her that he worries too. Time and again he suggested they go to the doctor at Fort Vancouver, but she wouldn't hear of it. He shouldn't have let it all get to him. But since those arrogant bastards came charging in, he's had so much preying on his mind. What he finally wormed out of Joe Meek has left him unsure which way to turn.

When he pinned him down the day before the wagon train pulled out, Joe acted ill at ease. As well he might; he'd been avoiding him for days. By then Angus saw no point in pussyfooting. "What's eating you, Meek?" he said, settling himself on the riverbank. "Seems you don't want to look me in the face."

Joe turned and stared at him point blank, to prove him wrong. "Naw." His voice was strange. "More like the other way around: you men don't want to see the writing on the wall."

"Truthfully, you're the last man I expected to see mixed up in such a dirty business."

"Dirty?" Meek looked surprised. "Nothing dirty it in, Mac. You've never even seen the place, so don't go judging."

Whatever happened to the man who wrestled grizzlies, murdered Blackfeet, loved three different Nez Perce wives? The very thought of Joe Meek farming was preposterous. But this wasn't what most concerned Angus. "So tell me straight," he said. "They really think that they can claim it all?"

"*We*." Meek gave him the queerest, almost pitying look. "*We* aim to make this territory bloom. It's not your country, Mac, it's ours—this great big country. We're stretching out in it, is all." A flash of the old Joe returned; he put a mitt on Angus's arm. "You can't imagine all the people at our heels." His eyes lit up. "The days are over when a man could roam and live off game, those wild and crazy days." He smiled, half-wistfully, and gave the arm a squeeze, but Angus simply sat there, numb.

"Not that I blame you for not knowing. Hell, you only just arrived."

It seems to Angus now that Joe felt Angus had been wronged. Old Doc McLoughlin knew the way the wind was blowing; it wasn't fair he hadn't told the fellows at Fort Hall. Joe's eyes had softened, Angus remembers three weeks later, driving his own pack train westward. "You've done all right for yourself, anyway." The former mountain man had smiled. "Your lady's quite the catch—real Nez Perce royalty."

Yet even then she was preparing her own flight. Angus could not hold her. The earth beneath his feet is sliding, tilting, everywhere.

He told Joe Meek the Company would never yield the north bank of the Columbia, nor cede their capital at Fort Vancouver.

"So they say—so they may even believe." Joe kicked the dirt bank with his boot. "But it isn't up to them, is it?" The kings and presidents would carve it up, and the rest was up to whosoever got their boots out on the ground.

His old friend looked hard at him then and dangled that lifeline. "You could always join us." His eyes were alive with their old crazy flame. "We could run horses, cattle, outfit all these greenhorns. Thousands, tens of thousands, all without a doggone clue! The land is going begging—don't you tell me there's a problem with the tribes. They'll come and go the way they always have."

"You want to strike it rich yourself." Angus's mind, his mouth, worked at half-speed. "Be your own man."

"Why not? No harm in trying."

For the first time he saw—he understood this man, these settlers even. Lighting out to make their own lives on their terms. While Angus was just a cog, with no more independence than a mule that turns in circles at a wheel. Goddamn them all, from London up to Stromness all the way to bleak Fort Hall: to drag him here, then drop him in the dust. He signed a contract though, he told Joe Meek, though privately he knew his five-year term was up.

"There won't be any firm left to be loyal to." Meek punched him in the arm. "C'mon, Mac. It'll be just like old times."

For days now it's been churning in his mind. All the difficulties that lie before him: not only rapids and ravines, nor ambushes and raging beasts, but the guaranteed resistance of his wife.

WHEN SHE ARRIVES all dusty and snapping with nerves, her mother takes one look at her and starts heating stones for the sweathouse.

"I see you grieve." Margaret puts a hand on Catherine's flat stomach, and she feels herself let out the breath she's held for all these moons. The whole way home she's felt a boulder on her chest. She's half ashamed at how she ran, and yet still furious—but most of all she's shaken. How easily these Yankees turn her upside down. Yet at the same time she wasn't entirely sure how her own people would receive her. Even now she can't quite tell. When Margaret takes her hand away, Catherine sees sparks.

Young George shifts awkwardly and she presents him to the people who emerge to look as a representative of her husband's Company. "My escort," she smiles, though both know it was she who led them. She was carried by the Salmon River's twists and turnings like her own blood rushing through her veins. Moving through the grasslands north, up past Lamotta, she was even gliding, lifting with the meadowlark that tells the traveler that their destination nears. Now she's here, though, she's tensed up again. The people look upon her with curiosity, as if they do not know her—Margaret, her deep eyes hooded, most of all.

The steam is soothing at first but then it's a red-hot poker in her center, blasting her apart. She cracks, her edges blurring, everything inside her draining out. A weak and mewling thing is all she is, completely emptied. Then her mother adds more water to the fire. She lays the herbs upon it.

"Now you are clean," she says. "Breathe deeply."

She fills her back up, with bay and mountain sorrel, bark of tamarack. She feeds her on the air, the soil, the oils from which she comes, in which she's always bathed. In that sharp tanginess there is a song she knows. "Kitalah." Catherine hears it like a whisper, though her mother's mouth is closed. "Open your throat, your womb, your heart." She feels a flutter, like a wingbeat in the hollow of her neck, and then the song is in her ear, the yellow-winged and black-barred song of long ago. She sees him clearly perched upon a twig, head cocked, beak parted, trilling. Warmth fills her from below.

When her eyes open Margaret is gone, the flap still trembling, and in the remnants of the fire there sits an egg. Its blue shell seems to glow but when she picks it up it's smooth and cool.

"The way was blocked," she hears her mother say. "The door was closed." This time her lips move as she comes back with a pitcher of cold water. Deeply, Catherine drinks. Her mother helps her up and they walk to the river, bright and swirling, running fast across the colored stones. And she steps into the knife of cold and is a child again, each morning scoured anew by the ice water of the Lochsa where it joins the little river, where she came into this world.

She's not cold, not here. The lodges on the banks of their small hollow ripple in a breeze and she can see the gardens all around, the young plants reaching toward the sun.

"You came alone." Her mother wraps her tightly, almost roughly. "He didn't object?"

"He didn't like it." At their parting he held her so tightly she could barely breathe.

"So you insisted."

"He would have taken me to their medicine. I said I wanted mine."

Margaret nods. She gazes off across the river, toward the camas grounds or maybe even farther. "You shouldn't push him too much, though. He'll only bend so far. And he has troubles of his own."

As always, she knows. How much she sees of all the things that Catherine's lived, her daughter never really knows. Enough. White women, white men, shadows in the back of Catherine's eyes. "I know," she murmurs. If she's not careful he'll choose one of his own kind. And to her own surprise, she finds that she would mind. She's come to care for him, this passionate and silly, stubborn man.

"How many Bostons were there?" Margaret asks. She tells her. Her mother's face sags; she looks more careworn now. "We hear the same from the Shoshone and the Crow."

"The Baymen are angry."

"Good." Margaret stands and stretches, arching her back, arms wide to the sky. "We'll need their anger as much—maybe even more—than their guns."

MOST PEOPLE HATE the Snake country, dry and hostile as it is. Burrs and brambles tear at legs and arms; in that parched air the sound of water maddens, flowing unattainable two hundred feet below. Not Angus. On this journey the harshness of the country echoes his own soul. He likes its otherworldliness: the black rocks jutting from the sage, red pebbles light as air that coat the trail. Far off, the dark cones of the mountains rear their crusted heads. He finds some comfort in this vastness. The earth is everywhere itself, indifferent to man—alive and beautiful in all its guises. He crouches to examine a green whorl that signals water. He sees a bunch of borage, shoots of goldenrod. Water, beauty, food. He's learned to look, he thinks with a slight twinge; and more than that, all this he learned from her.

From Hall to Boisé to Nez Perces—then what? Which of those forts will still be standing five years hence? While he and Meek are selling livestock to the emigrants, an image he still struggles to fix in his mind. At Fort Boisé Chief Trader Payette kisses him on either cheek. "*Mon vieux*," he says, "I've seen you looking better." François is low and fat and kind. He plies the men with cheese and salmon and begins to search for all their mail. He has it somewhere. "Apologies," he says, "it's all in a disorder." Indeed, the fort is a confusion of wide-open chests and boxes; in the yard, great sweating islanders are shifting the big bales.

"Moving?" Angus asks, and François nods.

He hooks his thumbs into his braces. "*Enfin.* I earned my rest, that much I tell you." He's off to his retirement at Red River and a new man is en route with the supplies. The sheer complexity of this whole Company, thinks Angus: well-honed web of men and furs and boats. Again he feels the sense of awe he felt back at the start. Surely such an empire can't just disappear. He carries in his pack his own short letter to McLoughlin, asking—no, demanding—to be told the truth. What future can the Company secure him, if these emigrants are right?

"Ah, here we are." François hands him a fat pack. The one on top he recognizes instantly: he clerked for Archibald for near a year and ought to know his hand. Angus slits it with his knife and reads it standing.

My dear nephew, it begins.

For once, his great-uncle's tone is warm. But this is not the only surprise his letter holds.

> *By the time you receive this we will be at the Boat Encampment I should think.*
>
> *Yes: Jenny and I at long last have taken that big step and set our sights toward the east.*

Angus blinks, looking out on the churn of men and boats, the glistening, treacherous river. *Et tu*, he wants to cry.

> *I cannot say that I am sorry, though it pains me to leave this fine establishment, erected with such pain and toil. And, too, our own beloved son Angus, resting atop the knoll. Still there is little left now to retain us. The Americans are baying for our necks. The fight ahead, I fear, will be long and vicious. Let the good Doctor and Douglas sort it out. You do well to stay out of it and ply your business where you are.*
>
> *I am sorry not to see you before leaving, and even more that we have not had the pleasure of meeting your wife. Please accept our most belated congratulations—we had expected to see you there or here before this. I hope that you will be as happy as I have been with my Jenny. There are few better comforts in this wilderness than a loving friend, companion, and the blessed gift of children, which I pray that you are graced with by and by.*

When we will meet again only the good Lord knows. Until then all of us send our fondest regards and I too trust that Providence will keep you well. As my old granddad would say, Slàinte mhòr agus a h-uile beannachd duibh. *Every good blessing to you.*

Archibald McDonald

For a long time he just stands there, staring. Payette, Archibald— McLoughlin, too, if Meek is right: one by one the Company's old men are cashing out. The world's gone mad, or maybe always was. There's no surety, no safety anywhere. Angus stands alone.

But would he feel much better out in Oregon among Americans, who do not think that highly of his kind? And suddenly he knows it in his bones: Catherine would never go. Not there. Across the wide web of the business, yes, but not to live among Americans. Why should she? He sees her again, eyes filled with fury. Her world is rich and full; she's rooted in her clan, as Angus once was too. He can't compel her, though a part of him insists a wife should do her husband's bidding. He takes a breath, another, wipes his face with his free hand. He should have talked to Richard Grant, the closest thing to kin he has, now Archie too is going.

"Everything all right?" He turns back toward the house, where Payette stands, his round face anxious. Suddenly two little heads appear behind him: his son and daughter by his Salish wife, who François calls his Petite Fleur. They paw at their father, patting his pockets for sweets and Angus watches, hunger sharp for just such sweetness. The old men all are leaving, true—but it was always thus. Whenever did they not give way, and leave a place clear for the younger, more ambitious men? And after all, why should he give her up, for some new, godforsaken life where he does not belong? This is the world he chose, these people, vibrant and alive. He thinks of Eagle from the Light, the nights before the fire, the days spent chasing buffalo, and then the Yankees, with their narrow, bitter faces and their judgments, and he knows. He smiles at Payette, answers, "No, I'm fine." And when he looks down at the other letters in his hand, he can't help but laugh. The next one bears the seal of Hudson's Bay: two standing elk, a fox, four little beavers. Emblazoned on the top: Chief Factor John McLoughlin, Fort Vancouver.

McLoughlin's note is businesslike. Mr. McDonald is informed that the Governors in London have approved his recommendation of a rise in rank. "I am aware," he writes, "that many have been infected by the gossip of Americans. Yet I would caution you to pay this little heed." It's true, he goes on, that the United States seeks to annex the Columbia District; their respective governments are holding talks as they've been doing for nigh on thirty years. "But this entire business will take years more to settle, and during this time we shall need such solid heads as yours. Your service so far has been exemplary." Angus feels a grin begin to spread. "It is therefore my pleasure to increase your pay to seventy-five pounds per annum and promote you to the rank of Clerk."

He's shaking his head, still amazed and grinning, as·he hands the letter to Payette. The trader skims it, hands it back, and with his other hand doles out dried fruit. "*Merci, papa!*" the children warble, dashing off. "It's not a bad life, after all," says François, giving him an understanding look. He spreads his hands as if to take in the whole fort. "What else would any of us do, hein?"

CHAPTER 10

FROM THE BIG River to the village of Flint Necklace is a journey of two hundred miles. A week's ride eastward, climbing out of the Columbia gorge. He can do it in four days if he pushes his big bay. Alone, he's twice as fast as the pack train he sent back with a note for Captain Grant. Rising onto the great plateau he finds the size of the sky suddenly astounding. The nights are a dense and wheeling net of light and he follows the line of the river she drew for him all those months ago. What the future holds he doesn't know and cares less with every day he rides. He only knows where he belongs: with this fierce and lovely girl who is his wife.

On the fourth day he plunges into the twisting canyon that leads to her home, picking his way along the river, cliffs looming overhead. This is an up-thrusting, pleated, riotous country, dense with wooded ravines and granite outcrops, cold rushing water and secret meadows. Bursting even now, in late autumn, with life. He can hear the rivers crashing together long before he comes upon their confluence. The one he follows joins with another that cascades down from the eastern peaks and finally he sees the flat clear pools she bathed in all her life. Angus stops and sniffs: he smells their fires; off the right bank on a little tongue of green he sees the tips of their crossed lodgepoles. Only in glimpses rushing past in a canoe, through the heart of this grand wilderness, has he seen such loveliness. He thinks he understands her better now. Kaix-kaix-Koose—Clean Water—puts even the Columbia, the Smoky Ground, and most of all the arid desert of Fort Hall to shame.

He rides straight to the painted lodge on slightly higher ground above a creek. The people know him, old women smiling, men squatted mending harnesses and bows. Flint Necklace embraces him as if he is a son, and something in Angus sets a burden down. "Your wife awaits," is all he says, with a glint in his eye, a warm and knowing smile. The chief prods him toward the shore below.

Catherine rises from the rocks as he clatters across the river stones. She looks different: brighter, lighter—or perhaps it's only the brilliance of the rays that strike the planes of her face—or even some new and corresponding lightness in himself. How could he not strive every day of his life to keep that joy upon her face?

She hoped he'd come before the hunters left, she says. Her mother said he would: she dreamed him on his white-blazed bay. Her fingers twine in his hair; her lips are butterflies across his cheeks and lips and eyelids.

"My love," he says, enfolding her.

She pulls back, scrutinizing his face. "I wasn't sure."

"It's all my fault. I was an ass to try to force you. Each day since you left I've felt such regret."

She nods, her face still serious. "I can't live all the year in the fort. I have to come home from time to time."

"I know it now." He pulls her to him and speaks into her shining hair. "I'll never try to force you—ever."

"Promise," she says.

"Never again. I pledge it to you, on my honor."

IN HER UNCLE'S lodge surrounded by the elders, he relates what he has seen. He tells them of the preacher's and the trapper's words, the torrent of soyapo surging westward. There's a preacher too in their land, Flint Necklace nods. Already he's taken many nimíipuu to the white man's god. "So the ancestors warned us." Margaret looks hard at her son-in-law. "Soyapo would bring their sticks of fire. Back then they didn't know the Bostons from King George."

If Catherine's people wonder why her trader has arrived without his goods, they don't say so. He's arranged, in any case, for Grant to send an outfit up to meet them at Big Hole—or so he hopes. "Then we will ride together," the chief decides. The leaves of the aspens are turning a deep golden yellow, like the cottonwoods along the bank; the swales are splashed with crimson, copper. Soon the lodges will be covered in their winter cloaks, while the hunters move off to buffalo.

Before they leave Catherine takes Angus a few miles downstream to where the river flows swift and broad. A cone of earth sticks up, some kind of mound, and she dismounts.

"You wanted to know where my people come from. This is where." She points toward the heap of soil, six feet high, ten feet across, covered now in autumn leaves.

"This is the heart of the monster from which *It'se-ye-ye*, the Coyote, created the nimíipuu. The hardened heart of our nation, which you have joined."

He slides off his horse and drops the reins. "It's our oldest story." Her voice is so musical. "How Coyote tricked the monster to save the animals and make the people."

"Will you tell it to me?" He slips his arm in hers.

"Too long." She raises one eyebrow.

"The short version then."

"All right." She steps away and plants her feet, summoning the firelit nights of winter.

"Coyote was building a fish dam down by Celilo, when someone called him to help the people. All were swallowed by a monster. He went there and saw a great head. He'd never seen anything like it. 'Let us inhale each other!' he cried. And he tried but couldn't inhale the monster. So he told the monster to inhale him, too, so that he wouldn't be so lonely, because he missed all the people.

"The monster didn't know Coyote had five flint knives and pitch and a flint. Coyote went in and found different animals and the bones of many, many people. He asked the way to the monster's heart. He went there and made a fire and started cutting it in pieces. Fox came and Coyote told him to fill the openings of the monster with the bones. He kept cutting the heart, every knife broke but the last and finally he had the heart. The monster died and all the openings in his body sprang apart so the animals kicked the bones out and went out themselves. Only muskrat was trying to get out the anus as it closed back up, which is why his tail is hairless."

She glances at him with a little smile. He smiles right back. It's no more nor less believable than a virgin who gives birth.

"Then Coyote cut the heart and spread the blood on the bones and the people came back to life. He spread parts of the body to the sunrise and sunset, the north and south, and where each part landed, he made a nation, the Cayuse and Blackfeet, the Salish and Coeur d'Alenes. When he was done Fox said, 'But you have given nothing for this part of the country!' And Coyote said, 'Why didn't you tell me before?' So he sprinkled the last drops of blood in the water, and with this bloody water he threw drops on the land around him. And this made our people, the nimíipuu, who the Frenchmen stupidly called 'pierced noses.'"

"You are part French," he laughs.

"But not the stupid part."

"No. Definitely not."

IT'S EARLY OCTOBER when they set out for Fort Hall in the company of her band's best hunters, horses and lodges and all. He watches Catherine look hard back at the village as they ascend the canyon on the river's northern side, as if to burn it in her mind. Up through timber and rock, dodging deadfall, over the pass they call Lolo and down. They move like a host out of dreams, sometimes silent, sometimes singing, strung out with the scouts far ahead, rejoining at night. Like a Highland regiment, he thinks, marching forward and threading itself back through its own lines. From the pass they turn south and parade down a valley more verdant than any he's yet seen. The Bitterroot, she says, the home of their allies and friends the Salish. In the Salish villages they collect more hunters and families and horses and dogs, and travel on, like snowballs that grow as they roll. Among them are Catherine's sister Kyuka and her man, her father Baptiste and his Salish wife, many other mixed families of Salish and Palouse and Nez Perce. The whole way through the Bitterroot to the southern pass that crosses the Great Divide, he sees the joy on her face to be among her kin. He rides sometimes with Baptiste, sometimes with Flint Necklace and the Salish chief, Victor Many Horses. For the first time in this country he feels at one with himself—at once apart and yet carried and nurtured by this clan. He whistles "Leezie Lindsay" as he goes, marveling at the ease he feels, this life that's come so unexpectedly. Like them he rides in moccasins and buckskin, his sash and flag stowed, lean and hardened by the saddle.

Catherine and he do not speak when at last they drop into Big Hole. They only look at one another with a smile and sneak off to the willows that line the creek.

"Just here," she says, stamping her foot in the soft mud of the bank where her uncle declared them husband and wife eighteen months before.

"Not here?" He teases her gently, pacing away, then returns and stamps his large foot next to hers. For an instant he sees their prints like petroglyphs, a proof of their passage engraved forever in the earth. Then the hollows fill and disappear.

The team from Fort Hall is not the only sight to welcome their eyes in that broad valley. Eagle from the Light too arrives with his hunters from the Salmon River. For three days they rest and feast: they race and gamble and dance. And of course they trade. When it's time to depart again Angus sees the people change and grow more serious. Even in winter, on the plains they contend for the game with the Blackfeet and Crow.

Weapons are cleaned; packs of cartridges and shot, along with clubs and bows, are tied onto their saddles. The men attach their special charms. The women break camp with low murmurs, boys herding the extra horses for the robes. Finally, in the chill of a late October morning, the time for parting comes at the edge of the great bowl. He and Catherine and the traders will turn south, while the large hunting party, now some two hundred strong, continues on to buffalo.

He is saddened to leave them, but to his astonishment not so his wife. Although she embraces her family long and hard, when she turns to Angus her face is serene. Not until the first night alone does he understand why. She knew already at Big Hole, she tells him. She heard the yellow bird sing, most mysteriously she adds. Her moon came and went but even so, already she knew. She is with child.

CHAPTER 11

LIFE DECIDES FOR us sometimes. His gram said that, when he and Duncan went to see her as small boys. One step at a time, she'd say, and shake her apron clean of crumbs. They'd spend days by the water, eyes burning, willing the monster to swim past. At Dores, on Loch Ness's pebbled shore. "He only comes when you're not looking for him," said his gram, and Angus thinks now that this is also true of life.

He'll stay a trader, then. In fact, says Grant when he gets back, there's an even chance he'll get his own post. McLoughlin has been talking about moving the post for the Salish trade further east and south. Angus's heart beats giddily. In no way did he foresee this, though he hoped. It's not so bad to be a part of something bigger than you are. He'll have a family to feed, he thinks, swelling with a sense of pride and purpose. The extra pay, as well, will help: he'll send a portion to his sisters for some gowns.

The only problem lies in what he is to tell Joe Meek. He hates to let the fellow down. He writes a letter filled with jokes, good wishes for fat steers and harvests, slender women, boozy nights—and ends by saying that he'll stay a "squaw man" after all.

▰

ANGUS IS ALMOST happier than she: from the minute she tells him, he can't keep his hands off her waist, her belly. "Little one," he croons, "our wee bairn, swimming in the deep." She rolls her eyes, though she's just as ecstatic. Her body awakens to this seed within, unfurling after all this heartache, all her fears and longing dissipating now like mist. Inside she feels the glowing; week by week her eyes are brighter, her heart lighter. She feels descend upon her a great peace. The first of a great clan in this extraordinary land, her husband whispers in the night, his hands upon

89

her, loving her more sweetly even than before. "What shall we call him?" He's sure that it's a boy; he lists the names of his own father, uncles, brothers: Donald, Archibald, Duncan, Alexander, John. "John," he says, and Catherine just smiles. Her mother will decide on his nimíipuu name when it is time. Outside the storms rage, then abate; she beads her cradleboard and hums the old songs as they wait.

When the sky grows larger in midsummer, and the deer and elk have dropped their foals, Catherine goes to the river to prepare. She makes a nest for them among the cottonwood and willow, lined in fur and sedge grass; she steps each morning in the sharp blade of the Winding Waters. She needs no midwife for this work: the child that enters life by its own will is strongest, she tells Angus. He objects, of course; how well she knows him now. His eyes flash and he tries to talk her round. It is too dangerous, he says; it is insane. *It is our way*, is all she answers, and he stops as if he has been slapped. He knows now to respect her power. When her time comes, she goes down to the glade, while up at the fort he stalks and wrings his hands.

For hours she walks and stops to bend, then walks again to let the wrenching do its work. Her body is a mountain shattering, rents pulled open in the earth. She steps into that rent and tells this child to have no fear. She will be there when he arrives.

Her face and palms are moist and she walks ceaselessly from shore to nest and back. The puffs of dandelion are white against the rich black loam and in her mind these blocks of black and white move like chunks of mountain, crashing, jostling for space. She doesn't feel the day pass. This work does not belong to time. When her womb heaves and hot liquid gushes down her legs she squats and holds a branch and breathes.

She's sticky and chilled; she lights the fire she has prepared. The world is smaller than a bird's eye now: she is inside herself, untangling the straining limbs. She feels a presence hovering beyond the screen of leaves, a woman's steady gaze but it's not clear if it's her mother or her sister or some woman from the village Angus sent to keep her safe.

She pushes her long hair aside, winds it in fistfuls. She grinds: she is the flint, the knife. She needs no more than her sharp breath, the trill she hears at intervals, her mother's whispered words. The pressure of the sky world bears down on her, and she pants and crouches, crying out. Her cries are not her own and she knows then that they are sent to help her bring this baby out. Each part of her is shuddering and working, throat and eyes and chest all squeezing toward the cavern opening below. She feels her mother stroke her back, hold back her hair. *Press now. Breathe deeply. Push again.* Her sister's throaty chuckle comes. *He floats just like the mountain sparrow.* Catherine thinks she hears a distant rumble of the weather then, and twists onto her side, draws up her knees. Her hand is reaching now to touch the sticky ball that's pulsing there, the slick crown of his head emerging. She cries again, exultant.

The child is battering the door between the worlds. It isn't she who pushes now, but he who clamors to get out. He shoots forth all at once, slithering and unfurling, and with one arm she's there to catch him in between her knees. The pulsing cord snakes after, up her belly, in between her breasts, as she brings the wet creature to her chest. And suddenly she's freezing cold. She feels the power draining from her, feels her self rise up and out of her own body. Looking down she sees the lake of blood still pouring from between her legs. Groggily she reaches for the knife that she has cleansed with fire and severs the still beating heart between them. She wants to tie his end first, but her fingers are too cold and stiff. She moans and wraps the rabbit furs around them both. *Mother,* silently she cries. *Husband.* Suddenly she recalls the water she must shake into his face and flings a hand and finds it, throws the drops across them both. He screams then, loud and shocked.

She's trying to put his groping mouth upon her breast when darkness overcomes her, and she dimly feels an arm about her back and underneath her legs. With monumental effort she pulls her eyes open and sees Angus, his face more frightened than she's ever seen it, rubbing her face and that of their son and harshly calling. "Catherine, darling, stay with me, stay—see, here's our lovely boy."

He swoops them both up, bearing them away to a place that's warm and safe. And only afterward does he confess that he had thought he'd lost her—and if he lost her, he would lose himself. There's nothing else, he murmured, stroking the soft brown scalp of their son: nothing but us, our blood united in this bairn, the only safe harbor in this shifting world.

A YEAR LATER, in 1846, the English and the Americans draw their line. One life starts, thinks Angus, and another ends. The British crown that sits so heavy on the Highlands does not fight to save him here across the ocean either. He cannot say that he's surprised. A treaty is signed: Britain cedes the whole Columbia basin to the United States. The Americans get everything below the 49th parallel; the British get Vancouver Island. They're still arguing over the islands in the Sound. "Queen and Country!" Angus snorts to Richard Grant. Her Majesty's government has sold them out. The Scots who still remain must clean the mess, take down the tents, before the Company is booted north of the new border.

It's a familiar story, one that picks at an old sore. And yet he's calm. He's not the man he was, though the resentments of his clan still bubble in his blood. He has been gentled by this child. He dandles him, he holds him in his arms and dances. He holds his hands out as the bairn attempts to stand and stumbles. John, they call him, as he wanted. No doubt Catherine has given him another name, but Angus doesn't ask. She'll tell him if she so decides. He finds he is astonished by her more and more.

When their baby was six months old a letter came from Scotland, and he wept to read the news it carried. His lovely mother was gone, all worn out by the effort of surviving. His wife held him and when his tears were dry, she took the letter from his hand and rolled it tight. "You'll see her in the sky world," she said. "I also long to meet her there." She opened up the pouch sewn on the richly beaded board, all blooms and vines, where John lay sleeping. Inside it was the dark and shriveled cord that once had bound this baby to her womb. That cord, kept safe, will bind their family in this life as well, she's told him. Now she slips the rolled-up letter in beside it. His mother Christina MacRae McDonald's life and death will always stay entwined with theirs as well.

Life flows on, ever-changing, unpredictable; he sees this too in how the Company reacts to the new border. There's no stampede. The Chief Factors, McLoughlin and James Douglas, tell them all to hold their forts. Nothing is to be relinquished until a price can be agreed for the lands and buildings they surrender. And yet their grip does loosen: one fine day the governors relent and send his boy back down to Richard Grant. He's a gentle soul who brings the life back to his father's eyes. And in that fateful summer, Angus too receives his orders, and he laughs.

"Some kind of madness," he says, "opening up when all is closing down."

"They take the long view. God only knows when these negotiations will conclude." Grant raises a glass. "Douglas will be damned if we concede an inch or lose a shilling in good trade until they do."

"How long do you reckon we have?"

His mentor screws up his eyes. "A few years, easily." He's so much lighter now, thinks Angus; a widow he fancies is also en route. "Enough," Grant winks, "for both of us to set down roots."

Angus departs the following spring, his little family safe with Grant and his boy Tom, Young George, the ever-present motley group that fills the fort. For her part, Catherine is overjoyed. It's not just that they'll be moving closer to her people. All in all their life is good. Their love is deeper now and stronger: like the honeycomb, far stronger for the spaces in between. She lets him go; she'll go herself to see her people. It will take months for him to build a home where they can live. And then she shares her secret: in six months she will bear another child. It's hard to credit, after all that pain, he says—so easily they seem to come now. Don't get too proud, she drily answers. It's not just him; her mother's medicine is strong. He has to laugh. This life, he thinks, contains so much that cannot be explained—one might as well just call it magic.

The new post is in fact an existing one he is to relocate closer to the tribes who hunt the plains. Now that the beaver are extinguished, the trade is there, in buffalo. Angus joins a man named MacArthur who's chosen a site in a glacial valley two days north of the Bitterroot, among the Qlispé, who the whites call Pend d'Oreille. It's the middle of May when he mounts the slight rise at the southern end of this valley and halts his team, amazed.

Before them looms a massive wall of snow-topped peaks that seals the valley on its eastern edge. Beneath them rolls a vast and verdant bowl of grassland, bounded and crisscrossed by lines of green from streams. The crest on which they stand, stunned into silence at the beauty, is a threshold—nay, a portal. All who cross it feel the power of this place.

There's something of the Highlands to it, like the slash of the Great Glen, thinks Angus, though these mountains are far higher, sharper, more majestic. Cleft by cleft and peak by peak they march in a straight line toward the north. He lets his breath out. Even in the southern reaches of the Rockies he has never seen tall peaks in a sharp line like these, each pointed summit brilliant, jagged, shining.

But beauty isn't why they picked this place. The Ql'ispé and Kootenai are great hunters as well—like the Salish, who the early trappers for some unknown reason called the Flatheads. The Company intends to trade with them all, as well as the Nez Perce passing through. McArthur has permission from the chiefs to build on a pretty spot along a creek. He leaves Angus to get on with it. He inherits an interpreter and two Kanaka to do the digging and a junior clerk called Antoine Finlay, along with the men he's brought. The plot is marked out with stakes but no work has started. There's precious little timber on the valley floor; the first thing, then, is to send them to the hills to fell some. The laborers are not gone more than fifteen minutes when they ride back, preceded by half a dozen Natives.

"*Mère maudite*, what's this?" Finlay calls to Angus.

The lead man is the brother of Chief Alexander of the Pend d'Oreille, the interpreter informs him. The fellow is powerfully built, about fifty years of age, wearing a broad-brimmed grass hat and a careful look.

"He wishes you to know you're welcome." Angus doesn't let on that he understands, though he learned Salish first, from the Skuyélpi people near Fort Colvile. "You're welcome here," the man repeats, "but also foolish."

Finlay turns to Angus and makes a face. "Hail to you too," he mutters.

Angus smiles and steps forward. "We're thankful for your concern." His Salish is rusty, but the head man seems to understand. "No Horses gave you permission," the fellow answers, referring presumably to his brother.

"Let's smoke," Angus says, nodding, "and then I'll show you."

They've packed in the weed, of course. Before anything else, tobacco. His pipe is a short clay tube painted with dots and stripes that was a present from Catherine. They all take turns to suck it. They're puffing companionably by the stream when the brother lurches to his feet.

"Not here." He sweeps his arm in an arc that takes in the water and the screen of willow. "Too easy to creep. The Blacklegs come down"—he points east, a blunt finger tracing the stream to where it trickles from the mountains—"and hide and shoot." He turns and paces, counting as the earth rises from the streambed to higher ground. At ninety he stops and turns around. He's dressed in everyday buckskin with its long fringe; his arms are spread, his long braids looped. He looks like some kind of scarecrow.

"Here," he says firmly.

In years to come Angus will say it was Sil-lips-tu, brother of Chief Alexander No Horses, who he could thank for saving his sad skin a dozen times over. Yet in the moment, his chief response is irritation.

"It's already laid out."

Sil-lips-tu shrugs. If white men are so stupid as to try to trade on the waters of the narrow door, he says, he has no choice but tell his brother to cancel the arrangement.

"When will he be back?"

"A moon, maybe two."

Angus walks back down to the twelve stakes marking a rectangle on the bank and pulls one out. "Well then," he says. "Time waits for no man."

BY THE MIDDLE of August there's a ten by twelve cabin and storehouse and fenced field cleared of stones high above the creek for the horses and lodges. Before he leaves for the hunt, No Horses approves Angus's request to buy hides and poles to build a lodge for his wife. Her people will come through here too, he hopes. The valley isn't directly on the Nez Perce route, but he'll make it worth their while to sell to him and not the Yankees, he tells the chief.

"We have no argument with King George's men." The sovereign now is Queen Victoria, but Angus just smiles. No Horses resembles a deer, long in the forehead and nose; he speaks softly but is renowned for his honesty and bravery. Angus is not the only white man the Pend d'Oreille welcome that year, either; No Horses gives the Black Robes some land to build a mission, too.

Angus McDonald is thirty years old, soon a father of two—in his way, he thinks, a kind of chief. He's master of his own post, Clerk in charge. In this powerful place he will found his clan. He looks around, heart singing.

The valley is a ballad of white glaciers and lodges shining against bright green grass. The tallest peak is *Coul-hi-cat*, or Jagged Mountain; its double horn is sharp and jagged as a fang. They call the whole range the Shining Mountains. But it's the valley's name that he most loves: *Sin-ye-le-min*, meaning "the surrounded," Chief No Horses explains. In years past, a herd of elk was surrounded here, then slaughtered to feed the people. The sense of shelter and protection is profound. Angus's family will be surrounded and enclosed by these peaks, in this great shining glen. He will not return to his homeland now. He thinks of the Ross-shire hills where, as a boy, he found a sense of godliness beyond the kirk and, most of all, of freedom. This place is like that but on a vastly grander scale. He'll call it after Strathconon, the glen of the river Conon. Fort Conon: it has a lovely ring, he thinks.

He sends word to Catherine via the hunters who go out through Big Hole. By September he's scanning the hills whenever he looks to the south. The baby she carries is soon due. He tries to banish his fears, in case the wind might carry them on, then chuckles to find himself thinking as she does. But still he worries, until one cloudy afternoon he sees a puff of dust far off. Like a shot he swings up, pounding toward it on the thin brown trail.

At a mile he knows her horse and figure, George, the rest of their small party. He whoops and hears a whoop in answer. They come together at a creek that slices the green plain and he sees a bundle wrapped across her chest.

"She wouldn't wait." Catherine peels back the blanket. He takes the dark-haired squirming girl and she turns back to untie the shawl that holds John to the cantle.

"I called her Christina." His wife tucks her arm in his. "She'll be strong and generous, like the *El'e* whose name she bears."

For a moment he is overcome. He feels his mother Christina's loving arms, her silent faith. His family is complete; he is complete. "Moràn taing," he whispers. Catherine glances, questioning. "Merci, it means."

There's a soft look on her face. They are together at last, and safe.

"And this is Sin-ye-le-min," he says. "The surrounded place."

"I know. We stayed here many times."

Catherine smells the grasses and sap; she hears the wingbeats of high birds. She's tired from giving birth and the long journey. She breathes in deeply. This land is abundant: it will sustain them. She has dug bitterroot and camas here, caught fish; she's bathed in those hot springs. She'll weave a garland of their blossoms, pink and violet, for her baby girl. She'll teach her how to spot the lacy fringe of carrot and the onion's poker, wind a snare of elk hair that can trap the vole. She surveys her new home as she rides in beside her husband. He's speaking of the mountains, happy streams of words cascading from his mouth. She scarcely hears them. She's seeing elk and whitetails in the foothills, bull trout in the rivers, serviceberries, huckleberries melting in their mouths. The only pity is the lack of water, he is saying when she attends to him again.

He doesn't know? The great Broad Water, only a day's ride to the north? Where the lakeshore tapers like a tipi? She clucks at him. He's much too happy to be bothered.

"I've been busy," he says, sweeping a fluff of hair from the baby's forehead. "I've been so busy, getting ready for you."

The trail rises after several miles and then she sees a glimmer of skinned logs above a creek, and passing over it, the place where they will live. The trading post is so new that sap still drips like tears, and on the roof the sod is dried and curling. Rain will chink and tighten it in time. There's a storeroom and to her relief two spacious lodges newly stretched upon the green grass of the meadow. Here they will stay and make it their own.

Through one whole winter and spring and summer the world lets them alone to dig their garden, sink their roots. She plants and harvests, teaches her son how to swim in the creek, her daughter strapped onto her back; the hunters pass bearing their skins and Angus bears them out again, along the river to Fort Colvile. And it seems to them both that this is enough, it's everything they could desire. Until the following December, when a lone rider at a gallop brings terrible tidings.

The preacher Marcus Whitman has been killed by the Cayuse at his mission, along with his wife and followers. Angus reads the note from the new Chief Factor in the saddle, having ridden out to meet the foaming horse and rider. McDonald is to bring his own people first to safety at Colvile, then continue immediately to join him at Fort Nez Perces. Fourteen at least are dead, but fifty women and children remain captive. God willing they'll arrive in time.

CHAPTER 12

The Cayuses, in a moment of despair, have committed acts of atrocity which without doubt you must have learned already. They have massacred Dr. Whitman, his wife, and the Americans who lived with him.

Mr. Brouillet, vicar general of this mission, who went to Waiilatpu, arrived there on Tuesday evening and heard the painful intelligence. On Wednesday he had the dead bodies clothed and buried, and before starting demanded of the Indians not to harm the women and children, whose fate had not been decided.

> *Your Excellency's very humble and most ob't serv't.*
> *Aug. Mage/ALEX. BLANCHET,*
> *Bishop of Walla Walla, Youmatilla, 21 Dec. 1847*

"Late Indian report says no women except Mrs. Whitman or children were killed, but all are in captivity."
     H. H. SPALDING, CLEAR WATER, Dec. 10, 1847

A BILL TO AUTHORIZE THE GOVERNOR TO RAISE A REGIMENT OF VOLUNTEERS &C.

Be it enacted by the House of Representatives of Oregon Territory as follows:—

Sec. 1. That the Governor of Oregon Territory be, and he is hereby authorized and required . . . to raise a regiment of riflemen, by volunteer enlistment, not to exceed 300 men.

2. That said regiment of volunteers shall rendezvous at Oregon City . . . and proceed thence with all possible dispatch to the Walla Walla valley, for the purpose of punishing the Indians, to what tribe or tribes soever they may belong, who may have aided or abetted in the massacre of Dr. Marcus Whitman, his wife, and others, at Waiilatpu."

APPROVED 10th December 1847 GEO. ABERNETHY

HISTORY HAS SHIFTS, Angus McDonald would come to believe, like hinges on the outside of a door you only see once you've passed through it. The Whitman massacre was one of these. The first whites who came to the Columbia were traders for fur—French or British or métis—who wanted one thing from the Natives only. Then a new kind came—Americans, whom Natives called Bostons, who wanted more than skins.

In every tribe there are good and bad, the upright and the downright crooked. He'd be first to say the Baymen were not uniformly saints. But these new men were of a different kind: first missionaries, then refugees and migrants time would style as founding pioneers. Farmers and miners and blacksmiths and coopers; hardy husbands and wives; chancers and drunks and thieves. And all of these people, regardless of background or creed, shared one cherished belief: they were better than the Indian—the benighted, savage, heathen Native—who must be shown the error of his ways.

Whitman believed this with extraordinary zeal. This, anyway, is how the new Chief Factor Peter Ogden explains it when Angus joins him at Fort Nez Perces just after Christmas. Ogden has brought a heavily armed group up from Fort Vancouver. The man himself is a legend, the hoariest of the hoary old traders, impressively huge and gray haired with a prominent beak. Angus has met him only once before. Fitting, Ogden says, eyes flashing, that this mess would end in his lap now McLoughlin has shuffled off to retirement.

"Keep your boots on, McDonald. We head out directly." He crushes Angus's hand. They have to get to the Cayuse village before the trigger-happy Oregon volunteers. Ogden has already been there to harangue the chiefs to release the hostages, but they're dragging their god-damned moccasins.

"How many are in this militia?" Angus asks.

"A few hundred. My guess is a few dozen will push ahead with Meek."

"Joe Meek?"

Ogden looks at him intently. "Know him?"

"Once upon a time. Years ago, on the Snake."

"Well, he's their marshal now." Ogden's face is grim.

An uneasy feeling jangles inside Angus. Joe never replied—a sign, perhaps, that he was irked Angus wouldn't join his venture. He's climbed quickly through the Oregon provisional government, become a leading figure—and now, apparently, a lawman. The thought is unsettling even before Ogden adds: "I worry about him and his men. Apparently, his daughter was among those taken hostage."

God only knows what will happen. Meek's killed Indians before for less, Angus knows for a fact; his volunteers are liable to shoot anything that moves. Riding east toward the mission, he's chilled by more than ice and cold. All the Company men have Native wives, half-Native children. All of them are at risk now, exposed. As they were in Sin-ye-le-min at his new fort, he understands. The Chief Trader was right. Tempers are running too high. Though Catherine objected strenuously, the whole family is now safe at Fort Colvile. The larger posts have palisades; Fort Conon has none. It couldn't even keep its name in that wild country. He smiles ruefully as he rides. Alexander No Horses tried to pronounce it, then Victor Many Horses, the Salish chief. "Conon," said Angus, his Scots vowels rich and round. Con-nah, Con-nah, they repeated helplessly back. So now it is 'Fort Connah' they have left behind beneath the Shining Mountains.

The first thing they see at Waiilatpu is graves cut in the iron earth, already drifted with snow. He can't help but shudder to think that not two weeks ago these people walked and breathed and now are no more, heads cleaved in or shot at point-blank range. Even now Angus doesn't really know what happened. He asks Ogden in a low tone so the men at arms don't hear. Apparently two Cayuse head men cut down Dr. Whitman, at first with clubs, disfiguring his face. One man escaped and made it to Fort Nez Perces to raise the alarm. In the meantime several others were shot, and Mrs. Whitman carried out and shot and somewhat mutilated. The rest they killed were men, fourteen in all, before they carried off the women and children. The Whitmans had a school there, but the Indians killed no children, as far as they know.

"Why did they strike?"

"Many insults over many years." Ogden's disgust is evident. He's traveled and trapped this region for decades; he has treated with every head man in every damned tribe. "We warned Whitman against settling there, but he wouldn't listen. He was harsh; he wouldn't pay for the land. That angered them from the start—the lack of respect."

"I heard something about an epidemic." Rumor linked the attack to a measles outbreak.

"Just the last straw. They were convinced Whitman was poisoning them. He couldn't cure their children, but somehow the white children survived. Chief Tiloukakit had buried his third dead child that morning."

It was hideous, horrendous—yet comprehensible.

"You know how superstitious they can be," Ogden adds drily. "I understand, in fact, we've relatives in common."

"Thick as thieves," Angus smiles. Ogden's son Michel, half Salish, half Scots, is pugnacious like his father and recently married Catherine's half-sister, Angelique. For the moment they're stationed at Fort Boisé.

Then they see tipis ahead and all conversation ends. Ogden dismounts and drops his reins. He looks like a cougar in an ugly mood. The rest of them wear their red Bay sashes as a kind of charm, but Ogden doesn't bother. They know him damn well, he growls and goes in. Four head men await and a bristling group of warriors. They look fierce; they speak a variant of the nimíipuu language. These bands have a reputation for wildness; for a decade the Company has watched the uneasy cohabitation between the punishment-prone God of the Methodists and the prideful, eye-for-an-eye Cayuse. It could never end well, perhaps.

"You know why I'm here," Ogden growls at two of the chiefs, one rolling with fat, the other a haggard old man with snow-white hair. He waves away the offer of a pipe. "These chiefs said before they didn't approve of the killing." He gestures at the two other head men. "They claimed the young men were out of control." There are murmurs; young warriors shift, and Angus moves his own hand to his pistol. "I say the same thing to you now: we are a different nation from the Americans. But they're the same color as ourselves, and our hearts bleed when you use them so cruelly. Haven't your young men pillaged and abused them as they peaceably make their way to the Willamette? As chiefs, do you approve of such conduct? You say the young men did these things without your knowledge. If you allow them to govern you—if you don't lead them—you're not men, you're half-men, unworthy to be called Chiefs."

He turns to skewer the braves next. "You're so proud of your courage, your skill at fighting. Don't be deceived. If you cause the Americans to commence war you'll repent it, for the war won't end until every one of you is cut off the face of the earth."

He folds his arms and studies them. Most look at the ground. Only a few stare back, defiant. His voice goes gentler. "I know you lost many to the sickness. Many die and no one knows why, but this has nothing to do with Dr. Whitman. He had no poison, not as you were told. These deaths are the will of Providence, which we poor mortals can't grasp." He runs a hand through his gray hair. "We can't promise there won't be war. We remain neutral. We simply sympathize with those poor people. If you deliver the prisoners to me, I will pay you for them, but I do this only on behalf of the families. So decide for yourselves."

The heavyset chief is clearly sobered by Ogden's words. "You white Chiefs are good, your men follow you." He makes a face. "Not so with us. Our young men are strong-headed and foolish." He gestures at the old man to his left. "Chief Tiloukaikt is here, speak to him." His lips droop as he heaves a sigh. "For myself, I'm willing to give up the families."

The old chief is helped to his feet. He shuffles toward Ogden, stopping a foot away. His voice is surprisingly loud. "Chief, your words have strength. Your hairs are gray. We've known you a long time."

Ogden nods; there is ruefulness in his look. Indeed, they are two old, grizzled warriors, face to face. How many hundreds of times has he been through these wooded canyons, Angus wonders—dealing with new men as they come up, swapping metal tools and weapons, flour and fabric for their fish and pelts? He was indeed Here Before Christ, as the old wags say—before the missionaries, before virtually any other white man, blazing and mapping the entire western interior. It's like watching God in motion, Angus thinks.

Chief Tiloukaikt glances from Ogden to the younger chief, then back. His red-rimmed eyelids droop. "I won't keep these families. I make them over to you, which I wouldn't do for anyone younger than you."

And that's it—as if it were a simple thing to save four dozen souls. Assuming the hostages are actually freed, Angus knows he's witnessed nothing short of a miracle. The Chief Trader intended this lesson. It's the concentrated residue of everything they've learned in the four decades since fur traders first set foot in the northwest. Deal fairly with the Native people, do not lie. Punish the guilty, and swiftly—but only the guilty. If punishment is indiscriminate, holy hell will ensue. Angus silently thanks the men who taught him these truths, Archibald and Grant and now Ogden. The Native may be uncivilized in their eyes, but has a finely balanced sense of right and wrong.

WHEN THE AMERICANS arrive Angus pulls back into a dark corner of the hall. Acting Marshal Joe Meek bursts in bitching at the holdup at the Dalles he clearly thinks is Ogden's fault. "Bastards demanded payment for the portage," he growls. Joe's still half-bald, head like a billiard ball, but he's heavyset now and florid, nothing like the nimble trapper Angus knew. Two others are at his heels, fellow travelers from that long-ago wagon train, fixed on Ogden like pointers on a duck. Ogden says, "Good day to you too." He raises an eyebrow. "I don't know a man alive who works for free."

"You paid them in powder and balls. They dance in our blood and you reward them with ammunition." Joe's face is as red as his welted ear. "I ought to haul you in right now." So that's how it stands, thinks Angus: overt hatred between the Company and the settlers. Well, two can play at that.

"Why don't you take me instead, Joe." He emerges into the firelight. "If being British is a crime."

"Well, how do you like that." Meek's face is a study in distaste. "If it isn't Young Mac, the pride of Her Majesty's squaw men." He turns back to Peter Ogden, snarling that he's now in charge, their presence illegal and unwelcome.

Angus half-listens, stung. How swiftly Joe turned. The men are arguing, feet planted, Ogden trying to dissuade Meek from taking his posse upriver. The hostages will be freed within a day or two, he says, and this enrages Meek even more. "What kind of deal did you make with those murderers? What did you pay them?" He puts his mug an inch from Ogden's.

"Surely the lives of these women and children are what matters." Angus steps forward.

Meek's second man sneers. "So those red devils know the price they'll get per head next time?"

"Gentlemen." Ogden signals for grog in an attempt to defuse the situation. "Let's just take a deep breath. We're in this together, for the present."

Joe Meek hunkers before the fire, back bent, and Angus leaves it for a while. Truth be told, his own feelings are raw. He has always tried to act with honor. After a while he walks over and pulls up a stool. "Bad business," he says, and holds out his cup, but Joe just leaves his hanging down.

"No thanks to you." He looks bitter now, slightly deflated.

"I'm sure she's fine." He'd put a hand on Joe's arm, but his old friend holds himself rigid, apart. "They wouldn't hurt the little children."

"You don't know that." Meek turns and his look is a slap. "You always think they don't mean business."

"You used to trust them, too," says Angus quietly.

"That was then." Meek takes a long drink, and Angus sees that his whiskers are wet, his mood dark and getting darker. "Things are different now."

"I wish it could have been otherwise. I was sorry I couldn't come and join you."

"You picked your side." Joe's head swings and his light eyes fix on Angus, narrowed, almost feral. "You had your chance to join the future, and you made your choice. You're either for us or against us now."

"That's not true."

"It is. You've overstayed your welcome, mate." Joe takes another drink. "When shots start flying, there'll be no in-between."

"The day I get my orders to clear out, I will. But not a moment sooner."

"There won't be any crying, I assure you."

Meek lurches to his feet and leaves. Angus watches his squat figure and feels fury twist inside. Joe never cared a whit, he thinks—not really, for the Natives. His matches were for lust, or else convenience. Else he would never throw his lot in with these trigger-happy colonists. These graceless louts who think this land is theirs to take, who think no more of clearing off the "savages" than clearing rocks from fields. Just like the English cleared his own land, hounded and removed the people. Angus McDonald feels his blood rise. How dare Meek decree that he has chosen the wrong side? He longs for Catherine, their children, then—and fears for them as well. In his own heathen way, he prays that his family is safe. *All is well, I am fine*, he whispers to her in his mind, half fancying that she can hear him.

And he *is* fine, entirely well and whole, he knows with a sickening lurch, compared with the terrible sight that presents itself the next day as winter darkness starts to smudge the hills. Someone shouts and from the palisades they see the hostages standing crammed in wagons, bumped and jostling, in thin and ragged clothes, a few tied onto horseback.

The women's long hair is hanging and matted, and even from this high Angus sees scratches and blotches of dried blood. The rude convoy is chillingly silent, except for a heart-rending whimpering from wrapped bundles that can only be the babes who've survived. Ogden is already in the yard, striding toward the gate, when the rest of the fort's occupants stream out behind him. Meek's posse springs out, priming their guns. Meek and Angus and the others are close on Ogden's heels as he spins to face them.

"Joe, Nesmith. Your men have to lay down your arms."

The Americans are incredulous.

"We'll have no accidents." The Chief Factor is firm. "The Cayuse must do the same."

Ogden opens the small door in the large main gate and they all strain to see. With a jolt Angus sees that these men's hate and fear instantly switches, no longer directed at the Baymen but with murderous intensity at these silent feathered figures in the dusk. Meek's face is the strangest mixture of all, half hopeful, half hateful. He's as afraid to know as not to know—afraid of the fury of his own vengeance, if his daughter is dead. Angus puts a hand on his shoulder.

"We'll all disarm," he says. "It's best."

Meek recoils but nods curtly, and Angus and another clerk move through the crowd, gathering pistols and rifles and knives. There's a large pile by the time Ogden reappears. "They agree." His voice is somber. "I watched them give their arms to one who rode well out of range."

And then the large gate creaks and the doors open inward to reveal the group of white women and children not fifty feet away, proceeding slowly toward them. The young, fat chief is in the lead, bearing a staff with feathers. It's the Company's bad luck that he's wrapped in a bright striped blanket of the Hudson's Bay. Then the chief drops the leads to the two horses pulling the first wagon, and someone drops the tailgate and women and girls stumble off and out, toward the gate. Several start sobbing as they slide from the battered wood and are met by waiting arms. But more are frozen, eyes dilated, bitterly used, surely raped. The children, several dozen of all ages, are a mix of white and métis and so shocked they too are silent. Angus sees the terror, the blank vanishing in their eyes. They have seen things no child—no human being—should see.

Beside him he feels Joe Meek start forward, as if he has seen his girl. Then Meek is running, in and around the desperate, terrified people, looking into each face, holding each small body by the shoulders before spinning away and racing to another, and another.

"Where is she?" he roars. "Where's my child, you murderous monsters?"

Ogden half-turns and sees him dashing in circles like a madman. The hostages are inside the palisade now, and the Chief Factor is overseeing the delivery of the ransom—blankets and shirts, rifles and tobacco and gunpowder. The Indians have lined up their horses to receive the goods, and it's toward this group Meek barrels now.

"You'll die, you filthy bastards," he screams. He starts to throw himself at the nearest brave, but Angus with his long legs is faster. He grabs Meek from behind, and the two of them skid and fall on the frozen ground, Angus on top as Meek curses and flails. He's still screaming "You're dead, you're dead!" as he tries to bite Angus, who wraps him in the tightest hold—so tight that he can feel the instant that Meeks' chest shifts and his screams turn into sobs. And he holds him all the tighter, saying "Sssh, Joe, it's okay, sshhh," rocking the broken and despairing father like he's rocking his own child.

CHAPTER 13

IT'S HARD WORK getting back to Fort Colvile in midwinter—pure struggle up and over the churned hills on the east bank of the Columbia. Rarely does Angus travel alone like this, though he's wintered enough with the Nez Perce to know the tricks: caves made of snow or, in extremis, the steaming gut of deer or elk. Nor is he really alone, he feels. All around as he plods north, he senses a presence—of the people, perhaps, wintering in their secret hollows, or else the pulse that animates the trees, the animals, the land itself.

Catherine can always tell when he is near, or so she says. She's first in the yard in any case when he bangs on the gate with the butt of his rifle. It's she who greets him, her face barely visible in the cowl of brown fur. They hold one another tightly without speaking for the longest time. Then draw back and look each other in the eyes. His beard is rimed with frost and she thaws it between her fingers. "How many days did you ride?" Six or seven, he answers and she leads him in. His feet are soon in a warm bucket of water. When the children hear he's home, John throws himself at his neck, a sturdy lad with skin of gold, and Christina climbs onto his lap. She's serious, dark-eyed; she has her mother's lips. And Angus's heart contracts to hold them, smell them.

"Joe lost his daughter," he tells his wife beneath his breath, shaking off the bairns and pulling her to his knee. He buries his face for a moment in her hair.

"The Cayuse?"

"Measles. She was sick already when they took them."

They look at their own two and feel the same chill. Their Indian blood makes them vulnerable too. But it's more than this. Angus can't shake the image of the hate-filled eyes of Joe Meek and his volunteer militia.

"We got the others back, though," he adds—though there's no hiding his concern. It feels like the whole country is suddenly against them.

"How many Bostons were there?" Catherine is pragmatic as always.

"Too many." She gives him a dry look. "A few dozen with Meek, but that's just his posse. Every year there are more."

Her face is still. Hundreds, even thousands come at a time, now they've forged a wagon route to the Willamette, the Chief Trader told him. Angus thinks back to the little map he drew for those first emigrants at Fort Hall; how bitterly he regrets it now.

"We'll leave as soon as it thaws." She's already planning. "As soon as it's safe."

He nods. At least at Fort Connah, deep in the mountainous interior, they do not feel this blind venom directed at their kind by the settlers and their priests. For they're considered a different species almost, he sees now, these mixed-blood families of the Hudson's Bay. They too must be made to see the light of progress. It's mainly the Protestants, like the Whitmans, who appear keenest to crack down. Like the preacher who appeared at Fort Vancouver the year before, one Reverend Beaver, as it happened, a most appropriate and ironic name, they all thought at first. Until he started hectoring McLoughlin and the rest of the officers to marry their Native wives in the Christian way. They were sinners, harlots, the usual, unless the sacrament could be performed—but McLoughlin refused, he'd been married by then for the better part of three decades in the custom of the country and he'd be damned if he'd accept such insolence.

Angus imagines that Ogden and Douglas, the chief factors, feel the same way, but he doesn't know for sure. It reminds him of how the Company brass came down so hard on Richard Grant. He doesn't feel the same judgment from the Jesuit priests who too are spreading through the Oregon country, trying to bring the tribes to Jesus Christ—including the brand-new mission on a knoll above Fort Colvile called St Paul's.

In that little chapel far above the Che Wana, in the winter silence when even the Kettle Falls are stilled, he discusses this strange anomaly with the new priest, Father Ravalli. It takes no genius to see that the Catholics sit more comfortably with those they've come to convert, Angus observes. He thinks, but does not say, that for one thing, none of them are dead. Ravalli explains that Jesuits do not require the Natives to embrace their faith before baptism. Protestants require conversion first; not so the Society of Jesus. They take all sheep into the fold and hope to bring them by and by to Jesus Christ.

Angus himself has no belief in any organized religion, he tells the sharp Italian in his long black habit.

"I've heard that said, but never yet met one who truly has no sense of some transcendence." Ravalli's dark eyes twinkle. He prays Mass for the Skuyélpi, the tribe along the falls, the first Indians Angus met when he came into this country. The new post trader is kind enough, but strangely enough Angus misses Archibald. He understands his great-uncle better now: the pride he felt in all he'd built here in this wilderness, and how that effort of surviving sometimes turned to harshness. And his heart weeps, too, for Archie and Jenny and their poor wee twins, who on the trail back to Red River perished of the smallpox. How fragile is this life, he thinks, how precious are these little people. And this is when it comes to him.

"I'd like the priest to bless our marriage," he tells Catherine early on a February morning, their bodies warm beneath the blankets.

"But we don't go to their house." She looks at him, surprised. "And my uncle and Captain Grant already have."

"It's just a ceremony. A kind of charm—to protect us all." He smiles, pleased with this analogy. He strokes her face, her fine carved lips. "Besides . . ." he feels her stirring toward him. "We could have another wedding night."

Her chuckle is throaty and he wants her again, as always. They are so good together now.

"Foolishness," she says.

"Not to the Bostons."

Her eyes are bright as a starlit night. The ways of Bostons make no sense; she's said it often enough. "If that's what you want." She pulls the cover over their heads and chuckles again. "I'll marry you as often as you like."

So they are wed in the Catholic way in the spring of 1848, in the rough log chapel of St Paul's. They hold John and Christina in their arms and Catherine observes the priest closely as he touches water to their foreheads, chanting in a language she has never heard. Latin, Angus tells her, an old tongue from an older world. The roar of the Columbia as the ice breaks up is like a consecration, too, thinks Angus, scouring them all as it surges past.

"Third time lucky," he says, and this time he produces a band of silver for her finger.

"Three is a good number," Father Ravalli agrees. "May the Trinity look upon you and protect you."

Five is more favorable, thinks Catherine, though she doesn't voice the thought. Instead she inspects the ring, which is carved with beaks and eyes and wings. One does not speak of one's *wyakin*, but still its avian spirit guides and comforts her. Five would be a ridiculous number of weddings anyway, she smiles to herself, holding out her hand to admire the winking silver.

By mid-April they're on their way back to Fort Connah, despite the ice that lingers on the trail. She can't wait to put the miles behind her, and Angus is anxious to see that everything still stands. Their home sits on the outmost edge of this retracting empire; whatever happens, he's determined to hold onto it. It's just a seedling, roots not deeply set. He brings tools and furnishings along with the trade goods and a big string of horses. His sights are fixed east now, toward the crop of buffalo. There are robes and leather goods, tack and saddle pads, meat and pemmican to procure. He's thrice-married to the same woman, with two young children—been ten years already on this continent, he marvels. How time races past.

Joe Meek's revenge, though, is more sweeping than anything he could have imagined. Angus almost respects him for it. Damned if the man didn't take himself back to Washington, DC, and convince the Congress to make the Oregon Country a bona fide United States Territory. No longer provisional, but part of the American experiment, with a capital and Joseph Meek, of course, as United States Marshal. There's just one newspaper in this part of the world, the *Oregon Spectator* out of Oregon City, and it makes great hay of this news. Angus sends Meek a note with the autumn returns to Vancouver, wishing him well upon his promotion. It will take more than Joe Meek to overpower a force like Ogden. Still, the Company can ill afford to have him as an enemy.

On the heels of this letter comes another from his brother Duncan in Dingwall. Their father has joined their mother in their long rest, at sixty years of age. It's the strangest sensation, Duncan writes, like standing alone on a mountaintop. He and Angus and Mary and Maggie are the older generation now. Someday, God willing, Duncan says, we'll see you again—though Angus can't quite imagine how. Their features in his memory grow dim. The world in which he lives runs downward, into the next generation, by the same gravity that drains the rivers to the sea.

Catherine's belly swells again and it seems to him their family is a caravan in which they ride together through the years. In Sin-ye-le-min they are mercifully distant from the struggle over this new place called Oregon Territory—which once seemed virgin to the traders, though of course it never was. They're caught between the very old and the heedless new, Angus thinks: between the duty to her people and the distrust in these settlers' eyes.

The following spring, in March 1849, Catherine gives birth to their third child. Her husband is away delivering the furs. There's still ice on the stream the servants call "Post Creek" as though it never had another name. She breaks this ice to wash them both. This birth was harder, more frightening than the others. She had to unwind the cord from around his neck and slap him hard. This boy, Duncan, is darker too, than the others—dark like her. He is the first fruit of this new union, blessed by a Black Robe. He suckles ferociously, as though there will never be enough, and she sees that he is a survivor, he will have a particular destiny. As her second son, many years later, will remark that he always guessed. He was born at the very moment the white man rushed off for gold in California—and if that were not an evil omen, and the source of all the ills to come, then Duncan McDonald, for one, could not think of any worse.

BOOK 2

BOSTONS

Oregon & Washington Territories, 1852–1870

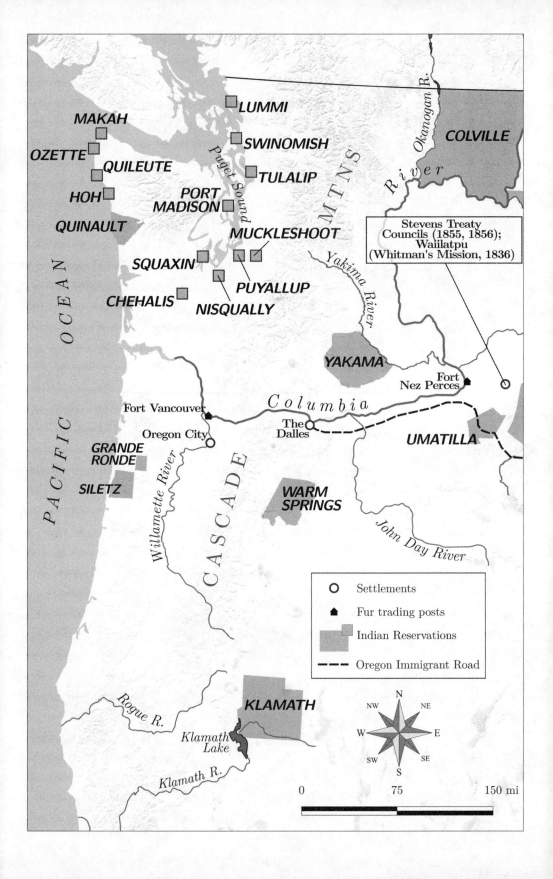

LUMMI

MAKAH

OZETTE

QUILEUTE

HOH

QUINAULT

Puget Sound

SWINOMISH

TULALIP

PORT
MADISON

MUCKLESHOOT

SQUAXIN

CHEHALIS

PUYALLUP

NISQUALLY

OCEAN

PACIFIC

GRANDE
RONDE

SILETZ

Willamette River

CASCADE

Fort Vancouver

Oregon City

The
Dalles

Columbia

Okanogan R.

COLVILLE

River

MTNS

Yakima River

YAKAMA

Fort
Nez Perces

Stevens Treaty
Councils (1855, 1856);
Waiilatpu
(Whitman's Mission, 1836)

UMATILLA

WARM
SPRINGS

John Day River

Rogue R.

KLAMATH

Klamath
Lake

Klamath R.

○ Settlements

⬟ Fur trading posts

   Indian Reservations

- - - Oregon Immigrant Road

N

NW   NE

W   E

SW   SE

S

0   75   150 mi

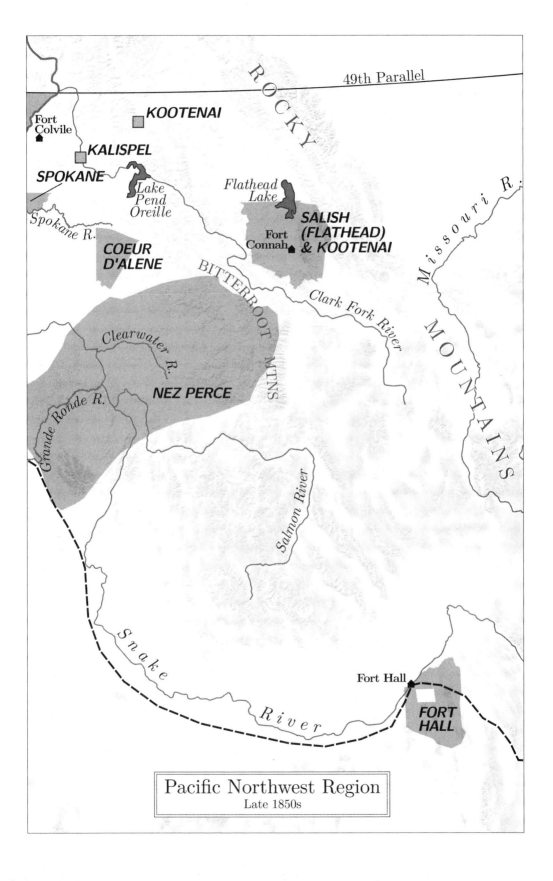

ROCKY

49th Parallel

KOOTENAI

Fort
Colvile

KALISPEL

SPOKANE

Lake
Pend
Oreille

Flathead
Lake

SALISH
(FLATHEAD)
& KOOTENAI

Fort
Connah

Spokane R.

COEUR
D'ALENE

BITTERROOT MTNS

Clark Fork River

Missouri R.

MOUNTAINS

Clearwater R.

NEZ PERCE

Grande Ronde R.

Salmon River

Snake

River

Fort Hall

FORT
HALL

Pacific Northwest Region
Late 1850s

"I have an abiding confidence in the future destiny of our Territory. . . . Let us never lose sight of the resources, capacities and natural advantages of the Territory of Washington. We have an interior soon to be filling up with settlements. Gold, in considerable quantities, has been discovered in the northern part of that interior. There are fine grazing tracts and rich agricultural valleys and that interior will fill up when these Indian difficulties are at an end."

—GOV. ISAAC STEVENS'S MESSAGE TO FELLOW-CITIZENS OF

THE LEGISLATIVE ASSEMBLY OF THE TERRITORY OF WASHINGTON,

THE PIONEER, OLYMPIA, WASHINGTON, APRIL 1856

CHAPTER 1

FORT COLVILE, WASHINGTON TERRITORY

1852

THE CANOE RUSHES through the bottle-green water and he's twenty-one again, Big Michel steering at the prow. Angus remembers clearly what Dr. McLoughlin told him that day as they arrived. Their sole purpose on this continent was to tread lightly, the Chief Factor said: to trade with the Indian and prosper, for Company and King and—beaver willing—for themselves. That job Angus has fulfilled to the best of his ability. And now, he thinks as they make the final sweeping turn to Colvile, there's one last duty to add: keep the lamp lit for the Hudson's Bay until they're booted north across the international border.

When he first arrived there wasn't an American in sight for five hundred miles. Astonishing, how in less than fifteen years, so much has changed.

He's packed his family in canoes for the journey down the Pend d'Oreille to where it empties into the Columbia somewhere near the 49th parallel. It's hard to tell if it's America or the British Possessions but it makes no difference to him or the land. He's filled with so many thoughts and memories, so much emotion. He's been transferred from Connah to run the whole interior from Colvile, a promotion that carries with it the rank of full Trader. It feels a bit as he imagines Hannibal might have felt, returning victorious to the home he left years before.

His heart jumps at the sight of the post, carved out like a green jewel on a bend of the river. An oasis in the wilderness still: the great farm Archie clawed from that gray clay. Here are the fields of wheat and corn and vegetables, the mill for the grain, the sawmill to cut the boards for the boats—and over everything the constant roaring of the Kettle Falls below. The place is emptier now that the furs transit overland to Fort Victoria, and the voyageurs have retired to farm in the valleys around. But he is its master, presiding over a vast and still rich realm. He will treat with the head men of the local tribes: the Okanagan, Skuyélpi, the Yakama and Palouse. Yankees or no, from the Cascades to the Rockies, Natives continue to bring him their hides to trade.

He looks to the other boat, where his wife sits wrapped in a shawl. The children wave and shriek but Catherine stares fixedly ahead. She didn't want this. The whole way she rode ramrod straight; she's more at ease on horseback. She's been happy at Connah: she has her garden, the children to teach and feed and clothe, not only John, Christina, and Duncan, but now baby Donald. Her people cycling through with the seasons, meeting as they come and go to share their news, to fish and talk and dance. Once a year she goes to Kaix-kaix-Koose. Both of them rattle back and forth across this land on their accustomed rounds.

"We're nomads, the lot of us," he joked when he received his orders, but she was not amused. Of course, he added, feeling bad, she's free to come and go. She'll hold him to that promise as she always has.

"Sin-ye-le-min will always be our home," he told her then. Chief Alexander told him on departing that the McDonalds were forever welcome on his land. Catherine, after all, isn't the only one who will miss that astonishing valley and its people. Angus, too, thinks often of the bonfires on the plains, the galloping rounds, his friends among the Salish and nimíipuu. But here at Colvile he has other worries, he soon learns.

Late the following spring the smallpox appears in the Skuyélpi village two miles to the south. Luckily Father Ravalli is a doctor of body as well as soul. When the fevers start, he brings the vaccine and tries to convince them to accept it. The needle terrifies them, the priest reports. But they see how "the stuck ones" do not get sick. Already the disease has taken dozens. Ravalli, of course, is vaccinated, but Catherine too is suspicious of this medicine. The way he comes and goes, the priest must carry the sickness himself, she objects. She's pregnant again, and in the first months she is always irritable, Angus knows. Only after much persuading will she accept the jabs for herself and the children—but still refuses to let anyone set foot outside the palisade. Even when summer comes, she does not relent. The children writhe and moan. They'll all go quite mad if she doesn't accept that the vaccine protects them, Angus says.

"It's on your head then," she says, cheeks flushed, one hand protecting her womb.

It's hot, late August: the baby is due any time. Even after all these years he marvels. She must use some secret medicine to space them out, one every two years like clockwork. Not until after the harvest and the birth of wee Annie do they look at one another with anything like relief. It has been quite a season of confinement, he remarks drily. Which is why the news of approaching Americans does not inspire the dread that it might. They are all—Angus first and foremost—desperate for diversion.

Two different parties are on the way, according to the scouts: one from the east and one from the west. They're surveyors, apparently, plotting a railroad from the Missouri to the Puget Sound. Angus and his wife exchange a look. The Crow have told them of this "iron horse," Catherine nods, looking thoughtfully after the departing messengers.

Remarkably, the two teams arrive on the very same day, a Thursday in October.

An incredible coincidence, considering the ground each covered. It doesn't occur to Angus until later to see it for what it really is: proof of the Americans' determined, ruthless thrust. He orders kegs of brandy and wine hauled from the stores. The Hudson's Bay Company will show off its strength and its welcome. Though the surveyors are bedraggled, his compliments are genuine. It's no small thing to bushwhack across these dense, high mountains. He, too, plays the surveyor, observing these visitors minutely. So this is the new governor of this huge chunk of the west which the Company was forced to yield, and the Yankees have now baptized their Washington Territory.

Lieutenant Isaac Stevens sweeps in as though the fort's already his. He's a short, good-looking fellow with dark eyes of the sort that make women swoon. He hands off his hat to a subaltern, fastidiously smoothing his blond hair, his mustache, and goatee. Instantly Angus dislikes him. George McClellan, the leader of the other team, is by contrast an American of Scots descent: tall and reserved, with steady eyes.

"The precision of the US Army is a marvel to behold," their host says, smiling.

Both are soldiers, though this expedition is nominally civilian. Angus will glean what information he can. He has to admit, at least to himself, that he also craves sophisticated conversation.

"A miracle, in fact." McClellan looks hard at Stevens. "I'd no idea you were this close."

The governor sets himself in the chair nearest the fire and gives them a wolfish smile. "Couldn't let the opportunity slip." He heard McClellan was on the opposite bank, he explains, the sly smile widening; he punished his horse to cross the last fifty miles in time. "And here we are, by God." His eyes are glittering as he takes a glass of Angus's brandy.

"A toast, then." The trader waits.

"To the railroad," says McClellan.

"To progress and development." Stevens tosses his back. "You'll not believe the lands I've seen and mapped!" He expels a minor roar of pleasure at the heat in his throat and holds out his glass for more. "The Bitterroot is by far the most lush, but there are many other valleys nearly as good."

"You found a route, then, to your liking?" It is Angus's policy, with Americans, to appear as blank and affable as he can.

"More than that! The railroad is only the means. Every stop is a townsite in the making. And I'd lay odds the place is stuffed with gold."

Angus says nothing. Secretly he's had the same thought. He's told no one of the ore Finlay found on a stream near Fort Connah last year, when he came back from prospecting in California. Uneasily he lets the young governor rattle on. Stevens is like a boy on a beach, building castles and moats and roads. After a while Angus goes to see to the rest of the men and their exhausted mounts. He's housed the grunts for the expedition in the empty bunkhouse. He opens a vat, fills a few jugs, hands the tobacco around. "Hallelujah!" one roars, and he smiles and returns to the house.

At table he surveys the dozen ranking gentlemen. There's an engineer and botanist and a scholar of ethnography and a former Company voyageur hired as a guide; there's an artist with a sketchbook full of penciled plants and animals—and Indians. Angus wonders if he's drawn Victor or Flint Necklace or any other of his friends. He returns to the main room with his children, scrubbed and brushed, and Catherine, her chin lifted, back straight, resplendent in buckskin dress and shawl.

"Well, well." Stevens rises. Angus is gratified to find the governor must look up to meet his eyes. "Your own little tribe?" His tone is almost mocking but Angus lets it pass.

"My children, gentlemen, and Catherine McDonald, my wife."

McClellan bows and chucks young John beneath the chin. Eight now, he takes this evenly, legs braced.

"Ma'am," says Stevens, lifting his glass but not reaching out a hand. He gives Angus a sidelong look. "I'd heard about your custom of the country." He turns back to Catherine. "They don't let me see their women, for the most part," he mutters. "Now I see why."

Angus could wipe that look off his face with one swipe of his hand. But his children are watching.

"My wife and I welcome you to Fort Colvile," he says tightly. "I'm sure there's much here you can learn."

Stevens strokes his mustache and they sit. The children flit back and forth, carrying bowls, using every opportunity to stare at these strange men with bushy beards of every imaginable color. Colvile offers up her harvest bounty: squash and corn and beef; tomatoes and salmon and melons and fresh-baked bread; and gallons and gallons of Her Majesty's claret. The men fall on the food, starved for anything that is not the stringy game on which they've subsisted the last few months.

From time to time, Angus catches Catherine's eye, and sees that she's on guard. He's placed her on his left, across from the artist. Perhaps this way he'll get a picture of his bride. Reassuringly he squeezes her arm. He asks Stevens which routes they took, which tribes he met. No formal meetings, the governor says, his mouth full, not yet.

"You came across the Lolo trail, like Lewis and Clark?"

"After scouting north and south." Stevens's lips twitch, as if the comparison grates. "They weren't looking at grades and passes, analyzing drainages, quite as thoroughly, of course."

"But you do know the tribes who assisted that expedition—who in fact saved their lives—were Salish and Nez Perce and Snake?"

"I did not." Stevens speaks with a privileged drawl.

"Sacajawea of course was Shoshone." Angus warms to his little game. "That's what the Snakes call themselves. And Nez Perce do not have pierced noses, as you can see from my wife, who is kin to their chiefs."

"I see." Stevens looks again at Catherine, who looks so regal with her fine bones and cool eyes that Angus nearly laughs; she holds the midget's gaze until he's the one to look away.

"I've always found it remarkable that the Nez Perce did not slaughter them on the spot, but saved the expedition."

"Perhaps," the governor observes, "it was Lewis and Clark who were equally remarkable."

Angus feigns a laugh. "In any case, you ought to see my maps. I don't imagine there's a bump or hollow in this drainage I don't know."

IN THE FORT yard there's horseshit everywhere, ground into the mud, sticking to their moccasins, its stench scraping their nostrils.

"Bostons don't clean up after themselves," says Christina with all the disdain of her worldly six years.

"Yankees," John corrects her. "Not Bostons."

"That's what E'le calls them," Christina retorts. John shrugs and shoulders his bow; Duncan crouches silently beside them. From the children's vantage at the kitchen door they can hear the crew carrying on in the bunkhouse. They creep to investigate. A big moon makes John's shadow tall as a man's, flitting to the storeroom, pausing to wait until they join him, dashing again toward the stable. They scuttle like the voles they've been cornering all afternoon in the tall grass of the meadow.

"Hell yeah!" one teamster is roaring as they flatten into the bunkhouse shade and fit their eyes to knotholes. Duncan has the best view, small as he is, where a mule kicked out a drain spout. There are a dozen muleteers and dogsbodies, drinking their father's wine, smoking his tobacco, playing bent and splitting cards.

"Queen of goddamn spades."

"Spades, yeah. Like to get me one of those dark shades."

"Not here. You missed the turnoff to Virginie."

"You blind?" A man hacks out a laugh. "Plenty dark and bitter, like I like it."

"You never. Not a squaw?"

"Naw." The voice a drawl. "A hog, fool. Porky like you are."

The one speaking is thin and stupid looking with eyes too closely set. The fat one spits toward the wall and John instinctively steps back.

"Sure, I done some." The fat man throws his hand down. "Squaws in every corner at Fort Benton."

"So how is it?" They can't see who speaks, though John has his whole face mashed against the board.

"Slick and twisty. Hot as Hades." The men hoot. Christina puts her hands on Duncan's ears, her eye still pressed against the knothole.

"Tell ya what, I'd do that juicy one he's got. This trader."

"Bitch is in heat and hurtin' for it."

"Squaw juice," the thin man rises, sloshing out another round. "Bet she don't wear nothing under, either."

"How's he mount her, you think?"

John looks at Christina, eyes huge. The men are raising their cups, chortling and thrusting their hips at one another.

"From behind like a dog."

John steps back, face dark but for the whites of his eyes. He slips the bow from his shoulder and puts his finger to his lips. Christina nods as he circles toward the doorway.

"You count them kids? He's doing her like doggies all the time."

"Has to hold his nose though."

Christina sees the arrow first, a little glint in the crack of the door. The fat one is disgusting, all slobber and piggy little eyes.

"Say it again," John yells as the man screams and clutches at the shaft sticking out of his thigh. "Say it again so I'll aim higher." She's never heard their brother shout so loud.

"Bleedin' hell!" the thin man is reaching toward his sidearm when the next shaft spears his palm against his thigh. The hand flexes as he looks dumbfounded down at the five fingers, curled and jerking like a rooster's claw.

"Shut your filthy mouths, or you'll get worse." The door slams hard, leaving Christina and Duncan to observe the drunken clot of them slumped and gawping, two bleeding and cursing and another laughing so hard his trousers are dark with piss. They watch a bit longer, hoping one is dumb enough to rip the tip from the wound without cutting the shaft first and working it out slowly as their father taught them. And they are dumb, far dumber than beasts or squaws or goddamn half-breeds as they hear them cursing their brother John, while the piss mingles on the floorboards with the fresh red blood and the lost contents of the over-turned, forgotten jug.

STEVENS IS TOO far gone to look at any maps that night. McClellan holds his wine better. Angus has long acquaintance with this grog, which helps keep him upright. He installs them by the fire, having cut some slugs from a wheel of tobacco. The governor takes command of the con-versation, despite his inebriated state, complimenting Angus on his tight ship, his well-appointed quarters.

"Rather far from the settlements, though," Angus responds.

"Never mind. You'll be headed north soon enough."

"Perhaps."

Stevens stares from under drooping lids. "I told Ogden this year is the last. You run your books from spring to spring, correct?"

"Correct."

"By spring then, the legislature will sit, and we'll sort out this mess."

"Which mess is that?"

The governor guffaws. "I have authority from Congress to wind up these forts and make deals over land with the Indians."

McClellan leans toward Angus. "The brevet lieutenant has a broad brief. Not just territorial governor, but Superintendent of Indian Affairs."

"Ah." Angus strokes his beard. "You'll have your hands full, then."

The prospect is worrisome. What kind of deals, he thinks, which land? In just one evening it's clear that Indians are little more than obstacles to this self-important little man.

"They can't imagine they can claim all of this country." Stevens pulls himself upright. "It's too big, too rich. Just look at Sutter's mill. Gold, I tell you—gold all over."

"They've struck on the Klamath and the Rogue." McClellan leans in. "Suckley hears there's another strike on the Yakama."

When Finlay showed him the golden flakes, Angus knew instantly what they were. He begged his old servant to keep the news to himself until he could think of a way to approach it. The last thing they needed were floods of miners pouring into the valley like the goddamned Napoleonic army. Nor would he welcome any such influx here at Colvile.

"Mebbe you could help me out." Stevens is tilting toward him now, his backside slipping out from under him. His voice is chummy, slurred. "I need the head men, see. We'll give 'em schools and civilize 'em." He stretches out the last words, his shoulder poking into Angus's arm. For an instant his head lolls. Angus looks at McClellan, who only shrugs.

"Need to get a move on," mutters the governor, by now in real disarray. As Angus rises, he twists and flops prone on the couch.

"Time for bed," Angus says, and the midget agrees.

"Lord, Mac," he says as Angus hauls him to his feet, "this is powerful wine."

Stevens isn't the only one who's ready for his blankets. But McClellan is still upright and gazing at the fire when Angus returns.

"Trust a Scot to hold his stout." Angus grins. They toast again. His people are from Appin, says the soldier.

"You've come a ways."

"Too far." He groans. "God love a proper bed."

"That hasn't stopped your friend," says Angus. It isn't clear, in fact, which commands the other.

"He's not my friend. You watch it, Mac. He has a way of riding roughshod."

"Damned Englishmen, eh." Angus laughs, pouring them both a final round. "Back in the day we should have cut their legs right out from under them."

"Those hearts that high with honor heave."

He raises his glass. "Clan Donald was in the charge."

"Me old ones fought, too, Mac," the soldier says, slinging his arm around his neck. "Me great-great-grandad, too, was at Culloden."

CHAPTER 2

THEY DON'T SEE her. These white men look straight through her, as if she's a ghost. Even curiosity is better: at least they see the children. They stare at them, in fact. Trying to see which part of them is Angus, which is her, what kind of creatures these might be. *Breeds*, they call them. Breeds, their blood crossed like that of the horses the nimíipuu breed— for strength and speed, resilience.

She feels sometimes as if she's fading away, paling like the moon when the sun arrives each morning. She watches the sky through the smoke hole in her lodge, remembering the tale of the warrior who died, only to return to his wife's lodge and hang right above it. He couldn't get to the sky world unless she burned his possessions. "Woman, you must let me go," he said, "or I will take you with me." He was a shade stuck between the worlds, like she.

When this Stevens looked through her, he saw only the land on which she stood; he and his kind do not actually perceive her or any of her people. She's the daughter and niece of great medicine women and chiefs. How dare he not see her? She was filled with rage when she left the table and had to walk for some time in the fields, around the horse park, before anything like peace returned. She whistled for the dappled gray whose coat in moonlight shines like silver. He laid his nose between her hands and she felt calmer.

Even Angus is different with these people. There was something in him tonight she didn't recognize. He was animated, like always in company: with her people on the plains, every New Year's when he plays the lord and his whistling bag. But tonight was different. She felt pulled from him, a string stretching out like the fibers of a bow. How easily he stands in that world—that world that does not see her.

She should have known nothing good could come of Colvile when

Christina nearly drowned on the journey there. She should have known the instant she heard the screams and sprang into the Pend d'Oreille to save her child. It happened at the very first night's camp, a clear omen. Even now she sees the dark head spinning, sweeping downstream, buoyed only by her tartan skirt. Only Kyuka really grasps the truth, she thinks. Her sister understands the way that Catherine's torn. How long must she wait until she can see her again? Already it's been two summers since they spoke.

It was the night before she left, the two of them like girls again inside the lodge. Kyuka wrapped her in her muscled arms. "Little sister," she whispered: "Many blessings go with you."

Their faces were wet; Catherine remembers her surprise. She thought her sister had shed all softness years before. She married a warrior; she herself goes to war; her power is equal to any man's.

"You think I don't know?" Kyuka stepped back, arms still holding Catherine's. "You're fruitful." Her hands dropped to her own waist. "I wanted them, of course I did, too. That surprises you?"

It did. "You got so much else," Catherine answered. Power, she meant, a place at council: a life free of this lacerating doubt.

Kyuka patted the cushion and they sat and she folded Catherine's fingers in her own. "I didn't choose any more than you." They smiled, conspiratorial. Their mother was somewhere outside, hectoring the men or the little children. "These paths came to us."

Kyuka can see into her very soul. It used to make Catherine want to run and hide. Angelique and she understand each other better; they're birds of a feather, married to these traders. But that night, her hands in her older sister's, Catherine felt an unaccustomed warmth.

"It's always there," she said quietly. "Like a worm being tugged from the earth, something tearing inside. I hold on, but it pulls and pulls."

"The strings of your heart." Her sister nodded. "Tied to your husband—and to us."

They heard the drums beginning, light taps with long silences between. Voices rising up in the stillness. The song of the nest she was leaving: her mother and Bonaparte; Angelique and Michel and their children; the hands at the fort, Ashley and Irvine; the women she spent her days with, planting, sewing, and tanning, Agate, Sarah, Antonie. She wouldn't see them for a long while, she thought, holding back the tears.

"Now." Kyuka placed a hand on her chest. "Everywhere the earth is our mother. She's always with us. To you she gave the gift of giving life." Her hand was warm. "It's her love in the shape of your children."

The sensation was like melting wax, Catherine's chest loosening, easing.

"Take the strings that pull and tie them in a bow," her sister whispered. "Enclose the ones you love and tie them fast around your beating mother's heart."

Now, hundreds of miles to the west, the sound of the falls is the only drumming Catherine can hear. She kisses her horse on the nose and returns to her lodge.

The older children are shining with excitement at the visitors encamped across the fort. Each of them hugs her hard, even her big boy, John. They nestle close and she tells them the first story that rises in her mind, the one about the homesick boy. The story that comes, her mother always says, is the story you need to hear.

East Country boy was living with his sister's husband's people across the mountains but missed his home in the west. Catherine speaks slowly, watching her children's eyes. The boy's family sewed him into an elk skin and sent him back to his western home. He was not to look out until they were past the five mountains. But he heard the sounds of buffalo and elk and other animals beside him and chewed a hole and looked. The animals fled back east. The next time they sewed him in a buffalo robe, even tougher to chew through, but again, just before the fifth mountain, his curiosity overcame him. He chewed a hole and the animals fled east, which is why there is no big game west of the great mountains.

As she tells it she's the homesick boy stitched fast into the skin, unseen. Only instead of animals it is white men who gallop in the night beside them, up and over all the five mountains, and it is she just before the fifth mountain who will use her sharp teeth to chew the hole, which will open up their world again and send the whites back to the east where they belong.

Her children listen intently, their dark eyes fixed upon her strong white teeth.

"*Yox kalo'*," she says. "That's all."

CHAPTER 3

HOW PEOPLE UNDERSTAND one another is the purest mystery, Angus thinks. He has his beliefs, of course—as others have theirs, these settlers included. Catherine, too, has her own view of the world, rooted in the thinking of her people. Even so he's astounded when shortly after the Bostons depart she says they must have another marriage. He has to struggle not to laugh.

"We have to marry again, baptize the children in their church." Her expression is firm. "The Americans do not truly see us." He looks hard at her, trying to understand. She puts a hand on his arm and he is moved by this appeal, though it has no logic he can see.

Marriage is forever, he tries to explain: it's a pact honored everywhere. He's given her his pledge again and again. She counters that this is neither straight nor good: she's seen how the Bostons regard them. She wants the new priest to bless them as Father Ravalli did before. Angus sighs and concedes. They'll be married again, for the fourth and—God willing—final time. He holds her face between his palms and tries to see inside. She has no concept of a law that stretches from one place to another. She thinks each time they move it loses force. At least, that's how he imagines the workings of her mind. But even now, especially now, as things grow more disturbed, he's not entirely sure.

KAMIAKIN, CHIEF OF the Yakama, is a stunning figure of a man. Angus doubts any of them have seen a person more majestic, even among the elegant Nez Perce. This late winter day he appears at the fort in full regalia, feathered and wound around with teeth and claws, a Hudson's Bay coat with brass buttons slung across his shoulders. Catherine stands taller, alert in his presence, this leader whose face and bearing prove the grandeur of the peoples of this land. But Chief Kamiakin is angry this visit, his eyes flashing—like Macbeth, thinks Angus, or Lear, some kingly fury out of Shakespeare.

"What right do they claim? They lie, they told us they would just move through." The chief's legs are spread, one fist holding his staff. His face courses with displeasure, breath flaring from his nose, long and sharp as the blade of a hatchet. The Yakamas' country comprises the whole Columbia basin, the huge inland valley between the Cascades and the Nez Perce to the east. "Soldiers trample my fields, stampede my horses. They scratch marks on the grass right up to the sacred mountain. Why are they scratching my land, Bayman?"

"They mark a place to put their railroad. The 'iron horse' McClellan spoke of."

Angus and he are equally tall. They look hard at one another.

"We've heard it snakes already through the plains." Catherine speaks in a low, hard voice.

Kamiakin tosses his head. The set of his eyes has always seemed haughty to Angus—though this may merely be an accident of Nature, the way his brows lift the thick domed lids, lending him an expression at once ironic and dismissive. "We've heard about it too. We don't want it in our country."

"They can't dig or build without counseling with you." Even Stevens must grasp this. "They have to buy the land, if you will sell it."

"The land isn't ours to sell. Did you tell him that too?"

"I wouldn't presume to speak for you."

Kamiakin is a complicated fellow. Half Palouse, half Yakama, keen yet friendly, with few enemies: he's had the sense to take a wife from every leading clan. Christian when it suits him and heathen when it doesn't—more farmer than warrior as well. Angus and Catherine have long wished to visit his village far to the south; it's said the chief's fields bloom like no other man's, his hillsides blotched dark with horses and cattle.

"Soldiers don't council, you ought to know." Kamiakin's lips press together. "No more than soyapo squatters do." He looks intently at Catherine, and it seems to Angus that something passes between them.

"They can't be trusted," his wife says. "I wouldn't trust them farther than this." She spits on the hard pan of the fort yard.

Kamiakin turns back to Angus. "Listen, trading chief. Take them a message: they can't take what isn't theirs. They can't take land, or dig it, or burn our neighbors' homes. The soldier chief at the Dalles used to listen, but no longer. Now they try to bring this iron creature. Tell them I won't accept it."

The chief must be worried indeed to come all this way north with the harvest not yet in. Angus nods. "I've met their chief. Governor Stevens. I'll send him your words." Stevens has set up a muddy collection of huts at the bottom of the Sound and called it his capital, Olympia. "Or we can go together to his village." Angus is due soon at Fort Nisqually on the Sound.

"I don't go to him like a beggar." The chief's eyes narrow. "Tell him to come to us."

"I'll do that."

"Soon. Every day they dig more."

"The only way to stop them is to kill them." Catherine speaks more loudly than she probably intends. Shocked, Angus turns—then sees her face.

Catherine McDonald looks fierce and livid, just as she did when they first met. Bristling in defense, no longer a woman of nearly thirty, the mother of five, but a warrior. He remembers this look on the face of Baptiste's daughter; despite himself he feels a stir of pride. How little any of them really knows the original people of this continent, he thinks. Yet when Kamiakin nods in agreement, a cooler part of him prevails.

"Insanity. You can't possibly kill them all. There are thousands, tens of thousands—they're like armies of ants."

"Yes." Kamiakin purses his lips. "Stinging ants that must be crushed."

"You kill one and thousands more will come pouring up from the nest. There are too many, I tell you. If you fight, they'll bring destruction on you all."

The encounter has barely begun; they still have a chance to shape it. Across what was once the Oregon Country there are at most five thousand settlers. It's a matter of finding some kind of compromise. The Company is trusted; they can broker some arrangement. They must do everything possible to keep things calm. There's no alternative. Any fool with the slightest intelligence knows how it's gone since the English landed on the eastern shore of this continent a hundred and fifty years before. Tribe by tribe, platte by platte, the scythe of settlement has moved ever westward, cutting its deadly swath.

"Then we have to strike first." The chief's voice is flat. He looks at Catherine and his lips lift in an almost fatherly smile. "We say you can't reason with a snake. You have to strike off its head first—then you can talk."

"No." Angus shakes his head. "I don't see it this way."

"You're white." Kamiakin shrugs. "Even if we count you as a friend, your eyes don't see like ours."

"**ARE YOU MAD?**" Angus wheels on her as soon as the chief is gone. "Inciting them to fight?"

"You always think your way is best." Her fury is a match for his. How dare he treat her like she has no say.

"Educated people talk things out," he says.

"I've seen more of their true nature than you. I've seen them kill. I know how Bostons are. When all you see is how they bow to you for your tobacco and juice." The words might sting, but he must hear her out.

"That's not the way that power works. You can't just settle it with arms." His face is filled with such distaste. "Educated people talk, they compromise."

"As if they care what Baymen say."

"They'll listen; they'd be fools if they do not."

But it's he who is naïve, not she. "That's what you think." She shrugs.

"It's what I know. It's called negotiation—parley, council."

"You heard the chief. You can't parley with a snake."

He shakes his head. "It isn't possible to reason with you, Catherine."

She laughs again then—harder, colder. "I hear things you don't. We hear from the sunrise, from everywhere, what Bostons do, the way they 'parley.' Parley won't keep us safe."

Again her husband shakes his head. He's been in charge too long; it makes him blind. Or else he thinks these Bostons will respect his words because he looks like them. But that's no guarantee. Didn't her father teach her, long ago, beset by enemies from every side? To climb up high and keep her eyes wide open, scanning always left and right?

Hudson's Bay Company
Fort Colvile
10 November 1853

Governor Isaac Stevens
Olympia, Washington Territory
Confidential

    Honourable Governor Stevens:
I trust since our mutual acquaintance at Colvile you have kept well.
Prudence suggests that I seize the opportunity for further communica-
tion before the passes close for the year. Hence this dispatch. Shortly after
your departure I was asked by Chief Kamiakin of the Yakama (one of sev-
eral chiefs of that tribe) to broker a meeting between the peoples of the
Columbia District and yourself. I'm glad to oblige, as you will doubtless
entertain this request with the gravity it requires. It's in no one's interest
to see friction between the Natives and the colonists whom a railway will
surely encourage to arrive.
    Might I suggest Walla Walla, where the Company maintains Fort Nez
Perces, as a suitable location? As to the when, as soon as practicable—al-
though naturally entirely at your disposition.
    I look forward to renewing our acquaintance, and your reply.

Cordially,
Angus McDonald
Clerk in charge

No sooner has Angus written to Stevens than he receives the quarterly dispatch from Chief Factor Ogden. Ordinarily these briefs consist of
orders to ship this here, that there—ensure there are horses and boats
enough along the trail. This one reads instead like a diplomatic cable.

The new US territorial government is proving extremely hostile to
the Company, Ogden reports. Stevens has ordered them to close Fort
Vancouver, accept a cash payment for their property and improvements
south of the line, and cease all trading with the Indians.

"Naturally, the Company will do so such thing. As I informed the

Governor, until negotiations conclude between our respective governments, we will continue operations as before.

"However," Ogden goes on, "Recent developments are of great concern." He doesn't wish to unduly alarm the remaining traders, as the conflict is far to the south, but settlers and Natives on the Rogue River are at each other's throats—and have been for some time. One newspaper has even carried a headline consisting of just one word: EXTERMINATE. As a result, the American government is moving aggressively into the area and has established a military fort of its own next to Fort Vancouver, with talk of another at the Dalles.

"In our estimation the trouble can be contained, provided cool heads prevail. You are instructed to continue operations, cautioning our representatives at the interior posts. Mr. Douglas and myself will monitor the situation and keep you informed."

The subtext is clear. Angus is to maintain a presence until the Company's financial claims are satisfied—however long this may take. He shares this news with Father Joset, who officiated at their latest marriage and is likewise alone at St Paul's, having replaced Father Ravalli. Their archbishop ordered these missions closed a few years before. But Father Joset is stubborn, like Angus, and more than that (and, worst of all, the Americans seem to believe) he too loves the Native people of this land.

WINTER'S UPON THEM when Chief Factor Douglas unexpectedly appears. He's sorry not to give warning, he says: he was at Langley and thought he'd swing down to gauge the situation for himself. He bows to Catherine while the children converge on the small brigade like chickens scratching after crumbs.

This Chief Factor seems old to her: his eyes survey them like an owl's. "Visit, my eye," grumbles Angus when he's settled the party in. "More like an inspection."

"It will be fine." Over the past few weeks they've circled each other warily, their argument never far from either mind.

"It's a test of some sort," he answers shortly, frowning at his reflection, tying his tie.

"Your returns were good."

"He'll expect you to dine with us." He turns and takes her in. Since Stevens came two months ago, Catherine has refused to share a table with a white man. Only a few have come through, mainly new settlers trying to farm the local valleys. But she won't do it; she's more like a rock than a woman these days, thicker, more obdurate. "Just this once. He's one of us, after all."

The Chief Factor, too, has a Native wife. Amelia—part Cree, métis like Catherine—like Douglas himself, born Scots and African in the West Indies. The family are old North-Westers, long in the fur trade, like Baptiste, the Ogdens, the McLoughlins—like the McDonalds themselves. For an instant Baptiste's battered face takes shape in Catherine's mind and she's surprised all over again to think they'll not meet on this earth again. Their father was crushed by a bull buffalo the year before; far too old to be out chasing game, her sister Angelique said. Angelique and Michel Ogden run Fort Connah now. They laid Baptiste's broken body in the Bitterroot, near his second wife's family's place.

Perhaps it's the memory of old days that causes her to choose the white buckskin dress. She still fits into it, just barely: it's the finest thing she owns. Oh, Angus has given her tartan and taffeta aplenty and ordinarily she wears a long blue broadcloth shirt over a simple shift. But she's among friends, among her people tonight; to her joy, Young George, too, is part of this group. She hasn't seen him in so long. She has Christina fasten the silver beaver necklace and stands a moment looking at herself in the long mirror. Catherine twirls for her daughter, who claps, eyes shining: the colored quills on the bleached deerskin softly clacking, the beads and fringe of her knee-high moccasins swinging and glinting in the firelight. She tucks two carved bone birds, one in the top gather of each braid, ties yellow feathers along the plaits, and takes up her best shawl, red and black and fringed with silk.

Angus entertains as he does so well. The party is relaxed, gay; the younger officers treat her with respect; everyone speaks French. She sits next to George, whom Angus managed to place at Victoria after their transfer from Connah. He's come far, George tells her, his face contented as a seal's: he has a wife now, a child. It's his greatest hope that Richard Grant will come north as well, when Fort Hall closes down.

And Angus and Catherine, of course. "I'll never forget his kindness, or yours." He smiles at the memories. "All our adventures: my first buffalo, the Smoky Ground!" He stands and kisses her hand when she bids them goodnight and she's pleased, so pleased. It's been ages since she felt such harmony and peace. She floats through the downstairs rooms extinguishing candles, buoyed and serene until she hears a harsh tone through the closed door where the men are smoking, recognizing the Chief Factor's voice.

"It was presumptuous."

"I wasn't aware communications were not in my purview." Angus speaks as though his teeth are clenched. She leans a little closer to the door.

"From this point on, all contact between the Americans and the Company will go through Mr. Ogden or myself."

"Understood."

"We have to toe a fine line, Angus."

"That I do see."

"I'm not entirely sure you do."

There's a momentary silence and she steps back. It's not her business.

"Our posts must be above reproach. You've let yours go a bit to seed." Douglas's voice is cool; her heart jumps.

"I do the best with what I have."

"I'd like to see . . . a bit more rigor." She leans her head closer.

"It'd be easier if I had half the crew requested." Angus is barely keeping his anger in check.

"Try harder, then, to keep them from running off."

"What would you suggest? Against three hundred twenty acres given free?"

"I know it's hard. But there's still business to conduct." There's a pause, a slosh, and clink of glasses. "We have to look the part, if we're to pry a penny from their bloody fists when we close down."

"Connah's a workhorse. I brought in close to five thousand skins last fall."

She imagines from the silence that Douglas nods.

"The Americans consult with me," Angus goes on. "Our pack trains pass their towns. It's not as if they're not aware that we're still here."

"But how you look, man! Where's the spit and polish? Sashes, uniforms? Anyone would take you for a ragged, shuffling band of Natives."

She presses her ear closer. Even so she barely hears her husband mutter. "I see."

"Half the Americans think we're in league with the Indians and priests to drive them out. They're gunning for us all, and every confrontation makes it worse." The glass cracks down.

"We have to keep things calm. You have to look the part. Wear the Queen's colors with pride, McDonald. You're not some buck; put on some boots. And get your wife to wear some proper clothes."

She starts back, stung. Tears blur her vision and she wipes them angrily aside.

"I beg your pardon, sir." Her husband's voice is tight. "Your comment is offensive."

"No offense intended. It's common sense. Our livelihood—even our lives—may ride on it. Fly the flag, show these Yanks we're British, first and foremost. Until this whole thing's over we cannot take sides."

CHAPTER 4

FOR A WEEK she waits to see what her husband will say, but he says nothing. The Chief Factor departs, and still Angus does not take her aside and tell her to wear white woman clothes. He wears his woolen trousers more often, she notices, though he complains they itch. Catherine can't say anything either. If she asked, she'd give away the fact she spied. Still, it builds up and she must know. The day before their New Year's party she lays out clothes like those Amelia Douglas and Julia Ogden wear: dark heavy skirt, white shirt with a tall, tight neck, the thin black gloves that Angus ordered her from England. She tries these carefully on. She's looking at herself in the mirror when Angus walks in, though she thought he was out with the horses.

"What on earth?" He stops short. Her cheeks heat up.

"I thought . . ." she says, and stops.

"Thought what?" He takes a step toward her.

"That we should be more . . . proper."

He looks at her, astonished. Then he throws back his head and roars with laughter.

"Proper, oh my Lord."

"You're doing it," she says, defensive.

"Oh, darling." Smiling, he approaches. "Hang them all. It's nothing to do with you."

"It is, though. Isn't it?"

He tugs her to him and puts his cheek on hers. "It doesn't matter what you wear. You'll never meet Americans again, I promise. Not underneath this roof." He strokes her hair. "I'd rather see you comfortable." He picks up a second skirt that lies on the bed and chucks it toward the corner.

He never said a word—because he honors her. Oh kindly, lovely man.

"Neither of us fits in, to tell the truth," he adds with a peculiar smile, and she sees he understands. The Yankees do not see him, either.

She starts unbuttoning the stupid bits of bone. "What do you say? Not fish or bird?"

"Neither fish nor fowl." He pulls her to him. She strokes the soft bit just above his beard. "I like it when you're here," he says. "I miss you when you're gone." Then he lays back, arms beneath his head, and looks up to the beams. He doesn't have it easy, either.

"I miss you too." She nestles toward him, leans and kisses him. And so they roll into each other, lazily and sweetly, right in the middle of a snowy afternoon.

Afterward, he stirs first. "I should be getting to the barn."

"First sing to me." Her voice is sleepy. "The one about the *braes*." She can't quite say it with that quiver of the tongue he can.

"Of Killicrankie?" Catherine nods. A *killicrankie* is an aspen wood, he's told her, like the ones she loves at home. And too, the song's a fighting song—and now she knows they both will fight for what they love.

He puts his lips close to her ear and sings it low.

> *Whare hae ye been sae braw, lad?*
> *Whare hae ye been sae brankie, O?*
> *Whare hae ye been sae braw, lad?*
> *Came ye by Killicrankie, O?*
>
> *An ye had been whare I hae been,*
> *Ye wadna been sae cantie, O;*
> *An ye had seen what I hae seen,*
> *I' the braes o' Killicrankie, O.*

ALL WINTER ANGUS waits for Stevens to reply. It's not impossible to cross this land in snow. The governor is busy enough rushing back and forth to Washington, DC. Still, he doesn't condescend to answer. Perhaps Douglas gave him to understand he need not reply to a mere clerk—if he was even granted an audience. More likely, he's put out by the Company's very presence. Stevens strikes Angus as a man who thinks he can wave a wand and get his way. A swaggerer who couldn't care less what others have to say. Day by day his indignation rises. Has the man no understanding of the relationships the Company has developed over all these decades? At the very least the midget might perceive the usefulness of his own knowledge of the tribes. Nor can Angus forget the sting of Douglas's words. He has never been found wanting before. They're all under threat, he begins to feel: not just the Natives, but the Company, his wife and children, and himself.

For some time he's been pondering the matter of their education. He'll teach the children himself; there's no other way. It'll be the first school in the whole of the old Oregon country. Education, at least, is something that can never be taken from them—unlike the things he suspects that Stevens intends to seize. So one freezing February day he asks Catherine to bring John and Christina to the big table before the fire.

"Lesson time!" Wonderingly his offspring take in the paper, the pots of ink, the long thin sticks. Catherine stands behind them holding Duncan, who struggles and kicks.

"I want to, too!" he whines.

"When you're older." Angus makes his voice soft and kind. The boy is not yet four. The elder two are ready, though—and so should be his wife. "I'll teach you as well," he says. She looks skeptically at the pen that he holds out.

"Why do I need that?"

"So you can come along." John and Christina are watching intently. "So your kids won't leave you in the dark." He knows just where to prick her pride.

"Come, mother!" Christina tugs at her. "We can draw together."

"Not drawing. Your letters first—then how to add, subtract. Reading and writing and arithmetic—the keys to the kingdom of the mind." He clasps his arms behind his back and sees himself a mirror of his old, crabbed master, in that drafty schoolhouse by the loch.

"It's of no use to me." Catherine's voice is flat.

"You'll wish you did, when you're the only one who can't."

"Mama." John kicks the table legs in his impatience. He's more like her, his father thinks: he'd rather be outside and making something with his hands.

"For a short time," she finally concedes. Duncan is dispatched to the nursemaid and they start. He shows them how to hold the pen and dip it, pull it lightly on the paper. "Not too hard." When Catherine drags it first, the paper rips; the children giggle.

"Step by step," he says, encouraging. "We'll start now with the vowel sounds."

He has them trace the letter *A*, and as he does, he tells them how he spent each winter day at school. Six miles there and back, but Angus never minded. "How I loved to read. Such a world you find in books!" He paces back and forth, touched by the way all three poke out their tongues in concentration. All winter he teaches them, and though occasionally Catherine bridles, by spring they can write their names and simple phrases on his blue Bay foolscap. *The deer sees the bird, the boat can float.* He reads to them in the evenings, tales from Scott or Shakespeare or those of his devising, for he too has begun to set some stories down. He will read about his hunts, or men in metal, banners, battles lost or won. Then Catherine will pull the small ones on her lap and tell the stories that she knows. She, too, tells of great battles and of beasts caught in the ice, the trickster Coyote and his troubles.

He could never force her to be other than she is, Angus thinks, watching the firelight play upon her face. A "proper" Englishwoman like the wives of the Chief Factors, forced into an uncomfortable mold. Why Douglas does it, who can know. Perhaps he, too, must pretend, to pass. Gazing at her shining skin he knows it's useless anyway. Anyone who sees her or their children sees the Native, knows their race. And should any try to harm these precious souls, they'll have Angus McDonald to reckon with.

CHAPTER 5

HIS FAMILY HAS been gone the entire summer when the world turns upside down. Angus is readying the furs for Nisqually when Morelle, his teamster, trots in from the north, his face streaked with exhilaration and cunning.

"Look here, boss," he breathlessly says that September day in 1854, tipping a little sack onto his calloused palm. Thin golden flakes slither out. "Washed out neat as you please at the mouth of the Pend d'Oreille."

Angus glances about. Instinctively he reaches to cover the bright mound. "Who knows?" he asks, bending toward this man he trusts above all others at the fort. "Who have you told?"

"Nobody." A muscle flares in Morelle's cheek and he flushes. "Well, I hollered, I guess. But only to the boys. They won't say nothing."

Morelle is a flat-nosed French Skúyelpi who was here in Archibald's day. A tough, unsentimental man as true to the Company as true can be. Still Angus must be sure.

"Is this the lot of it? You've not kept back a bit, as souvenir?" He bores his gaze into the teamster's eyes.

"No sir. Like I said, I shouted when I found it in the gravel, but then I knew I better shut my trap."

"Good man." He holds his hand out for the little canvas bag. "We'll keep it just between the two of us. Although I'll have to tell them at Victoria."

It's the same flaky ore Finlay found, a glittering treasure that probably snakes through the glacial moraine of all these mountain streams. Angus is half exhilarated, half struck with dread. He pours it out when he's alone and sifts it through his fingers. Funny how it makes your heart beat faster, this sparkling little pile. One thing is clear: if it's on the Columbia forty miles to the north, it's as likely to be in every tributary marching south, all the way to where the Yankees are.

He tells no one. He writes to Douglas, asking his advice. This letter he triple seals and sends up to Fort Victoria with his clerk. All it takes is a word, a syllable. The whole northwest is crackling with rumor. Since Stevens's surveyors arrived a year ago, the trails and streams are no longer silent, tread only by Baymen and Natives. Ordinary whites are on the move now, prospectors from the played-out California fields, greenhorns from the east, meeting and exchanging news. Gossip buzzes in the mountains like current in a lightning storm, crackling and rippling north from Sutter's Mill, Rogue River, the Blue Mountains.

Might as well try to stem the flow of the Columbia, though. He'll never know how it gets out—a slip of the tongue around a fire, a youthful boast, the sighing of the earth itself with all those ears pressed to the ground. It hardly matters. The whispers start whipping around. Douglas writes that their only recourse is to try to control the supplemental trade. Prospectors need shovels and grub and tents—in this way the Company, in the absence of any government, can keep some semblance of control.

They start appearing in twos and threes, skinny, bearded men with faces like foxes. They fell small trees to make rude boxes that they set into the mud. Not far from the mill above Kettle Falls, almost overnight, Angus discovers a sizable number churning in the shallows, rocking their rude cradles, sluicing the clear autumn water.

"Well, gentlemen," he says. "You might have asked."

"Don't need to." A red-bearded fellow answers, mitts hooked in his braces. "It ain't yours either, mister, far as I hear." Impudently he looks him up and down. Angus wears buckskin and plaid here in his own domain; he holds his rifle. "It's wide open now, that's all I know," the miner spits out. He turns to plunge his spade anew into the bank.

They look shifty, desperate. So much for the picture he'd built in his mind of a booming camp, a general store, himself presiding. When he returns to the fort, he tells the crew to keep out of their way. For the first time he posts guard day and night. Anxiously he sends a scout eastward, seeking news of his wife and children. They ought to be back by now. A day later he receives Pierre Jerome, the Skúyelpi chief, who demands that he clear these dirty creatures off his streams. Angus sighs.

"I can do nothing to stop them." The chief looks incredulous. "I've told you; it's the Americans you must ask. The country is theirs now."

Still, day after day the chief comes, bitterly complaining. "The water is foul; the people aren't safe." And Angus can do nothing. He's impotent, he understands at last. How bitterly it galls him. "My hands are tied," he repeats and repeats. "You must speak to their chief." But Stevens does not give him—or any of them—the time of day. It's just as Angus feared. At best he's got a few blankets, trinkets, food, and tools to trade. But in the greater scheme of things, he can't chase these gold diggers away. It's almost a relief when Michel Ogden arrives with the family and says the newspapers are full of the big strike on the Pend d'Oreille. At least now Angus knows where he stands: he's got a bona fide gold rush on his hands. His trader's heart revives. He may not be able to stop them, but he'll bleed them dry.

WHEN HER BROTHER-IN-LAW escorts them to the Clearwater this year, he's more cautious than usual. The Yankees are pushing up everywhere, Michel says, like mushrooms after rain. Catherine rides more alertly than she has in years, watching every trunk and leaf. Only when they arrive at Kaix-kaix-Koose does she release her breath. On the way she's decided: from now on her children will learn nimíipuu ways. They have to learn to protect themselves. Two days after they arrive, so does her cousin from Lamotta with his hunters and wives. Since his father died five years ago, Eagle from the Light has been chief of their Salmon River band. He walks with the same spring, though she sees chiefhood has marked him too.

"Kitalah." His face is even narrower now, his hair still loose and long, rippling like a flag. "Here we are, old and tired—one thin, one wide." His teasing is gentler, but still there.

"You try carrying children," she tosses back, and they both laugh. How good it is to see him, though his brow, like her own, has new lines.

"This is John, and Christina, and Duncan." They stand beside her, erect and still, and she feels a swell of pride at how they hold themselves.

"That's all?" her cousin asks, ironic, as she laughs and shakes her head, then leads her to his wife and his own children. Margaret will be happy to care for the littlest ones, Catherine says, for she and Kyuka are on their way too. Eagle from the Light smiles. "That I must see. I can't imagine auntie quite that gentle."

Life is indeed strange, Catherine thinks. Now it's they who are in their prime, they who lead. The elders may prod but will let them take the reins. Not just the two of them, but their other cousin too. The son of Flint Necklace—Looking Glass—is equally admired; he and Eagle from the Light ride together to the hunt.

"And your man?" her cousin asks. "I haven't seen him in too long."

"Back and forth to the ships, like always." They're like two ships themselves, Catherine sometimes thinks, coming and going, anchoring together for the winter storms. Angus accepts her need for the place she was born—the place their children must know, where the bones of their ancestors lie. Every winter she tells the tale of the Heart of the Monster, and every spring she's afraid she'll forget how home feels. But she doesn't. How could she? She's part of this land and it's part of her. She's the smell of birchbark toasting in the sun, the laughter of water on stones, the song of the lark in the meadow beside the creek. And now she watches in contentment as she brings her own children back and hands them to her family for instruction.

Margaret marshals them at the camas fields, winding their hands around small, forked sticks; she herds them in the mornings up the river to the deep green pool. She scatters the elder three to the four winds then, and occupies herself with Catherine's babies, wiping moss on their bottoms. Even Eagle from the Light takes an interest in these two-skin children, as he calls them. He can't fail to notice how her offspring track him, he tells her, a smile on his thin lips. They're in awe of your height, your strength, the fact that you're like them, yet not like them, she replies. Besides, they've learned to track with Angus.

"Since he's not here, I give them tasks." Their uncle winks. Whoever catches the most trout or collects the most feathers from the jay—to that child falls the right to make and light his pipe that day.

"Just like you to make it a competition," she says.

John nearly always wins and Duncan cries if he's not quick enough, collapsing in a fuming pile. He's only five. He wants to play like at home, he cries; he misses his Papa, his pony. Christina takes his hand: "Don't cry, Duncan." She glances with a bright smile at her mother. "I'll be Flora McDonald, and you can be Bonnie Prince Charlie."

And so they scatter again, and Eagle from the Light moves through the village consulting with Flint Necklace, preparing his weapons, shadowed by half a dozen darting figures, her boys recognizable by the dark kerchief they knot at their throats in imitation of their father. And she's free to sit or work with the other women, dying cornhusks or planting the kernels, the peas, training the young vines. The village is peaceful, industrious; the June sky is sometimes bright blue, sometimes showering the crops. She says nothing of the complaints of Kamiakin or the white men digging for their iron horse. These things seem far away, like thunder on a far-off mountain, and she's happy not to think of them here in the village—until the last hunters arrive from the south to join the party and she sees her cousin's face change. The muscles around his eyes tighten at the words these young men bring. Their Shoshone neighbors have attacked the Bostons, it seems. They're tired of white men trampling through their land. The traders' trail is a broad and trampled track now, from their moving houses.

"They cut the trees and foul the water and shoot the people, so the warriors trapped a whole long train." It's not clear if the speaker finds this good or bad. "They made a great example of it, in blood and fire."

Inside Catherine feels a strange mix of fear and pride.

"Men, women—even the children were killed."

Eagle from the Light growls in his throat, shaking his head. Later her husband will tell her the Shoshone speared the infants and roasted them, but she doesn't know this now, and even later doesn't think it true. Even so, the deaths of children twist their hearts. No one speaks for a long moment, until she does.

"There's fighting south of our trading house too. The Yakama are aroused." The nimíipuu are no great friends of the Shoshone, or the Bannock or those southern tribes whose names she doesn't even know—but even so, each people has a right to defend its land. "The Bostons push on," she adds.

Both she and Angus are right—they're like ants, and yes, the people have to fight.

Her cousin's eyes are closed. He opens them, looking briefly at the sky, then back at Catherine. "I must speak to Flint Necklace. Tell Whiskers he should come soon."

◄◄◄

EVEN BEFORE THEY cross the Spokan on their way home Catherine sees the changes: trees felled at the sides of streams, churned banks and riverbeds. At the ford where the old voyageur Antoine Plante has his ferry, she's told that Angus has sent word to stay until he comes to fetch them. The way is no longer safe. Diggers are everywhere in the woods. She waits, impatient to be home. Angus doesn't delay and she unwinds at the sight of his tall figure on the bay, his black Scots cap. He scoops them up in his long arms. Over the heads of the children his eyes seek hers, and she squeezes his hand. They're all right. The trip home is not long, just the length of the Chewalah valley. But as they ride he points out streams where miners squat. She can smell them even from the trail. And when they bivouac at night, she's glad that Angus is beside her, along with a pair of burly servants. These diggers are dangerous, she senses.

Angus claims he'll make them pay to come into this country. His face is strange: tense yet strangely alive, like men preparing for battle. Ten bucks for a shovel, he exclaims: fifty for a mule, five dollars a pound for flour. That'll show the bastards. Even miners have to eat; he'll bleed the buggers dry. As soon as they're back at Colvile he loads the bateau so full the river licks its oarlocks and Catherine just watches from the shore. He barks orders, flies the big red banner, tacks a bearskin to the pole. Chief Jerome stands at her side as they watch them push off. This is no way to drive an enemy away, he growls. But Angus won't listen to Jerome or her. It's his only chance to show who's in charge up here, he counters—to instill some law and order. Who else but the Company will keep the peace between these diggers and the people, he says, if the Bostons' leaders can't—or won't?

Still she's uneasy as they pole away. Someone on shore has the bright idea to fire the fort cannon, and they all jump—at least, the people with skin like her. A few days later Michel and Angelique pass through en route to Fort Connah with the goods. Catherine feels a wild desire to just turn around and go back with them and leave Colvile to whatever might come. It's never been an easy place for her. Now it's surrounded by hateful white faces. Angelique tries to reassure her. They'll meet again in spring, she says, though the trail along the Pend d'Oreille may be more difficult because of the miners.

And indeed when Angus returns, he confirms that the river mouth has become a roaring mass of tents and lean-tos, wood stakes marching up the hacked black gravel either side. Three, four thousand miners, he says, his face still filled with the noise of it. "Extracting like hell while we did what extracting we could ourselves. Douglas will have to stop his grousing now." He shows her the bags of gold powder, so heavy that one as big as her hand bows her arm to the ground. When he first spoke of this yellow earth, she knew she'd seen the same stuff along the Colorado as a girl. They found many lumps and threw them away; to them they had no worth.

She stands in their doorway as he strips off his filthy clothes. "You sell the river for a handful of dirt."

He looks up. "The river's not mine, or anyone's, to sell. They'll be gone as soon as they've dug it out."

"But now that way is blocked."

"By spring it may be different."

She looks at him, grimy, tired—yet buoyant. He doesn't want to see. Is the fear she feels so small to him? The thought pains her sharply. "It will never be different," she says harshly. "These men will never go away. They're still here, they didn't leave as you thought they would."

In the three weeks he's been gone the miners on the creek below the fort have only become drunker and more frightening, digging and leaving their casings on the soil like worms.

"You've been down there when I expressly forbade it?" His face is thunderous.

She clicks her tongue. Is this all he cares about, that she obeys?

"Pierre Jerome has informed me. Many didn't go up to the Pend d'Oreille. They foul the people along with the land; many already hang on their drink."

Angus doesn't move; his light mood has drained away.

"The chief is furious. He takes his staff at night to clear the filth. The women spread their legs for it—he doesn't like to think what the men do. He's disgusted, he'll have them flogged."

"All right." Angus stands and sighs. "I'll take men down there and drive them out." ·

But he's no more able to move a score of miners than he's able to protect his own employees. That same month the Shoshone, perhaps emboldened by the terror they inflicted on the emigrants, attack the Hudson's Bay Company too. Two of Angus's men are killed bringing furs from Fort Hall to Boisé: two old hands, one Scot, one métis, expert in the trails, long friendly with the Natives. Even that can't save them anymore.

Angus has to sit down when this dispatch comes. It might as easily have been him or any of his crews. The trade was always dangerous, but this is different. For the first time it feels as if the place is truly on the brink of war.

Chief Factor Douglas will take no more chances. Angus is ordered to close the inland forts. He writes the orders for the Snake posts, picturing the trail above the gorge now littered with corpses. Fort Nez Perces on the Columbia he'll close himself when he takes out the spring returns. Meanwhile he's still barred from contact with Governor Stevens. Like the rest of the population he gleans what he can from the territorial press. But these new papers from Oregon and Olympia only incense him further with their drumbeats of vengeance and hate. Never has the progression of mankind's vices seemed so clear: after miners and settlers come saloons and restaurants and whorehouses, hostelries and stables, and inevitably some itinerant half-educated man with a hand press, spreading a noxious mix of gossip, dispatches, and lies.

The old moccasin telegraph, as ever, is the more reliable source. In this way the following spring he learns that Stevens has summoned all the western tribes to a big parley—to "address these present difficulties," as he claims. Difficulties my eye, thinks Angus: Stevens told him himself he had authority to make deals for land with the tribes.

Foreboding settles on him. He'd like to speak to Eagle from the Light or old Flint Necklace, but neither he nor his wife knows exactly where they are. The date of this council is fixed for June near the Whitmans' old mission at Waiilatpu—as disrespectful a choice as there could possibly be, considering the blood spilled on that ground. He has a mind to offer his services as interpreter but knows Stevens will reject it out of hand. The advice—or interference—of the Hudson's Bay Company is not desired. Still Angus feels a mounting alarm. So far this year miners have shot and killed several Yakama; in reprisal their warriors killed half a dozen Yankees, while volunteer militiamen shot up a Cayuse village.

It's a sobered and anxious Angus McDonald who leads his family south that early summer of 1855. They ride together as far as Antoine Plante's; he dispatches four burly men to escort them into Nez Perce lands. By summer's end, he thinks, he may have to tell them to stay there, far away, where it's still safe.

Catherine grips his arm. "Warn my cousin if you see him," she says. Stevens's parley will take place within the week. He promises, holding her more tightly than ever. The northern trails are peaceful so far, but even so. The fear is permanent now—mineral, like blood on the tongue.

CHAPTER 6

FORT NEZ PERCES
June 1855

THE LAST REMAINING southern outpost of the Hudson's Bay Company is nearly empty. Its shutters hang open, casements gaping like vacant sockets. It will never be reprovisioned now. The clerk, Pambrun, gives him the key. Angus has half a mind to torch the place to keep it out of Yankee hands. He won't, of course. He knows his duty.

He needs more horses to get his load across the Cascades. This year's haul was good, oh irony of ironies. The western tribes are gathered thirty miles upstream with horses to spare. But he isn't welcome at Stevens's council. Shifting uneasily, Pambrum tells him that he's been asked, in fact, to translate for the governor. Well, Angus allows. A man has got to eat. He pays him his last wage and sends him east with the message that he's looking to buy some mounts. That way the nimíipuu will hear he's around, at least.

He waits impatiently on the arid shoreline. This whole sweep south to shut these posts is bitter—yet not half so bitter as what the Native people face. Well he remembers Stevens's belligerence. He alone can save the day, the midget seems to think: "saving" the Indians from certain extermination by separating them from the whites, and in so doing, no doubt, seizing large chunks of their land.

On the third morning he picks the horse with most heart and runs him east to the cluster of cabins the Yankees call Frenchtown, like every other settlement of retired voyageurs. It's a relief to gallop full out, wind whipping at his beard and hair. He shares out one last coil of tobacco, dispatches one last message, and sets himself by a tree in a meadow. It burns him: he ought to be there. He of all these white men knows these people best. But respect is the last thing the Yankees care to show: their game is power.

He idles in the noontime heat. After a while he pulls a ledger from his bag and starts to write, the same thing he's written every American he can think of. To whit, that peace can be maintained, but only with respect. Be fair: offer cash and progress for their land. In no case should you try to take each band's ancestral home. He waves the letter to dry it, folds it, walks a circle in the grass. The hours slip past. He's almost given up when there's movement in the trees across the way. Three men appear and he lifts a hand.

He and his friend have grown old together, Angus thinks as Eagle from the Light rides in. He sits his white mare loosely; his hair hangs un-adorned. There are pouches now, beneath the slate gray eyes that never missed a thing.

"I greet a chief, I hear." Angus smiles.

"And you still wear your whiskers." Eagle from the Light, too, smiles as they embrace. The chief looks weary. He wears a breastplate of long quills, tight bands of beads about his wrists. He waves at his companions and they sit and Angus lights the pipe.

"We met when it was morning," Catherine's cousin says. "Now the sun is going down."

"Not yet, I hope."

"You come with news? Or just to show your ugly face?" Thinly, the chief smiles.

"I know this Stevens. Maybe I can help."

"He didn't call you to his council."

"He cannot wait to see the British go."

Eagle from the Light looks hard at him. "So you have no more influ-ence. Your power is flown."

Angus feels his face flame. "I would not say so, no."

"Then tell me: can you push them back?" His old friend's voice is slightly mocking.

They stare at one another a long moment. "Tell me his proposition," Angus says finally.

"You know how they talk." Contempt fills the chief's mouth. "Bad men are coming; he can protect us. If we stay behind his lines, he'll send soldiers to keep them away."

One of the others spits on the ground. The chief's younger brother, Left Hand.

"Kamiakin and Yellow Bird won't listen to these lies," he says. "He doesn't speak straight, they say. He speaks to them as if they're children, or feathers."

"What does Flint Necklace say?"

Their faces darken. He's still at buffalo, they respond.

"They can't make a treaty without the head chief," Angus says, shocked, looking at each in turn, observing the fury in their eyes, their necks, their nostrils. Eagle from the Light makes a mouthful of spit and throws it out onto the hot dry earth. "Stevens doesn't care who leads. First, he talks to one, then another, then makes Lawyer head chief."

"And Lawyer—"

"Is for the white man's road."

"Not so the others, though."

Silent and dour, all three shake their heads.

'Twas ever thus: divide and conquer, separating clan from clan, the way the English did across the Highlands. Angus feels rage rise inside. The missionaries have divided the nimíipuu, put half on the white man's path, while the other half refuses. Lawyer's people and Timothy's and the rest who follow the Christian teachings have cut their hair and wear the white man's clothes, Eagle from the Light explains. They look down on the "longhairs," the buffalo hunters from the Salmon, the Wallowa, the Clearwater. His people. Catherine's people.

"And the Yakama, the Walla Walla?" Even as Angus asks, he knows these tribes too are divided; those who would resist may not hold out for long.

"They council today," says Left Hand.

"I've said what I had to say. Now others must speak." Eagle from the Light nods at the third man, who rises to prepare the horses for the return ride. "I told him I've had enough of white men. They killed my brother for no reason, and my father. We welcomed them—it was in our hearts to be friendly when they first came. But we were blind."

"We, too, welcomed our enemies into our homes." One last time Angus hands him the pipe. "Only to learn they were snakes." How do you ever trust again, if your enemy comes as a friend, then slaughters you in your bed?

HEARTSICK HE STARTS up the slope. The white cone of the sacred mountain dazzles his eyes as the pack train climbs the spine of the Cascades. *Tahoma*, Kamiakin's people call it: they send their young here to attain their power. As they do on Coul-hi-cat and other western peaks. Soon it will be John's turn, Angus supposes. How keenly he misses them and fears for them. But they are coming fine, he tries to tell himself: they're strong limbed, sharp eyed, crossed with the blood of the Nez Perce and the McDonalds. Half-white, half-red, descended on either side of a proud people. Each bloodline spurned as savage, too, at one time or another. Heat seeps through his hat brim and the insects are terrifically loud, and he opens up a space between himself and the brigade. He rides in a dream, his body alert though his mind feels scrambled. He's on a grade, it's high summer: once more he has shot a red deer of the Highlands that belongs not to him, but the laird. How that one action changed his life.

In the high meadows the oily tang of sage gives way to cooler pine and toasted smells, and he remembers suddenly that cougar hunt last winter with John. How smoothly his son moved through the woods, how coolly he plunged the knife into the animal's dead eyes so it would not perceive its fate and spoil the hunts to come. Angus showed him how to fire his flintlock down the open mouth to finish him off, so as not to spoil the pelt. Their children are the best of both of them, no doubt. John couldn't have been more than five when Angus understood that he could move without a sound. He'd stop his father's heart, appearing suddenly behind him. He's nimíipuu, smiled his mother. But something of the boy must come from Angus too: his ardor and aim, his firm belief that he is master of his fate. All of their children have this confidence. They've grown up at trading posts in full knowledge that they are princelings, princesses—sons and daughters of the head man of their little world. What future can he possibly ensure them now? Behind him all the men he loves are treated worse than dirt. Like children—or feathers to be dispersed—said Left Hand.

Why then has he been put here, just to watch them dispossessed? Is Angus's own life to serve no purpose? He turns in his saddle, looking back at the plain far below. How bitter is his impotence. How random, pointless, his existence. It's only by some fluke that he is even here. If that other John, aged twelve, had not escaped the slaughter in the glen, he—none of them, not Archibald, his gram, his father, Duncan, Maggie—would be here. In the darkness of his heart, he sometimes thinks it might have been better if they weren't.

DROPPING ONTO THE alluvial plain that stretches to the tip of Puget Sound, he's shocked to see the change. There are rough houses and fences and mules with plows along the dirt road leading to the post at Nisqually. Farms and cabins on the flat rich soil where just a year ago stood the lodges of the coastal tribes. The settlers look up, hands shading their eyes, as the brigade appears out of the mountains. Angus has the strangest feeling that to them he's an apparition—a spectral warrior at the head of some fell convoy. They shrink and gape and he salutes them as they pass. All that marks him out as white is his Scotch cap: he laughs to see confusion on their faces.

Chief Trader Tolmie only shakes his head when Angus notes how fast the flies have settled on their carcass. Not dead yet, he says, but might as well be. They've swarmed Company land on the point and at the Cowlitz farm, even squatted Fort Vancouver's pastures and fields. Took every stick of wood as well—fences, outbuildings—to use themselves. Heaven above, thinks Angus. Just get it over with—dispatch us with a mercy ball and let us go.

He reports what little he knows about Stevens's negotiations. Soon there'll be no one left to trade with, Tolmie observes. Already these new governors have shunted off the coastal tribes to inland "reservations." Of course the Company opposes confining the Natives, out of pure self-interest. They can't trade with people who can't hunt or trap. "But we haven't got a leg to stand on." Tolmie, a bright-eyed fellow with a curly beard, is the closest to a kinsman Angus has now in this whole country. They hail from the same small corner of the world.

"To Inverness, and the unknown," says the master of Nisqually when they sit down.

"Where will you go?"

"The only place there is to go. North."

Angus lifts his glass of homemade rotgut—cloudy, quasi-fatal, like this whole damn place. "So it would seem."

All along he hoped it wouldn't come to this. He can't imagine she'd agree. He tries and fails to picture his whole brood moved north across the line.

For the next week and a half he pitches in to keep himself from brooding. Unfolding, drying, counting, packing up the trade goods he will take back out. Respite is needed for man and beast alike. Last time he was here they caroused like the devil. He even paid a lad to serenade the fort at dawn with his own pipes, laughing like hell when the English clerk burst out telling him where he could stick those drones. But this year every day drags by. He can't shake the feeling of being surrounded.

The settlers don't come to the fort, but still it feels as if they're only waiting to invade. It's a siege, Angus thinks. Well, damn them. We were here before you were born. We were Here Before Christ—you've no idea what this western world once was. He'll walk where he damn well pleases. He roams the point, examining their fences and shacks. The settlement clusters around a mill on a creek feeding into the bay. The man who runs it is huge and blond.

"Come a long way?" Angus asks, but the man shoots back, "No farther than you, I'd warrant."

A stringy woman is hoeing a little way on, and he asks if he can trouble her for water. She puts down her hoe and nervously splashes some from a pitcher on the porch.

"My husband's up at the timber." She's incredibly pale, with blue eyes rimmed pink like a rabbit.

"Never mind." He smiles. "I don't bite."

"You're from the fort?"

"Aye. And you?"

"Ohio." They lean awkwardly at the rail. The view is beautiful, encompassing the choppy dark blue water of the Sound, the low green fields of the fort, the white cone of the distant mountain.

"Lovely," Angus says.

"I love it here," shyly she says. He looks at her closely. What kind of people are these settlers? Are they evil, or just ignorant? How can they not know they've taken someone else's land?

"So did the Puyallup," he says, and her face hardens.

He spies a newspaper folded on the rocking chair. "Mind if I take a look?" She nods and goes back to her work, too polite to refuse him.

The *Puget Sound Courier* is all of four pages, dated June 24, 1855—just a few days ago. His breath stops when he reads the headline on the second page.

Oregon, Washington Treaties Agreed;
Indian Reserves Determined.

The item is a communiqué signed by both Isaac Stevens and Joel Palmer, his counterpart for the Oregon Territory, reporting on the "successful conclusion" of negotiations with a dozen tribes from the Cascades east to the Rocky Mountains:

> By an express provision of the treaty the country embraced in these cessions and not included in the reservation is open to settlement, excepting that the Indians are secured in the possession of their buildings and implements till removal to the reservation. This notice is published for the benefit of the public . . . Oregon and Washington papers please copy.

It's not even two weeks since the council. The bastard. How swiftly he extracted what he wanted. The words "open to settlement" burn Angus's eyes—as they're surely burning every eyeball for a thousand miles. The whole goddamned thing is a farce: carte blanche to the plunderers, the thieves. Not a soul even knows where these so-called reservations even are, so how in hell are they supposed to leave the Indians in peace?

Oregon and Washington papers please copy.

He rips the sheet in two, crushing them into balls he lobs as far as he can. "Hey!" the woman shouts but he's gone, long legs burning up the distance to the fort, where he bursts in on Tolmie and tenders his resignation. There's no choice, he says, they've thrown the whole thing open.

The tribes are doomed; it's now or never—he must move if he's to protect his family, stake them any kind of future.

"It's all right for you, you'll just move north," he says. "But I—." He shakes his head. Catherine will never leave her people.

Tolmie smiles sadly, shaking his curly head. "I understand you, Mac, I do. But I can't let you go—or else the rest will run right after." He puts a hand on Angus's arm. "None of us can sink before the ship."

Angus stares, though he doesn't really see him. His mind, his heart, are lit with rage. He turns and bursts away, striking out again toward the water this time, the rock wall the voyageurs made. He comes to a field filled with cows and sheep. The bleating mindless sheep, mowing all that stands in their dull path. He swings his head toward the plank shacks. These people, too, are sheep, like dung-hung filthy Highland sheep, dumbly pushing onto land and mashing all that thrived before. He hates their small mean mouths, their primness and propriety, feigned innocence, entitlement. "These lands were never yours!" he roars and hates them with a clean bright fury that till now he'd only felt for sheep and masters as they wrecked the glens of Easter Ross.

"Bloody thieves," he mutters, advancing to the fence below the mill. The horses clomp toward him; the sheep lift up their baleful eyes. He lifts the top rail off with ease and hoists the ten-foot pole upon his shoulder, heaves it like a javelin beyond the millrace where it pierces the gray mud. And wrests another up, this one set tighter so he has to yank, but he is heedless of the splintered wood, the piercing of his hands, his whole self tearing down what they threw up. He launches it with fell joy toward the mill and only then does he perceive the yammering that fills his ears as human and the red-faced miller as impediment. A gnat, rushing at him, hollering and swinging. Angus spins, his elbow lethal, and with one blast he knocks the gnat, legs crumpled, to the ground.

"You have no rights here, hie ye hame!" he cries, Scots taking over as he fights the fight he tried and lost before. He turns and laughs to see the knot of men approaching, holding hoes and pitchforks, one a rifle trained upon his breast. A burning as of clear strong whiskey fortifies him, though he's stone cold sober. "Come and get me," he yells, taunting. "Not a man among you pussy farmers strong enough to wipe us out." It had to come to this, he thinks as they begin to charge, a half a dozen, more—his jaw whacked, then a boot into his stomach, iron taste of blood inside his mouth. *Scots, what hae with Wallace bled!* he sings inside as he swings back; we'll not submit, not this time, nevermore. These people are just sheep who grunt and do not speak and he is sure then they are brutes, and he's reciting Burns and Byron in his head still all the while. He's still connecting, hearing bone crack, then sharp pain in his right eye, and someone's pinned his arms. Heat everywhere, and light and some mad laughter he can barely hear that tells him it is over, he has done all that he could, and it will never be enough.

TOLMIE SENDS HALF the brigade ahead while he patches McDonald up. The miller, not content with nearly gouging out his eye, would see him clapped in irons. Tolmie applies his habitual plasters of coin and spirits, keeping Angus out of sight until he's fit to ride. Three days later he catches up with his men, who are idling in the foothills. Hostiles, they say, and he scowls at them with his one unswollen eye. The yellow bellies of the Yankees have infected even his own men.

It can only be the Yakama, he figures. If Kamiakin signed this treaty, it could only be a ruse to buy some time. He's told Angus plenty of times he'd rather die than give up his ancestors' land. Near the summit Angus feels the Indians' presence well before they show themselves. In his foul mood he barks in their language: "Who stands in my way? Show yourselves, or you are women." Nothing gets a brave like being called a woman.

A score of armed warriors steps out. He recognizes Kamiakin's nephew, a man called Qualchan. He looks monstrous, a thick band of red paint masking his eyes. "This isn't your road," Qualchan says as his men fan out along the pack train.

Angus dismounts. "Your argument isn't with me. Your uncle and father know it."

Qualchan sneers. "I do as I choose." He's barely twenty, but the weight of events is such that he surely believes his people's fate hangs in the balance. In this he isn't wrong. Angus steps toward him, hand raised, but Qualchan takes no chances, a thick blade instantly in his own hand.

"You can kill King George's men," Angus says softly. "But what good would that do? We've never been your enemies."

"What good is what you carry." The warriors' eyes rove toward the bulging packs.

He should have brought more men, but there were none to be had. Qualchan's knife is a bare few feet from his neck and Angus feels his scalp tingle.

"Look." He drops suddenly, squatting and marking a circle in the dirt. "This is the Company." He makes some marks inside the circle. "The traders you sell to, from the English kings and queens." Qualchan and his men watch coldly. "And these"—he draws lines raying to the left, "are the Americans, and these"—drawing a similar set of lines to the right—"are your warriors and allies." He stands and wipes the red dust from his hands. "We're not in your battle, as you see. We're in between."

"We don't want to kill you for your guns," Qualchan says, conversationally almost. The implication is that if he must, he must.

"I could give you all the guns and powder you want. But then as you see, the Americans will also call us their enemies. I don't think you want our blood on your hands."

This stops the young brave for a moment. Angus watches him think.

"You sell the guns to them."

"We don't. They have plenty of their own."

He turns to his clerk and tells him to unload packs containing goods he's willing to part with. It's a gamble, but all he has.

"I can give you everything else." Suddenly he remembers Ogden, ransoming those Whitman captives. "I know your quarrel isn't with us."

Qualchan must know that his father and uncle will have his hide if anything happens to the Baymen, or to Angus.

He opens a pack and spreads it on the ground—one of the better bales of hunting equipment, steel arrow tips, fishhooks, bone-handled knives for gutting. The young men mutter and he looks up sharply. "I give you all this for nothing. It's better than what you have."

They shift sulkily from foot to foot and Qualchan says, "More."

Angus nods. "Tobacco. Pipes. Flour. Flints. Ribbons. Dentalia." He enumerates each item as the packs are unrolled. The young men's eyes glint: they like especially to decorate themselves. They don't often get the shells and teeth the Company procures from the coastal tribes.

"A horse to take it home." Angus selects an elegant gray with black spots on the rump. "Take it with my greetings for your family from Angus McDonald."

So long as they feel they've saved face, he'll be fine. He swings up in the saddle and salutes them. "You are a fine force." He scans their powerful, naked torsos. "We've known you a long time. Your fathers and grandfathers should be proud."

Then he is off with his long snake behind him, hand held up in respect, holding his breath as he rides out of sight.

A LETTER IS waiting for him at Colvile from the Company man who interpreted at the treaty talks. He witnessed the whole sorry business. All told, the tribes signed away fifty thousand square miles—nearly twice the size of Scotland. Stevens bullied and threatened them, the interpreter writes: if Kamiakin didn't sign, the Yakama would bathe "in a river of blood."

"The priest and I saw how the chief put his mark—of 'friendship,' he later told us—biting his lips so hard they bled. His face was so full of hate it was clear to myself and Father Ravalli he won't rest until every Boston is dead."

Heading home Angus's brigade kept running across knots of miners with picks on their backs. They slunk with hostile looks to the side, or sometimes held their ground until it was clear he'd not slow his train to spare their lives, and they sprang back. At night by the fire he felt haunted by the burning in their eyes, that queer and insatiable lust for gold. And yet a part of him knew he was no different. He cringed to recall the way he hoisted his own flag and set off cheering to the mines. He heard Catherine's reproaches in his ears, far louder now. His own pulse, too, always beat a little faster at the sight of a great haul of fur. How brilliantly he oversaw the mining of those riches. Mineral or fur, they bring a man such power and pride.

Eagle from the Light once told him that this, of all the white man's ways, most baffled him. The earth's rich offerings were all around; they were enough. He almost thought soyapos lived in fear—of going hungry, never having all they needed. And this alone showed they didn't live in harmony with the Creator—for if they did, they'd live in faith that they'd be cared for.

By now it's August; Angus sends a note to Catherine on the Clearwater, telling her to wait a while. It stings to think that this is why he taught his wife to read. He'll ask Michel to take the Lolo Pass with his brigade, to escort her and the children safely home. A week later he gets a packet from the clerk who oversees what's left of Fort Vancouver. The newspaper type swims disconcertingly; he'll need some spectacles before too long.

The Oregonian reports that US Marshal Meek will provide volunteers to bolster an Army command sent up from the Dalles. There's no question, the paper opines, that "a war of extermination has been decided upon by the natives."

Bloody Meek. It was he who eventually hung the Cayuse who turned themselves in for the murder of the Whitmans. How did he just flip, decree that Native people had no rights? Angus drops the paper, staring into space. The preachers of the racial calculus are on the rise now, spreading hate. The worst of them a Scot no less, this noxious Robert Knox, a surgeon who lumps all the races darker than the Anglo to a life of slavery or else extinction. He shakes his head and picks up the next screed. The Americans are well advanced at this grim task—and not just with the Negroes.

The clerk has marked up a well-thumbed copy of the *Olympia Pioneer and Democrat. Nota bene*, it reads, with an arrow pointing to the item:

Indian Trouble: British Accused

We have evidence to believe a pack train was dispatched across the pass . . . [and] the gentlemen in charge of the train, whilst en route, made large presents of ammunition to these Indians, openly encouraging them to take up arms against the Bostons.

Following the murder of the Haylett family in the Walla Walla valley . . . there are strong feelings here that the Hudson's Bay Company encourages such attacks east of the mountains in order to keep Americans out and so gain control of the gold discoveries along the Columbia.

Is it not strange, that at all of the former British trading posts, the settlements of retired Scottish and Canadian workers with their half-breed families seem curiously immune to Indian attack?

CHAPTER 7

NO ONE SEES Duncan in the woods. He darts from place to place, too young to thresh the harvest wheat, too old to hover by his mother's side. He's six years and exactly half. Duncan watches and collects: a desiccated cricket and a hornets' nest, a piece of rock with shiny bits like those the Yankees dig. He builds a screen of willow by a rock cleft that he makes his secret cave above the mill. The salmon are running, and he squats to watch the young men haul them out in baskets, holding one another waist to waist above the spray. When he tires of this he steals along the ridge and spies upon the miners.

He's the exact color of pine bark and can stand so still that sometimes they pass right beside him when they climb the banks to shit. He smells their sweat and defecation, but they don't smell him. He wants to understand just how the water blasts the golden seams apart. He tried to pound his rock, but it just split and this was not the gold their father showed them, glittering and thin like scales of fish.

He waits for evening, when the men have stood and groaned and pounded at their backs and called to one another for a drink. Then he flits like a shadow to the last box on the bank and looks inside. He's seen them pour water in the top and watched the mud pour out below but now up close he sees a lace of metal fitted in the box. He glances toward their fires; he holds his breath. The gloaming comes and they no longer look below. He breathes a little easier and puts his fingers in the box, feeling for the place that holds the gold.

Mysteries are everywhere: the trees turn into wood and men turn rock to gold and he is always there, observing. The day before he saw some people in the woods by the Skúyelpi village signaling to one another. Not local people: others, speaking in another tongue. The miners, too, do strange things when they think nobody's looking. Two men were rutting like the deer in season, white bottoms flashing dark against the trees. Another time he saw a woman slip inside a miner's tent and come out later with a jug. He wishes he could creep close enough to hear them at their fire. He'd like to hear their stories. One day he'll write as well as Christina and he will write them down, the tales from Kaix-kaix-Koose he keeps inside his mind. His father's stories, too.

He rises on tiptoe, peering into the box but there's nothing in it but the rusted metal plaid. Probably the miners take everything out at night, he thinks in disappointment. He's halfway turned to slip away when a hard hand lands around his neck.

"What in the devil are you doing?" The voice is a harsh whisper.

"Nothing—" he whines, twisting, feeling his stomach drop into his pants.

The man pulls him close to see him in the growing dark. Duncan shrinks; the eyes are so red and squinting and the breath that blasts his face so foul. "I've seen you creeping, little boy," he hisses underneath his breath. He glances right and left and tugs him from the box and Duncan thinks he's going to roast him like they say. His water spurts hot down his left leg and he lets himself go limp; he's seen a rabbit do this in an eagle's talons.

"Aw," the man says. "There you've gone and pissed yourself."

He doesn't want to cry; he's a McDonald.

"I didn't mean—" he starts. But then the man appears to smile.

"You're from the fort, now, aren't you?" Mutely Duncan nods. Next thing he knows the man has grabbed him by the waist and slung him underneath his arm and with a little groan he's climbing up the hill.

"Not a peep, hear?" he says as they get to the trees, and he looks back at the camp. Then Duncan knows he's in real trouble. He starts to squirm and about ten paces on he finds his voice again and tries to shout. A dirty hand clamps his mouth hard.

"What did I say?" Roughly the miner sets him down, his hand still pinching Duncan's neck." You don't want that lot coming after you." He pushes back his hat with his free hand.

"Let's get a move on now."

To his relief and amazement the man half-drags, half-carries him to the door of the fort. It isn't shut, but even so the fellow bangs and hollers.

Maybe he's scared to step inside; maybe he's afraid of Father. And that's who appears, looming tall in the dark, and moments later, his mother.

"Got something of yours," the miner says, and thrusts him toward them. "You're lucky I'm the one who found him, that's all I'll say."

"As I live and breathe." His father's face is twisted. "Duncan McDonald, get your hide in here."

He's darting into the yard when his mother snatches him by the arm.

"He's not allowed to go down there," he hears his father say. "I have to thank you for your kindness."

"Naughty," his mother is hissing in his ear. "Foolish, naughty boy." His heart is hammering so hard with fear and relief he doesn't even care if she whips him with a switch.

"Got a boy myself, back in Frisco," the man says. "These creeps are rough. Your people ought to keep away."

"I've told them every day since you arrived." His father reaches out a hand and shakes the man's. "It's nice to know, at least, that there's a gentleman among you."

Duncan isn't whipped because his father won't hear of it, but still he will be punished. For two weeks he has to shovel the manure out of the horse park morning to night until his arms burn. If he leaves the fort alone again, his father says, his mother's punishment will be allowed. And you can count on it: she will not spare you.

MINERS AREN'T THE only worry. The country is filled with stealthy movements in the hills. Chief Kamiakin has been up to see the Spokan, the Coeur d'Alene, even the Skúyelpi. They've seen his warriors flitting through the trees. After Stevens went east, the Columbia tribes apparently met and pledged resistance to this treaty. The Yakama and Cayuse feel especially betrayed: outraged at these white men who immediately started swarming. The Boston chief lied when he said he'd keep these people off their land. Kamiakin is for war, others not. As ever, they are divided.

The Nez Perce have come out better, Angus and Catherine are relieved to learn: they managed to hold onto much of their homeland. Though they sympathize with the other tribes, they do not wish for war. In any event it will be a hard long winter. The leaves are hanging too long, the trees afraid to shed their coats, the elders note. Catherine, too, is on edge: he can tell by the way she watches the children, herding them more like hawk than hen. She jerks their hair when she combs it; she mutters under her breath. Something bad is coming. What? he asks. She frowns. She only knows her dreams are dark. If she were her mother, she might know better.

But it's not war, not yet. It's worse in a way, the thing that happens not a mile off. Angus is in the storeroom with his clerk when they hear shouting one steel-gray afternoon. A runner from the Skúyelpi tells him he must come. A girl is dead or dying in the woods above the creek.

He puts a pistol in his belt and calls the two biggest Kanakas on post. Catherine appears as he's mounting his horse and gives him a look that says she won't be left behind. Before he can speak, she's astride her own horse. Below the mill the Indians are clustered around something on the ground. They dismount and the chief parts the crowd. The girl's handsome face is streaked with blood, her cheek bruised, her lip swollen; the rest of her body is wound in a white blanket. She cannot be more than twelve, thirteen. Catherine speaks to the women on the edge of the crowd.

"She died only now," his wife reports. "They heard her screaming, up along the bank. When they got there, many men were running."

Many men. It turns his stomach. He's heard they boast about "pounding me a nice little Kettle," and he wants to rip their pricks out.

The girl's mother and father kneel at her side, mouths twisted and wailing. Catherine kneels beside them. She strokes the woman's arm, her hair. The father stands and raises his fist, and screams in a way that makes his words unintelligible. Angus looks to the chief, who stands with a dozen men a few feet from the wailing women. The chief is a mild man but no longer. His gray braids whip the air as he moves toward Angus. "We'll have the men who did this."

Angus nods. "I'll get Father Joset."

They're like a procession from old Europe, he thinks, when the priest arrives, and they advance upon the mining camp: a trio of sacred and secular power. There's comfort in the Black Robe on his left, the chief on his right. Pierre Jerome has striped his cheeks with black; Angus holds his rifle to accentuate his rank. Twoscore men and women follow: Catherine and the girl's family and armed men from the village and the fort. The girl had gone for water, higher up where the miners hadn't fouled it. She felt safe, in the daylight. It's a gray, cold day in mid-October, and somewhere in the middle of an ordinary afternoon one of these animals had spotted her, and thought it sport to violate her, and call his friends to violate her too. It could have been any of their wives and daughters. They don't know precisely why she died, why and when one of those men attacked her with a knife, but this is not the point. This rape and murder cannot go unpunished.

By now the sun is dipping and cold shadows lengthen along the shore. There's no center to this camp; it's a long string of tents like dirty wash upon a line. Angus determines to skirt it from behind and higher up the bank, so they'll feel them looking down on them. They ride to something like the midpoint, and he squeezes off a shot and barks "Any man of you who wants to eat this winter, you'd better listen here."

Some are pulling on trousers and braces as they step from their tents. Others are still bent at the water, and they straighten, turning, shielding their eyes from the setting sun. Those who know, know, and those who don't, don't, Angus whispers to Pierre and Joset. Keep your eyes on the ones who look shifty and hang back.

There's palpable hostility among the miners, who mutter, gathered in clusters, keeping their distance from the row of braves and Baymen ranged above them.

"What's the big deal?" calls one.

"Ain't done nothing," another yells.

"Call off yer wolves."

The Jesuit steps forward and speaks clearly and firmly, as if praying the mass. "A crime and a sin have been committed this day."

Silence.

"You are guests on this land." Father Joset speaks in a curious English, filtering the words that the chief speaks in his ear. "Some among you have broken our laws."

"What laws?" There's a general snigger. "Don't see no marshal."

"The law of God," says Joset, commanding and biblical, with his lean frame, his long fair hair. "The fifth of the ten Commandments: Thou shalt not kill."

Silence falls again. Angus is watching the perimeter of the group, the men who watch the ground. It's a pack, he thinks, a collection of mostly lone wolves. He hasn't been able to determine which, if any, one might call a leader. He spots the man who brought his son back, his cheeks aflame. Yet even in a pack there is order; in every band they'll yield the criminal to justice, however raw.

"A few of you are killers, and you know exactly who you are." He tries to pin his eyes on every face. "You attacked a defenseless child, defiling her, and then you killed her." He hears murmuring, the sounds of decent men registering disgust. "You have one hour to talk among yourselves and produce these killers to face justice."

"Justice!" There's a hoot from the back. "Savages got no goddamned justice."

Pierre takes several steps down the hill, flanked by four warriors. Uneasily Angus watches a few miners reach for their pieces.

"No man takes a life without punishment. The punishment will be decided by council and the Lord Jesus." The chief's words ring out, unintelligible to them yet clearly furious. Angus repeats them in his thick Scots accent.

"You got no law on us," one fellow shouts. "You redcoats better get up north."

"This here is the United States of America," pipes another.

Angus laughs and looks on them with condescension. "You don't do as I say—as the chief and the good Father say—and your stay among us will be short and bloody, I assure you." He looks back at the Skúyelpi ranged above these foul-mouthed brutes. "You don't turn in the men who rape and murder, know that you are on your own. No government will lift a hand for you. You'll face the wrath you deserve alone."

He sees the fear on their faces then, as they dart their eyes around.

Angus puts his gun back in his belt. "You have an hour to produce the guilty parties."

"I will stay," says Father Joset, "to take their confession and bring them to the mission."

The whole party pulls back a few hundred feet and lights a fire and waits. Angus and Catherine ride back to the fort to get a rope or chain to bind them.

"You can't kill them," she says quietly. It's not a question but a statement of fact. In former times he'd send miscreants to Fort Vancouver, where they'd face the Chief Factor as tribunal. But these Yankees do not fall under his jurisdiction—if he even has such a thing as jurisdiction anymore.

"I'm not a judge," he answers, and she raises a hand to his cheek.

"If they confess, they must face their punishment."

How clean that would be, he thinks: if the white man followed the same code as the red. If they owned up manfully and faced the music. In his experience, in the so-called civilized world, this is a rare thing indeed. Catherine's people govern the unruly with the firmest hand; they won't risk the survival of the band to shield a member who does evil.

"They might not confess," he says.

Her face is barely visible now the sun has set. "This isn't your work." She bends her forehead to his. "It's the chief's work now, and the priest's."

He understands she's warning him to step away. He's done what he can do, and now the laws of the people, their justice, must prevail.

This is why she returns to the Skúyelpi village with the Company's stout rope, but he remains in the fort, feeding and reading to their children as the night advances. It's why he doesn't rise as he hears the distant sounds of drums and cries, but instead composes a letter to General George Wool, commander of the Pacific Division in San Francisco, requesting a detachment of soldiers to protect the Americans who have ventured too far into this lawless interior. It's why, early the next morning, he walks up the three miles to St Paul's to see Father Joset. No man knows better just how far—and no further—the white man's law can reach. Climbing into the clearing before the log mission Angus sees three charred bodies hanging from his rope stretched between two trees. Most likely they were executed, then burned and strung up. Joset is praying when Angus steps into the chapel. After a long moment the priest turns stiffly and holds out a hand. Angus sinks onto the bench.

"It was wrong," he begins. "But I couldn't see—"

"My son." This is the man who married him, who says prayers for his soul and those of all his family, whether Angus wants him to or not. Joset puts a hand upon his head. "We cannot prevent all wrongs. We can only strive for an imperfect justice."

Angus turns to look out at the charred stumps.

"Did they confess?"

"Before their God, in their own way, they did."

CHRISTINA AND JOHN practice every day after chores. The straw bale just beyond the bunkhouse is a Boston. *Thwang* go their arrows, landing with a thud like flint in flesh. "Got ya, white man," says John, hazel eyes hard as glass. Duncan watches this, confused.

"They're not all bad," he says, remembering that miner.

"They are. They hate us all, especially Mother." John's glare is fierce. "I wish them dead."

All six children will be sent for safety to their mother's people as soon as spring arrives. Duncan clings in protest to her arm. "I don't want to go, if Father stays," he cries. He turns to Angus in appeal. "I want to stay, like you." His father shakes his head, and he holds back his tears. John's hooting, boasting of the buffalo he'll spear. Their grandpa Bonaparte has promised her a horse, exults Christina. The little ones are running here and there but Duncan stands still, rooted. Why must he go? Is he not also white?

Over that harsh winter, as they feared, the war begins in earnest. Magically, the miners leave; the settlers too, except some farmers who seek refuge at the fort. Angus has the space if not the welcome in his heart. These men would seize every stick and stone should Angus die. But there's fear on their faces and those of their wives and children—and for good cause. The Yakama are on the path of war.

First, Qualchan's men kill half a dozen miners who refuse to leave, then two others who rape a girl. In response the Yankees push deeper upriver, sending a battalion to the Dalles. They build a new fort on the Walla Walla. In November, young bloods put a bullet in the head of Stevens's brand-new Agent, gone out to see what happened to those miners. The US Army charges. Even so, Kamiakin's warriors keep the upper hand: they whip the soldiers, seize their Gatling guns. Finally, in December Stevens turns to Angus, summoning him to another council with the tribes who haven't joined the fight. But nothing is accomplished—nothing,

Angus exclaims, can be accomplished with such an arrogant, bullheaded man. Four days in a blizzard to get to Antoine Plante's, then all the bastard did was hector the Natives, accusing them of breaking their word, when any fool could see that Stevens broke it first.

Catherine beads in the firelight and listens to him rant. She's only waiting for the snow to go. Since the Skúyelpi girl was killed she's known: much as he tries, he can't keep them safe. It could so easily have been Christina. Her husband knows, though he doesn't want to say it. No parley now can possibly protect them. They've argued about it long enough; she has no more to say.

The last news is so terrible none of them have the heart to dance when the new year comes. Some fleeing miners caught the Walla Walla chief while they were escorting Stevens back to Olympia. Chief Yellow Bird, a man they all esteemed. They scalped him and skinned him, used his flesh for razor strops. They put his ears in some liquor, forced it down some poor grunt's throat. Barbarity is never only on one side. Angus McDonald stands at his front door on the first day of January 1856, dispensing kisses and cake to the ladies, decanters and handshakes to the men. There's nothing—absolutely nothing—he can do. He's useless, impotent—the head man of a dying tribe, a tinpot king.

CHAPTER 8

AT FIRST, HE thinks it's some sick celestial joke when the mailbag arrives the following May. In appreciation of his contributions to the Honourable Company, the governors have promoted him to Chief Trader. Angus is now a shareholder entitled to one/eighty-fifth of profits, estimated at an additional four hundred pounds per annum. "Douglas just wants to nail me to this post." He lifts an eyebrow at his wife. "The money will help though, for whatever comes next."

She looks at him sidelong. She's started packing for the journey—they'll be away a year, maybe more, this time. "It means he'll move you soon?"

He shakes his head. "I think not."

She's not deaf: she hears the clerks talking. They bat the choice back and forth: either stay with the Company and move north, or resign and stay below the line.

"The Bostons will never give in," she says.

"No. They'll take all they can. But we'll hold on just as hard until our claims are satisfied."

She nods, pursing her lips. Then it strikes her. "Don't wear your Scotch cap anymore, though, please. It makes you a target."

"I guess it depends on who's aiming." He has to make a joke of it, if he's to keep his spirits up.

He's planning to escort them all the way himself. Over the winter the Indians declared all land north of the Snake off limits to whites. In response the Americans have dug into their new fort at Walla Wa·'a. He and Catherine do their best to shield the children from the anxiety they feel, though the older ones perceive the tension in the air. Angus has imported a fresh-faced young Scot from Fort Hope to send along as their tutor. He tells the lad he'll accompany the family to the Nez Perce camp,

as gently as he can. "Even if I had it—which I don't—I couldn't in good conscience give you this."

Owhi watches, saying nothing: this is not his business. It's Kamiakin who's rich in herds, whose home is a blooming garden. Angus wonders if Qualchan told his father how he tried to fleece King George's men upon the trail. Most likely not, since he had failed.

"Seventy pounds then," Kamiakin says. His feet are planted; one hand slips between the buttons of his jacket.

"See for yourself." Angus strides toward the storehouse. "I have no powder, not for you or anyone else."

"Baymen have plenty of powder and shells and guns," Kamiakin growls. "Don't tell me lies." He barely glances inside.

Angus bends his head so only the head men can hear. "Don't put me in your war. I told Qualchan"—he looks at Owhi—"the same. It's not my fight. It's yours."

"Then why do the Bostons use your guns?" Kamiakan brings his face so close that Angus involuntarily steps back. "Why do the Baymen sell them Sharps and shells when all we have is old broken muskets?"

"I don't know what you mean."

Kamiakin sneers. "Then you're more stupid than you look."

Owhi nods. "They get them from the King's men."

"I'm not aware of this."

"Then you really know nothing," spits Kamiakin. "Your chiefs don't even trust you that much."

He turns without another word and strides away, his men closing around him. The palisade swings shut but at no point do they glance back in farewell. Angus hears them pound away. His face is hot. He stomps to his desk and scrawls a dispatch to Douglas, demanding an explanation.

"I don't doubt the allegations are true." He doesn't care if the tone is scathing. "But I am at a loss to understand. Neutrality is the only option here as you well know—or always claimed."

He's not naïve. They're making money hand over fist supplying the Yankee troops. Profit-taking in war—or mining or farming or any of these spreading and extractive businesses—is what good traders do, and lucrative as hell. Everything the Company can sell to the US Army it's selling: tack and tents and grub and horses. He gets the same reports as everybody else. But they have always drawn the line at arming either side.

"You risk everything we've built to tilt the fight in favor of Americans—even as they push us out. Have you no regard for our partners in trade these many years? Have you finally succumbed to the noxious fantasies peddled by the body-snatcher Knox?" He could write more, but he's disgusted. He closes by announcing his plan and sends the message north.

In all these eighteen years he's never once asked for a furlough—never once gone back to Scotland or even to Red River to see Jenny and her children. Truthfully, he never felt the need before. Life in the Rocky Mountains has been everything he could have hoped: fascinating, glorious, difficult, maddening—like any life, equal parts thrilling and dull. His toil has made him rich, respected. But now it stretches out before him, bleak with loss and compromise. He's tried to leave before and they resisted his departure. Even so, they can't deny him a year's leave.

Douglas minces no words in his reply. Chief Trader McDonald is reminded that he's pledged to the Hudson's Bay Company, a trading concern. Decisions on the goods to trade are made in London, not Fort Colvile. Since its inception the Company has sold armaments to Indian and white alike and will continue to do so. Between the terse words a clear warning against insubordination. Bitterly, Angus responds with a single line, asking when his replacement will arrive. He departs Fort Colvile for the east as soon as George Blenkinsop appears, just after the turning of the year.

CHAPTER 9

THREE FORKS OF THE MISSOURI

1858–1859

NOT SINCE HE was a boy has he known such freedom. He lives purely, freed from thought, in a city of tipis drifted with snow beside the clotted ice of the Missouri. He's released from responsibility, free to bask in the love that he feels for this woman, these children, their brightness and beauty and strength. He has drunk deep of joy, as the poet says, and needs no other wine.

He caught up to them in March 1858 at Horse Plains and followed the rhythms of the seasons as they moved eastward. Such a homecoming it was. He was sorry to hear that Victor was ill and would not join the winter hunt, but this is the only dark spot. All else is friendship and warm regard: Ambrose leads for the Pend d'Oreille, Moise for the Bitterroot Salish. To his great pleasure, Michel Ogden locks up Fort Connah for the winter to join them. Between the two couples they have a dozen little ones who've spent the summer as wild as otters in the streams of Sin-ye-le-min—which, thanks to the new mission of the Jesuits at St. Ignatius, the Yankees have taken to calling Mission Valley.

They meet the Salish at Hell Gate and follow the road to buffalo. For the first time since he has been in this country, the mood is not fierce but elated. Despite the many ills Stevens has caused, his treatymaking has accomplished one great thing: the Blackfoot Confederation has agreed to peacefully share the buffalo plains. There will be no war this winter, no raids or death. It's scarcely to be believed. They exist in a blessed and suspended moment, Angus thinks: his year away from the worries of the district, the miracle of intertribal peace. The chiefs set up camp just north of the Three Forks. The business at hand is buffalo, of course, but these winter hunts are so much more. He remembers how he first saw these gatherings as pageants, with their songs and dances. He tries to convey this to Catherine and she laughs. "It's just life." She tweaks his beard. "Your people are too dull, they don't know how to enjoy themselves." She's smiling as she says this; she's so much happier here among her people. But perhaps it's the opposite, Angus reflects. Perhaps Highlanders make too much of hopeless causes and waving banners; it makes them wistful and romantic.

Everyone, it seems, is here. Catherine's people are a tribe all their own, descended through the trade in fur: in their veins flow the blood of Scots, French, and Iroquois, Salish, Nez Perce, and Pend d'Oreille. He's always admired and slightly feared Margaret, who presides at this camp with Old Bonaparte, her second husband. Catherine's sister Kyuka has a lodge of her own and is grown fat from gifts received in thanks for her great power. He's a little wary of her too. In their own lodge he entwines with his wife in a place that is snug and familiar as a cocoon. They scatter their children like goats and lace up the tipi. He needs her smell, her warmth; he sometimes thinks he could live forever coupled like the mayfly in flight, safe and ecstatically alive. In his cooler moments he's aware that he's clutching at the things he most fears losing.

It was a good idea to send a tutor along with them too. Since he engaged Tom Mitchell at Colvile, the lad has browned up and filled in, and seems to have charmed both Duncan and Christina. He's dashing enough that they vie to please him. The week he arrived, Angus slipped in to observe their lessons. The older three were reading aloud from *Rob Roy*, after which they were to write their impressions of life at Osbaldistone Hall. Donald and Annie were drawing pictures of animals, while the tutor helped them trace the names. John, who's shot up in his absence, read hurriedly and without great interest, while Christina held the book in a lively fashion, altering her voice to suit the different characters. Duncan is the keenest reader of all, the tutor later told their father, though he doesn't like to read aloud. They're all good at sums, but John is the fastest—though Angus suspects this is mainly because he would rather be outdoors. The look on the boy's face when he gets his first bison is so radiant, he wishes he could frame it. All his children rode horses before they could walk, and can shoot an arrow at full gallop, girl or boy. He sees no reason to differentiate between the two.

The nights are biting but inside the lodges they are warmed by fur and bodies and especially the tales. They go from lodge to lodge, some nights to Margaret, some nights to Moise or Ambrose. Everyone is rolled in buffalo robes, but as the night progresses the air inside grows hot and heads emerge from wraps like turtles. The elders tell the stories their parents told them, and Angus is fascinated by the variations, the characters who change from story to story, tradition to tradition. Each of the plateau peoples has its own tales: sometimes these merge; sometimes they are distinct. He tries to fix them in his mind and sometimes jots notes. But with the hunting and the children and the camaraderie of the fire, there's little time for solitude, much less for writing. He'll save that for a future winter at Fort Colvile.

Catherine sometimes drops in, too, to watch the children learn. She gave up herself when the teacher came. She'd rather spend what free time she has with her mother and sister, when they're done with the butchering and tanning. She has her little girls, Maggie and Annie, to look after besides, and another baby on the way. Her mother approves—another strong member of the band—but Catherine's more tired now than she used to be. She doesn't have the strength she did. Increasingly, Margaret asks her pointedly what Angus has done to push the Bostons back. Why the Company has not prevented this war or intervened with these Bostons seizing the land. Her sister, too, is dismayed. "Why is he here?" Kyuka said snidely as soon as Angus arrived. "A warrior stays when there is war." They all trusted him to take their side. What is this Chief Trader good for, if not that? For once Catherine's relieved not to see Eagle from the Light. His fury is said to be immeasurable. She knows they're baffled and disappointed. She feels the same. But unlike them, she sees how hard Angus tries, and knows he suffers, too.

▧

IT'S LATE JANUARY when a new band straggles into the camp. The wind is unrelenting and the tented area where the women tan the robes must be constantly swept of snow. The hoots that signal strangers is surprising, to say the least. But nothing is more surprising than who this stranger is and how he looks.

Chief Kamiakin leads no more than a score of people, including his three wives and five children. He rides directly to the lodge of Moise and doesn't notice the McDonalds as he passes. Angus stares at him, then looks at Catherine. She's holding her hand across her mouth. Indeed, if they didn't know him, he'd say the man who passes is a ghost. It's only eighteen months since he last saw him, but Kamiakin is completely withered and collapsed. It's as if the flesh has melted from his large frame, and the bones have bent with the effort. He stoops now, favoring his right leg as he dismounts and vanishes inside. They wait until they're summoned, watching as space is cleared for the newcomers' three lodges—no more than three and the ragged bodies who erect them.

"He was sent away." Catherine looks as shocked as Angus feels. "They wouldn't come alone, if not."

When they're called, they see instantly that Moise is upset. He remains standing, his face shuttered, while the camp's leading men and women take their seats. Since the summer they've had only confused reports of battles between the Bostons and Kamiakin's warriors. A combined force—Yakama, Coeur d'Alene, Spokane, Walla Walla, Palouse—defeated one regiment, some reported. Yet there has been no fresh news since November. It's obvious from Kamiakin's face now that this news can only be bad.

He waits for them to settle before pushing himself to his feet with a stick. Then he walks slowly around the circle, bending and looking each person full in the face. The bones of his skull are extremely prominent, his hair lank and lips cracked, but it's the look in his eyes that gets to Angus. It's like a gaze from beyond the grave: devoid of feeling, a solid beam that moves from face to face as if to capture their resemblance for all time.

"You choose the white man's path, but I will not."

It's a harsh thing to say first off. Everyone seems instantly offended.

"Where's Owhi and the rest of your people?" The frown hasn't left the face of Moise, baptized Moses by French priests. At this moment, large and glowering, he looks much more like his own real name: Steit-tisli-lutse-so, Crawling Mountain. "You come here alone, like a beggar."

"You're the beggars, begging them not to steal your land."

"Plenty Horses warned me you wouldn't see sense."

At the mention of Victor, Kamiakin stiffens.

"Is it sense to give up every tree and stream and stone of our forefathers? Plenty Horses wasn't forced to give up his home as I was."

Moise nods. Ambrose mutters, "That's true." The tension abates just a bit. For the outcome of Stevens's treaties has been very different for different peoples. The Nez Perce retain most of their homeland; the Salish have held onto the Bitterroot; Alexander has kept the Mission Valley for the Pend d'Oreille. The more westerly tribes have borne the brunt of the relocations so far.

"I don't force anyone to take my way," Kamiakin says next, more accommodating. "But I take nothing from the white, not a blanket, not a horse, not even tobacco. If you take anything from them, they'll say they've bought your land."

His eyes rove around and rest for a moment on Angus, who feels them like a knife. Even had he armed the Yakama, what good would it have done?

"And Owhi?" insists Ambrose. "Your warriors. Why are you alone?"

Kamiakin sinks, toppling slightly to his buttocks, his bad leg stretched out. He looks down at a spot on the rug. "We were scattered, the soldiers had long distance rifles." He touches his leg. "I escaped with a few wounds." He looks around. "We fought hard. Then some agreed to make peace through the priest."

"Joset?" asks Angus.

Kamiakin's assent is more of a growl. "But they don't even respect their own priests." There's a pinpoint of fire in his black eyes. "Their chief promised there wouldn't be any hanging if we made peace, if we let their people through, and their white road." He falls silent.

"You didn't make this peace?" Moise speaks harshly, too harshly. Angus looks at him, perplexed. The old chief is broken, half-starved: why do his brothers treat him this way? Angus's heart contracts as he grasps how deeply the wedge has been driven between them.

"I ran away." Kamiakin rubs his eyes. "I didn't trust those devils, so I lived."

Owhi was more trusting, he tells them. He went to the meeting with the priest to ask for the same good peace that the colonel gave the Coeur d'Alenes. The colonel Wright said yes, if only he would bring his son Qualchen.

"In front of his father they hanged him." Kamiakin's voice is bitter. "Owhi was hostage; later they shot him dead. Then went the Walla Walla. They too"—he strangles his neck with one hand. "I don't know how many died by hanging."

The silence in the lodge is profound. No one is aware of holding breath, but there is no breath expelled. A sickness of heart and soul drapes them as completely as the poisoned blankets the settlers once gave them, saturated with invisible death.

"But they promised no hanging." Angus addresses him directly. He doesn't doubt it's true. Still he needs to be completely sure.

"Every word from their mouth is a lie." Kamiakin shrugs. He has no life left, no will to fight. Nor will he accede. Angus pictures him wandering now, for the rest of his days.

THE CHILDREN WATCH the Yakama chief with enormous eyes. Why? they keep asking. Why is he withered like a tree struck by lightning? They remember him in the front hall at Colvile, Catherine says quietly to Angus: shining and proud and larger than life. They sit with the older three—fourteen, twelve, ten years old now—and try to explain.

Christina and John bristle with indignation. "The Bostons did that to him, didn't they Mother?" Christina says. Catherine nods. Duncan says nothing, face screwed up with the effort at understanding. He's sensitive, too sensitive, Angus thinks: he's always trying to understand. "But why?" he asks, his eyes pained. "How can they be so evil?" His distress is intense.

"Men do this to other men." Their young faces are somber. "It's been so from the dawn of time. One group tries to rule another—even those sharing the same skin and beliefs."

Angus has never told them his family's story, but now he judges is the time. "It happened even to my own clan, to our own blood, in my great-great-grandfather's time." Ordinarily their eyes would glisten as he started a tale, but with Kamiakin's destruction so evident they shrink a little. "I'm not speaking of open warfare but of treachery."

It happened in the dead of winter, he tells them—like now, in February of the year 1692. Unimaginably long ago. His clansmen were tucked into their cabins and crofts in their ancestral valley called Glencoe, which means the valley of the River Coe. Except that the English king had conquered the Highlands—Angus looks at each in turn—the same way the Bostons are trying to conquer this country now. King William decided each Highland chief had to pledge his allegiance by a certain date—the end of that January, in fact.

"Our clan chief didn't turn up in time—he tried to take his pledge, but to the wrong place, and was denied. But it didn't really matter. The McDonalds were considered troublemakers, you see, and the King's men had already decided to make them an example. They'd be crushed to show the rest of the Highlands what was in store if they didn't bow before the King."

Catherine stirs, intrigued. Why has he never told her the full story before?

"They sent a rival clan to punish us." He touches each child gently. "A regiment of Campbells marched into Glencoe and asked for shelter. Now, it's a code of the Highlands that no visitor is refused a roof." Thus, the Campbells were billeted all around the village, men in every house. A week went by and the McDonalds let down their guard; these people seemed friendly after all.

"Until one morning before dawn they rose up and started shooting us all. It was a massacre, pure and simple." He softens his voice at the shocked look on their faces. "Thirty-eight of my people were killed that bloody morning, including the chief. Many escaped, including my ancestor—my gram's grandpa, a boy of twelve called John." Here he stops, his eyes seeking those of his eldest son. "Who with his mother by some miracle survived. If he, too, had died, none of us would be here now.

"Except your mother, of course," he appends with a faint smile.

"I, too," she quietly puts in, "am only here because I escaped in battle."

Their children sit cross-legged, stunned, and Catherine reaches to squeeze his hand. They're more alike than she ever dreamed.

"Yet you're one of King George's men," she says.

He shakes his head. "He was never really my king."

CHAPTER 10

FORT COLVILE

1859

THEY'VE COME TO cut a gash across the earth: a line from the sea to the mountains as thick as the height of two men. They're cutting the trees and digging their roots to make this wound, a day's ride to the north. Where is there anywhere such a straight line, except the lines that mother earth cuts herself—her cliffs and trees that reach straight to the sky world? Catherine remembers how the Colorado looped and swung and feels her anger growing at the way the white man with his tools divides the earth. He'll divide her family, too.

Already Angus takes Christina to the cutters' camp, these "Royal Engineers." He's overjoyed, in fact, to see his countrymen. Catherine doesn't like the way he seeks them out. She plaited this girl's braids and taught her how to form the dough and strip the roots. But now Christina rides in plaids and skirts, enamored of the trade and these machines. Already these children are torn between the white man's world and hers.

It's her own fault: she let her husband take the child. Catherine gave up her place at his table years before. Young as she was, Christina took her place, counting his furs and even helping him deliver them. And now she looks into the cutters' star-tubes and their image-boxes, dazzled and delighted. She shines with the beauty of youth and Catherine thinks it's not too soon to find a boy of her own kind. When they bring their box to the fort one day, she sees how the British bow and smile at "Miss Christina." At her daughter's urging she puts her eye to it. Her house is suddenly miniscule. She steps back, startled, and even Angus can't persuade her to sit before it. He puts Christina and baby Alexander and even Catherine's own half-brother Red Ox before its peculiar eye. But these white men have never really seen her, and now she doesn't want them to—and certainly not in this terrible way, frozen for all time.

ANGUS IS THE last Chief Trader left on this side of the new border. His orders are to stay until compensation for the Company's property has been agreed. In other words, he's the one to lock the door and blow the lamp out when they leave. It's assumed he'll move north like everyone else, along with his mixed-blood brood. But he has always been contrary—insubordinate, in a word.

Quietly, he's written to the government of Washington Territory to put in his claim for the property at Colvile. At the same time, he's written directly to the Governors in London, asking if there's any prospect of further promotion. He hasn't made up his own mind what he will do. He's not yet forty, after all. If he goes north, he'll get his own post and keep his share of profits. If he stays here, who knows?

Lately, Catherine's been talking more insistently about returning to her people. It's understandable, of course—but what then, he asked recently, would he do? At least up north he could provide.

"And be a servant of King George." Her tone was cutting. "Who you, and all your clan, despise."

"Whose Company has fed and clothed us all these years," icily he answered.

Neither of them tried to hide their anger.

Sometimes it feels she holds him by the balls.

It often feels to her he cannot see the way his world erases her.

There's a line between them, they both think, more cutting than before.

WHEN BABY ALEXANDER gets sick the following summer Catherine thinks instantly of the prophecy. After the land, the children will be taken too. She lifts his hot, limp arm and holds the burning forehead to her cheek. Angus paces back and forth outside. He's sent to the soldier fort but no one has yet come.

She doesn't want their medicine. It seems to her it is malign, emerging from the line they cut into the earth. The evil seeps into the soil, the air, traveling on the wind to this lodge where the baby lies. He's only a year old, the first of their seven children to sicken—and then to die.

They bury him in the fenced yard at St Paul's. Angus called him Alexander, but she will call him the one who is snatched away. Father Joset prays in his dead distant tongue: Jesus Christ will care for him, he says. She was ready to picture their Christ in the sky world, before. Heaven is just another name for the world where the ancestors walk, she believed. But now she won't let them have him. It's their sickness that killed him. Before Red Bear met the soyapo, it was foretold that the rivers would run red with blood, and so it has transpired.

All the deaths Angus has seen have been violent: sudden errors in judgment or fatal wounds. He's sidestepped his own a time or two. But never has he watched life flicker and fade like the ember on a wick. The tiny body he holds too might be made of wax. Tears roll down his face. "Poor mite," he whispers, "little child, light of my eyes." He hands the bundle to Father Joset. The mother of his children stands weeping above the red hole in the earth. Joset mutters and the children snuffle all around them. In truth they've been lucky so far, he thinks, and is instantly ashamed of the thought. A life is a life. Catherine leans into him and he braces his legs to hold her. She is heavy, dense as an oak with her loss, unreachable. She carried this life inside her all that time.

For the first time in a long time he recalls his own mam, worn to the bone with the effort of life. Catherine, too, is filled with darkness. And yet loss begets loss, it seems. No sooner have they laid Alexander in the ground than Angus receives word that his petition for land at Colvile is denied. And then they receive an urgent summons from Kaix-kaix-Koose. Flint Necklace calls a council of war—for the Bostons have turned their sights now on their homeland. Gold has been discovered in their mountains, too. The nimíipuu, in their turn, are overrun.

The children may not cross the river to its northern bank. Their grandmother will whip the one who disobeys. There are miners there, on the Lochsa that crashes down into the Clearwater. So they stay on their own bank, lying flat on the wide warm stones, watching the water choked with salmon heave.

These fish have their own strange existence, Duncan observes. They ram their red-streaked bodies in a block that moves like ice, except it flows upstream. His mother says Coyote made a place for them to squeeze through the weir once the people had been fed. His father says some mysterious signal causes them to return to the very stream in which they were bred. Of the two theories, he guesses his father's is probably right. But still he wonders if he is anything like the *núsux*, the Chinook—and if so, to which stream would he return? To the Columbia or to the waters of Sin-ye-le-min, or here to Clear Creek?

John is up in the Bitterroots, two days away. Looking Glass, the son of Flint Necklace, led him there to get his *wyakin*, his power. Christina and Duncan are not yet old enough, though Christina protested that she was fourteen. So they're in camp and the other children, after a few days of suspicious observation, begin to include them in their games. They swim with them far upriver where there's room for both fish and humans. They fish, but Duncan doesn't. He likes to watch the salmon leap instead— likes to imagine himself gliding as they do in the silent world beneath the surface. The water's so cold it feels hot; he's cold-blooded then, like the fish, muscular and fit and so relaxed he can ripple and bend as they do.

In the woods he's like the others, a normal boy. He makes friends with a thick-set kid who likes to whack him and laugh, as if they are brothers. But Eel-ah-wee-mah is every bit as quiet when they hunt, so quiet his father once thought he was About Asleep, so they call him that. About Asleep asks Duncan his nimíipuu name and he's embarrassed not to know it.

"I don't have one yet," he announces the next day, relieved. His grand-mother will give them their names soon, his mother said. In the mean-time there are huckleberries to pick, and they gladly rush up the deepest canyons on the south side of the river, a band of children with bark bas-kets and three elders to ride herd on them. Christina and Donald and Annie have new friends too, and Duncan feels a great relief, laced with guilt, to escape his own family for once. Here in the heat of September in the pine forest he's someone other than the third in line, the middle of a squirming mass—he's himself. This is why, he's certain, he and About Asleep are granted this encounter.

Even here on their own side of the river they've been warned to look sharp. It's not the miners they must fear, but the grizzly, aggressively stuffing himself for his long winter sleep. They should yell and sing and make noise from time to time. It's not natural to either of them, making noise. Duncan fills his basket, takes it to the gathering place, returns to pick some more. About Asleep is above him on a needle-slick slope, holding onto the branches. They look at one another across the bush, gulping as many as they pick, and then the berries are flying as they try to throw them in each other's mouths. They're giggling, which ought to be noise.

But in the time it takes for the crashing sound to reach their ears and their giggling to stop, the bear is above them, giant paws pedaling as he plunges down the slope.

"Hah!" erupts from Duncan's throat before he even knows it.

"Yee yee!" About Asleep has never looked so scared.

The bear, until now, they understand in a flash, has not even seen or smelled them, so intent is he on his feast. He freezes, tall on his hind legs, front legs flailing in reverse to halt his slide, turning his head from side to side. His eyes are tiny, and all the boys see is snout and skull and slaver and a silver-brown coat so enormous it could wrap up all the McDonalds.

The bear is a prophet, a being of great power—the master of this land he shares with the nimíipuu. His appearance in dreams brings the dreamer great strength; his appearance in life is the worst nightmare they can think of. Duncan feels his knees buckle but knows he must speak. "Great bear," he manages to squeak out. "Lord bear, we greet you."

The grizzly twists its massive head. Its eyes are yellow, suspicious.

Slowly, carefully, Almost Asleep raises up his basket. "Here," he whispers. "Eat fully, O bear."

If they bolt and run, they both know they're goners.

The black nose wrinkles, spit dangling in long strings from its black-tipped gums. The teeth are two rows of yellow knives. And then it lets out a sound that is halfway a groan, halfway a yawn. It stretches out a paw, and Almost Asleep bows and places the basket on the ground. And they begin walking, slowly, backward down the hillside, miraculously without slipping, as though their feet are held to the steep slope by magic, or, as Duncan will later relate, by magnetism, a concept he has just learned. Over the hammering of their hearts they hear slurping and then they're a hundred feet, two hundred feet down the mountain, staring at one another, mouths agape, hammering each other on the back and exclaiming that they're bear brothers now.

▃▃

THE DANGER ON the north side of the river is much worse than bears. A year before, soyapo miners tried to dig east of the root grounds, fleeing only when Flint Necklace's men chased them off. Like foxes they snuck back—with help, some muttered, from those tribesmen sucking at the teat of the white Christ. And there they found the yellow rock. In the papers the discovery is hailed as the new El Dorado. Within weeks they built a camp along a stream they call the Oro Fino. That camp is swollen to a thousand miners now, only two days away. With the spring and summer these diggers have started fanning east and south, grubbing in every stream bed. Armed prospectors roam the canyons in packs, a menace to everyone, not just the girls and women.

Flint Necklace's village only looks calm. Inside his lodge, the air is thick. Red Owl's band repulsed another group not five days back; they killed one miner, but two of their own men were wounded. The chief did not agree to admit these miners. Nor have any of the other chiefs he's called to council, Flint Necklace tells his niece and her Bayman. The chiefs who follow Christ might take the white man's gold, but he won't. He'll never allow them on his land.

So much has changed since the Yakama were thrashed. Angus and his family saw it on their eastward journey: the people cowed and herded in between the lines established by the treaties. The Army doing all this herding, building forts, while Stevens picks more agents to administer these "reservations." The kind of men these are, Angus has no doubt: rank opportunists. And then there are the missionaries, in the case of the Nez Perce one Reverend Spalding, who's turned half his charges into model Christians who despise their brothers who still follow their traditions. It's like a scene from a play, Angus thinks: all the players in place, this magnificent backdrop—then suddenly, GOLD.

It's everywhere across the northwest, from the Columbia to the Rockies, far north into the British Possessions. He's had his part to play in the

189

whole mess. The only saving grace is that when they're done, the miners usually up and go. Even the new Yankee fort near Colvile has less to do with protecting the Indians' rights than ensuring the access to gold. Brevet Major Lugenbeel of the Ninth Infantry Regiment is also charged with "restraining the Indians lately hostile" in this part of the world, Angus has read. Their military fort not ten miles from his establishment was called Harney's Depot, then Colville Depot, and now they have the cheek to call the place Fort Colville—as if Angus is already six feet under. They refer to his own place as "Mac's old pile of logs." You could at least have had the courtesy to spell Colvile right, testily he told Lugenbeel, who was actually knocking back Angus's good brandy in April of this year when the news arrived on a half-dead horse. "Fort Sumter is fired on!" the rider cried. "It's war, sir, with the Confederate States."

Four months later all the American soldiers have left for this civil war. In their place the authorities have dispatched a disreputable lot of volunteers, many "recruited," as Angus understands, from the prison on Alcatraz Island. With such friends, who needs enemies? Gladly he and his family saddled up and headed to the Clearwater, for even his fort no longer feels secure. And this is the main point—the only real news he can bring to his wife's people. There's barely a uniformed officer left anywhere west of the Rocky Mountains, not a single trained soldier to stand between the nimíipuu and this invading horde.

ANGUS ISN'T PART of this council, just an observer. Nor are women allowed, though those of high rank send their messages in from outside. He catches his own wife slipping away from Eagle from the Light as he arrives. Once inside the lodge he's surprised to see how few they are. From the Clearwater, Flint Necklace and Red Owl; from the Salmon River, Eagle from the Light and White Bird and Spotted Eagle; from further downstream Bald Head. "Thunder Going Across the Mountains would be here, but the Bostons attack him, too, in the Wallowa," Flint Necklace says.

His age weighs on him, Angus thinks. Catherine's uncle is entirely gray, his skin slack on his bones. The hand that holds his rattles to his chest is skeletal, almost; Angus wonders if he is ill.

"This is all the fault of Aleiya, the Lawyer, and Timothy," he goes on in a monotone. He wasn't asked—he didn't sign, but apparently there's a paper now that says soyapo can share the country the nimíipuu claimed from Stevens, and mine it for gold.

"Which Bostons made that agreement?" Angus asks.

"The agent. And his father in Washington, I'm told."

Red Owl scowls, his round cheeks drooping. "The Boston chiefs did nothing to stop the diggers. Even the soldiers did nothing."

Eagle from the Light jumps to his feet. "And these are the soldiers they promised to send if the bad men came." His voice is cutting. When he turns, Angus sees that his eyes are thin with rage. "The soldiers are gone to a different war, so Whiskers tells."

Angus nods.

"So you see." Eagle from the Light swings his head back. "We have only ourselves. It may even help, that the soldiers are gone. We can strike now, push them back."

Flint Necklace makes a face. "Spoken like a young chief. There are many of them, well armed." His own son, Looking Glass, nearly twenty, sits beside him, listening but not speaking.

"We could pick them off like rabbits!" Red Owl grins. "They run like women, let me tell you!" He has the broader, more open face of his Salish mother and an infectious laugh. Several others smile.

Flint Necklace squints at the other chiefs. "What do your hearts say?" he asks.

The answers are halting. Angus watches as they uneasily shift. They are outnumbered by the miners and they know it. Besides, this is not their fight, not yet—for the moment only the lands of Flint Necklace are threatened.

White Bird stands. "It's no good fighting," he says in a sonorous voice, removing the eagle's wing he otherwise holds before his lips. He's tall but broader than Eagle from the Light, and a great medicine man, as Angus understands. Both are related somehow to Catherine's mother. He speaks with great authority. "We can only defend where we are." He gestures to the north. "We can make a line along the river, tell the Bostons they may not set foot over here."

"But the paper is there. The other chiefs have signed it."

"Then they must be shown they don't speak for anyone here."

Eagle from the Light's face twists. "Will you just let them take your land?"

"You can't hope to beat them." Angus didn't mean to speak but can't help himself. "You saw the way it went with Kamiakin."

His wife's cousin wheels on him. "It's not your fight." His voice is cold. "You, in the end, nothing will happen to you. They'll kill us and take our land, but nothing will happen to you." His eyes rake Angus. "I don't listen to your words! Would you fight them with us?"

He plants himself before Angus in challenge.

"It's folly to fight. I've always said so."

"I didn't think so." Eagle from the Light sneers openly. "You have the same skin."

Angus hears Ogden's words then, from a dozen years before. *The Americans are the same color as ourselves.* Must this be how it always ends?

He looks his kinsman in the eye and nods. Then he stands. "I've given what help I can," he tells Flint Necklace as he bows and slips out.

Waiting for the council to end he walks the riverbank. He picks up stones and skips them. Bit by bit his anger abates. There's nothing he can do. The Americans will continue to push; the Indians will fight, or else they'll comply. Eventually the tribes will splinter, each warrior, each band, go its own way. He's beaten too: he and the Company, no less than the nimíipuu. Each must think of his own family, his own future. He straightens and retraces his steps. It's time to be getting back—if not to Colvile, then to Connah. The children will be safer there, if fighting comes to the Clearwater.

He goes in search of his wife and finds her with the other women pounding berries into dried fish to make the sweet-salt paste he loves so much. He swipes a handful, begs her for a minute. Christina looks up, a pestle in her hands, and he is startled for an instant. How beautiful she is in her smock, how much she looks like her mother when she was young, shining and dark. She winks at him and he smiles.

Catherine wipes her hands and comes to where he stands, and they walk out into the open meadow threaded by a silver streak of creek. The sky is blue, the sun is high; they could be forgiven for imagining their world is whole.

"It'll be safer with Michel and Angelique," he says quietly. Eagle from the Light's rebuke still stings. All his days in this country he has tried to take their side. "We should think of heading out."

She looks at him, this woman he wed half a lifetime ago. He sees love in her eyes and for a moment he's tempted to confess his despair.

"We must fight." Her voice is equally quiet. She puts a finger to his lips to stop him. "You'd do the same. You'd fight to save what's yours." He's shaking his head, but she goes on. "This paper is a lie we have to fight, to save our home."

"It's much too dangerous. For all of you—especially Christina."

"Ssshh." Catherine is strange: neither defiant nor cold, as so often before.

"You think they won't attack them with the rest? You'd put them at such risk?" He grips her by both shoulders.

"Sssh," she says again. "This is their home as well as mine."

"Your home," he says thickly, "is with me and our children."

The look in her eyes, he sees suddenly, is sadness.

"No."

"No one is safe in their home when those in power wish you dead." He tightens his grip. "No one knows it more than a McDonald."

"You'd do the same for your glens, your . . . killikrankies." He catches the ghost of a smile, then again that disconcerting sadness. She puts her hands up, tries to loosen his. "I won't lose any more. We've already lost so much."

"You think you're the only one whose life has been destroyed?" He wasn't going to tell her but a desperation fills him. "They strip it all away, you know—not just the post, but now the land. They won't let me have it." It was a mistake to tell her, instantly he sees.

"Then stay with us." Her face is lit now, with conviction. "Defend our home, our real home, here. Be part of us, as you have always been."

"You know I can't. I have to stay until the whole thing's done."

"Then what?"

"I don't know, Catherine. Goddamn it."

The light in her extinguishes and he can see her fill with bitterness. "I know. I see." Her voice is harsh. "They'll take them all away—or try to."

"You'd rather they died in war."

"They won't die. You think we haven't lived through wars before?"

She's her mother's voice then, recalling battles fought and warriors felled, the brutal bloody mayhem of their world before. Time rushes strangely in his mind.

"It's madness," he repeats.

She shakes her head. "I won't leave."

"You won't keep my children."

She laughs, hard and low, and his rage is so great he has to keep himself from striking her. "You never want to see the truth. The whites don't want them. Some, perhaps—not all." Before he can speak, she rushes on. "Let's ask them, then, where they will go. They're old enough to choose. Your people, anyway, will make them choose." She stops, eyes blazing with challenge.

His head feels like it might explode. "No." She wouldn't do it—she couldn't rip their family apart. "You wouldn't do that to them."

"It's the truth," she says, and he shakes his head. Good God. What mother would force her children to choose?

"No," again he says. Her nostrils are flared, and he knows he will never sway her. "You're a hard, hard woman."

"I fight for what's mine."

"And you think I'd leave them here, in danger's way?"

"Angus." She bends her head to his; he jerks away. "That's why I keep them here." She puts a hand to his cheek and feels him flinch. "Here with my people I don't feel fear."

CHAPTER 11

THAT WINTER IN his den, alone, he paces—turning, twisting, coming always in the end to the same ugly conclusion. He's failed not only in her eyes but in his own. He pledged to shield them from all harm. He takes his pen up by the fire and tries to write, as ever, to dispel the darkness. But this darkness lies too deep within himself. O fool, to think that he could hold the wolves away. He can't write to her, not yet. Instead he'll pour out his own miserable soul. This winter—the harshest, it will turn out, in the long memory of the tribes—he'll set the story straight, so those who come after him will know. Call it, he thinks, filled with venom, what the world has always been: *A Brief History of Dispossession.*

He drinks too much, but it has always helped the ink to flow. Here he sits, the last one left to witness, like the servant in the book of Job. The last of his kind in this whole part of the world. Not of Cooper's fantastical Mohicans, but those blind and idealistic Scotsmen who came to trade for fur.

The history he has in mind connects his present to that past. He scorns the view, so widely held, that the great tides of change are somehow fated. This is a feature of the rosy lens of hindsight, an excuse that every colonist will use. Imagine, for example (he will write), the English crown had let the Scotsmen rule themselves. If they had not seen fit instead to subjugate and seize the land and turn the Celtic peoples of the Highlands and of Ireland into vassals?

Imagine, just imagine: The Bruce at Bannockburn and Bonnie Prince Charlie might have met the English kings as equals, were the Scots not spurned as savages, barbaric, tribal. His own clan would not have been slaughtered on the banks of the Coe if the English had considered the Highlander a human being and deserving of respect. A boy escaped, and Angus McDonald was granted an existence. And now, in the year 1861, as eastern boosters bloviate about their manifest destiny to colonize the west, he's sure that though his Native kin are of a different hue, the trap they enter will have much the same complexion.

Unable to protect them, he's a mammal in a metal jaw, spinning and biting to free himself. He should have stayed with them. The glass keeps dropping and he sends word to the Skuyélpi that any who wish can take shelter at the fort. At least here he might help in some way. But only a few arrive; they keep to themselves, not unreasonably, hoping to avoid removal to some reservation. Nor is there a priest at St Paul's. He would have liked to pass the bitter nights with Ravalli or Joset—discuss it all with those good Catholic fathers. If there was more they could have done to protect these people of the Columbia, these generous and intelligent souls. Not one of them, secular or sacred, has been able to prevent this catastrophe.

"*The graves of empires heave but like some passing waves,*" he murmurs to himself. "*Between two worlds life hovers like a star.*" He goes in search of his Lord Byron, and it strikes him to the quick, how apposite the verses are.

> *How little do we know that which we are!*
> *How less what we may be! The eternal surge*
> *Of time and tide rolls on, and bears afar*
> *Our bubbles; as the old burst, new emerge*
> *Lash'd from the foam of ages; while the graves*
> *Of empires heave but like some passing waves.*

He weeps then, for his life. He's not so blind he doesn't know he mourns not just the Native way of life, but his own little trail. His great adventure, too, has ended, and the world is taught its mortal way. He thinks of all the nights that he sat frozen, wakeful, his brain shriveled from sleeplessness, awaiting the enemy's blow; of the times he watched the wolf cannily select his prey; the woeful moans of the deer when eaten alive, now scratched forever in his ears. He must sit with her, he thinks suddenly, and take down the story of her one great voyage down the Colorado. Such a thing will never be heard of on this earth again.

He feels a great affection for her but also a great loneliness. He knows her world better than she can ever know his. She stands her ground, she'd take him with her, but a gulf remains. He could never have stayed in Scotland; that at least he knows. His brother Duncan is a postman, his sister Maggie a spinster and poor as a mouse. He himself is rich beyond his wildest imaginings. But what good has it done? What safety has it secured, absent a home in which he and his family belongs?

By December the snow reaches halfway up the palisades. At least, he thinks, this arctic blast will keep the miners away. He half pities the fools who leapt upriver with just a shovel and the shirts on their backs. The nimíipuu, of course, know well how to warm themselves. He thinks of his wife, rolled up far away, unreachable. He's extinguishing the torches in the yard, distributing blankets to a group of Okanagans who have taken refuge there, when he feels dark eyes on his, a deep, familiar heat. He takes the young woman to his bed, to warm his emptiness and loss—may all the deities above rest his black soul.

SEASON AFTER SEASON the Union Army battles the Confederates. Elsewhere time ticks on, apparently unrecorded. So much the better, if the US government has forgotten him, up here in his remote corner. With the snowmelt Angus writes to his family. He's reassured that there's no fighting by his children's own sweet letters back. Nature's fury blasted the miners, Christina says: the nimíipuu keep stumbling over their blackened, thawing corpses. The danger seems past and she misses him, they all do; they wish they could soon be home.

If not for their love, he doesn't know how he would have carried on. That winter without them was the darkest he has ever known. And it's his dear bairns, too, who insist that their mother let them come home. How Catherine feels he doesn't know, but the eldest three especially hammered and nagged until a full year later, they return.

The tornado of hugs and kisses subsides, and he turns finally to his wife. Each is broken, he thinks, in a way they were not before. He's gaunter, brown from work in the fields, more silent after all these months alone. Young Marie is long gone, back to her people the Okanagan, but the sight of his wife revives his shame. Catherine is broader, her face more lined, her hair shot through with silver lines. She also seems calmer, even happy to see him. Their children rule the roost now, she says with a rueful smile. She felt like a piece of wood that they dragged like a legion of ants over brae and dale.

"You kept them safe, anyway," he says.

"Like twigs and branches in a dam, we'll withstand." She cocks one eyebrow. "I was for fighting, like my cousin, but the fight didn't come this time."

"It still could."

His wife nods, surveying the screeching children in the yard. "They need us together, too."

"Do you?"

"I never changed my mind. It's you who tried to change me."

"I never wanted to."

"Don't your poets say love is blind?"

He smiles. She's always known more about him than she lets on. For twenty years, now, more. She, too, smiles, briefly, before the smile fades.

"If you choose the north, I can't go with you," she says.

"I know."

They look so deeply in each other's eyes that for the first time he feels he sees inside her mind—sees even the spider-silks that join her to the things she loves. Her family, her village, children, home. And him. He nods. "I pledged a long time ago that I would never force you."

"I remember."

He recalls suddenly what Tolmie said when Angus confessed he wasn't sure that he'd go north. "Good Lord, man. Have you gone entirely Native?" Yes, he thinks—he surely has.

"You've come with me this whole long way—even when you didn't want to." She waits, lips slightly parted. "So now it's only fair. There's nothing for me up there. I've always said it, haven't I? My home is where you are, you and the children." He puts a hand to her shining hair.

Her face is suddenly radiant. She seizes both his hands. "You crazy man. You made my breath stop for a moment."

He laughs and folds her in his arms, rubbing his face to hers. "Perhaps they'll leave us be in our exile, then," he murmurs. They hear the children hoot, but they are not ashamed.

"We've always been exiles." She wraps her shawl around them both. "Both of us longing for the lands of our fathers."

"Then let us be exiles together, for the rest of the trail."

BEFORE THEY KNOW it their eldest are grown. In 1864 John is twenty, Christina eighteen, Duncan sixteen, and so down the line. All in all they haven't been bad years. Animals continue bearing pelts and the Natives continue bearing them to Angus. And life is rich in joy. The riotous lot of their children brings them both such happiness. They're the stuff of stars, proof of life's stubborn continuance. Angus knows Catherine views them this way, the ancestors carrying on in their clean, strong minds and bodies. It does seem the strong survive, as this Mr. Darwin has recently proposed. Offspring are unpredictable, enduring—a source of wonderment, along with the usual frustrations and delights.

Christina has taken to the fur trade like a bird to the air, her elder brother less so.

John's a bit feckless, even his father must admit: so handsome every girl in miles has a cricked neck from craning to look at him, or worse. On brigades to Connah he's been known to ride well ahead. It wouldn't surprise Angus if he's left a bairn here and there. Still it's hard to remain angry with him: his ways are so winning, his zest for life so infectious. He's kind, if not particularly ambitious, and this must count for something. Duncan is more of a mystery, studious and intense; he's equally handsome in a more private way, though from a young age incurably curious.

Truth be told, Christina is her father's favorite, and his constant companion. For the last few years she's delivered the furs to Forts Hope and Langley with him. In her mixture of buckskin and tartan, she's a credit to her mother and father both: pluck and strength and beauty and intelligence, along with nerves of steel. If he's to have a follower in the trade, he guesses, it won't be his sons but his daughter. As time passes, she blossoms and becomes as striking as her mother was. The Royal Engineers used to call her the belle of Colvile, and it's even truer now. He'll have to drive the lads off with a pitchfork, he tells her. "I won't let you go as easy as that, my girl."

"Nor would I leave you, papa," she responds, squeezing his arm. Still, he sees how his own clerks blush and fumble when they're around her. Be kind to them, he thinks—be gentle. They're only star-struck, like us all.

He gets the newspapers from Olympia and Oregon City and twice a year Michel Ogden brings news from the interior. Angus is nearly fifty and slowing, like an old stag whose flesh runs to fat, his mane streaked with gray. The news is usually bad, but even so it's news: he's a man who can't live without the broader view. Ideally, he'll die in the saddle, cresting some range with a panorama spread before him. Richard Grant died this way, bringing home his supplies from the Dalles—just closed his eyes right there on the trail. And then there's the disappearance of Eagle from the Light. Catherine's cousin, it appears, first gave up his chiefdom—and now has vanished as well.

She grips the arms of her chair as her brother-in-law relates what he knows. It wasn't long after she returned to Colvile, he says. Her cousin, in his turn, saw his own lands overrun—but the gold rush on the Salmon River was massive, far bigger than at Oro Fino.

"Ten thousand miners, so I hear." Michel is tired; they can both see it. He, too, is fighting back, protecting their patch in Sin-ye-le-min from the Indian agents and priests. "He tried one last time to rally the chiefs to drive them out, but they were too far outnumbered."

Catherine listens, her face drawn. "So they took Lamotta too."

"Not completely. White Bird is head man now, deep in the canyon. Some say Eagle from the Light is living with the Shoshone, that he's taken a Shoshone wife."

Nor is this the only grievous news. Old Chief Flint Necklace, too, has died. Catherine bites her knuckles. So goes a great chief, Angus thinks. He was probably happy to go, Michel says, given the treachery faced by his people.

"The government forced that treaty down their throats. The 'Thief Treaty' they call it." The Christian half of the tribe sold it all to the Yankees—every place that yielded gold, or that the settlers coveted. The whole Salmon country, the Wallowa; they cut the Nez Perce reservation to a tenth of its size.

"And Clear Creek?" Catherine bends toward him, stricken.

"Still inside. At least for now."

They lie silently that night, each wrapped in dark thoughts. In her distress Catherine has barely spoken. She's lit herbs for her uncle, chanting under her breath. He'll make inquiries, Angus tells her; he'll discover exactly where things stand. She rolls to her side. This is exactly their way, to divide the people, cut them apart. "The cutters," she whispers.

How they slice and slice. Last year Lincoln chopped the Washington Territory in two; now he has sliced off another chunk. Angus lived first in the Oregon Country, then the Washington Territory, then the Idaho Territory. And now his old post is in a place they call Montana Territory—while all this time he has hardly changed his position at all, circling year after year across the same five hundred miles.

CHAPTER 12

HE GIVES A ball every New Year's. A *kay-lee*, he calls it—Scots for a night of dancing and music and tales. Everyone comes for miles around. All their old friends who've retired to fish and farm, slicing through the snowy darkness on their jingling sleighs. When they were first married Catherine joined in these revels. But then it all changed. Her home was thrown open to white men with no knowledge of their world, the world of trappers and traders and fur. Angus welcomed all with open arms, of course. He draws people to him, Native and Baymen and Boston alike. So of course they always came, the surveyors, the soldiers from the new Boston fort, in their shiny uniforms, eyes wide at first, then focused, surveying the girls.

It would be different this year, he said. He gave her that doe-eyed look he sometimes uses. No Americans. No British, for that matter. Like old times. He lifted her hand to his lips and kissed it. *Auld lang syne*. He taught her those words, years ago. The children will so love to see you there; there'll be boat songs and dances on swords. She laughed then. "I know. I've been married to you for quite some while."

So here she sits in a full skirt of navy taffeta, a shawl with roses, her yellow feathers in her hair, in a row of chairs pushed back to make the most of the large storeroom. Earlier she stood with him at the gate under gently falling flakes and greeted them all: Lapierres and Boisverts and Finlays and Irvines with their extensive families, all those Ignaces and Marys and Jeromes baptized by Father Joset. He, too, has returned; he wouldn't miss this evening for the world, the priest says, ice forming at the tip of his long nose. Of course Angus slips away, the better to make his entrance, pipes blaring and kilt swinging, notes drilling through their heads. She's not the only one to cover her ears, even after all this time. It strikes her how fitting his instrument is. The very opposite of modest:

bagpipes command; they draw attention to themselves. Like Angus. How he loves to lead a parade, whether human or a horse brigade. He's handsome and clever and still slightly vain; he likes the brightest light trained on himself.

Before long the fiddles are struck and dancers are shedding their vests and shawls. The music gets into her toes and she jiggles them softly, so as not to wake the bundle in her lap. Archie is eighteen months old, her solace after losing Alexander. How deeply he sleeps. John is juggling knives by the hearth, his face flushed and laughing, playing court to an eager band of children and girls. Other young men pose casually, one foot against the wall, as if they do not care, though they envy the way he attracts every eye. Like his grandfather Baptiste; like his own father—her eldest is a showman too.

And then she sees Christina standing, extending her hand for a dance. Oh, she is beautiful, her daughter: she captures the light. She has high cheeks and full lips and that arresting expression in the eyes she shares with Duncan, as if she were permanently surprised—or just uncommonly alert. All evening Catherine has watched how the men approach her: the old voyageurs who've known her all her life, bending and smiling, their wives smoothing her long shining hair, and then the younger men, Angus's head clerk especially, James—who does not seem to take his eyes off Christina the whole night long. From time to time as her mother watches, sipping her hot drink, she sees too how Christina's eyes seek his out. And a feeling comes over her of great sadness, inexplicable until she sees how beautiful her girl is and how she's moving away from her toward that other place. As Catherine herself once had—to marry a white trader as her own mother required. And where has that left them now?

The room is hot, stoked with grog and fire and wild notes leaping, all the bodies flushed and whirling. Christina dances on the arm of James Mackenzie and Catherine takes inventory of her brood. It's approaching the hour now, and none will go to bed until it strikes and Angus leads them in the old mournful tune. The little girls dance together, and the younger boys pretend to whip their legs out in the Highland Fling, arms bobbing up and down. Only Duncan sits with her, shy with people as he's always been. Together they watch their family and she's comforted by their density, their presence all around her. They're like thigh-high grasses softly lapping at her, the boulder in the center, frozen like a figure from the legends. Then Angus is before her, all pink-cheeked and smiling, tugging at her and nodding, and Archie is shuffled into Duncan's arms and she's on her feet, tugged into the hot mass, spinning and dipping with this crazy soyapo as they still can do, rekindling their old abandon.

⌁

IT'S JUST A nick, a nothing, they think at the time. She isn't even aware of it until John comes over to sit down, his finger wrapped in a cloth. Duncan saw it, though: the way his brother's attention faltered for an instant, and instead of grasping the hasp he caught the blade. The two of them go out to the yard to dunk it in the snow and stop the bleeding. The next day it's swollen and oozing. Angus pronounces it diseased and jokes he'll have to cut it off. They do not worry unduly; they've seen worse. Until the next day when the hand goes numb and Catherine sees red streaks up the arm like the scratches of a cat and she's afraid then, for the very first time. Angus sends to the Bostons for a medic but there's none around. He curses himself, as he's done before, not to have one at the post. At least before they had Father Ravalli, trained in medicine— not so Father Joset. All he can do is pray. The old Catholic fool is entirely useless.

John lies very pale on a pallet in the front room, as if his fire has drained away. They don't understand. It was just the smallest cut. She makes a poultice of yarrow to draw the evil out, but this doesn't help. His skin is cold to the touch, yet he complains that he's burning. "You're not to take it!" he shouts when his sister or brother come near, then his body will writhe and his face contort as he gasps, "Father, father!"

They must plunge him in cold water. Now. She looks wildly at her husband, but he's shaking his head, No.

"Roll him in the snow then!" He bars her with an arm. She weeps and calls to her mother in her mind. She was there when John was born, but now Margaret can't hear. There are too many people between them now, too much disturbance.

Angus holds their boy by the shoulders as he thrashes, sponging his

204

forehead; Catherine spoons bitter tea down his throat, which he spits up. There's no night or day, only the endlessly burning candle and the sweat-soaked youth alternately jerking in pain and slipping into some more distant place where they can't follow.

His heart beats like a hummingbird's inside his laboring chest and they can do nothing. Each breath he rasps feels ripped from her own lips. He doesn't speak any longer—hasn't spoken for many hours. Joset hovers and Angus bats him away.

"You won't deny him last rites," the priest says finally, desperate and sorry. Angus looks at Catherine. She's sunk somewhere inside herself, arms wrapped around her elbows, rocking slightly. From time to time she places her cheek on John's own. Though she feels her husband's regard, she does not look back. They've banished the children but whenever the door opens, he sees their frightened faces, their enormous eyes. He nods.

"Very well. Do it quickly."

When the mumbling is done, he stands heavily and goes to the door. "Come and kiss your brother," he says, with a crack in his heart. "We shall not see him again, I fear."

Only when the last rattle leaves his chest and he breathes no more does his face return to its own sweetness, its peace—once again the laughing, loving boy they both adore. Before anything Catherine sings him back to the time before creation. She sings him to the sky world. The notes catch like knots on a rope she pulls out of her throat.

They're weeping, the rest of her children, her husband; Angus buries his head in his hands and howls. Duncan stands, his face ashen. He goes out to strike the frozen earth and dig his brother's grave. Yet there is more that must be done. Catherine rises and goes to the winter room she shares with the father of her son. She pulls out her own knife and begins to cut. The hair falls like cornsilk, with a swish, to the floor, until her face is the center of a dark, jagged ruff, as spiky and demented as her heart. Only then is he gone, and a part of her with him, and she can begin to mourn.

It's not only her firstborn she mourns. Her heart too, cut out of her chest and dumped here on this iron earth that is not hers. All these years every cut in the trees and the soil was a cut in her own body, and the bodies of those she bore. All are butchered now, cut from their mother, their source. Her son is dead and there is no clan, no tribe but she to sing him home. Her soul rises up and races to the river where her mother formed it from the soil, but they're all gone, too. The enemy will wipe them from the land as if they never were.

SOMEHOW SPRING ARRIVES or so it must be, for a horse can get through with a summons. Angus is required in Victoria to testify for the commission winding up the Company's affairs. The world is so painful and cunning he almost laughs. He rips the paper up. They ought to have bordered the damn thing in black.

Christina finds the pieces and presses them back together. "Goose," she says. British and American Joint Commission, Relative to Claims Arising from the Oregon Treaty of 1846, it says.

"My whole career here was apparently illegal." He sneers bitterly.

"Now, Papa." She tries to smile. Such a comfort she is, and brave. For she too is lost, like them all.

Grief is a cave with space for only one. Each sorrowing creature must dig its own hole. For his part, he's not ready to leave the den that holds him in its grip.

"Write that I'm unwell."

"I will not." She tilts her head at him. "I'll go with you. That'll do it. We'll make our own little brigade."

As if by magic, she eases his heart. It's true, he should escape this place. Catherine's preparing her trip to the plains. His eldest daughter is right: movement and air are the best of medicines.

They set out in the hack with his snappiest driving team. Christina dresses in plaid skirts, a jaunty feathered hat; she carries a small grip filled with gold powder. Travel requires more forms of transport now. They leave the gig at the Snake and take a steamer, switch to another ship at Celilo Falls, then to a portage road and another pair of steamers to Portland and then Astoria. Each time his daughter opens her satchel and plucks a handful out, the distrustful captains jump right to. The graying fellow in buckskins is suddenly known. Ah yes, Mister McDonald. Indeed, Mister McDonald. His daughter is tender to him, yet firm—better by far than either parent. All children are, he supposes, this miraculous blending of two essences. Every thought leads him back to John.

Christina sees how her parents drift. Neither father nor mother will ever be the same. Nor she, nor Duncan—but here she is, steering him down gangplanks and into hotels. Here she is, holding him up as best she can. In the hotel at Astoria, they meet the tall attorney for the United States, a Mr. Johnson. When her father sees black crepe in a band on his hat he's momentarily confused.

"It's for President Lincoln, papa," she whispers.

On the bluff above the Pacific all that's left of Fort George are two stumps of chimney and indistinct bumps beneath the sand. Angus squeezes her hand. "My name is Ozymandias, king of kings," he says beneath his breath.

They return to Oregon City where they make lists of the buildings and acreage and fittings of the many forts Angus has personally managed. He stands, his hands at his back, staring out the window, spitting out the figures while Christina writes them down. The city is unrecognizable to him: the activity below leaves him dazed. He thinks he catches a glimpse of Joe Meek from his window, that squat bullet of a man, but it's just a figment in his brain. He sees John everywhere, too, in a certain cock of the head, a leaping stride. How tragic, he thinks, that the tall president had ended that civil war and not even had a week to relish it before some madman put a bullet in his head. He catches a glimpse of himself, gaunt and tall in the wavy glass and sees the resemblance. He, Lincoln, John— they're all ghosts now.

He leaves Christina with Dr. McLoughlin's widow, Marguerite, and sets sail with Tolmie and a handful of men from what was once the Columbia District. Of the proceedings in Victoria there is little to say. He finds the dark fir forests of the island oppressive, the officiousness of all these lawyers absurd. He no longer fits among civilized folk—if he ever fit at all. The whole notion of civilization makes him sick. But when he returns to collect Christina, he finds her transformed. How she loves the dances and the cunning restaurant rooms with their running water and pomades. "Let me show you, Father—I've met the most interesting folk!" she exclaims. Her dark beauty marks her out in these parlors and pews, on the sidewalks where every head turns. She's in her element, he sees, as at ease with this bustling new world as a fish in a stream. While he cannot wait to return to his den, his river, his mountains. To his own little mixed-up clan, peculiar and out of step as they've become.

THAT FALL HE decides to go to Fort Connah himself to collect the furs. Catherine and the children are there; besides, it may be the last time. Christina laughs and says he always told them to keep their eyes on the trail ahead, not behind.

Only now he knows he lied. An ambush can blindside you from any direction: front or back, left or right.

Sin-ye-le-min is stunning in October, tamarack like flaming yellow torches on the hillsides, scarlet splashes of maple marching toward the bright white glaciers. He salutes the notched crown of Couhlicat, the bright line of the Shining Mountains. People at the post look up as he and Christina climb the slight rise. Then there are figures running toward them, and Catherine is standing, one arm raised, beside her lodge.

"You didn't stay in the north," she says with a little curve to her smile.

"I couldn't breathe in that place."

"So then—"

"Bide a while." He opens his arms to her. "The game isn't over yet, my darling."

The authorities will dither a while yet, he's sure. All he knows for certain is that for some unknown reason they've forgotten all about Fort Connah.

Together they all sit at the close of day surveying the sweep of the valley, painted now dark green and gold and rust. There's a continuous rush of geese swooping south, the chitter of smaller creatures in the brush. Now and then they hear the bells of the church Chief Alexander allowed the Jesuits to build.

"There wasn't a word, not a mention in all that testimony," Angus says. "Just a note that Flathead House was closed—as if this post never even existed."

"Fitting," says Michel Ogden with a crooked smile. Angus figures nobody noted the new name and location back in 1847. The Oregon treaty was already signed, after all.

"So the post remains—at least for the time being."

Michel takes this moment to say that he's been thinking. It's a good time to set up in ranching, before the Bostons grab all the good land. There's a piece he's been looking at up near the lake. Angelique holds his hand; both look nervous and determined. Angus lights his pipe, an ordinary one, not ceremonial in any way. Still he hands it to his brother-in-law, with a gesture to puff and pass it on. They can council in this way, his little clan.

He doesn't mind, he says. So long as Michel finds a good man to take his place. The shadow swoops across them then, as he imagines it always will. For some time now he and Catherine had been talking about sending John.

Later when they lie together, he tells Catherine all that fills his mind. That Christina will marry soon, if he has eyes, to his clerk James Mackenzie. That the two of them could easily run this post. Except.

"He won't want to come here."

He nods. "He'll want to make his way in the firm."

Catherine rolls onto her back. Their daughter will leave them, go north, melt into that great arctic whiteness. She's long known it in her heart. Their girls are clever, beautiful, born and bred to the rigors of the wild. Men will seek after them, soyapo men—of this she has no doubt. "Then you must send Duncan."

"He's too young."

She laughs. Among the nimíipuu, a boy his age is full-grown. As suddenly she sobers. "He's my son. The best we have." She doesn't say more, but knows he understands. If all that's left to them are their children, then that has been her destiny: to give back to the people, to carry them on.

She turns to face him. "You've done what you could. I know it." She holds his face in her hands. "It's their turn now."

Each child is a twig in the dam she builds. She thinks he grasps this now. Each one a member, a warrior to swell the band. Some will be lost, but more will survive.

Angus thinks how strange it is that life goes on. For months he's tried to keep John's image in his mind, and yet already it is slipping. Life perseveres, no matter what; the strong prevail; the generations succeed themselves. They hand the torch, and it goes on.

BOOK 3

THE SHINING MOUNTAINS

Montana Territory, 1867–1878

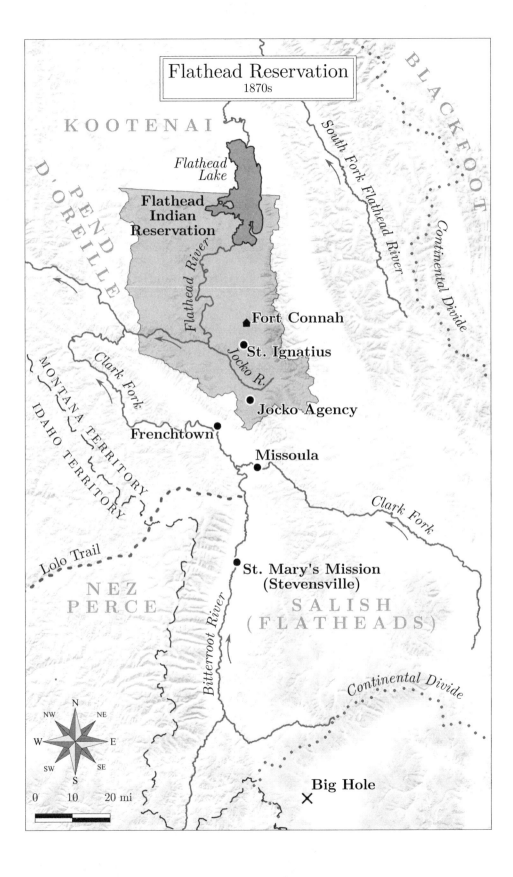

Flathead Reservation
1870s

KOOTENAI

BLACKFOOT

PEND D'OREILLE

Flathead Lake

Flathead Indian Reservation

South Fork Flathead River

Continental Divide

Flathead River

▲ **Fort Connah**

● **St. Ignatius**

Jocko R.

Clark Fork

MONTANA TERRITORY

IDAHO TERRITORY

● **Jocko Agency**

● **Frenchtown**

● **Missoula**

Clark Fork

Lolo Trail

NEZ PERCE

Bitterroot River

● **St. Mary's Mission (Stevensville)**

SALISH (FLATHEADS)

Continental Divide

N
NW NE
W E
SW SE
S

0   10   20 mi

✕ **Big Hole**

"I warn the whites not to kill any more of my Indians. I would not mind if you were killing Indians who are trying to do something wrong, but it seems you want to kill my best men, and for this cause I will not stand any more murder. I did not ask you to come and settle in my country. If you do not like us, keep away."

—THUNDER TRAVELING OVER THE MOUNTAINS,
CHIEF OF THE WALLOWA BAND OF NEZ PERCE,
KNOWN TO AMERICANS AS CHIEF JOSEPH, 1876

CHAPTER 1

FORT CONNAH, MONTANA TERRITORY

December 1867

IT SHOULD HAVE been John in this saddle, coming into this valley, taking charge of this post. But John is gone, undone by his own tomfoolery—as perhaps he always would have been, one way or another. And though Duncan loved his brother with an intensity not far off idolatry and misses him like a limb torn from his own body, he can't help feeling fate intended this. Christina is happy married to her clerk, so it falls to him to take their father's mantle. Truth be told, he's more suited to the job than his brother ever was. But the thought is disloyal, and it shames him.

He relieves a man called Edmunds who's going north across the line where a British subject isn't loathed. He pats Duncan on the shoulder as he hands him the key to Fort Connah. "Luck, boy," he says. "Better you than me." And off he goes. Duncan is eighteen years old.

The line is imaginary yet entirely physical. They watched the Royal Engineers hack it out from west to east. Their father sang and raised his cup to old Britannia; their mother kept her distance. The earth is a gift from the Creator and cannot be sold, much less divided. Even so, she acknowledges that the border has power. To the people of the plains— the Blackfeet, Sioux, and Crow—it's the "medicine line," the most bizarre and magical of the white man's inventions. An invisible barrier between the country of the Bostons and the country of the Queen, where Yankee soldiers may not chase them. Nearly all the Baymen have slipped north across it now, except a handful on the coast—and the McDonalds.

Duncan puts the key in his pocket and turns to the south. This valley is his immediate concern—his own glorious domain, protected by the Shining Mountains. Sin-ye-le-min, the Surrounded. It's a foot deep in white powder glazed to a crust this day before Christmas. He's too excited to care about a celebration his parents never had much time for. The New Year's *cèilidh* was the thing—though this is now irrevocably tarnished. He hears the bells from the new mission, as though the belfry of St Ignatius were beside him and not six miles to the south. It's well below freezing and utterly still and he hoots back in answer, picturing the sound that travels from his lips as crystals sliding on the pure clear air.

He and the post assistant and two servants unload the winter trade goods and see to the mules and horses. He takes inventory of his little fiefdom, then sleeps rolled up in his blankets, his rifle beside him. Angus likes to tell how the Blackfeet tried to ambush them one time. But Duncan has no fear: he's bred and born of this place. He can hear a hare in the fields at thirty yards, the wind sawing at the feathers of the eagle far above. He was the first to come into this world on this very spot, on a day in late winter. No one knows exactly when: his father was away and his mother didn't know the day. But he likes to tease her whenever they are here together. He'll take her arm, pointing to the green-gray mud along the creek. "Was it here, Ma?" The willows up the bank, branches bent like crooked arms. "Or here?" She'll laugh and he will too. It doesn't really matter. He's made of it all—the earth and plants and air.

In the morning the sun makes an appearance so dazzling he understands why the Greeks called it a blazing chariot. The peaks flash salmon, purple, pink. The valley shines and he knows he'll need to ride down to the mission and the settlements below, where white men have set up towns along the path to buffalo. But first he feels a need to reintroduce himself to this place. He dresses in woolen trousers and a clean white shirt, his Company greatcoat. He'll make a practice of the white shirt, he decides, to mark himself as the new trader. Angus wears a tam o'shanter or Glengarry cap, but Duncan is American by birth. He wears a black felt hat with a wide brim to shade his eyes and sets out up the creek, his mare picking her way around the stands of alder. He sees the bare-branched dogwood, red limbs flung up like flames. He hears a twit-twit and spots a pair of finches with red splashes on their cheeks and breasts. Everywhere he sees flashes of red—russet, cinnamon—against the white.

Rising into the canyon he spots a gray bush on the cliff and recalls how they'd been warned by Father not to touch that leaf, or one that looked much like it. And how even when Angus left to see the mines, and his brother again told him not to, his young self took that leaf and rubbed it on his face, just to prove he could—to set himself apart, perhaps, from John, the one who never seemed to put a foot wrong. And Duncan's whole head swelled up like a melon, eyes and mouth so fat he couldn't see or eat and that was all he saw for that whole trip to the famous Pend d'Oreille mines.

He'll keep his eyes peeled and wits about him this time. He turns to look back on the valley. Wisps of smoke rise from clusters of Native lodges and a few scattered cabins. It's a different place, no longer the wild paradise of his childhood. Now it's the "Flathead Indian Reservation" with lines around it and new people coming in. He might be the only one who gets the joke: there are Kootenai here and Ql'ispé, who the whites call Pend d'Oreille, along with the Salish and Nez Perce passing through—but not a single so-called Flathead. The actual homeland of the Salish is the Bitterroot, three valleys to the south. They no more have flat heads than the Nez Perce pierce their noses.

He arrives at the lake set in a saddle of the foothills, ringed by moraine and granite. The people have stories of this place; there's a trail that leads to the summit of Coul-hi-cat, to the sacred place they go to get their power. Duncan hasn't done it. He might have, had he been among his mother's people when he came of age, but the chance did not arise. Their rhythms were disturbed by the encroachments of the miners, and then John died. Even so, he's never really felt the need. He's a McDonald, tall and brown-haired like his father, though with his mother's deep, dark eyes.

In the blue cold of a winter's morning he's the only human for miles. He sees a place more worn, a gap that clearly whispers *Here. The path is here*. The land does speak; it also listens. That's all he's ever needed for religion. Not medicine power, nor Christian creed—just a sense of life's great mystery and preciousness. He didn't know how precious it was before. Again and again he thinks of John. It feels so strange to be alone. He's spent his whole life surrounded by others, always following, as water fills a footstep, his older brother John.

He doesn't notice he's stopped while all this courses through his mind. A movement catches his eye then from across the water: a family of whitetails, mincing their slender fetlocks through the snow. The stag stands guard while the doe and fawns drink, and he thinks of Angus. Duncan won't take these creatures out of life. He'll leave them wild, in tribute to their spirit. He'll take it as a sign instead, he tells himself, of the abundance of these climes, his own success in this new life.

IT ONLY TAKES four days for the authorities to come sniffing around. A man named McCormick presents himself at the trading post as the US government agent in charge of this reservation.

"I thought Edmunds was to close it down," he says when Duncan introduces himself.

"Apparently not." Duncan had the presence of mind to put on a tie when he saw the rider kicking up the snow.

This Indian Agent is a lanky fellow with roving eyes. Duncan offers him coffee, which he accepts, all the while peering at his bales and bundles. Lucky he hasn't unpacked them yet.

"Well, then." McCormick puts down his cup. "That puts us in a pickle."

"How so?"

"This reservation is on US territory. That means I regulate the trade, and only licensed traders are allowed. The Baymen had their day, but we're all Americans here now."

"Then there's no problem." Duncan fakes a broad smile. "I'm as American as can be. Born right here in this valley."

"It's the Company you work for I can't allow."

Thankfully, he's been well tutored. "Here's the thing." He pours on the friendliness. "This goes higher than you or me. My instructions come from London. Under the treaty, we can continue operations until our governments settle."

"That's not how the Governor sees it."

"It's over our heads, so I'm told." They haven't heard the settlement is done, then. According to Angus, the cash has already changed hands. Their ignorance might last a season or two—in which time Duncan can still take some profits.

"In the meantime, I might be of some use." Duncan rises and peels back the wrapper on a bale of flour. "I hear you didn't get the rations you were due."

McCormick's laugh is short and mirthless. "You've done your homework."

"Let's just say we're good friends with the tribes."

Angus's old friend, Chief Alexander No Horses, is dead. The new chief of the Pend d'Oreille is Plenty Grizzly Bear, known to white folk as Michelle. Duncan went to see him first thing, near the mission where the bulk of his people are camped. Things are bad, Michelle told him: they're down to a hundred lodges and food is scarce. For the Kootenai by the lake, half their number, the situation is even worse.

"The Indians in your charge are hungry, I hear." Duncan speaks softly. "If you can't provide food or ammo, maybe I can."

"So I see," the agent says sourly.

He wouldn't like to be in the fellow's shoes. From what Duncan hears, he has neither goods nor cash to give the tribes. Hardly any of the treaty pledges have been kept since the government installed its first agent ten years before. There's no school, no doctor, no houses—not a tenth of the cash and tools for farming the chiefs were promised in exchange for their land. According to Michelle, nearly all the agents have been incompetent or crooks. Most lined their pockets from the meager sums, the shoddy, insufficient goods that were sent; this fellow is the eighth to cycle through.

"Thing is," McCormick is saying, "I already have a fellow wants to open a shop by the mission."

"The more the merrier," Duncan lies in answer.

"I'll have to report you to Washington, anyhow." The agent pulls on his coat and steps outside. He's tugging on a muskrat cap when he spies the pelts—of fisher, fox, lynx, deer—hung out to dry. He turns to Duncan, scanning him a bit too long.

"You Native, too?" he asks.

"Part."

"What part?"

It's a strange question, one he's not been asked before. "A quarter or so, I guess." He shrugs, to show it makes no difference.

"On your mother's side, then." The fellow is getting on his nerves.

"Yes."

"What tribe?"

"Nez Perce." He could insist he's more white than red, more French and Scots. But something in the ugly separating of the parts disgusts him.

"Not Kootenai or Pend d'Oreille?"

"What are you driving at, if I might ask?"

"Just verifying, so I know where we stand."

"Verify all you like." There's a trace of sneer on the fellow's face that gets his blood up. "When you're done, let me know."

He pauses so the agent has to look back. "I have goods to sell. And as far as I can see, you've got people you're supposed to feed."

NOT A WEEK in, and he's made his first enemy. Well played, he tells himself. Still, he won't be condescended to. Walk like you own the place, his father always says. Which the Baymen did for quite a while. Just how little they do now is hammered home when Duncan starts to make his rounds.

His first stop is Frenchtown, a hamlet two valleys south, outside the reservation and west of the new town of Missoula. The settlers are starting to fill up this plain where he used to run races with the Salish and Nez Perce before their summer hunts. He skips over the lovely valley in between, called Jocko for Jacques Finlay, a fur trader so ancient even Angus never knew him. The Jocko is where the government's Indian agent sits in his lonely compound, waiting for the government annuities to arrive—or not. Why they located it here, and not among the actual Indians, is a mystery only the stupidity of Yankees can explain. Duncan rides past so early that not even a dog lifts a questioning ear.

He intends to meet the Frenchman who runs the mercantile, one Jack DeMers. According to Michelle, Telesphore Jacques "Jack" DeMers runs what amounts to his own private state; half the whites, and most of the Indians too, are in hock to him. Duncan's looking for a short fellow with a big red beard but inside the store there's only a dark-haired chap who smiles when he asks for the man in charge.

"That would be me, for the present." He stands and puts out his hand. "Robert Baird." He's not much older than Duncan, good-looking in braces and necktie but no apron. "Jack's out . . . prospecting, you might say."

"Duncan McDonald, from Fort Connah."

"Edmunds's replacement?"

"That would be me, for the present," Duncan parrots back and they both grin.

Baird is Jack's clerk, which means he runs the store. DeMers, he says, is rarely there. Too busy building up his empire. More than this Baird's too loyal to say. It takes Duncan some weeks to learn that Jack's got stakes in some mines, a share in the stables in Missoula, and five or six teams he runs up and down the territory, as well as the Frenchtown mercantile. He's Duncan's competition, in other words.

"Care for coffee, or something stronger?" Baird sits back down, gesturing at a stool by the counter.

"Drink doesn't agree with me."

"Doesn't agree with most people, but that doesn't stop them."

"True enough."

Duncan's eyes flick over the bolts of fabric, the hanging hams, the upright open sacks of flour and coffee and rice, each with its own pewter scoop. There's a side room filled with tack and feed, and out back, something that smells suspiciously like a still.

"I'm of Scots blood too," Baird says. "Where's home, then, to you?" Duncan judges him not much older than himself. The man has a friendly face, black hair, and dark blue eyes. "Seems like everybody wants to know." He grimaces a bit. "I was born at the fort."

"How about that." Baird pours them both a coffee. "Only arrived last year myself."

So many new men blowing in, Duncan thinks: hungry to make it, stake a place out, strike it rich. Hungry and eager—like him.

"Still, I bet you know the lay of things. Who the big men are, who to watch out for."

Baird gives him a long, unnerving look. "I work for Jack."

"You don't strike me as a grocer," Duncan replies, and Baird laughs.

"Nor do you, for that matter."

They smile at one another. A trader is more than a grocer, Duncan thinks: he's a reader of men, a stalker of game, a diplomat—a fellow you could use at your side in the long, bitter northwest winter. "Anyhow I imagine there's enough for all," he responds, feeling the power of the Company, the unlimited resources behind him. He can afford to be magnanimous. Baird nods and tells him there's a good deal of business being done at Hell Gate, where a fellow named Woody has a store, another called Bonner & Eddy a few miles west near the mill at Missoula. Plus two saloons and a blacksmith, a hotel, a little school.

"Enough for a poker game, anyhow." Baird smiles.

"And the agent," Duncan says, "this Indian agent. McCormick."

"What about him?"

"He claims he's in charge of the trade. At least on the reservation." Duncan pushes back his hat. "He wasn't very friendly when I met him the other day."

"I wouldn't worry." Baird's tone is amused. "He'll be gone before long."

"You don't say."

"Jack will take bets on it."

The merchants of Frenchtown and Missoula have seen these agents come and go, Baird tells him. They rack up credit and disappear as soon as a sweeter government job comes along. Or else they're relieved for dereliction of duty. And indeed only two months after this, McCormick too is gone, accused of siphoning off the Indians' funds to build a new house for himself in Missoula. By which time Duncan has dug himself into their little society. As winter turns to spring, he plays poker with his fellow traders at the fort or down in town: Jack DeMers and Baird and a fellow named Andy Hammond, who clerks for Bonner; the sheriff, Mose Drouillard, who knew his father way back when; and when he's not skint, Duncan's own clerk Dupree.

When they finally meet, Jack makes clear that Duncan in his little fort is hardly competition. He's barrel chested and pugnacious, married to a Pend d'Oreille woman. "I don't mind if you mop up," he ribs him right away. "Someone's got to clean up after." He grins. He means to win the big game, corner the trade to the Fraser River mines, Baird tells Duncan on the sly. Jack reminds Duncan of the old-time French-born trappers who filled his father's halls. But those men were modest, loners for the most part. DeMers is a man with ambition as grandiose as himself, with his matching team of bays, his wad of Yankee bills, the red-and-gold lettering on his dozen gigs and wagons.

M

IN EARLY MARCH Chief Michelle sends a young hunter to Fort Connah under the cover of a starless night. The people starve; they need ammunition, he signs with his hands. Duncan astonishes him by replying in his own tongue.

"Tell the chief I'm glad to, but doesn't the agent provide?"

Immediately his visitor's face turns spiteful. "He's afraid," he hisses. "He ties us with iron and asks for more guns for himself."

"But he won't give you ball or shot?"

"The chief sends me to get it from you."

Duncan doesn't need to reflect. These past few months he's seen why Jack couldn't care less about the reservation trade. There's hardly any. The people hunt but still go hungry; they bring only a handful of skins to exchange. The game is dwindling, or warier perhaps. He hadn't realized they hunted mainly with bows. Of course, he tells the young man, who's called Red Horn. Without their hunt they have no food and he has no pelts to take to Colvile. Better yet, I'll come shooting with you.

They pack two dozen Sharps rifles and two fiftyweights of ball and powder and ride that very night to the chief's lodge a half-mile from the mission. After a brief discussion he understands that they're of one mind. McCormick and the agent before him strongly opposed their summer and winter hunts to buffalo. "Their" Indians should stay and farm on their reservations, the agents maintained; the settlers are unnerved by their wild parades. This winter, as a consequence, they did not go—and as you see, the chief says, we are starved.

Duncan himself has seen and shot pronghorn sheep and deer and elk on the peaks, more than enough to feed them. If the Shining Mountains are not theirs, he doesn't know what is, he tells Michelle. So he goes with them up to Coul-hi-cat, his hat pulled low. They fan out and he and Red Horn hunt alone. The first crack of the rifle brings an exultant whoop to the young hunter's lips. A cat falls, maybe, or a fox; both coats look red against the snow. When Duncan takes an elk doe at two hundred yards, Red Horn raises his fist.

They shout across the distance, sound refracting like the light. He hasn't felt such warmth since he hunted with John. When they return with meat for the tribe and a promise of fine dressed pelts for him, Duncan builds a fire and dries his clothes and considers how a man survives—not in the wilderness, but in the world of men. How to decide who he can trust? Discern who tells the truth, who lies? Jack and Hammond are both men on the make; they wouldn't hesitate to step on him to get ahead. Same with the agent, who clearly has orders to block the Hudson's Bay. Only Baird and Red Horn seem to him men of their word: Baird is more educated, Red Horn more exuberant, but both are men you can rely on. He laughs a little as it strikes him. Of course, the ones he most trusts are the Scotsman and the Native. The two halves of himself—the very halves which the Americans, he'll learn soon enough, will do their best to tear apart.

CHAPTER 2

The Fight on the Marias
A Blow for Peace

The northeast frontier of settled Montana is the worst exposed of all to Indian depredations. . . . The Blackfeet, Bloods, Piegans, and all manner of savages and half-breed mongrels have their haunts close up to the settlements, familiar with every trail leading into and through them. . . . Scarce a month passes without predatory excursions, resulting in the capture of stock, and, as in the recent instances of Malcolm Clark and Tingley, massacre and torch. . . . Since last spring Gen. de Trobriand has been in command of the district. He has talked practical sense about Indian management. The cavalry force of Montana was augmented by troops from the East and . . . a winter expedition determined upon. It was detained by severe cold weather until the 19th of January, when it, according to Helena papers, surprised Bear Chief's Piegan camp on the Marias, and killed men, women, and children, giving no quarter. . . . The net result was: one hundred and seventy-three Piegans killed; three hundred horses and forty-four lodges, with all winter supplies captured, and the Blackfeet, with the refugee Piegans, driven in panic into the British Possessions. . . . Considered in a military view the expedition was a complete and brilliant success.

February 25, 1870
THE NEW NORTH-WEST, Deer Lodge, M.T.

A Washington dispatch of the 22nd [Feb] says:

The Indian Commission announce that they have the sickening details of Col. Baker's attack on the Piegans in Montana.

Out of one hundred and seventy-three Indians killed, there being only fifteen fighting men; ninety were women; over half were more than forty years of age, and there were fifty children under twelve, many of whom were killed in their parents' arms. The whole village has been suffering for two months with the smallpox—half a dozen dying daily.

—*THE NEW NORTH-WEST, Deer Lodge, M.T.*

February 4, 1870

AS A RULE Duncan avoids the territorial newspapers. He only sees them tacked on a board at the courthouse when he rides into town. This winter afternoon there's a cluster of bodies craning there. He reads over their shoulders, conscious of the way they sidle and shrink away. From the start he's been repelled by the venom and lies he encounters in these lines—from Helena, Fort Benton, Deer Lodge. But this is the worst he's seen so far.

The deaths of two white men are a "massacre," the revenge murder of one hundred seventy-three Blackfeet an "attack." Beneath his buffalo coat sweat cascades down his back. He turns and retrieves his reins. They'd call him a half-breed mongrel, too, if they dared to brave his knuckles—which most don't. In three years he's managed to piss a line around himself to protect his patch. But even the ferocious, battle-hardened Blackfeet couldn't draw a line around themselves.

Blood is shockingly raw against white snow—in Montana or Glencoe. As a boy he shrank when his father told the tale. Duncan couldn't stop his own imagination: how easily he pictured the children screaming, the flames from the soldiers' muzzles, the bleeding, fleeing bodies hanging from the doors and windows. But there are no windows in a Piegan lodge. He worries at this detail, as if it matters somehow. Did they shoot right through the hide or did the people stumble out before they mowed them down? And when he has ridden back in the direction from which he came, his errand entirely forgotten, he retches at the side of the trail. Bile fills his mouth, like the poison that starts as words and ends in murder.

He remembers vividly his shock at the destruction of Chief Kamiakin. A boy's first taste of cruelty—evil, even—never really leaves him. That mighty frame had seemed so crumpled. How his father raged that winter on the plain. Even the founding document of their United States, he cried, is steeped in hate. "It's in their bloody goddamned charter! In writing they accuse King George of 'bringing onto the inhabitants of our frontiers the *merciless Indian savages*'—as he described them, yes, he wrote this, their great Jefferson—'whose rule of warfare is destruction.'"

Well, look who's destroyed now.

Duncan will have to bear this terrible news to the chiefs at the mission. And, he thinks heavily, he'll have to start reading these scurrilous sheets himself. He's their trader—now it's his job to interpret the world outside as well, it seems. It's not a role he relishes. The fact was hammered home to him none too pleasantly when he unexpectedly ran into Eagle from the Light last fall.

He was startled, of course, to see him—few had seen him for some years—but even more startled at the venom his kinsman spewed. Duncan was provisioning the autumn hunt at the place they call *In-may-soo-let-tqui*, the place of ambush, where the river bends around a cliff and Blackfeet once attacked from overhead. Hell Gate, the Yankees call it. Chief Victor of the Salish and some Pend d'Oreille and Palouse were there, when to his astonishment his mother's cousin appeared. Once a chief, always a chief, Duncan told himself, recognizing that haughty bearing. He tried to memorize the sunken cheeks, loose hair, the thin gray eyes, so he could tell his mother.

"You come to sell?" The man he once called uncle held no love for him in his cold eyes. "See the trader," he said mockingly. "Kitalah's son who wears soyapo clothes."

Duncan was too stunned to answer. Victor was old but still in charge. "We welcome young McDonald," he said reprovingly. "No one forces you to trade."

"Uncle." Duncan answered in Nez Perce. "I haven't seen you for a long time."

"By choice. I have nothing to say to men who let the Bostons take our country."

Duncan stood rooted, silent. But this only enraged his mother's cousin more.

"Speak for yourself!" His mouth was twisted. "Do you defend your father? Do you defend your precious Company? They, too, did nothing. No white man can be trusted—not the Bostons, not the British, not soldiers or farmers—or traders."

Duncan glanced at Victor, his son Charlo, a dozen others, and saw agreement on some faces. It was a point of immense pride with Victor that he managed to keep peace with the whites. But what had it brought them? The buffalo were vanishingly rare, the promised seeds and tools never arrived. His people were haggard and harried, while the settlers in the Bitterroot agitated to have them removed by force.

"We should have killed them when we had a chance," Eagle from the Light hissed, "but we were women, like the whites who claimed to be our friends." He threw a hand out in dismissal, looking Duncan contemptuously up and down. His final words were what stung the most: "If you were my son, you wouldn't dress like the enemy," he said. "You'd choose the path of honor and not lose yourself along some middle way. In war there is no middle way."

Duncan had been shaken, then furious. Yet increasingly he grasps his kinsman's meaning. The whites have picked at him from the moment he arrived. Jack's brother Alec now sells up at the mission; each new agent scans Duncan's skin and asks what quantum he might be. Yet neither is he a full blood Native. He brings the terrible news of the massacre on the Marias to the Pend d'Oreille, thinking of the myths Angus read to them when they were young. The messenger is Hermes, he thinks, neither man nor god—trickster and patron of merchants and trade, forever flitting between two worlds.

FOR AS LONG as the elders can remember, wild horses have been on the island in Broad Water—black and bay beauties the Salish stole from the Crow and drove across the winter ice. Now in summer the lake is dark blue and choppy, and everyone gathered on the shore feels the weight of what they have to do.

There are perhaps forty wild horses left. From time to time in years past they rounded up a few to sell to the Baymen or exchange for cattle. Now they need the whole fine crop. It's not their imagination, the chiefs grimly say: the woods are emptying of game. White men shoot as much as they can and drive the rest away.

Antille, second chief of the Pend d'Oreille, and his counterpart Arlee of the Bitterroot Salish give the signal to start. Behind them on the shore women make frybread and men string ropes for a corral. Every soul for fifty miles has come to watch. Screeching kids and barking dogs stir the air. The Americans who've come to buy stand some distance off.

Duncan and Red Horn and a dozen others will swim across with their mounts.

They urge their horses toward the freezing water, along with Finlays and Coutures, Beaverheads and Deschamps and Big Knifes, most of whom Duncan's related to by blood or the Company's sinews. Except, of course, Red Horn, who's pure Q'lispé and the most competitive bastard on the planet.

They've coiled and recoiled their lassos. Each has his technique for keeping it dry. Red Horn uses his saddle, cinched high on the withers, winding the rope around the pommel. Duncan goes bareback, rope coiled in the brim of his hat. Afterward there will be racing, dancing, drumming, food, and drink. The herders' horses are wiry and small compared to the wild mustangs. With a shout they swim them into the big arm of the lake. Duncan and Red Horn aim for the east side of the island where the shortgrass rolls down nearly to the shore. By the time they scramble up the bank and their horses shake off, nearly tossing Red Horn's lasso back into the lake, they're whooping, along with others they can hear at points around.

Then they fall quiet, speaking to each other in sign. The noise will surely drive the herd toward them. They knee their horses into some trees and then the drumming comes at them, the earth quivering, a fan of horseflesh flashing, galloping flat out then turning sharply like a flock of birds, dashing and careering. Duncan and Red Horn kick hard into the open. They gallop stretched out, aiming for the ones at the front of the wild bunch, their dark coats rippling, hooves sending sparks from the rocks. Duncan lets fly at a black shiny neck, cursing as the loop glances, reeling back as fast as he can. Red Horn has a big bay now, he's leaning back with his legs splayed to slow the stallion, and on the second try Duncan's catches and he's nearly hauled off by sheer force. The herd shies, rolling off to the left, shedding its captured members like a single creature shaking water from its mane. Nearly all the riders have a writhing devil dragging at their ropes, but he only sees his own captive, muscled, furious, resisting. He knots the rope to his bridle, drops down, and reels it in hand over hand, pulling himself as he pulls the horse, whispering and chanting, "whoa now," "hush now, there's a good girl" to the angry and eye-rolling mare.

Heaving she turns her neck away, then swings back, teeth bared, and tries to bite him. He takes a fistful of her mane and puts his hand across the bar between her eyes. Rubbing hard he brings her head down, pinching above the flaring nostrils, talking the whole time, tightening the loop beneath her chin and walking her, or dragging her, as every few steps she rebels. In this way he brings her close to Red Horn, who has done the same with his stallion. Red Horn takes the wild horses, a rope in each hand, hopping and leaping like a madman as they prance and rear, while Duncan tethers their own. They can't swim back with both. Besides, there are many more mustangs.

It's hard, exuberant work, kicking and stroking while guiding the mare across the channel. He hands the horse off to Michel Pablo, turns and plunges back into the water. He emerges on the sand, lungs burning, the sun now high overhead. Red Horn pretends he's been waiting all day, but his torso, too, is shining wet. They grin at one another and slap hands. This goes on all day until there's just one left—a wily dark brown stallion. Some want to leave him there, a lone free spirit. He'd die of loneliness, Duncan objects. It makes him think of Angus: his father wouldn't have survived without his family either, if he'd gone alone to the north. Though it'll be hard here too, forced into an early retirement. Duncan hangs back as the rest vie boisterously to catch the last horse. Maybe the two of them can do something together: ranch or run supplies to the mines.

As soon as the mustangs are in the enclosure Jack DeMers ambles over and offers the chiefs fifty dollars for each stallion, forty for each mare. "Broke, of course," he adds, eyeing the milling, furious beasts. He'll wait until August, then drive them north and sell them at the mines. Duncan sidles closer to the Indian side.

"Cash," Antille is saying, but Jack shakes his head.

"Haven't got it. I'll give you credit."

Antille is a gentle giant, not easily angered. But his broad face creases in displeasure. "It's too far to your place," he growls. Indeed, Duncan thinks: a long day's ride just to trade for whatever Jack will sell.

The merchant makes a face. "Fifty a mare too, if that's a problem."

In rapid Salish Duncan whispers to the chiefs: "I can't pay quite as much, but my place is a whole lot closer."

The Kootenai chief grunts his assent.

"Hey, I know," Duncan says brightly, turning to Jack. "Why don't we split the difference?" He addresses Arlee in Salish, which Jack, too, speaks: "Your people can make it to Frenchtown, yes? And the folks up here can trade with me."

The chiefs seem satisfied with this arrangement. Not so Jack.

"Who's to say how many horses belong to each tribe?" He's got a truculent look in his eyes.

"They'll sort it out, I'm sure," says Duncan evenly. He reaches a hand toward Jack, who grips it as hard as he can.

"That's the last time you run off my customers, Mack," he says fiercely beneath his breath.

Duncan just smiles and crushes his hand in return. He waves at the other merchants, Hammond and Higgins, who, disconcerted, wave back. They must have come just for the spectacle, he thinks—to watch the "savages." Since the Blackfeet were murdered, these white settlers are more emboldened. Recently in the new town called Helena he saw fresh signs on certain businesses: *No redskins allowed*. Hammond and a few of his pals, meanwhile, are putting up cabins on the reservation. They've started fencing land and running cattle. Rough elements are running whiskey down from the British Possessions, though it's strictly forbidden to sell to the Indians. Come to think of it, Jack DeMers is probably mixed up in that business.

He strolls over to where Red Horn is watching the dancing. The settlers' threats don't bother him. We'll outlast you, he thinks—we were here before you came, and we'll be here when you pack up and go. You've no idea of the people you're tangling with. Once the McDonalds are back and joined to the tribes—pureblood and mixed blood and white—we'll be a force to be reckoned with.

HE'S STILL BASKING in his slick move with Jack the next time he stops by the Frenchtown store. You should have seen the boss, Baird chuckles; the S.O.B. was apoplectic. Robert's just waiting to bust out of this lousy job; he and Duncan want to do some prospecting of their own. Duncan's expounding on how they'll have to tear him out by the roots if they think they can get rid of him that easy when Baird gets a funny look in his eyes.

"Best settle down then." He winks. "Sow some seed."

Duncan feels the blood rush to the roots of his hair. Bachelorhood suits him just fine, he retorts. The truth is, he keeps the question locked deep inside. He's had his offers, of course. But he remembers the look in his mother's eyes when Christina went north on the arm of her clerk. Either way he'll hurt one or the other, it seems to him: whether he goes with a Native girl or a white.

"I know!" Baird rocks forward. "The fillies all come to Riley's dances. There's one tomorrow, in point of fact."

Duncan's heard of these revelries held in a Frenchtown hall, the half-Irish half-Salish Ignace Riley on the fiddle. Half of Missoula County piles in, farm girls rubbing up against the rougher elements among the Frenchmen, Chinamen, the Native men, Black freemen, Krauts and Micks and Poles fresh off the boat. Everybody drinks and dances up a storm, while behind Jack's they all get soused. DeMers is the only place that sells Indians liquor, it being banned in town and on the reservation.

"Not my cup of tea." He hates how people act when they're drunk and he's not.

"Never find a girl unless you look."

He has no other plans; Baird knows it. "Only if you go too."

"Wouldn't miss it." Once more Baird gives him that merry, mocking look.

Duncan looks down with some dismay at his clothes. "We'll sort you out," Baird laughs, and that evening after closing they make free with Jack's stock.

It stays light and warm until close to ten o'clock and they eat their supper out front like two old-timers. Life could be worse in the long run, thinks Duncan, two old friends sitting and chewing the fat. He doesn't actually know what it's for, this life—hasn't given it much thought. Now the question seems more pressing.

"Living," is Baird's answer. "In a couple years you'll see, there's not much greater meaning to it."

"Unless you aim to get rich," says Duncan, thinking of Hammond and

DeMers, men who make no secret of their desire to stride like colossi and control the world.

"Comes and goes," Baird shrugs. They both know plenty of men who've made it and lost it and made it again, only to fall right back down to the bottom.

"I feel like the land is the thing," Duncan says slowly. "My small bit of it, at Connah."

"Better find a girl who wants that, then."

THEY HEAR THE fiddle yammering before they head over the next evening. They've slicked their hair with tonic, turning their heads to and fro in an old, tarnished mirror. He's little bit dashing, maybe—though nothing compared to Baird. Duncan's hair is lighter now in late summer, a blondish brown, his skin darker than Robert's, but then he's an outdoorsman. Stay too long in this store, he warns his friend, and you'll start looking like a vampire.

Two musicians are sawing up front, jigs and reels bouncing off the whipsawed floor. He and Baird lounge against the wall among men in striped shirts, white shirts, vests, and polished boots, as if they're waiting for a job or a handout. The women cluster like clumps of columbine against the opposite wall. A fellow behind them is delivering himself of a running commentary: "The actual composition of the feminine population of this territory is as follows: you got your farm girls, your merchants' and barkeeps' girls, your schoolmarms and your horny wives, your half-breeds and your full-blood squaws, and don't forget the whores."

"Who could forget?" someone says.

"In your dreams." All eyes return to the chattering prospects across the way. The bolder men step across.

"He missed the cousins from Illinois and Iowa," Baird whispers. "A whole nest of 'em down in the Bitterroot, I hear."

And indeed there are a surprising number of proper young ladies turned out in pale frocks, satin sashes at their waists to accentuate their curves. It's the style to button clear to the chin, a most unfortunate fashion, Baird adds. It makes Duncan a little less nervous, seeing so many fellows in his same plight.

"Act like you're a catch." Baird elbows him and starts to move. "Illustrious pioneer, prosperous salesman, crack shot." He grins. "Crackpot."

Duncan's still smiling as they come up to one pair of girls.

"What's the joke?" asks the blonder of the two.

"I was just thinking it's worse than the Jocko in April. You take your life in your hands crossing here."

They laugh, showing white teeth, looking from one man to the other.

"You ladies must be twins," Baird says gallantly. "Or at least sisters."

"No—" says the first one, "we only just met, ourselves."

"In Missoula," puts in the second, who like her friend wears her hair bunched in curls at the back of her neck. Her hair is darker, honey colored, but both have open faces, laughing eyes. Their eyebrows look surprised.

"Robert Baird." He's so smooth at it, pressing each proffered hand.

"Duncan McDonald." He bows slightly and feels himself color.

The blonder one is Elizabeth Gallagher, the darker one Lydia Wood. They're here to teach in the public school. Miss Gallagher has been here six months already; Miss Wood has just arrived.

"From the east, not the west, I assume," Baird drawls.

"From the railroad in Utah, which is technically south," says Miss Wood. She puts up a hand to mime a swoon. "Five hundred of the most hideous miles—I don't know how you call those things coaches."

"Or roads," Duncan smiles.

After a few minutes they run out of banter. Elizabeth lifts her hand toward Baird and tilts her head. He knows the drill and off they go. Lydia looks at Duncan, and before he can stop himself, he shrugs. Such a wonderful impression, he thinks as they step out on the floor. The tune is one he knows, "Farewell to Erin," and it's a little too slow. He moves woodenly; he knows it. Her eyes are encouraging, and the next number he picks up the pace. He tries to imagine himself leaping after game in the woods and feels a little more fluid.

"Try to look like you're enjoying yourself," Baird hisses as he swings past.

They break after another tune and Duncan and Baird fetch them huckleberry cordial. Waiting to pay his nickel he surveys the crowd. The hall is jammed now and the early birds from town are looking flagged. The new contingent is fresher, wilder: he sees a whole posse of DeMers. Now the faces are not uniformly white but fill the spectrum from light to dark. He sees young people from the scattered homesteads who occasionally trade at his store. One of Jack's daughters looks much like his younger sister Annie, with that same sweet, square face and observant eyes. She's sixteen; she'd like this, he thinks, and then remembers the faceless man's words. He's never thought of her as a half-breed—nor Maggie or Christina. It's a despicable thing to separate people that way, he thinks as they move back bearing their ruby-red drinks.

Lydia Wood is clearly the sharper of the two. Beth, as she asks them to call her, pays scant attention to anything once she's got her hooks into Baird. He looks at Duncan over her head as she pulls him back to the floor, a look that says plainly "You owe me."

"You're friends of long standing, I guess," Lydia says.

"A couple of years. That's long, for Montana."

"Ah."

"People come and go. Robert and I both keep shops—though mine is my own."

"Where's that?"

"Up north, in the Mission Valley." He watches her for some sign of recognition; there is none. "About thirty miles from here. I was born there."

She looks at him more closely then, as if trying to work out the math. Her eyes are a blueish green. "Remarkable." She smiles. "Romantic. I come from Erie, Pennsylvania, though perhaps that doesn't mean much to you."

He shakes his head, feeling foolish. "I imagine you'll have your hands full at the school," he says, "but I'd be happy to introduce you to my country."

"You speak as though it were a living person."

"I suppose I do." He laughs, caring a bit less now what she thinks. "In a way, I suppose it is."

CHAPTER 3

CHIEF VICTOR MANY Horses of the Bitterroot Salish died that same wild horse summer of 1870 on his way back from the buffalo plains. He was buried along the trail and the chieftaincy passed to his son Charlo, Claws of the Small Grizzly. One day not too long after, Duncan is in the corral when he sees a delegation approaching, leading a tall gray horse with an empty saddle. The warriors present it to him gravely. Victor's widow Agnes has sent them, they say. On his deathbed, the chief bequeathed his favorite buffalo charger to Angus McDonald as a sign of his friendship and regard.

The emotion Duncan feels is immediate. He sucks in a breath and tries not to well up. One of the men is not so restrained; his tears flow freely. Duncan receives the animal—magnificent, a speckled gray at least seventeen hands high. Such thanks, he thinks, such respect in both directions between his father and the people among whom he once dwelt.

The gift is waiting for Angus when the whole family arrives in Montana at long last the following summer. He knew about it, of course, but it's not the same as greeting this noble beast, its eyes both quizzical and calm. Angus feels Victor's spirit, his humor and grace and charm. He saddles the horse in equal good humor, breathing the clean air of Sin-ye-le-min. He's someone still; he's not forgotten. In a way, Victor has given him another chance. And even before he left Colvile the sting of his losses had begun to lessen. The fort existed no more. He'd sent the post records to Victoria with Christina, headed herself to Fort Kamloops with her man. Now he and Catherine and their remaining children are back where they began—back where they belong. Duncan has built them a fine new house near the stream beyond the post, with three new lodges pegged beside it. Angus smiles at the memory of Chief Sil-ips-tu. No Blackfeet will creep among the willows and murder them now.

His wife's face is shining at the sight of the little oasis, and he understands finally that he's chosen—this woman, this Indian life, unlike any other trader for the Hudson's Bay. He could never take her from it, force her to live among those who demean everything she is. What is ambition, after all, compared to this long, surprising love, so unexpectedly resilient?

CATHERINE EMBRACES HER tall son fiercely. How handsome he is, how strong. She was right: he's the one. Riding into the valley she saw the white steeple of the Black Robes' church and recalled it clearly. Their priest blessed that marriage, their third—the marriage from which this boy was born. It pained her deeply to leave John in the silent pine forest above Colvile; she wept, too, when Christina rode north. But now Duncan stands holding her arm—having embraced her, actually lifted her up and twirled her around. This ardent, often silent boy who fought to draw his first breath but has found his place here now beneath the Shining Mountains. He's the one who will carry them on. They've lost enough already.

Their four youngest boys are leaping like crickets while Annie and Maggie soberly greet their older brother. From the yard Catherine sees what might be a mirage if her heart didn't know differently. Dozens of people flow toward them from the village to welcome them home, dark ribbons sliding across the golden grasses. For years she and her friends were scattered—their Company family, her sister-cousins from St. Ignatius—but now she stands in the center of the meadow drawing them on. The wind whips her face, swooping down from Coul-hi-cat; the beloved country sighs as the strings inside her unwind.

"Home sweet home." Angus catches her by the waist—this waist that's thick now but not so thick she can't still bend and dance. She's still the same girl, still young inside. She walks a square forty paces by forty behind her lodge and declares that this will be her garden. She hands the shovel to Duncan and laughs at the mock-salute he gives as he starts to dig. She'll plant squash and melons, beans and maize. It's Hoplal again, the season of cold weather coming, the tamarack turning yellow. But she can prepare the soil, so when the first leaves appear, curled like tiny fists, her new life will also begin. Maybe her mother, too, will come to stay. She tingles with pleasure to think of days with Angelique, Michel, Kyuka, and her man. When the bitterroot blooms, her clan will come, too, from Kaix-kaix-Koose, flowing toward the sunrise, surrounding her as the soil surrounds and feeds the roots.

"RIDE WITH ME," Angus tells his son. "Show me the lay of the country now." They circle the valley in one day and at evening camp high on the hills that enclose it from the south.

"All this is America now—lock, stock, and barrel. Hard to believe it, but still." He turns toward Duncan. "You ought to get the papers, too, become a citizen."

They have to think of protecting themselves. He's left Donald, now nineteen, at Colvile in hopes of holding onto some part of that property. Being officially American will help. It's not as if they were ever all that British. Angus grins. "Just a bunch of upstart Scots."

"Maybe." Duncan takes off his hat. "I'll tell you though: the people here are sharks."

They bathe the next morning in the Jocko River and ride down the canyon toward the cold spring plain where the settlements are springing up. The past is still so alive to him. Everywhere, Angus sees ghosts, the traces of the world before. Here, he tells Duncan, a Kanaka called Koriaka led McArthur's brigade and was slain. "Ambushed by Blackfeet—so we called it the Coriacan defilé." Here's where Richard Grant had his latter-day ranch, near what they now call Frenchtown. Here, in the great bowl of bunchgrass criss-crossed with new fences and roads, is where Angus himself sang the *San-kah-na* one summer's night long ago, riding with Victor's people in a thundering round on the eve of their departure for the plains. "All flesh is grass. Man comes and goes." His son reins in to listen. "Man comes and goes, and some will not return." How that age-old lament pierced his father then, preparing with his friends for the hunt, the inevitable battles and deaths.

And then they come upon the colony the settlers call Missoula. Nearly twenty-five years have passed since Angus arrived here from Fort Hall. The place is unrecognizable. The Salish call it the Place of Bull Trout, but now the river is hemmed in by rows of low wood buildings and hardly to be seen. Two hundred white people live here, Duncan says, plus three hundred more in the Bitterroot. They ride past saloons and mercantiles, stables and a church, a jail, a courthouse. A laundry with Chinese letters and a new Masonic lodge. It's market day and the streets are filled with conveyances. Horses stamp at the rails; their owners stamp in and out of the shops. A few ladies drift past, lifting their skirts from the dust. The buckboards of the Bitterroot farmers stretch toward the water where, Duncan says, pointing, "now there's even a bridge."

Angus touches his cap as the ladies look up. He's finally old enough to admit he always liked to make heads turn. He's wearing his black silk scarf and beaded buckskin, his black Scotch cap; his beard is now striped with two white blazes like a badger. Let them think him eccentric. He damn well is—a relic of another age. They hitch their mounts and step inside a store. Inside the customers are three deep so Duncan takes him to another shop across the way. Higgins & Worden was the first in town, he whispers as they enter.

The proprietor is bald and wrinkled as a nut, with a snowy mustache. "Mr. Higgins, meet my father, Angus McDonald."

"A pleasure, sir." Angus grips his hand.

"How do you do." The shopkeeper screws up his eyes to get a better look.

"Mr. Higgins came in, what—sixty, sixty-one?" Duncan says.

The grocer shoots him a dyspeptic look. "Long before that, young man. I was here back in fifty-three, with the Governor's expedition."

"Imagine that." Angus takes him in more closely. "I knew Isaac Stevens too."

"You a trapper?"

"After a fashion." He'd planned to stay incognito but hadn't reckoned on Duncan.

"My father was here well before this place was even dreamed of." There's a queer heat in his voice and Angus thanks him silently for it. "Here Before Christ," he adds, "trading for fur with the Hudson's Bay."

"I guess Christ got the better of you then," the grocer remarks tartly.

After they steer themselves back out, Angus whispers in Duncan's ear. "Stevens still speaks from the grave, it appears. Couldn't wait to wipe us out." He may have been shot to pieces in the Civil War, but the former governor's legacy is well cemented. They move through the town, Angus observing his son. Duncan dresses like these settlers; he knows their names and greets them. But even so they don't like him, his father senses—nor any of the brown and half-brown people who remind them daily that their new town is built on someone else's dispossession.

There's a sad line of shacks on an island in the river where ragged dark bodies flit. Shacktown, Duncan says: the only place Indians are allowed to live in town, so they can pick up pennies sawing wood or scooping dung. Angus turns homeward feeling low. When they stop to rest in the canyon, he's still thinking of Grant and McArthur and the rest gone to the happy hunting grounds. You're getting morbid, he thinks, and shakes himself. Here's Duncan, bright and determined, here's the future, youth. He must help him to prosper as well as he can.

"You expect to keep trading, then?" he asks.

"As long as I can."

"As long as they let you, I guess." His son stiffens and he knows he's hit a nerve.

"I don't quit that easily," Duncan says.

Angus stuffs his pipe and pulls out his flask. He offers some but Duncan's never liked the stuff. Makes him dizzy, he says. Angus suspects it's because John liked it too well and liked the ladies besides. He's seen none of that so far in Duncan.

"Best settle down. Play it both ways, take some land like the rest of them." He screws up his eyes against the smoke. He doesn't know quite how to say it. "Take your place with pride—after all, you're more than half white." His son's nostrils quiver. "I know. It's ugly to think of it like that." He feels ugly himself saying it out loud. "But that's the way these people think."

Duncan leans forward. "Damn the way they think."

"Unless you play their game, they'll squeeze you out. They shoot to kill." Angus notices he's brandishing his pipe and lowers it. "I'm just saying the world has changed, and we'd better change with it."

"What do you suggest?" Duncan's voice is cool.

"You've got a girl in the valley?" He sees blood suffuse the boy's face, turn the skin rose gold. How old is he now—twenty-one, twenty-two?

"No."

"So. You might do like Christina, marry white."

"You didn't." The answer is instant and sharp.

"No disrespect to your mother, but it *was* an alliance—that's how her people saw it."

And yet, Angus wonders now. If he'd known how it would turn out—if Catherine or he had seen this coming—would they have brought these children into this unhappy world? What future will they have, these offspring of two different races? It was selfish, perhaps, to mix their blood, leave them neither fish nor fowl.

"But there wasn't ever really any choice." He smiles at their silent son. Love does prevail, after all. "The fact is, I was crazy—still am—about that woman."

"WHERE DO THE stars go in the day?" Archie looks up at her solemnly and she laughs and swats him on the bottom. "Run after your brothers. I'll tell you tonight."

The nimíipuu say they're the cannibals Coyote threw into the sky once he thrashed their sorry hides. They daren't show their faces in the daylight. Catherine watches her boys scramble two at a time onto the patient mares and dig their heels into the barrels of their bellies. My, they look fine, dark hair combed and shining, white shirts visible for miles. Though Angus was horrified when she informed him they'd go to the Black Robes for their schooling.

"Pour that claptrap down their throats?" His eyes were pinpoints underneath the bushy brows. "You'd see them bow and scrape to flour and wine?"

She snorted. "The priests are not American, at least. Besides." She drew herself up. "You said yourself they have to fight. You made us learn, remember?"

The only way to hold these Bostons off—to keep them out of this last place they've been left—will be by using their own tools. How long it's taken her to understand. Not one of them is purely anything—not she herself, not any of these half-blood children. Only Angus, blind as he's ever been to this cold fact. "They'll have to live a foot on either side, like Duncan."

"Like Duncan, aye."

"He does his best."

"All right." He strode away to huddle with his cows.

It's his turn now to see the way it feels to be unwanted and unseen, the head of no one but himself. While she has found a place here for herself in Sin-ye-le-min. She won't set foot in their white settlements; the only white men she will see are European priests, inside their chapel with her friends. They sit and listen to the words and song and prayer. At least the way the Black Robes treat them is respectful. The missionaries in the Clearwater are far harsher, says her mother: they make the people throw their clothes in holes they dig, then burn them. And then they cut their hair. At St. Ignatius the music makes her chest swing open while the light streams through the colored glass to wash the pain away.

She returns to her work. The new baby, Mary, isn't strong like the others so Catherine keeps her at her side, propped in the shade in her cradleboard. By late afternoon the boys will come home, along with some friends. It's high summer and she has bread and jam and honey and meat pies in the icehouse by the creek just crying out to share. There are always families stopping by. Already thanks to the boys she knows half the people who live at the mission, and her greatest pleasure is welcoming them at her open door.

How lonely she was at Colvile; how broad and deep is this net of her community now. Even Angus will find his place eventually. He strides out straightaway each morning to his corral, as she does to her crops. Duncan helped him assemble his herd and her husband cajoles the red and black cattle with cooing words. He blushed one time when she overheard, but they've been married so long they can't really be embarrassed. Nearly thirty years. They've been to the point of rupture often enough to know they never really want to part. She told him as much when he accused her of holding him hostage, when his Company tugged him toward the north. He talked like a white man, she teased. He of all people should know that her people had a different way. She chooses for herself—as he would have to, too.

It overjoyed her, of course, that he chose to remain and weave the rest of this life with her. Though it's hard for him, no longer being chief. He's always writing, sending his thoughts to men he knew before, traders and soldiers and the people who make their laws. And Duncan is good, always asking his advice, taking him along to Missoula and visits to the other chiefs.

When she stops for a cold drink, she sees him returning from the range and raises her arm in greeting. He raises his cap to her, but signs that he will see her later. For an instant they're young again, sending messages across the air. It hurts him that Victor's son Charlo doesn't want his counsel. Angus could help him write to the President, get the reservation question settled finally. But Charlo said even well-meaning white men don't help his people. Catherine isn't privy to the Salish councils, but she imagines they're like those her uncle held, and his son Looking Glass now holds. She sympathizes with these chiefs. Every tribe the Bostons made treaties with has faced the same wall. They have only two choices: trust the white man's words and watch their homelands disappear. Or refuse and resist, holding to the ancient ways like her own people. It's wrong to blame any for the choice they make. Some trust the Bostons; others choose to keep out of their way. In either case, they're dealing with cannibals—and no one believes anymore that Coyote will come to save them, tossing these invaders back into the night.

IN DUE COURSE Duncan lets it be known that he's taken the new schoolmarm out a time or two. Baird says Lydia's the kind of girl who likes to handle the wares before she buys. Duncan doesn't mind—in fact he kind of likes it. He's never been the object of a lingering appraisal. It must mean something positive, he's thought the whole summer long. Privately he pictures her soft arms, her thighs, imagines what she feels like underneath those skirts and whalebone. It seems to him the whole time he pays court to her—learning which music she likes, which food she prefers—she's doing the same. She quizzes him on the flora and fauna; she asks him to explain the local tribes; she pesters him to take her up to Fort Connah. Even so she hasn't let him kiss her. Once or twice the thought has crossed his mind that he's mainly a curiosity.

But she's smart. She likes to banter and laugh, and bit by bit he's softening. More than anything she wants to see the fort and St. Ignatius, she coos. "It's all a mystery, like you." She flirts with him and he's taut with yearning. Through the autumn she brings it up whenever they see one another, which is rarely. Duncan is ranging further to trade and she's busy building up the school. By Christmas he knows it is time. And once Angus learns she's never been to a cèilidh, his father insists that he bring her to the ball.

They hear the pipes warming up all the way from the Jocko fork, cresting the rise in the elegant trap Duncan has hired for the occasion. Lydia's wedged between him and Baird, and Duncan is aroused by the smell of her—a tanginess beneath the rosewater and talc. A few weeks ago Beth was thrown from a horse and broke her leg; Lydia seems to like having both men to herself. She turns sometimes to him, sometimes to Baird. Her face is a pale oval, her lips red, wisps of honeyed hair sneaking out from under her mink hood.

At the house he hands her down and follows her into the hall, festooned with pine boughs and red satin ribbons. The family will eat together, then repair to Duncan's post for the dance. Their finery is so blinding that for a moment he gapes: his whole family is wearing Glengarry tartan, some in kilts, some in plaids across their shoulders, all the way from Annie at eighteen down to three-year-old Angus Colvile. His mother, not to be outdone, wears a black taffeta skirt with a gray bodice, a magnificent shell necklace, and tall moccasins, ornately worked. His father plays the Scotch laird to the hilt in kilt and jabot, escorting Lydia to the blazing fire and plying her with bread and cured salmon, a dainty glass of brandy. He must have wiped out half the inventory of the Scotch House in London, Duncan thinks, laughing to himself at the horsehair sporrans and silver buckles. It's clear what his father's up to. By contrast Duncan's own get-up is drab, though he took pains with the gray pin-striped trousers and white tie. When no one's looking Baird convulses in merriment outside.

It doesn't matter. The night is grand in a way it hasn't been since John died. Angus pipes them in with "The Green Hills," and Dave Polson and young Tom on their fiddles keep everyone hopping. They get his younger sister to bow when they play "Drowsy Maggie," and Lydia to dance a hornpipe with Baird. And of course there are stories, in Gaelic and En-glish and Nez Perce. He keeps his lips close to her ear, translating. He wants the green-eyed girl then, more intensely than before. But when they stand for the next dance, she swerves from his grasp.

"Will you bring me a drink?" she breathes. Dutifully he trots off. Re-turning, he hangs back and watches her watch his mother. Lydia's bright eyes flicker as she scrutinizes the older woman who sits fanning herself, teeth flashing and color high as she laughs at something Maggie says. He follows Lydia's eyes and imagines how Catherine McDonald must appear to her, broad and loud in her get-up of taffeta and dead deer and feathers, and he feels a strange embarrassment—then anger and shame that that he should feel embarrassed about his own mother.

Lydia turns to him with her eyebrows slightly raised and he catches her hand and pulls her to him. He feels her fast heartbeat, light bones; he kisses her startled lips. Then he spins and leads her toward his mother and sister and leaves her there so she will speak to them, be forced to see them eye to eye.

That night she sleeps in a private room in the house, he and Baird in his cabin. The first day of the year dawns clear and bright. The pair of them are half-inebriated still when Duncan piles them into the gig and takes the turning to the mission. He prays that the Pend d'Oreille are still wrapped in their blankets as he makes the promised tour. From the backseat his white woman peers between yawns at the lodges and simple cabins that ring the church.

"How many fit in one tipi?" she asks. "Why do they all face southeast?" She's turning her wide assessing eyes this way and that when Red Horn steps out of his lodge, stretches, scoops snow to rub into his face and sees them.

"Hey!" His face is bright as he raises his hand and Duncan is torn. If he stops he'll have to suffer her curiosity, that strange, ironic look he thought he saw on her face last night. Baird lazily raises an arm in greet-ing, then pulls his hat down and slides back beneath the robes.

Duncan raises his arm then, too, and signs, "I have no time." He makes what he hopes is a rueful look and twitches the reins. Red Horn will stand looking, he knows, until they disappear beyond the grade, but even so he turns the team back toward Missoula.

CHAPTER 4

THERE ARE BEGINNINGS and there are endings. Time isn't a constant flow, his father says, one hand heavy on Duncan's shoulder as they haul the old flag down. The older you get, the easier it is to see the breaks and hinges. Together they fold the HBC flag with regimental reverence. It's faded and frayed but still potent, the sign of a once-great empire. Neither can think what to run up the flagpole in its place, so they leave it empty for the moment.

Fort Connah had been overlooked, a blank spot on some ledger. But now it, too, must close. Duncan has had no fresh supplies for a full year. You can expect a thing, he thinks—yet still feel some surprise and even grief when it transpires.

"And so it is," his father declaims to the small crowd, "that in this autumn of the year 1871, as the northern rivers start to freeze—closing the thousand tributaries that were our lifeblood all these years—our Company's great adventure in America comes to its end. We had a grand, grand run." He speaks with gravity and feeling to the mingled Scots and Indians and Frenchmen who have come to watch—old Colvile hands like themselves and other former Baymen and their families. "The world won't see our like again." He closes his eyes and sings, one hand beating the time like the oars of the voyageurs: "Alouette, gentille alouette, alouette, je te plumerai."

"Je te plumerai la tête, je te plumerai le bec." Duncan turns, surprised to hear his mother's husky voice respond. And then the rest join in, sweet and guttural and sad, many dashing tears away. Baptiste used to sing it when she was a girl, later she tells him. "I hunted beaver, too, you know."

Duncan watches his parents in the evening walk hand in hand through their field toward the creek and wonders how one picks up again when a chapter closes. What held them together then, what will hold them now?

He thinks of John as always, and Christina up at Kamloops. Now the post is closed he, too, will have to strike out on his own. It's not as if the last year has been easy. He underestimated the way Jack's new shop at St. Ignatius would hit his sales. Without the Hudson's Bay, he can't buy wholesale at a better price than Jack—or Hammond or Higgins for that matter. Regretfully, the chiefs have made it clear: they like him well enough, but every penny counts.

And he's not the only one they're trying to push out. It's a crime how the Yankees treat the Bitterroot Salish. For fifteen years Victor and now Charlo have been waiting for the government to fulfill the treaty terms. Their valley was to be their reservation: they wouldn't be pushed north to the reservation for the Kootenai and Pend d'Oreille. According to Angus McDonald, who had it from Victor himself, Isaac Stevens agreed—provided a survey was made to determine which valley was better suited to the use of the Salish.

Of course there has been no such survey. Nor have settlers been kept out as the treaty pledged. Quite the opposite: the President himself last fall ordered the Salish removed to the north. Homesteaders continue to squeeze the tribal pasturage and plots along the bottomland. Pressure is mounting. Two weeks after they close Fort Connah, a senator by the name of Garfield—who will in time become President himself—officially visits the Bitterroot. His party fishes and shoots and throws blandishments and reason and threats at Charlo, but in neither hunt are they particularly successful. "Recalcitrant," they call him. "Stubborn as a mule."

"He shows them their hypocrisy, that's all," Angus growls. He's seen it before: white settlers seething and afraid, terrified the "reds" will finally strike back. So has Duncan, he reminds his father. He was here when the Army massacred those Blackfeet two winters ago. This time around it's the *Missoula Pioneer* that claims Charlo's people plan to seize the land. The settlers are digging in; militias are forming. Angus figures they'd better go down and see for themselves.

The air is filled with the sound of wings, the birds, too, heading south. Duncan packs every last blanket and piece of equipment he has. He'll either sell it or give it away or set up somewhere else. Maybe the Jocko, he tells his father. Maybe Missoula. He doesn't say that much as he loves his family, he feels a little stifled with them all clustered around him at Post Creek.

"Closer to the action, eh?" Angus gives him a sly look. Neither mentions Lydia, but he knows what his father's thinking.

They make short work of it: half a day to Missoula, another half to the bank of the Bitterroot River north of the Lolo fork. Angus complains at the ache in his bones but brightens as they ride. He points to the Lolo trail dropping out of the Bitterroot mountains. "Years ago we rode with the chiefs in a long parade," he says. "Your mother and I, to the place of ground squirrels." He says the name in Nez Perce. "The 'Bostons'"— his father smiles—"call it Big Hole." They pass scattered farms and great stands of cottonwood, see fences, tipis, cabins, cattle, fields, the blue-green entrances to distant canyons.

"Gold," says Angus, surveying the peaks to either side. "All the trouble in this world that stems from gold."

He shakes his head and Duncan wonders if he even sees his own role. Well he recalls that cannon shot at Colvile, when the York boats set up the Columbia to take supplies to the miners. The Bitterroot, too, has seen numerous strikes, most of which are since played out, but the settlers stayed for the richness of the valley. It's been a year or two since Duncan was down this way, for Angus even longer. They gaze around in wonder. The store porches and smithies are busy with people coming and going, animals stamping, Indian and mixed-blood and white. The mood doesn't seem all that tense. At the edge of the next town a wooden sign proclaims they are entering Stevensville, Montana Territory, and Angus stops for a moment, his lips working. Then he spits and rides on.

Charlo isn't at his place on the west side of the valley. An old woman says he's hunting. He'll look in at the mission then, Angus says. "Ravalli will know." So they cross the river to a little chapel in a clearing ringed with garden plots and lodges. Angus slips off his hat as he enters the log building.

"My dear friend." The upturned face of the old priest is nearly transparent. "A blessing, after all this time." He tries to rise but can't quite manage it.

"Father." In a stride Angus is at his side, crouching and grasping his hands. "Dear Father Ravalli, the pleasure is all mine." The priest is stringy as an old chicken, eyes large in his bony face. "You remember my son, Duncan." Duncan shakes one papery hand.

"So many healthy children, Angus, the Lord has been generous."

"And some he has taken."

"And safeguards them in Heaven."

His father stands. "Father Ravalli married your mother and I." He looks at the priest with an expression of great fondness. "At Colvile."

"For the third time, as I recall." The priest smiles.

"It seems to have held. Did Joset ever tell you that Catherine convinced him to renew the rite?"

They both laugh, the low dry chuckles of old men.

Ravalli pushes himself up with some help and they move to a table outside. His arthritis is bad, but he treats it with infusion of willow bark, he says. Angus smiles. "If anyone can heal the sick, you can."

Rarely has Duncan seen his father so tender. He's never been a church-going man, but he's sensitive to questions of the spirit. His God, he once said, was the God of all Creation—firmament and earth and all that dwell within those planes. Duncan has followed that path. The Creator can as easily be called Jesus or Hunyawat, Mohammed or Amot-Kan. If a supreme being walked the heights of Judea, why not Sin-ye-le-min? His father has always despised organized religions, but he obviously respects, and even loves, certain priests.

Now he's questioning Ravalli closely about this senator's visit. The priest translated for the chief, who wouldn't be swayed—though Arlee, his second chief, agreed to sign the deal. "Charlo says he's like a tree with its roots in this ground, and only a hurricane will move him." Ravalli's dark eyes take a mischievous turn. "He calls Arlee 'that Nez Perce renegade.'"

Duncan snorts. Arlee is half Salish, half nimíipuu. Some full-bloods are suspicious of such men as they, though many Salish are the same. The tribe would have faded long ago had they not found men of other tribes to replace those killed by battle or disease.

Angus is still pumping Ravalli for information. Garfield promised to build them houses and schools and pay them fifty thousand dollars a year for ten years for their land, if they would move up to the Flathead Reservation. Equally worrying, the Montana legislature has just banned hunting for nearly half the year.

Duncan breaks in. "Where's Charlo now?"

"Across the divide."

The valley doesn't feel poised for insurrection. A gentle peace pervades St. Mary's Mission. Why in hell can't they let them live together? Charlo is a fair man, respected by his people and the whites alike. When his young men get drunk or fight or rob the whites, he has them whipped within an inch of their lives. He worships at the Catholic Church; the white men worship the skins his people barter for coffee and sugar and flour. Yet all the while these same settlers are secretly petitioning the President, attacking the "savages" for what they call their lazy, spendthrift use of this verdant place.

"I've tried to convince him to go up to that good country. There won't be another offer of such good land." Angus looks up toward the peaks and sighs. "If not, time will finish them off."

Sharply Duncan looks up.

"He's a man of strong beliefs," murmurs Father Ravalli.

"There are only two paths." Angus speaks harshly. "Submit, or fight and die."

"For years I have prayed for a different answer," the old priest nods. "But God hasn't shown me that light."

"Greed and pride." Angus stands. "Vanquish these and the Indians might stand a chance."

The farewells are warm, though Duncan only goes through the motions. In truth his mind is shocked. He has always believed his father would fight for the right. Not out of sentiment but principle: in opposition to injustice. Now he just sounds defeated—as if the days of the Native people are numbered, regardless.

THEY PRESS SOUTH, passing campsites long cold, ascending the narrowing valley. The next morning they reach the cleft through which the trail crosses the great divide. It's lower and less grand than the crown of their own mountains. But the sight it reveals is so majestic their hearts can't help but open: a vast golden platter of undulating grassland, touched with patches of blue shadow. At the foot of the slope beside a stream they perceive what must be the Salish camp.

"So much smaller," his father murmurs.

They ride in to whoops from the boys tending the herds and Duncan counts maybe forty lodges. Chief Charlo receives them at his fire, burning brightly despite the early hour. His small grandsons feed the flames, spinning the dried buffalo dung with looks of mischief. Charlo is eating and gestures at them to help themselves. His hair is unbound except one braid to the side; his dark skin is taut across the bones of his cheeks, his powerful nose, and mouth. When they have eaten, Angus produces tobacco.

"I saw Father Ravalli," he says. The chief emits a soundless puff. "He told me about this Garfield."

"I'm glad my father didn't live to see it." Charlo sucks deeply and hands back the pipe. The Claws of the Small Grizzly is only forty years old, but already has the visage of a much older man. "He fed them and gave them tools and helped them farm and now they lick their lips, coveting our land." He looks coolly at Angus. "They've always spoken with two mouths."

"So it is."

"You know Stevens called my father an old dog, because he wouldn't sign."

"He'd call you worse if he were alive." Angus smiles. "Your father was a great man."

"Yes." Charlo regards him and Duncan can't help feeling he's weighing Victor's high regard for this Scotsman against the incontrovertible truth: few white men can be trusted now. They smoke in silence. Duncan drinks in the silence of the lodge he's known for his whole life. White men find it awkward, try to fill it.

After a while Angus asks, "What do you hear of Eagle from the Light?"

"He went by In-may-soo-let-tqui. I don't know where after that."

"How did he seem?"

"Bad. It's the same for them. White Bird's still in his canyon but Washington stole Joseph's land."

As Angus is digesting this, Duncan leans forward. "How's the hunt?"

The chief thrusts out his lower lip, which gives him an evil look. He makes the sign for strangling. "Worse and worse. Every season less." He means not just the buffalo, but elk, longhorn, deer. "So you see," he says to Angus, "I have no choice but to hold onto the land I have."

The next morning the dew burns off before the sun even lifts above the hills and they can tell the day will be a scorcher. The band is headed homeward. Charlo will trade with Duncan back in the Bitterroot; he doesn't trust this open country. Not so much Crow or Bannock but "farmers, miners, with long distance guns," he says.

Before they leave they fire the grasses. The whole camp is mounted, lodgepoles and covers and what game they've shot lashed tightly to their travois. They watch as the four appointed to the task fan out on horseback. They taste the wind to see the way it blows and circle farther. At some unseen sign all four lean out and sweep their flaming brands along the ground, and then they're galloping, tracing the lines of flame toward one another until they meet and fall back toward the waiting throng.

Two hundred Salish men, women, and children watch the licking line of light as it sweeps away, eating every stalk that stands. They can't really see the fire, only the black earth left behind as it sweeps toward the distant hills. There's a cloud forming now, lifting and billowing, and the people turn the other way toward home. All that's needed now is the rain that will come in the afternoon as it nearly always does, the mountains tossing the light and thunder back and forth. Rain will fall and quench the fire and prepare the earth for winter and the fresh spring shoots to nourish them for one more season.

BY THE TIME they near Missoula Duncan has decided. He's pursued her for nearly a year. It's now or never. He tells Angus he has business in town and they part. He turns westward, plucking as he goes. Orange flames of sumac, rabbitbrush with yellow fluffs, tight coils of red berries: he makes her an autumn bouquet.

Lydia lodges with Beth now in a cabin on the Frenchtown road. "Like two old spinsters," she told him gaily. "Maybe we'll stay that way." White women seem to view life with a man differently from how his mother and sisters see it. Annie says they're raised like flowers and expect to be tended. He doesn't entirely agree. Lydia prides herself on her mind, her schoolteacher's wage. But certainly, as Angus has pointed out, the settlers' views on this, as so much else, are different from everything Duncan knows.

He'll steal in and steal her heart—catch her unawares. He hobbles his horse and moves silently toward the cabin. Their dogs know him well and merely raise their muzzles and prick their ears. It's a Sabbath afternoon, appropriate he thinks for answering a prayer. His throat is tight, his palms slick as he moves toward the door. He can't help but overhear the women talking inside.

"Pretty," Beth is saying as he lifts his hand to knock.

"It's from Duncan." Lydia's voice is soft.

"You going to wear it to that ball?" Beth has a nosy way that Duncan never liked, but now he thanks her from the bottom of his heart.

"I'm not . . . sure," he faintly hears her say. Then he can't stand there any longer like a thief and has to knock.

Beth opens and lets out a little cry. "Well, speak of the devil."

Behind her Lydia sits with a lap full of tartan and lace, the Glengarry shawl he gave her for her birthday. Her green eyes are startled, even shocked. She rises, still clutching the fabric cascade.

"I might ask that myself," he says smiling, melting at the sight of her fair bare arms on this hot afternoon.

"Why Duncan—I . . ." She looks around for a wrap and finding none, winds the bolt of blue and green and red about her.

"Would you give us a moment?" Duncan turns to Beth, who gives them both the slyest look before stepping out and sharply shutting the door.

"I—wasn't expecting you." Her honey-colored hair hangs loose and perspiration trembles on her lip.

"I know." He's never seen her this exposed, this tender. In one step he stands before her, wildflowers dangling. "I had to . . . come." He wills his voice not to shake. "Had to know."

He reaches out his empty hand to stroke the hollow of her throat.

"If I will come?" Her eyes look frightened almost.

"If you will be my wife."

She takes a half-step back, fingers whitening on the tartan. "Oh, Duncan," she says.

He waits as she just looks at him, eyes traveling the height and depth of him until she whispers as if strangled, "I can't. I just—can't."

He drops the flowers he supposes. Blood roars through his head. "You can't?" He's incredulous. "You mean you won't."

"It's just . . . not possible." He hears the pleading in her voice then, feels her hand upon his arm. "I care for you, I do. I *do* admire you, find you marvelous, but . . ."

With burning clarity he understands.

"You just can't see beyond my skin."

She flushes as the arrow hits its mark.

He feels such pain, as if a hand has reached inside his chest and squeezed. And then the pain and shame ignite and harden into fury. She's weeping, face all blotched and wet, and he has half a mind to seize the shawl and strip her naked. Her face is ugly now, all twisted by the ugly things she thinks. They're all alike, they'll fight like anything to keep the rest down and ensure they stay on top. How could he have thought a woman such as she would choose a man like him? He takes one last look at her room and sees the big chest where she keeps her special things. He crosses in two strides and flings the heavy top back. He digs his arms beneath the pelts of mink and beaver, rabbit, ermine—wraps and hats he skinned and tanned and stitched for her—and smells the snow, the air of the high mountains deep inside the fur. Without a word he gathers them all up and turns to bear his whole self out, all skin and claw and broken heart.

When the old year ends, he stands by the fire with his sister Maggie. They've invited no guests this New Year. Their brother Tom fiddles the old tunes by ear, and for the first time Duncan notices how many Scots melodies are laments.

When they toast, Maggie tells him she knew the instant she met Lydia. It was the way she looked at them, she says: with fascination, the way one looks at a new toy or pet. "They don't see us. We might as well not exist." Maggie's just eighteen, with a firm jaw and long and pointed Highland nose. Her complexion is sallow, her expression sad. "No one will marry me ever, I'm certain," she whispers as she draws him out to the floor, where their brother is sawing away at the first cèilidh dance.

CHAPTER 5

A TERRIBLE FIGHT

Gen. Custer and his Nephew KILLED
The Seventh Cavalry cut to pieces
The Whole Number Killed 315

From our Special Correspondent
Stillwater, M. T., July 2nd, 1876.

Muggins Taylor, scout for Gen. Gibbons, got here last night,
direct from Little Horn River with telegraphic despatches.
General Custer found the Indian camp of about two thousand
lodges on the Little Horn, and immediately attacked the camp
Nothing is Known of the Operation of this detachment, only
as they trace it by the dead. Major Reno commanded the other
seven companies and attacked the lower portion of the camp.
The Indians poured in a murderous fire from all directions.
Custer, his two brothers, a nephew and a brother-in-law were
All Killed
and not one of his detachment escaped. 207 men were buried
in one place and the killed are estimated at 300 with only 31
wounded. . . . The above is confirmed by other letters which say
Custer met a fearful disaster.

—EXTRA, HELENA DAILY HERALD
July 4, 1876

Custer dropped squarely into the midst of no less than ten thousand red devils and was literally torn to pieces.

—*NEW YORK TIMES*
July 6, 1876

THE FOURTH AT PHILADELPHIA

Philadelphia, July 4.–Strangers are flocking to town in a great multitude. The centennial parade of the Grand Army of the Republic, which took place this morning, was one of the most imposing demonstrations witnessed here for some time . . . At the conclusion of the music, General Hawley advanced to the stand and made the following address:

Fellow-citizens and friends of all nations:—One hundred years ago the Republic was proclaimed on this spot, and we have come together to celebrate to-day by peaceful and simple observance, our wonder, our pride, and our gratitude. These presences to-day proves the good will existing among all nations. To the strangers among us, a thousand welcomes [Applause]. To the land we love, liberty, peace, justice, prosperity and the blessings of God, to all time.

—*HELENA WEEKLY HERALD*
July 13, 1876

IT'S THE GODDAMNED mother-loving Centennial. That's what shocks them most when the dreadful news comes in on a blown-out horse just after midnight. The parade is long past and the drinking at full tilt, Main and Higgins a crush of puke and horseshit and paper wrappers. Hallelujah to the greatest nation on earth and all that. Then: *Custer's Command Cut To Pieces.* Duncan and Baird aren't the only ones to feel their guts drop.

They hear a volley of gunshots. Men all around them are muttering "Holy hell" and "Christ A-mighty," faces draining white. Near the courthouse someone screams, "Slaughter the goddamned savages!" Duncan's scalp starts to creep. The Lakota Sioux under Sitting Bull are the tribe that left no soldier alive. Not Salish, Pend d'Oreille, Nez Perce. But when did such distinctions ever matter? The "red devils" are massed across the Yellowstone not four hundred miles from Missoula. A hooker clings to her john, eyes ringed like a raccoon, screeching, "Oh my God! Oh my God!" Around him faces are purpling. Voices ricochet like bullets.

"Lynch every last one. Exterminate the vermin."

"Trust a redskin, you'll regret it. Savages will stab you in the back."

"One thing's for sure, this will embolden them. Best watch your backs."

It takes an instant for the last voice to register. That low, cool, northern drawl. The crowd had pulled them apart. Duncan lifts on his toes to be sure. It is. It's Baird. His flesh turns to ice. What does he even really know about this man?

Baird turns, blue eyes catching his; Duncan sees him flush. He starts to wade toward Duncan, but the space is gelatinous, a churning chum of arms and heads. Like salmon spawning, gaping eyes and mouths. Then Baird's at his elbow, babbling. "I don't mean you. I'm not talking about you. You're not that kind of Indian."

"What kind then?" He pushes Baird away, his blood rising—in his chest, his face, turning him even darker, more violent—more "savage." "Get your goddamn mitts off." He turns and shoulders through the white men.

"Mack! Hey—wait!" Baird sounds ashamed. He ought to. How d'you like that feeling, Robert—shame? You're welcome to it—hope it sticks in your craw. Duncan unhitches and swings up, looking with contempt on all these drunks. Full or half, redskin or breed, it makes no difference. They'd shoot him first, ask questions after.

He rides home under a moon so bright he's a target but he doesn't care. They're too drunk to even hit a barn. He'd take them out first, anyway. He's an Indian, after all: invisible and silent and deadly if that's what they want to believe. His mind clears as he rides and when he gets home to the Jocko, he wakes no one, not even the dogs. The agent's still in town; Duncan saw him passed out before the news arrived. He'll wake up hungover and mean, that much is guaranteed. This latest one, Medary, is a paranoid and bona fide lush. The twelfth, by Duncan's count, of these apostles of impotence and greed.

After the spring melt he discovered dozens of empties squirreled behind the outhouse. The fellow tries to hide the drink but can't conceal his spleen. Like every agent before him, Medary fancies himself a little king, dispensing charity to "his" grateful Indians. Like his predecessors he's continually thwarted by nonexistent cash and goods, resentment from the Natives, and—most galling of all—indifference from the "squaw men" and "half-breeds" who know he'll be gone before too long. Jack De-Mers and the McDonalds, for example. Duncan smokes on his porch and waits for the dawn. Whatever Medary does in response, he's certain to become even more unhinged.

Sure enough, overnight the coward in the man emerges. He returns raving that the bloodbath at the Little Bighorn is only the start. A bigger outbreak is imminent: the Blackfeet are coming across the divide, and his own Indians will rise up to join these demons of the plains. No one's safe, least of all him, alone in this godforsaken place. He's pasty, a tic flaring beneath one eye. Even on a good day Medary's pallor gives him away. Two weeks later the panicked telegram he sends to the Commissioner of Indian Affairs is published in the *New North-West*. In it, he predicts the "possibility of wholesale slaughter of the people of Montana" and demands two hundred troops and a military fort to control the Natives.

All this Duncan relays to the chiefs. They're not fools; they've kept their people close since the Custer attack. Some of the young men strut, eager for a chance to prove themselves in battle. But the older head men still control them. It's a powder horn, says Chief Michelle. Foolish people can spark trouble. But on one thing all agree: the agent is out of his mind. No plan is afoot to massacre the whites. The tribes worry more about what it means for the hunt—and their immediate survival.

The Indian Situation

The first great error was in recognizing the proprietary right of Indians to the soil. The right of conquest is a fixed principle among nations, and the higher civilization must rule.

We started wrong; treaties are in existence; where they have not been violently broken the government must keep faith. But no more treaties under any circumstance should be made. The Indians who violated theirs and become hostile should be whipped into perfect submission and all their treaties declared canceled. . . .

It should be made a capital offense to sell or give breech-loading guns or ammunition for the same to Indians. Traders should be allowed, only one to a post where there is an agent, be directly responsible to him and held under heavy bonds and confiscation if he violates the rules. This may appear a harsh system to establish, but it is the only way to secure peace and stop the butchery of American citizens. We are probably well into an Indian war, and the theater of it will be on the frontiers if not in the settlements of Montana . . .

—*THE NEW NORTH-WEST, Deer Lodge, M.T.*
July 14, 1876

AS SOON AS he sees the group heading his way Duncan knows what they're after. A black fog covers the fields; the hoppers chewed up half the corn before they got the smoke pots lit. So much for the winter crop. So here they are lurching through the gloom, three men beating a straight path from the agent's cabin.

Medary won't give them ammunition for the hunt, so they turn to him.

Chief Arlee leads, wearing the top hat he affects on formal occasions. He's grown fat since he agreed to move onto the reservation. Chief Michelle, more crippled than ever from an ancient fall, moves painfully beside him. Trailing slightly behind them is a taller, younger man, nose and mouth covered by a cloth. Duncan springs up, delighted despite himself.

"Who darkens my door?" He hasn't seen him in so long. "Red Horn."

A brief flash of joy lights his old friend's face and as suddenly vanishes. "Look at you," Red Horn shoots back. "I think I see a ghost."

Duncan embraces him, startled at his thinness, the sunken rings around his eyes. Everyone's threadbare these days, hunting and farming are so poor. But Red Horn looks like something chewed him up and spat him out.

The two chiefs install themselves on Duncan's bed. This time there's no friendly silence. Before Duncan even lights the pipe Michelle says, "The agent says he has no ammo."

Duncan looks at Red Horn, who nods. His eyes are bloodshot, he sees now.

"The trader at the mission won't sell it either," Michelle goes on.

"Or Jack," says Arlee.

"Though we know they have plenty." Red Horn grimaces.

"How much did you offer?"

"Twice the price." They eye him beadily.

"I don't have any either." Duncan lifts his empty hands.

Arlee chuckles. "Trade for them then. Aren't you a trader?"

"Ay-jen-see trader," says Michelle, molding his lips around the English word.

"Agency means agent. I can't go behind his back."

They only look at him with that mixture of derision and pity he's seen so many times. Poor pathetic white boy. Doesn't know how to grab what he needs.

"Come on the hunt, then," Red Horn says. "Bring cartridges for yourself. And some extra." His eyes are glittering in the strangest way and Duncan feels badly for how little he's seen him this last year. Since he moved down to the agency, his work has taken him far from the valley, and Red Horn rarely comes this way.

"You have ways to get them." Arlee nods. He's an expert himself at angling to his advantage. Since he arrived with a quarter of the Salish, the agent appointed him head chief, much to Charlo's fury, and he's wrangled what cash he could for his rump of the tribe.

"You know they'd string me up." Duncan shakes his head. "It's a hanging crime now to sell you guns or ammo."

Michelle purses his lips. "Ride with Red Horn like before. No Bostons will know."

Duncan's chest is tight. If they don't hunt, chances are they'll starve. Of course, the whites don't care—in fact, they'd welcome it. Nor is the army any keener to see Indians armed. The generals want to limit them to muskets instead of breechloaders. "I thought they said you couldn't go." He hedges, buying a bit more time.

Even before the slaughter of the Seventh Cavalry, the Indian Department had ordered its agents to keep the Natives on their reservations. The settlers and their elected officials have had enough of their "roaming" across the territory, their habits of dismantling fences and burning fields, shooting the occasional steer—their so-called depredations.

"He says we can go with soldiers like the treaty says." Medary, to his credit, at least defends them in this regard. Stevens specifically granted them this right in 1855, to hunt at will on their ancestral grounds.

"That's not the only reason he wants soldiers," Duncan says drily, and Red Horn laughs.

They stare at him, waiting. Of course he has munitions he could sell. They're cached in the woods in the Native way in a hole he dug and lined with straw. He sighs. Whether he supplies them for the hunt or fails to, one side or the other will wish him dead.

"It's a hard thing you ask." He stands. "Let me think on it." As they start to leave, he touches Red Horn's arm. "Stay a while." Red Horn shakes his head. "Later, maybe," he answers, pulling his scarf back up across his face.

No sooner have the chiefs disappeared than Duncan hears Medary bawling.

"What in the good goddamn are you up to, McDonald?" the agent shouts, striding across to his picket fence. "Don't think I don't know you're cutting some kind of deal."

Duncan looks at the man's wasted face. Jesus Christ. "Never heard of people dropping by to say hello?"

"You don't lie well."

"I don't get your meaning."

"I tell them no dice and right away they seek you out. You'd be insane to sell them ammo, though." Medary's eyes are unusually vicious and bright. "Unless you have a death wish."

"And you'll be giving them food and blankets to last the winter, I guess." He doesn't hide the acid in his tone. "You know you haven't got a damn thing to give them."

The agent's braces are down, his collar unbuttoned; he was planning on kicking back, a drink in hand. Instead he has to do his job. Fury sparks in Duncan, and a desire to see this bastard's back. But this is nothing to Medary's own ire. He leans across the porch rail and spits, "You do it and you're done.

"I'm warning you. I put up with you, I let you trade without a license.

Precisely so they will not starve. But you start selling guns, and I will march you off this reservation. Understood?"

He ought to keep his mouth shut, but he can't. "I'd like to see you try."

Medary's face is a mottled slab, his mouth a wet pink asshole, Duncan thinks as he begins to yell. "I'm sick of the lot of you," Medary snarls. "You meddlesome breeds and squaw men. You and your father and De-Mers—not one of you is even Flathead. You haven't got the right by law to live or trade here, and I'll see you go. I'll run you off."

"We were here before you." Duncan shrugs. "We'll still be here long after you're gone." He turns and goes into his house and shuts the door.

HE SPENDS THE afternoon inventorying his flour and salt and blankets. In the evening he rides out and waits until dark to return with the cartridges, four dozen boxes, forty to a box. Most everyone has a carbine. There's no light at the agent's and Duncan breathes a sigh. He starts packing, winding the boxes in blankets, spreading out the tarps. He's nearly finished when he hears the sound of footsteps sliding through the dirt outside. He throws a blanket over the remaining ammunition and opens his door a crack.

"Who's that?" he says in a menacing tone, holding the pistol he keeps on the sill for just this purpose.

"One you called a brother. Once . . ." Red Horn pitches into the sliver of light, his vest undone, stumbling as he tries to mount the step. Stinking drunk. "Ooof," he grins, clutching at the rail.

"Jesus Christ." Duncan tucks the pistol in his belt and reaches out, but Red Horn ducks to the side, brandishing the bottle before cradling it hard against his chest.

"Whoa, there. Watch yourself." Red Horn grins, a terrible sight, his teeth brown in the dim light. "Wanna drink?"

"No. And you've had plenty." Duncan lunges for his arm and manages to spin him to the door. Before he knows it, Red Horn has him pinned against the jamb. He's still incredibly strong, despite the wreck he's become. He hid it earlier but Duncan sees it now. The man he knew is gone, replaced by this hideous slobbering creature, simultaneously bloated and starving.

"Big man now." Red Horn's voice is hard. He pokes him with the neck of the bottle. "Big whiteboy chief."

"Get inside," Duncan hisses, glancing at the houses on Agency Square. They grapple for a long moment, silent but for their wheezing, until Red Horn collapses suddenly like a heap of sticks.

"Poof! You disappeared." His eyes seem momentarily clear. He spins his hand, watching it rotate with a fixed expression. "No more hunting, no visits. Nothing." Sadly he shakes his head.

"I've missed them too." Duncan pries the glass from his hand. Still the reproach strikes deep. "You could have hauled my ass up to the mountains." Red Horn's look is so mournful Duncan's not surprised when he starts to cry. Somewhere in that welling shame is some that belongs to him. "Sssh," he says. "It'll be all right."

"You say so," Red Horn spits with a flash of venom. "What do you know. You're just like the rest."

Turning his back, chasing white girls, white riches, white phantoms. Duncan sees how it could look. His stomach burns. "What can I say." He gets him in the door and scoops some water, holds it to the dry cracked lips. "Except I'm sorry."

Red Horn drinks, eyes unblinking on Duncan's face, obedient as a child.

"Brother," he murmurs as his head drops back. By the time Duncan has scooped up more he's fast asleep.

Before dawn Duncan rises from a fitful rest and tiptoes to Arlee's. "Delivery," he hisses. Arlee's brother springs up as if he was waiting; together they move the packs. "Get them out of here pronto," Duncan instructs, and returns to his own place. Red Horn's still passed out and he busies himself with the rest of his preparations. He's due to take Maggie to Missoula to pick out some fabric. He'd planned on riding up to the ranch and returning with his father's gig, but Red Horn complicates things. Watching his chest rise and fall, wind whistling through his ragged lips, he's filled suddenly with rage. Not at Red Horn, but at the drug, the numbing and seductive stopper for their pain that white men pump into the reservation. It's illegal to sell an Indian liquor, but that never stopped them. He knows they run it down from the British Possessions, Jack and his brother Alec and probably even the agent—any number of others besides.

By the time he's got Red Horn in the wagon it's light enough to bang on Medary's door. He looks green in the gills and this gives Duncan some satisfaction. "I'm taking this fellow back up to the mission." He nods with his chin.

"Drunk?" The agent's eyes flick toward the wagon.

"Easy enough to get, as I'm sure you're aware."

Medary passes a hand across his face and nods.

"It needs to stop." A pure flame of vengeance cuts through Duncan. "You know who it is. You handed them a trading license."

The fool doesn't even realize he's standing on thin ice. Nobody's allowed to sell liquor on the reservation—no one can even possess it, not even the agent. God only knows where Red Horn got it—entirely likely from Medary's own stash.

CHAPTER 6

RED HORN'S WIFE spits through the open lodge flap. With a sigh Duncan hauls him to his parents' cabin. Surely they and his sisters won't turn him away. His father leaps to his feet, then smacks his son on the back of the head. "You give him this poison." He glares at Duncan.

"He doesn't need me to find it."

Still he knows how he looks in his dark coat and trousers, hair cut close beneath his hat. He's even wearing a tie. To keep trouble away, he rides in his white man disguise.

It makes his grandmother nearly double over laughing when he gets to Post Creek. "Ha! Fancy pants!" She came in the spring to live with her daughter and man and take these children to hand.

"Not you too." Duncan makes it a great big joke, although it stings. However he presents himself, he's a target.

His grandmother's lodge is hung with skins and feathered staffs and filled with objects held in careful bundles and drawers, each object with its own story. She dispatches his little brothers with a clap of her hands, and they leave unwillingly, tugging at Duncan.

"You're looking well, anyway," he tells her.

She points to the boys outside. "From chasing those little monsters."

He's always amazed at the way life streams from her like sunshine pouring through a hole in the clouds. Margaret's face is battered like an old copper pot, but her teeth are strong and white, her hair in braided loops as bright as the hammered silver discs she wears around her neck. They were a gift from her second husband; he won them at cards or in a race, she can't recall. She's outlived them both, Bonaparte and the rascal Baptiste, she laughs. She has no further use for men—except, perhaps, she told her daughter slyly, this Angus and their boys. Her son-in-law treats her with the reverence she deserves.

Duncan thinks she came mainly to ensure they were all raised properly nimíipuu. She's interested in who these children are. There are things they must learn, she says, pulling the younger ones to her, holding them by the jaw, investigating their power to resist her eyes. Each is summoned, prodded, interrogated, and released like a fledgling back into the wild.

"Everything good?" she asks, holding his own chin now, patting the rug beside her.

"Same as ever. I scratch out what I can."

"No nimíipuu is a chicken in the yard." Her expression is dismissive.

He could tell her that none of them trust him entirely. Neither the Indians nor the whites. To no one is his friendship uncomplicated. But he knows what she'll say. He tried it once years ago, whining about some broken thing or other. "Don't cry over it," she snapped. "There are worse things to cry over."

"Things are tense, though. The Bostons are trigger-happy. It's not safe to move around."

"When was it ever safe?" She tilts her head. "I've seen more killed than you've seen alive."

"No need to tempt fate, even so."

At this she scratches her nose and smiles. Fate is her special province. The first weeks she was in the valley, she gathered them around and gave them their Nez Perce names. He doesn't know if John and Christina had theirs; he supposes so. She stood for long moments, her hand on each head, eyes closed, communing. He can't remember anyone else's, but his is *Tim-mina il-pilp*. Red Hart. "Fleet and dashing away." She grinned wickedly. "Flashing your white tail."

He leaves her lodge and goes to the house in search of Maggie. Annie's married now too, to a nimíipuu man. They live on the reservation in Idaho Territory near Kaix-kaix-Koose. Maggie has taken up the role of jollying their father, keeping him humming the way Christina did, then Annie. Now she barrels across the hall, nearly knocking him over in her excitement.

"I've been waiting for HOURS," breathlessly she exclaims.

"Get your things and give me a minute. I haven't seen Mother or Father."

Their mother is on the porch turning cornhusks into a bag. "You didn't sleep," she says, reaching up to pat his cheek.

"Not enough," he agrees.

"You worry too much." She resumes her weaving, face placid. A change has come over her since Margaret arrived, Duncan thinks. Her family is together at last; the village on the Clearwater, too, is at peace, safe inside those soyapo lines. She's even thinking of sending the younger boys there next summer, though Duncan's not so sure that's a good idea.

"The agent is out for my scalp."

"Then stay here." For a moment he thinks she's right, they'd all be better off retreating from the white man's hate onto the reservation. Then he chides himself. He's mostly white, goddamn it.

"Maggie would kill me." He kisses her on the cheek. "Need anything from the store?"

She looks at him impishly. "Your father keeps me well supplied."

His latest gift is a newfangled beater for eggs, a metal whirligig that she laughed at, then marveled at, and now keeps in a special case. When the children are naughty, she takes it out and pursues them, cranking madly and laughing at the wind it spits in their faces.

His father is upstairs in his study, doubtless writing another in his endless stream of letters demanding justice and fair play. "Mail call," Duncan says when he enters and sees he's right. Who is it now—the President or General Sherman, or some Army officer Angus once knew? His father looks up and unhooks his spectacles and rubs his eyes.

"Fripperies and fabrics, more like." They embrace and Duncan sits for a moment, though he can hear Maggie whining "I'm ready" below.

"I hear the hunt is held up," his father says.

"Arlee asked for an escort, but no one will sell them the ammo."

Angus gives him a penetrating look. "Including you, I hope."

"I watch my back."

His father harrumphs. "And here I go pledging there'll be no trouble."

"You know damn well the trouble doesn't start with them."

Angus nods. "Keep yourself clear of it, anyhow."

Duncan just looks at him. "How exactly am I supposed to do that?"

"Like I did. Head high, take no side."

"Easy for you to say." A bitter laugh breaks from him. "Jesus, Father."

"Why on earth not?"

He's raising his eyebrows in that imperious way he has, and something in Duncan snaps.

"Because to them I'm a red." Can't the man at least grasp that?

"You're not. You're half Scots."

"You never want to hear it, but the Indian in me is all these bastards see."

For once his father is silenced. A peculiar look glazes his face.

"I'd better be going." Duncan holds out his hand. "There's something you wanted sent down?"

Angus is still regarding him fixedly. "We'll talk about this later," he says, shaking himself. He slips a note into a leather pouch. "For the judge. Just leave it at the courthouse."

THE WHOLE WAY to Missoula his sister gaily chatters. She has a new bonnet for which she needs some lace. She'll sew vests of worsted for her brothers for the winter; their aunt Angelique has shown her some fancy stitches. Duncan nods absently. Maggie doesn't notice. She's too thrilled to be going into town; she hardly ever gets to go, she says, dark eyes lively in her narrow face. After two dusty hours he hitches the gig in front of Bonner & Eddy and buys them both a juice straight from the cooler on the counter. Andy Hammond raises a hand in greeting from the storeroom and Maggie starts to swoon before the fabric. So Hammond's back from wherever he went; they heard he'd gone west to scout for timberland. He's a man with big eyes, like Jack. Duncan ducks out so he won't have to chat.

It's a beautiful August day, white clouds sailing like frigates across the big blue sky. Maybe he should ride away too, head someplace where they don't know him. The door to the saloon next to Bonner's is open and he's angry all over again at the stink and waste of that drink. What future does a man like Red Horn have if he can't hunt? What future is there on a reservation anyway? Just so time will do them all in, as Angus told Father Ravalli? Duncan remembers his father's letter then and crosses to the courthouse steps. Bitterness eats at him—that even his own father can't see the truth of things. He sits up there in his nice house, his white skin, and writes and writes.

Duncan should give the letter to the clerk, but a malicious twinge impels him otherwise. He sits instead and slides it from the pouch.

H.B. House

23 Aug. 1876

Hon'ble & Dear Judge Knowles

I hear the Army and most particularly Genl Sheridan will not allow the Indians to use any but muskets on their hunts, in fear of them putting better weapons to some other purpose. This is non-sense as far as the confederated tribes of Missoula County are concerned. Try speaking to the agent and you will hear words and no action and meantime the harvest moon pales. I think the government takes a foul advantage of the Indian here. They have never asked for anything but to be let alone in their lands. That Sioux business is bad but the animus of the Montana papers only makes it worse. Let the Indians of this territory but know that the farmers are out to exterminate them, and Montana would be an entire wasteland in a few months.

One of the old bloods and most eloquent savage of the west was my friend and a close relative of my wife and he it was who said they should have risen up against us long ago. Let them hunt, and properly, as they will not sit by and idly starve. From your lofty spot on the territorial bench, dear sir, is there nothing better than can be done?

Sincerely,

A. McDonald

Post-script: I forgot to advise Mrs. Knowles to anoint the skin of that fox with something such as rum or camphor to help preserve it as its ills will come out in this warm weather if not.

DUNCAN READS THE thing again, two, three times, his chest tight.

Most eloquent savage. A relative of my wife.

His father's handwriting too is eloquent—as eloquent as the savage he doesn't name. But then who needs names, if they're all just savages?

His heart beats erratically. He rubs his eyes, the grit of his sleepless nights, these hate-filled days, stuffs the screed back in the pouch. His father's own wife, his own children—Duncan, too, is a savage, then, half-savage anyway. Angus should have sent this crap with someone else—someone white. He laughs harshly to himself.

"Not that kind of Indian." Baird ran after him, too, face all white and stricken.

They have no goddamned idea.

Maggie sees him across the way when she pokes her head out and stamps her feet for him to come. He's the one with the cash, after all, the greenbacks that make their sick little world go round. He rises heavily and comes across. There's a clot of low-looking fellows by the bar but he pays them no notice. He peels off a few bills for her packets tied up in string and then they're done. He unties the team and is holding the bundles while Maggie clambers up when one of them yells "Hey, Bonner served an Injun!"

His sister freezes. The hooligans pitch toward the rail, one brandishing a bottle. "A little squaw in lady clothes."

"Why don't you take your red ass home—"

The second man breaks off as Duncan's fist connects with his front teeth. He splits another lip and kicks the first man in the balls and then he hears glass shatter and perceives the jagged bottle end approach. He can hear Maggie screaming as he twists and jabs to grab the arm that holds it. The man who touches her is dead, he thinks with great lucidity. "Say it again," he's shouting. "I'll rip your filthy tongue out." His mother's face appears, John letting fly that arrow. The glinting murderous glass is still inches from his cheek and he's being kicked now in the ribs. He drops and rolls beneath the wagon, coming out the other side.

"Sit down, Maggie," he orders, his sister ignoring him, standing and yelling her lungs out. "Help! Somebody help!"

Then the barman's outside, yelling at Tom and Art and God knows who to cut it out, calm down and for Christ's sake put that bottle down. Duncan stands, his face sticky where some bastard nicked it. Over their heads he sees Hammond standing there outside his store, just watching like it's a goddamned rodeo performance.

"Say it again and you're dead," Duncan spits at the ugly knot of them, hauling up onto the driving board and jerking Maggie hard so she sits down. He lifts the Sharps he keeps on the floorboard and stands looking down on them. "Got that?" Nobody says a word but they don't have to. He knows exactly what they're thinking.

HE KEEPS TO himself the whole next week. The hunters depart with some soldiers rustled from Fort Shaw to keep the peace. What Maggie tells his parents Duncan doesn't know. She wishes they were never born, she cried onto his shoulder on the long ride home. Life is only misery for half-breeds. He remembers how she said she'd never marry and suspects she's right. Indian or white, men largely choose their own. There are enough white women now, besides. It stirs up memories of Lydia, her ripe, deceitful mouth.

He takes off for a number of days deep in the woods. He eats berries, fish; he sleeps beneath the stars. On the last day of August he returns along the river to the agency, lying listless on its little rise, its mill along the Jocko broken as it's been for half a year. A fiction of a town is Agency Square, mill and smith and doctor, agent's house—not a stitch of it remotely fit for purpose. Arriving at his own cabin he's startled to discover a young woman sitting there. A Pend d'Oreille girl wearing her best dress, a shawl wrapped tightly around her. She stands. "It's Red Horn," she says quietly. "He needs help." Duncan looks more closely: her heart-shaped face is familiar.

"Who are you?" he asks, dropping his gear.

"Quil-see. His sister."

Ah. He remembers now. She was littler then, this sister. Red Sleep.

"What's wrong with him?"

"He's sick." She has bright eyes and a pointed little chin; she must be sixteen, seventeen. She squares her shoulders in the same stubborn way as her fool of a brother.

"How long have you been here?"

She waves her hand, impatiently he thinks. "A day. I could wait."

He gives her food and water and listens as she tells him the elders won't let Red Horn stay unless he mends his ways. He's been whipped but it hasn't helped. "He has nobody else." Her eyes are solemn and shaped like teardrops.

Duncan thinks for a long time that night as she sleeps in one corner. In the morning he tells her he'll come in day or two, and she presses his hands and climbs on a little pinto. He can't do it alone. He sends a boy to Frenchtown to find Baird. God knows he won't go there himself. Nor is he all that keen to call on Baird. But he doesn't see any alternative.

Robert has done nothing but apologize the few times they've crossed paths since the Custer affair. Not that it's really helped. Trust is a coin that once spent is not easily recovered. Duncan is aware that in some part of himself Baird loves him as he once loved Baird. But the truth is Baird can't see beyond his own white skin. It's painfully clear to Duncan now that he is a mere honorary member of this privileged and superior tribe, the whites. At any moment this privilege can be revoked.

Baird is happy to help, and that's all Duncan needs to hear. They ride up to the mission and find Red Horn. He's all bone; they gather him up like firewood. He resists until Duncan pulls his forehead to his own and hisses, "You'll do as I say, or never see the inside of this lodge again." They ride bareback up into the mountains, Red Horn in front, slumped against Duncan's chest. They bring a spade, poles, some hides, up Post Creek to the lake where Duncan first saw the trail up Coul-hi-cat, the Jagged Mountain, nearly a decade ago. He can't believe it's been that long, so many summers and winters and hunts, yet here they are, three men laboring alone up the mountainside. It strikes him as funny, the endless sameness of life, for all its storm and bluster.

They scramble above the tree line as the horses drip foam. He won't leave them to be stolen below. He searches out grooves in the granite, semi-horizontal pleats that lead steadily upward, around and around the upper reaches of the double peak. Sweat pours from them in the heat, the harsh glare off the rocks, and Red Horn moans. Duncan whispers in his ear: *the time is now*. The disease has not yet utterly wasted him. He holds him with his left arm, the reins in his right, his body both prison and embrace. They struggle up and drop suddenly into the bowl between the two horns of the mountain, a sheet of ice nine thousand feet above the valley floor. Between the pointed schist of the southern peak and the lip of the glacier there's a band of crumbled rock and gray-green vegetation and they make for this and start to dig.

They build the sweat lodge as Duncan's grandmother has instructed. From time to time as they climbed, Red Horn heaved hard and emptily, emitting dribbles of bile. He's sticky, glassy, dead-eyed as they strip him and roll him inside. Now they'll burn wood and boil water and wait for as long as it takes. They've hauled up what wood they found along the trail; they chip ice from the sheet and melt it. The day dies, the night passes, and in the morning, Baird goes down for more wood. The scrub here is oily and burns badly, except in ceremony, resinous and sweet. In any case Duncan uses no herbs, no prayers. Just the heat and the steam.

Every hour or so they haul him out and cool him down, rubbing his arms and chest with a rag dipped in cool water. The first night Red Horn strikes out at him, cursing in his language, spitting in his face. One hand snakes out and grabs Duncan's hair, jerking his head back, but Duncan just holds there, speaking softly as he would to a flailing colt. He's better than this; he's a hunter, a warrior; they will stay by his side. Baird, alerted by the scuffle, sticks his head in and Duncan signals with his eyes. They get a spoonful of broth between his lips, tap patiently with the spoon on his teeth until his jaw and his grip release and he falls back. They let him sleep, take turns watching, and sometime later they build back up the fire and the steam. They pour water into him and watch it come streaming back out, sluicing out the poisons, the impurities, carving deltas down his arms and chest.

The air at the peak is so pure Duncan can feel it cleansing his own head and heart. It's more than likely that Red Horn has been here before, as a boy on the verge of his manhood. Now Duncan asks the wide sky that he be rebirthed once more. He does not pray; he only gives his friend back to the earth, the sky, the forces that made him in and of this place. Let his soul be at rest; let him find his true home once more. He thinks of the years beyond number, the people who have climbed and crossed these peaks, sat on the blue ice of this glacier, this rim of rock, listening to this wind, like him. There is a hawk; there, unbelievably, a pair of yellow butterflies, mating in the air. Even this high up there is greenery and life.

At sunset it's still possible to love this world. Red Horn shivers, but his eyes are clearer. He takes some broth that stays down. They wrap him in a blanket and prod and push him up out of the lodge, where he stands feebly, supported on either side. They survey the darkening teal of the sky, the bands of orange and pink to the west behind the Red-Topped Mountains, the snippets of first stars, and Red Horn begins to cry. They hold him as the grief washes out of his heart through his eyes. Duncan, too, feels changed. A cool, calm resolve blows through him, powerful and light. They are of and from this air, this soil. It gives them strength. No interloper, white or drunk or both, can wrest away this birthright. Not leastways without a fight.

CHAPTER 7

SOME WEEKS LATER Red Horn's sister appears again at his door. This time he hears her leap off and patter up to rap with gusto on the doorframe. Her face when he opens is bright; she seems close to bursting, holding something behind her back.

"Whoa," he smiles, but before he can say more, she's rising on tiptoe—this Quil-see is short, though compact—smiling widely and pressing something against his chest.

"In thanks." She steps back and watches him, and he's amused and also a little embarrassed at the intensity with which she regards him. He unwinds the fabric and a bridle falls into his hands. His breath catches as he carefully lifts it. It's heavy, entirely encrusted with beadwork in an elegant pattern of repeating diamonds. The edges of each diamond are formed of red-dyed quills; in the center of each, a moose tooth hangs. The ivory glistens and clacks as he turns it, marveling. This gleaming decoration covers every strap, stitched to the hide; the reins she made of bison hair, twisted and then braided.

"You like it?" He looks up amazed and sees that this girl too is shining. "The four points," she explains, "are the four directions that you ride."

He's never seen a piece of tack more fine. Her hands are deft, remarkable. For the first time he looks at her closely. Quil-see looks boldly back and he can feel the blush creep on his hairline. She's an attractive young woman, her cheekbones high and round like pommels, her eyes and eyebrows dark against that shining skin, a striking shade of russet gold.

"You didn't have to do this—" he says finally. "It must have taken—"

"The whole summer. Yes." Her lips part, pleased. "It's the least thing, for a man's life, don't you think?"

Impulsively she darts forward and puts her lips to his cheek. Then she bounces back and laughs. He's laughing too, startled but hardly displeased—with barely time to call his thanks before she's back up on her pinto. "Stay a minute," he calls, but she shakes her head. Her teeth are a flash of light, her face with its small, pointed chin exactly like a heart. He watches, still surprised, then thoughtful, as she goads her mare to a gallop and disappears along the Jocko.

THE MISSION VILLAGE hardly changes and yet it changes utterly. Here are the same scuffed tracks between the cabins and lodges arranged in a ring around the church; the yellow owl clover pushing up along the fences; the mill and plot the Sisters of Providence planted years ago. Even so it feels different. The white church looks smaller as the industrious Jesuits expand. There are boarding schools in St. Ignatius now, one for the Native boys and one for the girls: two huge buildings with stained glass and ornate roofs that look like arks left stranded on the valley floor. A few months ago they hauled in a big new printing press to produce the gospel in Salish and Kalispel. Antille, the second chief of the Pend d'Oreille, has moved his large family into three side-by-side houses, halfway between the creek and the nuns' bunkhouse.

It was at Antille's that Duncan left Red Horn to recover, under the eye of the man who controls the Native police. As many rings around his friend as he could build, he built. None of it's worth a thing if Red Horn doesn't believe in a future better than the hell where he's been. Antille and Red Horn's family are the rope that must hold him now. All Duncan did was toss him back like a fish returned to his home water.

It's enough to see his smile when Duncan lifts the latch. Since Red Horn came back he's been put to work making halters and lariats and girths. A family affair, apparently, thinks Duncan; his own gelding wears the resplendent new bridle. Red Horn's slim fingers, like his sister's, are skilled at braiding the long chin bison hairs. He sets the work aside and rises to embrace Duncan. He'd never complain that it's women's work, he says. He's happy just to wake up every day. He's quieter, less jocular than he used to be, but he's alive.

"Empty-handed," Red Horn tsks. "I expected better."

"I keep secrets, you should know that." Duncan half-turns and pulls at the rope threaded through his belt loops that is in fact a snake of prime tobacco. "Nothing but snoops and beggars, if I come with packs." He drops the loop in Red Horn's lap.

They go out into the November day, which is cold and blustery, the north wind making tumbleweeds of the bulbous clouds. They have a wide view of the village and the corrals where Duncan's left his red-gold horse to mingle with the others. As they smoke they compare the heart, the wind, the power of the various animals—this roan, that yellow, that gray one with black spots.

"Which will you take?" Duncan asks.

Red Horn doesn't immediately answer.

Antille told Duncan the last time they spoke that he'd discuss the hunt with Red Horn. Shame has kept him from rejoining his fellows, or perhaps he doesn't trust himself. But it can only do him good to ride out with the band, thinks Duncan.

"I'd go if I could," he adds.

"I spoke about it with my father and uncle." Red Horn's lips worry at one another. "I don't want to hold them back."

"When have you ever held them back?" Duncan shakes his head. "You need a partner, that's all, someone you can trust." His cousins were the ones who led him down the garden path. "Antille will put you where you can't get into trouble."

"So he says."

"Then you should go. So the question remains—which one will you take?"

Red Horn's teeth flash white, a flicker of his old mischief.

"Thought I'd take yours. He's running to fat, like you are."

"Bastard," Duncan says softly. "You want to meet me at the creek?" He grinds his knuckles into Red Horn's crown.

"I'd beat you still." Red Horn has him by the bicep, then, squeezing tightly, a funny light in his eyes.

"What the hell?"

"She's right." Red Horn chuckles. "Says you're hard in the head but good at heart."

"Who?"

"You know who."

"Quil-see?"

"You never see what's right in front of you. Always trying to be something else."

Duncan feels shame then for the way he neglected his truest friend, running after these white women and white men.

"Nobody wants a mongrel, though."

"Ha." Red Horn lets go of his arm. "Your head is truly sick, you know that? Some count your drops of blood. I count the times you stood beside me. Blood has nothing to do with it, my brother."

Fleetingly Duncan recalls the bear who scared two small boys witless in the woods. "We're not getting any younger," he admits.

"You're not allowed to give up." Red Horn slaps him on the back. "Don't you remember what you said?"

He doesn't. Red Horn breathes it in his ear. "The only excuse for giving up, my friend—you said—is death."

SHE MAKES HIM feel alive. That's it—that's all it is. So simple. When in the middle of a winter day he stops to see if she is free to take a walk, she dazzles him with her audacity, her joie de vivre. She'd rather ride. "Let's race," she says, "up the canyon to the lake, and take some food, too, for a picnic." Just seventeen and yet already she is wise in how to live life to the fullest, suck each drop out of the days.

Louise Schumtah, Red Sleep, streaks before him, looking wild-eyed when he draws abreast, pumping her pinto hard. He watches her out the corner of his eye. The hands that stitch so delicately grip the reins and he finds himself imagining those fingers on his skin. The shore is rimmed with ice; she winks and pulls a line of gut out, throws the hook in. They squat and wait and within minutes she is pulling in the trout—one then another and he makes a fire to cook them on. They lick their fingers and discuss the sheep they see high up the crags. She thinks an arrow is the surer way—for the shot, if missed, will only scatter them. He tells her that her bridle is a marvel he doesn't deserve. He'd like to give her something just as fine. She flirts with him then, with a wicked look. "We'll see," she says. "First let's see if you float or sink!"

And off she dashes, garments flying as she taunts him, standing naked at the edge of that cold lake, her compact body full and firm. And she dives in. She's testing him, of course; he strips as rapidly and runs right to the edge and knifes his body in. The cold is brilliant, scything, and they gasp and laugh as they both surface. Quil-see pops out, dark head sleek and silky and he swims toward her, puts his arms around her body, churning fiercely with his feet. They splash and nip and dive and chase each other like wild creatures till the cold has penetrated to the bone and they must flee the water for the shore. He gazes at her, one hand holding hers as they stand dripping, freezing—burning with the joy of life. The lining of his coat is sable and he lays her in it. She pulls her own of rabbit tight around his shoulders and they start what he is certain is a lifetime's worth of loving in the shelter of the fur.

DUNCAN SETS OFF with his younger brother Archie for Clear Creek the following June. He's taking the boy to his elders at Kaix-kaix-Koose, as he and John and Christina were taken years before. It's been ages since he saw his mother's young cousin Looking Glass, even longer since he saw Almost Asleep. They were all boys and young men together, he tells Archie as they ride.

This brother looks so much like John. At fourteen he's thoughtful and quiet, but even so he makes Duncan feel old. He's nearly twice his age and had begun to think good things had passed him by. Until this life unexpectedly ignited. He rides down the wide new road to the Bitterroot, smiling to himself.

Quil-see. Red Sleep. Louise. He sees her heart-shaped face, and feels her soft warm hand in his the whole time as he rides. When she thanked him, he saw a love and loyalty to something larger than her brother or herself that moved him. "What's ours is yours," she said, and he had cracked wide open. Everything he does now feels so natural, as if he's wakened from a sleep. His place is in these mountains and valleys, with the people who were born here, as he was. When he went hunting that winter Duncan shot a ram and brought her family the golden-yellow horns. Over many nights he sawed and sanded, cleaned and purified them in the fire.

He gave one oiled and shining vessel to her father, one to her mother. He pledged to fill her life with plenty. When he returns, they'll stand together for the blessing: Duncan McDonald, Quil-see Schumtah and their baby in her swelling belly.

His eyes are closed to better smell the pines, the bitterroot, the moss and water welling. He could go on like this forever—except that someone's tugging, shouting in his ear: "Duncan, Duncan! Wasn't that the trail?"

He shakes himself and laughs and they backtrack to take the Lolo trail westward through the canyon into Idaho Territory. The journey should take five days or so. Each has a bow and arrows. Your first challenge, he told Archie: see if we can catch enough to eat.

The trail's cluttered with downed timber, rough enough in places they have to lead the horses. As they climb, the canyon opens onto sweet green pockets he recalls from long before. All around the land and air roar with life. The noise is constant, thick, fecund, whirring: the rhythmic beating of wings, staccato and slow laid over one another, pushing and pounding the currents. The buzzing of insects in tall grasses, the large animals audible by their crashing, the snapping of deadfall and sighing of leaves as they pass. Only the fish are silent but not really, for as they crest the range the fish, too, leap and splash in the bright water, showering the surface with a patter, then falling back. And in this whole buzzing, roaring, clicking wealth of life, he and his brother, too, move and make sounds heard by every other living creature.

At night while Archie guts fish or skins a hare or, one lucky night, a wolverine, Duncan builds the fire. He smokes and points out the constellations and Archie draws them in his little notebook, noting the names. "I'll make a map of the sky," he says earnestly, "and all the stories of the stars." When the boy sleeps Duncan pokes at the embers and thinks of Sin-ye-le-min. Life can shift so suddenly. He was so angry before; now he feels invincible. Even his father's failures rankle less. One day he'll take him to task for his views, but not yet. They've been busy, driving the agent from his stinking nest. Medary sued Jack for selling liquor and Jack stung him right back, got him indicted for theft by the grand jury. It gave Duncan enormous pleasure to translate for the chiefs on that occasion. Arlee blasted the agent the same way he'd blasted him in a letter to the President: *Eighteen years and still no government school. Such an agent, led by the nose by Jesuits, we do not want. He's a thief and a drunk.* And so on. The Commissioner ordered him recalled. Twelve agents in all since 1855. The next will be there when he gets back, Lord help them all.

On the western slope they start to see signs they're not alone. Marks on trees: lines and triangles and arrows, the secret language of the people as they move. *Here three lodges camp, beyond two rivers. Below the waterfall, a cache.* And to his practiced eye some branches snapped within a week or so. Even so they encounter no one and it strikes him as odd. It's still camas season; they ought to be digging someplace near. Even when the trail flattens on the north side of the river, nothing. Just when he thinks he's taken them the wrong way, they spy the village and his chest relaxes. It looks smaller, but then everything does: the lodges set back in a meadow just across the water, the gardens and corrals he recalls on either side of the stream that feeds into the Kaix-kaix-Koose, which the Yankees call the Clearwater.

They splash across and up into a strange calm. The herd is gone; only a handful of lodges have fires. Nor does he see the chief's lodge, which was his father Flint Necklace's before him.

"Too late," a voice says, and they crane right and left, accompanied by soft dry laughter. The man who speaks is so wizened and brown he melts into the hide of his lodge. "Looking Glass is gone to Split Rock."

Archie looks at his brother, disappointment on his face. Duncan drops his reins and approaches the elder.

"I'm Red Hart, Kitalah's son." The old man nods and makes a sign of greeting.

"I see you."

Duncan knows better than to launch in with questions. He sees an open space up the creek and asks with his eyes for permission to pasture the horses and lay their bedrolls there. They draw water and make fire and after a short while a few others emerge. Only elders and some pregnant women have remained.

It's like this, the man explains. The whole band has gone down to the lake on the prairie. A great powwow, he says, one final time to bid farewell to that powerful place. Duncan frowns. His informant's face is grave. White Bird and Joseph and Toohoolhotoze and Bald Head have bowed to the White Father, he says, along with their bands. They'll leave their homelands and come onto this reservation. Even now, as the sun falls in the west, they should be coming, Looking Glass with his cousins and friends, the rest of the nimíipuu, on the trail to Lapwai.

The news sits like a stone on them both, and the old man sighs. "The soldiers require it. Hearts bleed, but there's no other way."

Duncan has never been to Lamotta, the canyon of his mother's Salmon River people, where Eagle from the Light once led, and White Bird now is chief. Nor to the lower reaches of the Clearwater, or the Wallowa Valley, the ancestral homelands of the other bands who refused to sign the thief treaty that stripped them of their land. So why have they capitulated now?

Only Looking Glass can tell him, he supposes. He tells Archie the fun will begin in a few days, and in the meantime, they must make the best of it. The dell is a gentle place, and they are weary from their travels. They'll rest and see. His little brother busies himself, humming softly as he collects plants, feathers, bits of antler, arranging them in dioramas he then draws. Duncan smiles to recognize the kind of boy that he himself had been and volunteers his strong body to gather wood and fix fences for the old aunties left behind to tend the gardens.

Two days pass and on the third there's a thundering sound of many horses, and they spring to their feet. Around the high knob of boulders at the meeting of the waters the riders swirl like a current rushing the opposite way, scores of men and women in a bright mass of color. They ride in and he sees his cousin on a white horse at the column's head, fringe flowing from his shoulders, a black stovepipe hat on his sharply sculpted head. "Looking Glass," he whispers to Archie. They stand at attention as the cavalcade sweeps into the village. The chief looks neither left nor right and the expression on his face raises the hair on the back of Duncan's neck. He has never seen such a look: more than rage or fury— thunderous, murderous, he'd almost say.

Duncan waits to be summoned and when it comes, he girds himself. They've always dealt cordially, but coolly.

"The trader comes," says the chief to his men with the faintest smile. "Hold onto your things."

"I come empty-handed." Duncan holds both out. "Except for my brother."

They chuckle but the meeting still feels strained.

"You pick a bad time." Looking Glass holds out a hand and someone passes him a pipe. He lights it, looking all the while at Duncan with his strange light eyes. He's angry still; his neck is taut.

"So I've heard."

"You heard wrong." His eyes glitter. Smoke rises around his face and Duncan keeps his mouth shut, waiting. "Tell him," the chief says.

Another warrior leans forward. "White Bird's young men made war the night before we were supposed to go." He glances at the chief. "The son of Eagle Robe and some others went wildly to kill whites. Now blood is spilled. We wanted no part of it, so we left."

"I stand for peace." The chief's braids jerk like angry snakes. "White Bird must pay."

Duncan looks between them. "When did this happen?"

"Three, four nights ago. Already soldiers are chasing White Bird back to his canyon."

"And Joseph? The others?"

"Like us, he refused to fight." The other warrior snorts. "They called us women when we wouldn't join their battle."

"They'll be slaughtered by the soldiers, and for what?" Looking Glass looks less angry now. His thoughts seem turned inward.

Duncan knows little of this territory or its politics. "But they were planning to move onto this reservation?" he asks. That in itself is surprise enough.

"The soldier chief showed them the rifle in a peaceful council. That's why the young men broke." Looking Glass almost growls it. To show the rifle—bring weapons—in a peaceful negotiation breaks every rule. This much Duncan knows. He'd like to know more, ask why the chiefs agreed to move, but this isn't the moment. That autumn of the bear fifteen years before flashes back into his mind—that dangerous autumn when Flint Necklace let no one cross the river, either. "It sounds bad," he murmurs.

"We're safe here." Looking Glass speaks firmly. "We have no quarrel with them here, inside their lines."

Duncan hopes he's right. But something in that gruff assurance makes him wonder, as he goes to sleep that night, just how well his cousin grasps the white man's world.

THEY SLIP EASILY into the rhythm of the village. They start bringing in the crops and Duncan figures he'll wait to head back with the small group that still hunts on the plains. He installs Archie with the family of Almost Asleep, who's entirely different from what he remembers: alert and a hard worker with a family to support. His old friend's shy, at first. Then one morning they go upriver and strip off and dive into the freezing pool below the cliff and the shock of it's so exhilarating it's as if they're boys again. They grin and say "bear brothers" and Almost Asleep tells Duncan to put his bedroll by his lodge. Duncan thanks him but says he sleeps better beside the stream. He thinks of Quil-see and wishes he could send word that he's well. In fact, she'll get news even sooner than he thinks.

The fourth morning after the band's return he awakens to the happy smell of frying meat. Dawn's breaking and the birds are belting out a chorus; he lies there feeling the warmth in his veins. These smells are tickling his nose this Sunday morning from the chief's own lodge. A few people left the night before to worship in the Dreamer church downstream, but Looking Glass is not among them. Duncan hears horses and voices and pulls aside his tarp to look. Five armed white men are pulled up across the creek, two of them uniformed soldiers. Swiftly he tugs on his trousers. The elegant warrior whose name is Bird Alighting emerges from the chief's lodge and walks with purpose toward the creek. Duncan can't hear what they're saying but one of the men prods Bird Alighting's chest with the butt of his rifle, and he knows this will be serious. He stands, glancing across to the hill behind the men. He sees glints of sun on metal higher up, a line of blue and brown half-hidden in the trees.

Intently, with no hint of speed to betray him, he walks toward the chief's lodge. Archie is his only thought. His mother will kill him if anything happens to that boy. People are stirring, looking up from fires, eyes fearful. There's a general sense of shrinking, falling back. He shakes his brother to wake him and hisses at Almost Asleep: "Soldiers! Be careful." And tows Archie behind him, circling behind the lodge of Looking Glass. Bird Alighting has an old man with him now, not the chief—the same old man Duncan and Archie met the first day. Old Kalowet, waving a white shirt tied to a stick. "Stay on your side," Bird Alighting is saying, his face drawn. "We want no war."

Almost the minute he says it a shot rings out. They see the puff from the rifle, held by a man in a plaid shirt. Settler not soldier, Duncan registers instantly as he drags Archie down. The group of mounted men wheels and rides back uphill and in another instant the whole line of rifles up above them is alive and shooting fire. Bullets smash into earth all around him, slap and sting on the lodge skins like hail. He hears a man cry out, then another, sees one of the herders fall. The soldiers are boiling down the hill now and Duncan grabs Archie by the waist and they run flat out toward the horses, clutching at any mane they can and swinging up. "Stay low," he hisses. Behind them they hear screams and the bellowing of aggressors as they pound into the village. He glances back and sees people scattering, fleeing with their children up the river for their lives. The soldiers' horses are trampling the gardens and the lodges and then a ball of flame explodes, and he and Archie are upon the herder who lies moaning in his blood.

"Help me," he calls, and they lean out, one on either side as he weakly lifts his arms. Clutching tightly to their horses' manes, each grabs an arm to drag him up toward the trees. His leg is hit but that's all. A whole phalanx of mounted bluecoats is pounding toward them, directly toward the herd that circles and roils in panic between the trees and the creek and Duncan knows if they don't escape now, they're dead. They abandon the horses, and he hauls the wounded man on his back as they scramble panting up the eastern hillside, the acrid smell of blood and smoke in their nostrils and eyes. When he judges it safe, they stop and wait. It's an orgy of butchery and destruction down below, Duncan thinks, winded and sick, as he holds his brother close. They remember to bind the man's leg with the cotton of Duncan's shirt. And then they just listen.

He doesn't know how much time goes by. Archie is so shocked he just rocks back and forth, and Duncan rubs his back. He whispers that he'll go scout and Archie clings to him and he sinks back. Above them he hears branches crack and knows there are other survivors. Into his head comes a picture of a boy and a woman, struggling up through wind and snow. Here it is silent finally, the trampling of the herd erased as if they never were.

They creep back in ones and twos into the smoking mess, lodgepoles twisted and blackened, fences and garden plots obliterated, food and pots strewn and smashed. He sees the chief near the shore, bending over a body. Old chief Red Heart is dead, his face contorted, one hand at his chest. Others, too, a young man, a young woman and her infant who sank in the river, shot or drowned. Bird Alighting sits dazed on a stump. The herd is gone, the village destroyed. He hears no weeping, no sound, just the most awful empty silence.

Looking Glass is untouched, but his face is incandescent with hate. He swings in a circle, long arms spinning as if to ask why, and raises one fist toward the west. "You make war? You want war?" His eyes pull the eyes of his warriors toward him. "Then it will be war."

CHAPTER 8

The Nez Perces
THE HISTORY OF THEIR TROUBLES
AND THE CAMPAIGN OF 1877

The writer, a relative of Looking Glass and White Bird, has entered into arrangements with the NEW NORTH-WEST to prepare a series of papers giving the Nez Perces' version of their troubles and their remarkable campaign. It is a condition of the publication that the views shall be related from their standpoint, and as full particulars as possible will be given of the tribe and their great expedition.

It will be remembered that in the year 1847, Dr. Whitman and wife were murdered by a Cayuse Indian named Ta-ma-has. This murder resulted in a conflict between the US Government and the above-named tribe. After the Indians were defeated, the Government demanded the murderers, and Ta-ma-has and several others were hung in Willamette Valley, Oregon. At the time the Cayuse were engaged in this war, a young man of the Nez Perce nation named Yellow Bull abandoned his parents and tribe. Ta-ma-has had a young and beautiful daughter, loved and respected by all who knew her. Yellow Bull, by his coolness and personal bravery, had won her affections and the confidence of her father, and it was soon agreed that the two should wed.

After Ta-ma-has was hung the young couple came back to the Nez Perce country and shortly after the girl gave birth to a son. Little worthy of note transpired regarding this couple until the boy reached the age of manhood. One day, whilst convers-ing with his mother, he asked her if he ever had a grandfather, and, if so, he would like very much to pay him a visit. Hesitating for a few moments, the woman told him that he had a grandfather and that he was dead, he having been hung by the Americans a long time ago. This same young man was one of the three who committed the depredations in Idaho last summer.

—*THE NEW NORTH-WEST*, Deer Lodge, M.T.
April 26, 1878

The family has heard not a word since Looking Glass joined the fight. Since Duncan returned to Post Creek there's only been silence—except for the ceaseless roaring of the Yankee press. The "hostiles" in Idaho are clashing repeatedly with the Army, the papers report. These "renegade Nez Perce" slaughtered settlers over there; any day now the savage horde could come pouring over the ridge into Montana. The *Weekly Missoulian* drips with hysteria. Its editor, an unctuous fellow called Chauncey Barbour, published an anguished appeal to Benjamin Potts, the governor of Montana Territory, a few days before. It read in part: "The people of Bitterroot are fleeing in terror from their homes. Danger is imminent not just from the Nez Perce but from the Flatheads here at home, who will undoubtedly rise up to join in the attack."

To his credit, the brand-new Indian agent on the Flathead Reservation doesn't immediately leap to this conclusion. Peter Ronan appears to have more sense than that.

"Ran a newspaper myself," he shrugs to Arlee and Michelle, with Duncan interpreting. "Half what's printed isn't worth the price of the ink." Ronan has the look of a judge or a cavalry officer, with his erect carriage and luxurious brown mustache. Notably, he's brought his wife and children and seems steadier than any agent they've seen before.

Still, by the middle of June 1877, in post for barely two weeks, the man has a full-fledged crisis on his hands. He rides ceaselessly around the reservation, taking the pulse. How likely are your people to rise up to defend the Nez Perce, if it comes to the worst? he asks. Not likely, the chiefs say. Privately they're not so sure. After so much loss and hate, will they be able to restrain their young men any better than did the chiefs of the Nez Perce?

Who started it—and how—seems the most pointless of questions to Duncan now. All he can say for sure is that it didn't start in Idaho, or this summer—but years, decades, generations before. For the first time in a long time he remembers the Yakama, the first tribe in his lifetime to be crushed, and feels his blood run cold. He'd never felt panic for another human being until he fled back across the Lolo pass. He was clammy with fear—for Archie, for Quil-see, their baby to come. When she cantered toward him, he couldn't help scanning the hills for volunteers and vigilantes, bracing for the whine and snap of bullets. In dreams he sees their snarling faces and strikes back, writhing and kicking until she calms him. White people are terrified of anyone whose skin is dark—so they obliterate this source of their blind fear. He clutches his wife and keeps her close; he keeps his pistol on him at all times.

A week after his return the papers report on the "battle" he witnessed, and he measures its lies against the evidence of his own eyes. "The Looking Glass band fired the first shot, thus starting the fight," it claims. Seventeen "hostiles" died, but the Army lost not a man, and took a thousand horses besides. Another week passes and he's knotted with waiting, eyes dry from peering up the Evaro canyon. He tries not to think how his mother and grandmother are worrying up at Post Creek. It's almost a relief, then, when something finally happens. Late in mid-July he spots a large party emerging from the southern woods. Flashing color and barely any dust: clearly Native people. His stomach clenches. It must be the Salish—there's no way the Nez Perce could have crossed the mountains this fast. He calls Quil-see to take shelter in the agent's house, in case these visitors don't come as friends.

Agent Ronan is already on his porch, a glass held to his eye. "Who is it?"

"Hard to tell." Duncan shades his eyes. "A good number anyway. Forty, fifty, perhaps a hundred horses." He watches the agent obliquely, to gauge his fear. But Ronan gives nothing away. He's not a large man but carries himself as if he were. He disappears and reappears with his white collar up, advancing as he knots a black cravat.

"Doesn't look like Charlo," Duncan adds, eyes trained on the tall, bareheaded leader.

He's made a point of shooting straight with Ronan, presenting himself as an independent trader at the agency—a businessman, impartial and honest. He even went so far as to report the Idaho unrest to Barbour in Missoula—to show them he's as much part of this community as they are. As the strangers advance, the agency's residents gather: Chief Arlee in his top hat and bear-claw necklace, Mary Ronan with children peering out from behind her skirts, faces bug-eyed and blanched. Quil-see stands tensed at his side.

"Michelle brings friends," Arlee says, and Duncan finally sees.

"Nez Perce—but not those who fight," he whispers in Ronan's ear. His bowels have instinctively tightened at the sight of Eagle from the Light and his small band. What trouble does his mother's cousin bring into their valley now?

The chief is thin and gray as wire; Chief Michelle of the Pend d'Oreille rides with him. The agency translator begins to speak. Urgent things to discuss, but first they'll smoke and share greetings. While he's talking Eagle from the Light takes in the shrinking crowd. His eyes meet Duncan's and their look is a vise.

"*Leehe'y we'et'u 'ee he'kin*," Duncan says. Haven't seen you for a while.

Peter Ronan looks at him sharply, but Eagle from the Light's face lights up.

"Young McDonald." He answers in English. Then he signs, so the Salish speakers too can understand. *I hear you shoot well, for a white man.* His right hand swipes a line across his forehead, pokes an index finger straight out from his stomach: the sign for soyapo, man who wears a hat.

Duncan turns to Ronan with a shrug. "He says he hears that I shoot good."

Always the same crap, from either side. Ronan's look is hard, but he tells him to come inside in case the translator needs help. After twenty minutes they get to the meat of things. Michelle tells the agent he invited the Nez Perce chief onto the reservation. Eagle from the Light wants nothing of this war, Michelle says; his friend will cause no trouble. Duncan is scrutinizing his uncle's expressionless face. He's never played a simple game. He spoke against the treaties at the start: one he signed; another he refused. He broke at last with his band when they wouldn't rise up to drive the miners from their lands. So why does he bolt onto the reservation now?

Duncan watches the intelligent eyes, remembering the hostility with which he last received him. Agent Ronan doesn't know how closely related he is to these "hostiles." When it's his turn to speak, his kinsman stands and juts his chin at Duncan. "Tell my words to this Boston." Warily, Duncan complies.

"I don't stand for this war. First the whites divided us from the land—then they divided the people. Those chiefs might fight, but I will not."

Ronan, too, stands, a head shorter than his guest. "When I met you two weeks ago you were headed across the mountains—to tell your people to come back and keep out of the fighting. You said you'd stay at the Missoula fort."

"Our people live here."

Ronan's expression is sour. "We agreed you'd pitch your lodges at the fort and wait the trouble out."

"We wish to camp here until the war is over."

"That won't be possible."

Tell him. The chief's voice is calm, entirely reasonable. "There won't be trouble. We'll camp right here where he can see us. We don't share our brothers' hearts. I left my tribe because I opposed war."

The words leave Duncan's lips like tiles plunked on a board: true-false-true-false. Ronan twists at his mustache, frowning. He addresses the other chiefs.

"You bring this man here as your guest." Unthinkingly he laces his hands behind his back, tilting forward like a schoolmaster. "It's your right. But just for a short time—one week, say. Not for months. Agreed?"

"Agreed," says Arlee.

Ronan turns back to Eagle from the Light. "Soon you'll have to camp somewhere else. I'll speak to my chiefs." His face takes on a hawkish look. "I'm sure they can find a spot for you at Lapwai." The Nez Perce chief doesn't blink at the name of the main outpost on the hated reservation. He bows his head instead, as if in acquiescence. Then he turns to leave. Arlee and Michelle press forward, faces bright with pleasure. Only Duncan sees the sign as he passes onto the porch: the swift strike down with his right fist that means *to kill*. He's still pondering this as Ronan's voice comes like a whip.

"McDonald."

"Agent Ronan."

Mary Ronan sits on the black horsehair settee she dragged by mule and cart across half of the country. She watched it all from a side door. "My word." Her eyes seem twice their normal size. "What an . . . imposing man."

"The point is, what to make of him." Ronan strikes a match. "I don't like the look of it."

He's barely scratched the surface, Duncan thinks. Barbour recently pulled Ronan aside to warn him "his whole damn reservation" was lousy with no-good Nez Perce. The agent discussed this with Duncan, who thought it only politic to reveal that his own mother belongs to that nation, as does the mother of the Salish second chief, Arlee.

"What's the real story?"

A complicated question indeed. "He broke with Chief Joseph, and with Looking Glass, some years ago. He used to be a very big chief, even over White Bird and his band."

A bare month ago these settlers had never even heard these names. Now they appear in every paper under headlines reading "NEZ PERCE MENACE." Duncan feels the sweat run down his back. "A long time ago, when there were fewer settlers, he wanted to fight." He spreads his hands. "Now it's too late, he says. For him it's over."

"A likely story." Ronan grimaces.

"One person might know." Duncan is loath to draw suspicion on himself or Quil-see or his mother. But one man has always relished the central role. "My father has known him for nearly forty years. If any white man knows the mind of Eagle from the Light, it would be Angus."

SUBTERFUGE ON SUBTERFUGE, he thinks as he escorts the Nez Perce chief the next day to Post Creek. Eagle from the Light says what he thinks the white man wants to hear, while his true purpose remains secret. Duncan, too, has learned this art. For it's not entirely true that Angus knows this once-great chief—not anymore. Who can truly know the way that loss and exile, anguish and despair, combine and twist inside a mind?

Duncan glances at his wife as they ride, gracefully balanced despite her great belly. She's going to her mother for the birth. She glows and he feels blessed that this daughter of the Shining Mountains chose to make her life with him. Whatever happens, they will have each other. She leans across and puts her lips to his cheek when they reach the turnoff to the mission. "Listen to your heart, not him," quietly she says. She, too, knows Eagle from the Light brings not just news, but some more complicated choice.

His mother's watching from the gate nearest the road. Her breast flashes silver and her arm goes up when she sees them coming. Catherine McDonald scours her cousin's face with eyes that hold every possible feeling. "Tipyehleneh Kaupu. I didn't think to see you in this life."

"So it would seem, if this is all you give me as a greeting." Behind the mocking tone, the slightest smile: a flash of the old friend.

"My mother felt you would come." Catherine nods at her son.

And indeed, as they lead the horses in, Duncan's grandmother is waiting. For the first time Eagle from the Light smiles openly at the sight of this old woman leaning on her stick. Margaret is no longer as tall as her nephew, but her face is every bit as carved and lovely, still unlined despite her years, which number seventy-five. The chief embraces her, then turns to Angus. They grasp one another by the forearm, a hand on a shoulder—formally, it seems.

"So," says Eagle from the Light. "We meet again, near the end."

"Let's hope it's not." Angus's smile is strained; they're both pushing sixty, more or less, these men who once were closest friends.

Then Duncan feels his own arms grabbed from behind and turns to find Maggie.

"Where is she?" She looks past him.

"At her mother's."

She pouts. "Then come and help. We've got a beef to finish spitting."

Their younger brothers are set to tending the horses, eyes round as they approach the warriors who serve as the chief's men at arms. These young men stand with legs apart, plaid shirts unbuttoned in the heat, hair twisted into tails, Winchesters dangling. With great care the boys take the reins of their mounts and lead them toward the barn.

Duncan takes a moment to savor the scene. The two-story house he built with his own hands faces the old post and storeroom. Yellow meadow spreads from the paddocks toward the creek that rises toward the peaks. Thin lines of smoke rise from a half a dozen lodges. He looks, and loves the peace, and feels a sudden fear run through him—that this charmed world of theirs could somehow founder. And then he feels himself hauled back; he feels his mother's presence, and her mother's.

"You bring her much gladness." Catherine smiles. He bends to kiss his grandma. She's seated now, snowy white like a queen; she raises her stick as if to beat him with it. "Why only Tipyehlenah Kaupu? You think I don't also want to see his brothers and their wives?"

The chief tosses an answer back. "There will be time. If all goes as I hope."

"Ah." Margaret nods. "So you'll tell us what they are, these hopes."

THEY WAIT FOR the heat to abate before gathering. Margaret sits in her lodge on a hay bale draped with fur. Duncan makes tea, a clump of yarrow for each cup. His mother stands, gathered as if waiting to spring. He's never seen her simmering with such power. It streams from her mouth, her hands, her eyes, pinned like a beam in the night on their guest. She doesn't sit until her cousin breaks that gaze and sits in his turn next to Angus. Only then does Margaret speak.

"You bring bad news."

"Bad, good." He shrugs. "I don't judge."

"But Looking Glass is alive—and fighting?"

"Yes. They're beating the soldiers. White Bird fought strongly at Lamotta."

"It was White Bird's men who started this war." Duncan can speak; he's entitled to now. "Looking Glass was furious at them, before he was attacked."

Eagle from the Light gives him a shriveling look. "They're beating the soldiers," he repeats. "They left the soldier chief choking on their dust and are coming now across the pass."

Catherine turns to her mother. "They're escaping, then. We can help them when they come." In an instant, her face clears. "We'll help them escape." Duncan sees the relief wash through his mother; the look she turns on her cousin now is benevolent.

"They'll be pursued like the rest." Angus speaks flatly. "You know it."

Margaret says nothing, only looks at Eagle from Light, awaiting the rest of his report.

"You know me." The chief's voice is soft and persuasive. "I tried to lead our people. Again and again I tried. Now I was friendly, now not: still the soyapo came. I left because they wouldn't fight. And even two winters ago, when the chief in Washington said, 'No, Joseph, you must leave the Wallowa, it's no longer yours,' I said to them again: we have no choice now, we must fight."

His face grows hard as he recalls, and Duncan feels that for once he speaks the truth. "But my brothers, White Bird, Joseph, Red Owl—they won't do battle. They choose to go like cattle behind the white man's line. They agreed to it at the last council."

"And so . . ." Margaret says grimly, "some broke loose."

Eagle from the Light rocks back on his heels. "At Split Rock Lake. Where they gathered to say farewell." It seems to Duncan he's not aggrieved but proud. "My nephew decided to avenge my brother's murder."

Margaret's lips tighten. "Stupid. Brave perhaps, but stupid. Eagle Robe warned against that, as he breathed his last."

"He did."

"But his son has started one." Catherine breaks in, her voice acid. "And now they flee toward us." Her gaze moves to Angus. "My husband is right; the soldiers won't rest until they're punished."

"Then we must resist." Eagle from the Light's nostrils flare. "Your way—" he looks coldly at Angus—"has failed. You thought the nimíipuu would be spared, we'd be safe inside their lines. But that, like everything they say—your own son even says—is a lie. After Cayuse, Yakama, Blackfoot, it's nimíipuu they hunt now. We must fight or die."

"It's true, daughter's husband." Margaret swivels toward Angus. "They won't rest until we're all in the ground."

"You're badly outnumbered." A muscle throbs in Angus's cheek.

"Not all of us together." The chief's eyes blaze strangely. "Together we can crush them worse even than they crushed the yellow-haired general. Crow and Blackfoot and Lakota—we'll even call Sitting Bull."

They stare at him. Since the Lakota chief destroyed Custer's command, he's been in exile in Canada, across the medicine line where US soldiers may not follow. Yet now their own kinsman invokes that blood-soaked name—and the collective uprising of every tribe across plateau and plains. It's the worst nightmare of every settler Duncan knows. So this is the plan Eagle from the Light has harbored all along.

"Kamiakin thought the same." Angus is angry, although still contained. "He, too, had powerful allies, but he was still destroyed." He stands and begins to pace.

How old he looks, Duncan thinks: old and impotent, still clinging to the hope of some middle way. Then his father is barking at him: "What does the agent say?"

"He trusts our chiefs. Charlo and Michelle pledge to stay neutral if the nimíipuu come across the Lolo."

"No one can stop them if they come this way." There's no mistaking the pride in the voice of Eagle from the Light.

"Kitalah." Margaret speaks with urgency. "You have boys you can send as scouts."

"The chiefs have already posted some," quickly Duncan answers.

"Even if they come this way, what possible aid can we give?" Angus's voice is sharp. "They've killed settlers and soldiers. You know how it will be. They can never surrender." A shadow passes over his face and Duncan knows he's thinking of Qualchan and Owhi, all those Yakama strung up like dogs.

"They have to escape across the medicine line." His mother's voice is firm.

"And Looking Glass, White Bird—what are their hearts?" Margaret hasn't yet betrayed her own view. She sits there, head turning like a judge, her grandson thinks.

"Looking Glass will find help among the Crow." Eagle from the Light looks at his aunt. "My counsel is to join the Crow on the plains, for they're not afraid to fight."

Margaret nods.

"And risk the war continuing here?" Catherine pitches forward.

"He hunts with them." Margaret nods again. "The Crow are good friends."

"No better than the Salish or Pend d'Oreille." Duncan shakes his head. Are they mad? The Crow to the east have not always been reliable allies. So his mother, too, thinks; she slaps her hand onto the mat.

"Not to the Crow." Her mouth is set. "The way there isn't safe. They must go north across the medicine line—to Grandmother's country, where they will be safe."

Angus is the only one who hasn't shown his hand. "If they go north, they can never return," he says slowly. Stony-faced, Catherine nods.

Now it's Eagle from the Light who slaps the floor. "That's why we must fight."

Angus looks long into his old friend's face. The chief's disdain must hurt. "You'd rather they died? Cut down in battle?" He speaks harshly, without hope of convincing. "They can't win, you know it. The Americans will hunt them down."

"We've always fought for our people." Margaret leans forward. "It's better to die fighting than be enslaved like a dog."

Her face is so fierce Duncan is chilled and it bursts out. "You've said it since I was a child. Even if you killed them all, even if you killed their great explorers, other whites would keep coming. You can only ever slow them; they'll never stop."

His mother clenches her fists. "To fight them is suicide."

"We must defend our people." Margaret stamps her staff upon the ground.

"My son can lead them to the old woman country," Catherine growls.

"No. I stand with my nephew." Margaret speaks with finality. "If they come into this country, they must seek help from our brothers on the plains. Red Hart will deliver them this message."

The elders decide.

Catherine rises, thunderous and silent. She looks hard at her mother, her cousin. Then she turns her broad back to the circle and stands for the longest moment. Angus looks stricken. But he, too, rises; he, too, turns his back to show they don't share in this decision. Eagle from the Light smiles grimly as he bows to his aunt and leaves the lodge. As his parents turn to go, Duncan sees tears of anger on his mother's cheeks.

He bends to his grandmother and takes her grizzled hands. "You send me on a hopeless errand."

But she's as strong as she's ever been. She pulls his head toward hers. "If you think it's without hope, Red Hart, you don't know your people."

CHAPTER 9

The Nez Perces
THE HISTORY OF THEIR TROUBLES
AND THE CAMPAIGN OF 1877

Wal-litze was the man who fired the first shot in the late Nez
Perces war. He was the son of a well-to-do farmer named Tip-
piala-natzit-kan [Eagle Robe], who is a brother of the once favorite Eagle from the Light, and who was murdered by a white
man four years ago.

Tip-piala-natzit-kan was well known throughout the tribe,
and his duty it was to call the councils together. . . . The father
of Wal-litze was a farmer, and in good circumstances, peaceably inclined toward all, accommodating and undoubtedly
desired the settlement of the country in which he lived. About
a year prior to the murder of Tip-piala-natzit-kan a white man
came to his house and stated that he would like to take up a
piece of land and requested of him to show him a piece of land
unclaimed by anyone promising him (the Indian) to be a good
neighbor. Tip-piala-natzit-kan, liking the appearance of the
man, at once granted his request and proceeded to show him
the unclaimed land. No difficulty arose between the white man
and the Indian until about a year afterward, when the white
man wanted to fence a piece of land that the Indian claimed.

It seems that early one morning the man was engaged in
hauling some rails, a short distance from the Indian's house,
when the wife of the Indian roused him up and told him that his
white friend was putting some rail upon their land. Tip-piala-
natzit-kan at once aroused the other Indians who were living in

his house, and asked them to accompany him, as he wished to talk with the white man and find out what were his intentions, and said that he was afraid to visit him alone. But it seems that no one wanted to accompany him and accordingly he went alone. Upon reaching the designated place he asked the white man if he had forgotten the promise he made to him during their first interview, and asked him in a friendly manner not to put any rails on his land, but put them on the land that he was owner of. The white man at once became wrathy, and taking his rifle from off the pile of rails shot the Indian, wounding him mortally.

—*THE NEW NORTH-WEST, Deer Lodge, M.T.*
June 7, 1878

I give below a list of the Nez Perce Indians killed by whites before the war of 1877.

Chief Bear Thinker was poisoned; Juliah was killed near Bozeman without cause; Taivisyact was shot while passing a house on horseback near the Missouri River on the road to Bozeman; Took-kay-lay-yoot, Lapwai, by a soldier on account of liquor; Yalmay-whotzoot, Lapwai, was killed while looking for horses; Him-p-augh was killed on account of buying a pistol; Tipyahlanah achino-mouch at Elk City, cause unknown; Koy-otes was killed on a spree with supposed friends at Slate Creek; Maltze-qui was killed because he was falsely accused of stealing a bottle of whisky; Eya-makoot, a woman, was killed with a pick on account of her dog whipping a white man's dog; Cass-say-u was accidentally killed by the son of their own minister, Spald-ing, who shot at another Indian while gambling and killed the wrong man; Took-ooghp-ya-mool on Salmon River; Usaykay-act was taken away by a white friend and never seen again; T-nan-na-say, a councilman, was shot by a soldier in a council south of Yakima; Tipyalahnah tzi-kan because his field was taken from him; Willatiah in the mountains near Wallowa. As I have stated before, none of the murderers of these people were ever arrested or punished.

—*THE NEW NORTH-WEST, Deer Lodge, M.T.*
Oct. 18, 1878

IN THE FADING light Duncan sees his father standing at the paddock. Angus rests a foot on the bottom rail, observing his herd, and the anger his son has kept in check burns through the shield he's wrapped around it.

"So that's the best you could do—the best resistance you could mount?"

His father doesn't turn.

"But then, the *savages* don't stand a chance, so why bother?"

Angus swings his head around. "Watch your mouth."

Duncan gives a caustic laugh. They might have swayed the elders if Angus had argued half so forcefully as he's glaring now.

"It's true. You said as much yourself. They're doomed to fade away."

"It's not up to me if they decide to make a stand."

"Just let the Yankees finish what you started."

His father's face is angry now, and Duncan's glad.

"Stop talking rubbish."

"You never see your part in it. You and your precious Company, you opened up the floodgates." They're all so innocent—they didn't have a hand in any of it.

"As if." Dismissively his father flicks a hand. "We didn't open anything—the horse and gun did that, and long before. We were their partners, nothing more."

"Of course you'd say that." None of them accepts a shred of culpability—loggers, trappers, traders, settlers all. Convinced their every move is foreordained and righteous, blessed if not by God, then weaponry and might. "You used them for your own ends and you know it. I did it too—for you." His own complicity offends him just as much.

Angus says nothing, although his jaw works. His son watches his eyes flick across his fine herd of cattle.

"*Civilization*. It's all a fraud." If only his father could for once admit it. "Here we are now—all of us—hunted. Your own children, all of us *savages*."

Finally his father has to turn and face him. "This is about you, then. Not White Bird or Looking Glass."

"For Christ's sake. Full-blood, half-blood. All of us. You chose to bring us into a world that only chews us up and spits us out." He sees Maggie's tear-stained cheeks, the fear on Archie's face.

Angus rubs his forehead. "It was better before." Heavily he shakes his head. "In my day, in the Company's day, though you won't credit it. We lived together, never tried to change them."

"You knew how it would turn out."

His father sighs. "No one can see the future, Duncan."

"But you knew from the start! Before I was even born. The British had already lost this land. And even so you kept pretending."

"We tried—I tried—to limit the damage. I did my best to protect them, I tried ceaselessly to get the Army to enforce the treaties."

"Your motive was always profit."

Angus expels a breath. "The curse and brilliance of mankind." He looks evenly, almost despairingly, at Duncan and they both stand there, stalemated. It's such a pointless and circular argument, thinks his son. He admired the Baymen so much as a boy, revered his father, his power, his Scottishness. Only now does he see the trade in fur for what it always was: the vanguard of a larger, far more brutal force.

HE WAITS IN the evening for his wife to arrive, trying to calm his mind.

Fat is frying, smoke rising, horses nickering, a baby crying.

First slits are cut in the nap of darkened sky. Starlight behind.

He hears a burbling of nasal, glottal, clicking voices, some low singing, a note held, then silence. He smokes and watches from a far paddock as bodies gather near the fire. Everyone is here from half a day away. The sounds, the smells, the laughter, mangled French and Salish, English and Nez Perce and Gaelic. He's swept back to Colvile and the campfires of his childhood. O sweet world, so marvelously mixed—how could it pass away?

Without a moon he melts into the dark. As can they all. They're all hunters who can hold their bodies still as death. He sees Rileys, Finlays, Ogdens and Revais and Baptistes—his uncles Alexander Big Knife and Red Ox and his own mother—all that generation save his aunt Kyuka. Each a mixture of that old world and the new, blood stirred in a vat by profit and the appetite for fur. Each formed by that blind impulse known as empire.

He scratches the stubble at his jaw and watches down the darkened road for Quil-see. She's pure Q'lispé. No white girl ever could begin to know him, not deep down—he knows this now. Duncan hears the hooves of her pony on the hard-packed dirt as she turns in, distinctive in its gait. Clop-clip-clop-slide. He'd know it anywhere. They kiss; he holds her for a moment longer.

Everything all right? her eyes ask and he shakes his head. He takes the reins and walks her toward the light cast by the fire.

"Hey papa," cracks Frank Riley, né François. "Got one in the oven already. So quit your skulkin' around."

Men grin and pass a jug. He sees Alec DeMers there, guzzling Angus's good grog.

The balls of him, he thinks. Then out of the dimness comes Maggie McDonald, eyes lighting at the sight of Quil-see. She brandishes a pan, slapping its handle in her brother's hand. "Go make yourself useful," she says, elbowing him toward the fiery circle.

When they're sated and lying in twos and threes, he hears the drums start up. They push themselves upright. The fire has been built higher. His grandmother, Margaret de Naie, is seated at the north side of the fire. The flames carve shadows in the hollows of her cheeks, above the jutting sockets of her eyes. When she stands and raps her stick against the ring of stones, all talking stops. Her white hair hangs to her breast and shines in the light of the stars and fire.

"My children." Her voice is low and sinuous. "It's not the time—and yet it is."

She breaks with tradition, he thinks with astonishment. She tells a story in the summer night and not in winter ice—as if the old rules have been overthrown. Her youngest grandchildren lie propped, intently watching. Her voice grows in strength as she begins to speak, her hands moving with it, swooping and darting, making signs: river, mountain, white man, horses, each concrete thing a picture in the air.

My children. You are the children of the Lam'tama and the Tookpehma, sons and daughters of the river Tamonmo, which the white man calls the Salmon. We nimíipuu were there, from long ago, until the Across Water people came. I'll tell you how it happened, how the soyapo first came into our country.

"May they go back where they came from!" A hoarse male voice shouts.

Margaret dips her head, a smile on her lips. It's Red Ox who interjects; he grins and looks around. The story will continue in this way, nipped and added to like layers on a quilt, by those who hold another stitch, a different thread.

In my father's time there was a girl of the Lam'tama who lived in Lamotta, the place reached by long and weary travel. One day, while her people were hunting near the river of the White-Colored Waters, she strayed off and was captured by Blackfeet.

"Aiyee. So many lost to those Blacklegs."

They didn't keep her, but sold her to another people. Who they were we don't know. In time they sold her to people with pale skin who came from the far north. These people treated her well. But she missed her home. So she ran away and came after a long time to the land of the Salish, who fed and cared for her. On the way her baby died.

"We've taken in many like this." Quil-see nods at Duncan's elbow.

When she returned to her band, she was called Wet-khoo-weis, she who is Returned from a Far Country. And she told the people how the white-faced people had been kind, and this was shared with all nimíipuu. Now, when the soyapos came with their half-dead horses into the camp on the Wieppe from the direction of the sunrise, Wet-khoo-weis was in camp. Hohots Ilppilp, Red Grizzly Bear, was chief at that time. Even old as I am, the Highest Mystery hadn't yet set me on the earth.

"Your father was there. He remembers. He hears you now, from above and from the ground." All eyes turn, acknowledging the words of Eagle from the Light.

Margaret looks up at the streaks of stars. The longest day is not long past, the air still warm. She nods.

My father was a young man of fourteen when these men came. They were called Clark and Lewis. He said the people were afraid. The chiefs were all gone hunting, only women, old men, children were there. When the soya-pos came into the valley, the people talked and said they must kill them. And they would have, but Wet-khoo-weis told them NO.

"We should have killed them then and ended it." Once more, the voice of Eagle from the Light.

These whites were good, said the woman Returned from a Far Country. She put her hands to the bows and pushed the arrows toward the ground. And then Red Grizzly Bear came and they smoked the pipe to show they came in peace. Our people gave them food and trees to make canoes and kept their horses for one year. When they returned they gave us metal things for our arms and necks. Later we found out these were cheap.

So now you know it. Hear me, my children. It wasn't the nimíipuu who first shed blood. We greeted them as guests in our own country. Wet-khoo-weis, the Returned, was peacemaker. We didn't make war on them, though they make it now on us. This we remember. Our ancestors remember. You remember, too.

That's all.

CATHERINE WATCHES HER son rise and slip away at the sound of his father's bagpipes. On his face is this look of desperation that's only grown since she returned to Sin-ye-le-min. Only Quil-see ever wipes it completely away. Catherine hears the groan of the pipes, wobbly then taut—full at last, the bag releasing its shrill notes—and thinks that life can clarify in just this way. The muddy comes clear, the action shown that you must take. She and Angus share the same thought; her mother and cousin take another way. She doesn't blame them. Each chooses the course that their heart instructs them to take: to fight, or to escape.

Angus has his whistling bag to remind him of his home. She, Tipy-ehlenah Kitalah, has the song of the mountain meadowlark. It's filled

303

her ears at the darkest times, giving her strength and courage. She, too, rises, slipping from the fire. The stars are so bright tonight, the sparkling plain so near she could reach and pluck one for a guide. She thinks of the Spanish Indian who guided her and Baptiste by these selfsame stars. Her ancestors are very near. They lived so she can live and carry the people on. As Angus's ancestor, too, survived. She knows what she—and only she—must do. The defiance in her has ebbed; she's steely, calm. There's only one path now.

Duncan is watching the horses gently bumping into one another in the dark.

"He does his best," she says.

"He's weak." He keeps his face from her.

"Not like us, eh?"

And Duncan sees his mother smile, her face beneath the stars a mirror—shining, calm. "All mixed up—and you the most." With a dry laugh she pokes his side. "Tobacco and Kin-nic-nic—French, Lamta'mah, Mohawk, and Glencoe.

"Come," she says next. "Walk with me. We must talk."

They circle around the house, toward the north, dropping down to the creek.

"Here," she says, pressing her foot into a crescent rim of shore. "Exactly here, is the place you were born." She closes her eyes. "Fighting and struggling. This struggle formed you, made you strong." She turns to him and sees the pain that defines him, the tenderness he hides. "You will tell Looking Glass to take the northern way, across the line—and not the way the others say."

He draws back, astonished. "You'd defy them?"

"The way to the Crow isn't safe." Her fingers tighten on his arm. "You take him this message, from me, from all of us. Tell him it's our advice."

"But your mother, your cousin . . ."

"Will leave us soon. It's not for them to speak for the future." She hears the distant sound of the feast, the chirping of crickets, a slight rustle in the willow like the flapping of wings. "It's for the children—the children's children—we must act."

CHAPTER 10

The Indian Menace

Well, there's a good even show for a fight in Missoula county. Joseph's or White Bird's bands have reached a point on the Lo Lo trail near its entrance to Bitterroot Valley. Overwhelmed in Idaho and driven on the Lo Lo trail, there is but one recourse for them—they must get through to the buffalo country. They profess to desire peaceable transit, but avow a determination to go fighting if they must.

However deficient [Captain Rawn's] force he must treat them as hostiles. Although largely outnumbered, we do not believe the Indians can dislodge him from his entrenchment in the canyon. . . . There [are] 110 rifles in the hands of the regulars and volunteers at the front with Rawn, and 330 hostiles. Men were being sent out as fast as they could be armed and mounted. The Indians, we believe, have their entire camp of squaws, children, and horses, and are very much encumbered thereby. We think it more than probable they will send all but the warriors back to gain exit by some other side trail. . . . The principal danger apprehended in Missoula seems to be from home Indians, some of whom have proclaimed if the hostiles are not allowed to pass peaceably through Montana they will assist them. . . .

—*THE NEW NORTH-WEST, Deer Lodge, M.T.*
Friday, July 27, 1877

AGENT RONAN WORRIES about those Indians unfortunate enough to find themselves in town amid the growing panic. They have to get them back on the reservation, he says, enlisting Duncan's help. The operation reminds him of that last lonely mustang on Wild Horse Island—even his father's boyhood, sent up the braes to find the "bloody sheep." Everywhere, masters lock in other creatures, supposedly to keep them "safe."

They ride fully armed toward Missoula with a string of ponies. The country is unnaturally silent; beneath the canyon canopy they scan for movement. As they enter the gorge, Duncan pictures their track from the eagle's point of view: two men heading south, hundreds of Nez Perce heading eastward over the mountains toward them. At some point these lines must converge. Since Custer's defeat the settlers have succeeded in securing a rudimentary fort, thrown up barely three weeks before. Not that it could hold the nimíipuu. Fort Missoula is just a few hasty barracks southwest of town; Ronan stops there.

"You go on ahead." He gives Duncan a peculiar look. Uneasily he waits until the agent spits it out. "You might have told me you were kin to these hostiles."

"You knew my mother is Nez Perce."

"Not that these are her relations."

"Everyone's related to everyone else." Lightly, he shrugs. "It's not so surprising. People intermarry, now the tribes are so reduced in size." Thanks to your guns, your diseases, silently he adds.

"Even so. Some things I need to know."

"I don't know any more than you." It's mostly true. They read the same reports: that Looking Glass has joined with Joseph and White Bird and "the hostiles," fighting General Howard's battalion. A week ago they were both at the agency when three Nez Perce youths turned up, scouts for the Army who'd skedaddled to see if they were needed at home in Idaho. As he translated Duncan scrutinized these young men with cropped hair and Army-issue rifles, members of the Christian bands who signed the treaties. This trouble doesn't concern their kin, Ronan said: not those who stay put, obey the law. Just the so-called non-treaty Nez Perce, the "hostiles."

Duncan struggled to contain himself. What kind of man tracks his own kind for an army intent on their destruction? It sickens him, the way whites turn brother against brother. He knows they think there are two kinds of Indians: those who can be "civilized," and those, as he read recently, who "must perish either by violence or decay." His mother's people—his people—are those whose extinction is ordained.

Ronan jogs on. "What worries me is if they head north through the reservation."

"I'd tell you if I thought there was any danger," he answers smoothly. Things should be calm, so long as the settlers let them pass.

"I notice you sent your own wife north, though."

"She wanted to be with her family. The baby is due any time."

The two men eye one another. Mary Ronan grows more pinched and pale by the day. No one knows anything, except that the hostiles are coming—with their lurid tales of atrocities and scalping and rape, the butchery on the Little Bighorn fresh in every mind.

"I should have offered Mary and the children refuge at Post Creek," he says. "I wish I'd thought of it before."

"Never mind." Ronan gives a weary smile. "The chiefs will post men at the agency."

"No Nez Perce would attack a Salish or Pend d'Oreille." This Duncan firmly believes. "They're the closest of allies."

"Let us hope so," Ronan says. He reins his horse toward the fort. "Go ahead into town. I'll catch you up."

On the outskirts of Missoula, Duncan stops and pays a boy to mind the horses. Already he can hear a great hubbub. Main Street is a crush of wagons and buggies so crammed the teams are half-rearing, bug-eyed and baring teeth. Along the sidewalks men press together, bodies cocked like pistols. Eyes dart every which way and every last man is armed; he can smell the panic. All the women and children in the outlying farms have been brought to town, it seems. They've looped a chain at the bridge across the river heading south and it takes everything he has not to smile. It'll take more than a chain to stop the Nez Perce if they're determine to come through.

He steps onto the wooden plank outside Wordens and hears a steady murmuring from every shop and hotel, the rise and fall of women's and children's voices. In the store the room is ringed with ladies fanning themselves. He tips his hat and waits to put in the agency order. Old Higgins takes the list without touching Duncan's hand and disappears into the back. Duncan moves to a spot in a corner where he can see the whole room and waits, aware of the ladies' unease, their rapid glances. His skin is always darker in the summer. Even dressed to the nines, he's an Indian.

To his relief the agent doesn't tarry. Ronan sweeps in, sweet-talking the ladies, gesturing at Duncan. Higgins comes out from the back, bowing and scraping this time. "Quite a load," the grocer says, and Ronan nods. "Need to get them through the winter." So he won't allow them to hunt, Duncan understands. Higgins's rheumy joints now appear to work just fine. He bends toward Ronan, whispering like a conspirator. "I hear they're moving out." Duncan guesses he means the troops. "Gonna block the buggers." Higgins smiles benignly, the halo of white hair belying the bellicose glimmer in his eyes. "Keep 'em up in Lolo till they starve." He drops his voice. "Any idea how close the hostiles are?"

Ronan puts a finger to his lips. "A day or two," he mutters.

When Ronan is done Duncan puts in his own order. Quite a crowd now in the Jocko, he says, plenty of customers. Higgins's mouth is tight, but he takes his money all the same. "No ammo, at least," he says, scanning the list.

Duncan snorts. "You know I know better."

He's counting on rivalry between Missoula's merchants to keep his secret. Andy Hammond's little brother sold him a gross of cartridges several weeks before. Even then Duncan guessed he might not be able to procure much more. As they leave, he sweeps off his hat, secure in the knowledge his purchase is safe stashed at Baird's.

And then they fan out in search of those they've come to find. Some are at the mill stacking lumber, a couple hauling out trout by the Shacktown bridge. More idle in the sun before the ramshackle huts, enjoying the heat and unaccustomed calm. They move among the Indians, spooling out Ronan's promises of food, tobacco, shelter—safety, most of all.

"You don't want to be here if fighting breaks out," says Ronan, and there's little disagreement in their eyes when Duncan repeats the words in Salish. Still the active are harder to convince than the idle; two Pend d'Oreille men who make a nickel for each barrow of offcuts protest.

"The mill won't run once the hostiles approach," Ronan says.

"You don't want to get mixed up in this," Duncan adds. By the way they look at him he can tell they're only half-decided. A few Pend d'Oreille are bruising for this fight. Some have crept across the mountains already to meet up with the Nez Perce on their push eastward. They nod reluctantly and he glances at Ronan, striding away. Then he asks quietly if they know, in fact, where to find the camp of White Bird and Looking Glass.

"Just above Traveler's Rest," one mutters.

Such ugly irony. Traveler's Rest, so called by Lewis and Clark when the Nez Perce first conducted them safely to that exit from the Lolo canyon.

Grumbling, the stragglers head toward the waiting ponies. Duncan walks slowly behind. At least he knows now where to find them. So deep is he in thought he doesn't see the barrel-chested man who spins and strides toward him. The first he knows is someone's bashing into him, and hard.

"What the—" he belts out, hand to his pistol until he hears the guffaw. Bastard. Jack DeMers.

"Nice running into ya." Jack's grinning widely, whacking and dusting him at the same time. Duncan steps back. The man's hands are like butchers' hands, puffy and red.

"What the hell, Jack."

It was real fear that tore through him. Real fear lying coiled inside, just waiting for a trigger. He's livid that Jack—rich, callous, manipulative Jack—can so easily do that.

"Surprised to see you sneaking down here." Jack's blue eyes are small but shrewd.

"Here with the agent."

"Really." Jack folds his arms. "Thought you were up to no good, fool that I am." He gives him a look of pure knowing calculation and Duncan's stomach tightens. Jack glances around and bends toward Duncan's ear. "We both know you got ammo from that pup Hammond." He pulls back; the look of hurt bafflement he assumes is entirely fake. "Why you didn't get it from me like last year I can't imagine."

"Pure fantasy." Duncan smiles. Since they joined forces to run the agent Medary off, he figured he and Jack were even. The enemy of my enemy is my friend and all that. Apparently not.

Jack chuckles but his look is mean. "Really hurt my feelings." He's been waiting, Duncan thinks; ever since the roundup he's been looking for a weapon he can use against me. "All I can figure is you didn't want me to know. And that worries me, Mack, that really does. I'd imagine it'd worry the whole town."

"Good thing there's nothing to that rumor then. When we've got bigger worries on our minds."

Jack walks alongside him right up to the string of horses. The man never shuts up, Duncan thinks, one foot in the stirrup. And sure enough he's still at his knee, hissing so low only Duncan can hear: "Thing is, Mack, wouldn't want anyone thinking you're on the wrong side. My advice, you'd better get out—start ranching with your old man."

Duncan scowls and Jack steps back.

"Medary was a drunk and a fool," Jack DeMers says, smiling genuinely now, delighted as only a bully can be. "But he got one thing right. You've got no right to trade on this reservation—and you can bet Ronan knows it too."

HE'S TEMPTED TO ride down to the mouth of the Lolo and see the fortifications the Army has thrown up—if only to sneer at their uselessness. But it'd be a waste of time. If he's to get through to the Nez Perce camp, he'll have to come at it from the north. He peels off from the agent and continues toward Frenchtown. Baird's still Jack's clerk, imprisoned in his store. Duncan doesn't mention Jack; it's not Baird's fault he has to work for the man. The clerk's mood is foul in any case. He ought to be down in Missoula and not stuck out here, he says, shrugging and looking away.

Duncan understands. He feels a duty to stand with the white men joining the volunteer militia. He just can't say so to Duncan's face. Instead Baird waves an Extra edition of the *Weekly Missoulian* at him. "Fresh off the press," he says.

HELP! HELP! COME RUNNING! WHITE BIRD DEFIANT! the headline screams.

"Come running!" Duncan rolls his eyes. "As if a few farmers can hold them."

"Easy for you." Baird's mouth draws down. "Nobody expects it of you."

"So go. No one will miss you." The burg is so silent they can hear the rushing of the river half a mile away.

"Not too keen on shooting Injuns." Baird smiles thinly.

"I wouldn't worry, they'll shoot you first." Duncan smiles back. Best to make a joke of it. Then he sobers. He can't—it's too damn serious. "Jesus—they're not looking for a fight. Can't anyone see that? They're traveling with every stitch they have, their wives and kids, grannies and grandpas, all their dogs and horses. Thousands of horses!" He's jabbing his finger, he notices, and drops his hand. "Nobody's looking for war."

"Looking Glass offered to surrender their ammo if they'll just let them pass, that's what I heard from Jack." Baird nods. "They want to move in peace down the valley."

Amen, thinks Duncan. Thank you, Bobby boy, for that.

"Captain Rawn parleyed yesterday with them and they're meeting again today," Baird reports next.

"They should make you the newsman."

Baird snorts. "I'm only telling you so you don't go stick your nose in." His look is penetrating, and Duncan wonders how much he suspects. He draws a breath as if to speak, and Baird interrupts him, almost angrily.

"I don't want to know, either. The less I know about what you're up to the better." His face goes hard. "I better find the goods exactly where you left them, understand? Don't think I won't tell if they vanish—it's war then for certain. And I'll have no part in that."

Duncan nods. "You have my word."

He slips out so early the next morning no one will even know he was there. No one sees him tie sacking to the gelding's hooves, leading it out like a ghost. At four in the morning even drunks are dead to the world. They ford the river and start up into the mountains. He doesn't know this tumbled part of the foothills well and struggles to find a path. Brambles tear at his shirt, limbs whack him in the dark. He slips off and gives the horse its head. Now and then it stops to regard him quizzically. "Up boy. Up." He pats him. By the time the sun lifts above the eastern peaks they're ten miles south and fifteen hundred feet up. They've crossed three ridges, the last the tallest; the Lolo canyon cannot be far. It's a fine, fantastic view, the grasses rimmed with fire as the sun's rays touch them. To his left the peaceful, shadowed valleys, to his right the swales and jagged outcrops rippling upward, vanishing from sight. The Lolo pass he traversed with Archie just four weeks ago is harsh and cluttered and narrow. And now the nimíipuu flee the same way, running for their lives—a whole huge camp struggling through the gorge. Goddamn Lewis and Clark.

Now he can see what looks like a deep cleft in the earth ahead. He's still a few miles distant, on the shoulder of the tallest point thereabouts.

It's full morning and he figures he should angle westward to come to Traveler's Rest well above the camp. He feels his blood quicken in anticipation. He presses his horse a little with his knees, sees its ears prick, knows it sees something farther even than he can see. Scouts from either side, most likely. He slips back off, half-crouched, braced for anything except the incredible sight he sees.

Along the ridge before him, partly silhouetted, cut off by the edge of hill, a line of people slowly moves. They're on the far side of the ridge, bodies and horses obscured; all he can see are heads and shoulders, feathers, dark hair shining in the sun, the glint off breastplates made of bone and hammered metal. He puts his hand to his eyes and strains and sees the people, all his people, babies in their cradleboards and children behind mothers, old folks, flicking ears of pintos, appaloosas, roans. Every ten horses or so there's a warrior flanking them, a rifle at his shoulder. He stands there watching them, amazed, so moved that he could weep. Looking Glass has taken the high road: he has taken his people up and out of range of the soldiers, above and around the danger. They thread their way along the ridge, then disappear again, back down toward the valley floor. There are hundreds of laden animals and the unmistakable dust of the travois they drag behind them, heavy with lodgepoles and hides and canvas. And after this he loses count of the herd that the boys drive before them, two thousand, maybe three, magnificent animals, the pride of the Nez Perce. He watches them pass for as long as they move, for hours, immobile, erect upon his horse, listening intently to the distant jingle, the wind blowing the sound of their hooves toward him. At the end he sees a rearguard, a strong band of some twenty tall men who sweep behind, waving their hats and plumes, enclosing the final stragglers, and only then does he permit himself to rise up in his stirrups and raise an arm and whoop loudly, the pride within him bursting forth.

AT TWILIGHT HE judges it safe to descend. The soldiers have long since deserted their earthworks. He would've liked to have seen their dismay as the Nez Perce paraded past. The governor was apparently even planning to ride out to see these "hostiles" trapped.

From the fork where the trail joins the road he sees campfires across the way, flickering in the birch groves across the river of In-shew-te-shew, Red Willow, which whites call the Bitterroot. He fords it easily, a seam down the center of the valley, flowing northwest to empty into the Che Wana where he lived as a boy. How connected they all are, Duncan McDonald thinks as he crosses the marshy bottom and passes through the outermost row of lodges. Children and women return from the river with jugs. Not once is he challenged and it unsettles him, this looseness in the camp. They ought to be more careful.

He's stopped finally by a pair of men who catalogue his coat and boots with their eyes. "I'm here to see the chiefs," he says in sign, and they look surprised.

"Give us the gun," one says, and he shakes his head. The words flow from him in his mother's tongue. "I'm nimíipuu, like you, cousin of Looking Glass, son of the Eagle Rising Up." Satisfied, the pair leads him in.

At first, he can't quite believe it's the same man, so hollow are Looking Glass's cheeks. But there's a look of softness in the hunter's eyes and a smile as he stands and wraps his arms around him. Duncan didn't expect such a greeting. But his kinsman is relieved, on top of the very world, he tells him, sweeping his eyes around his warriors and closest friends. They have passed out of Idaho.

"War is over!" They're safe at last. "We tricked the soldier chief but good!" He laughs. "I thanked him—I did!—on our way past."

The whole camp will celebrate; it's only right, after so many weeks of hard fighting and loss of life. "And then?" asks Duncan. He has messages to convey to the council. "Then we'll see," his mother's cousin says. "We'll hear you, and all the chiefs."

He goes to the lodge of White Bird to present his greetings. The chief of the Lamta'ma is still an imposing man, despite his great age. His shoulders stoop and his hair is white but he holds his head up, chin jutting, neck drooping like the pelican for which he's named. His father knew him in his prime as a great hunter and medicine man, Duncan thinks, and bows in acknowledgment. When the chief hears that Duncan's brought a message from Eagle from the Light, his face wrinkles up like an old chamois cloth. "What can he say?" he mutters, frowning. "When it was his nephew who started this war?"

There must be four hundred nimíipuu, Duncan guesses as he moves around camp. Five different bands, from every corner of the Nez Perce homeland. United at first by refusal to abandon their ways and now bound by this fighting and flight. Still, they are in no way a mass—instead a whirling collection of single hearts and minds. He watches them laughing, making food, feeding fires; he's both delighted and afraid. It won't be easy to forge them into one.

They meet in the lodge of Left Hand, who looks so like his brother Eagle from the Light that for a moment Duncan thinks he's been fooled, and the chief has whisked himself down here somehow. Then he shakes Left Hand's arm. Some twenty men pack in, the chiefs in the center on the ground. All of them three forks, his grandmother would dismissively say: two legs and one penis and barely a brain.

He stands nodding at those he knows, struck by how handsome they are, almost to a man—uncommonly so. How clean and sharp the bones of their faces, how clear their eyes. Chief Joseph, his brother Frog, forelocks stiffened and swept elegantly up; Bird Alighting with his cleft chin and full lips; Red Owl, delicate with domed, sleepy eyes; the gnarled and stately White Bird; Looking Glass; even short, fiery Lean Elk, part French like Duncan himself. Some are fleshier, but in the main they are splendid specimens of manhood.

He's thinking it must have to do with the hardness of their lives when Looking Glass starts to smoke. The pipe takes a long time to go around. The chief bows his head slightly when Joseph says, "It's Looking Glass who led us to safety, we are thankful." The young chief of the Wallowa has a square face and narrow eyes and an expression of almost unbearable sadness. "We were never for fighting," agrees Bird Alighting of Looking Glass's band.

"It's over now, we left the soldiers behind," says Red Owl, and there's murmuring and nodding before Duncan bends forward.

"Unfortunately not." He wishes he spoke his mother's language better. "The soldier chief will pursue you. Even now Cut-Arm"—their name for the one-armed General Howard—"is coming toward the Lolo."

"They let us pass. They accepted our pact of peace." Bird Alighting speaks for Looking Glass, it seems. The chief himself looks displeased.

"They let you pass because they knew they couldn't stop you." Duncan takes a breath. "But they'll still hunt you." He turns his gaze to the two youngest men, hidden in the shadows, the hotheads who started it all. These boys, too, are his kin, he thinks. "It's foolish to think they won't make you pay for the deaths you caused."

White Bird removes the gray wing of the eagle he holds lightly before his mouth. "What you say is true." He bores his eyes into Duncan. "Is this the message sent by Eagle from the Light?"

"Our people in Sin-ye-le-min are worried." He has to be diplomatic. "They want to know which way you'll go. They send me to say the safest way is north, to Grandmother's Land."

Looking Glass snorts. "What should I do in the white Queen's land? This is my country. We hunt here every season. We're going to our friends the Crow."

"I can lead you across the medicine line. To safety, with Sitting Bull and the Sioux. On the plains you're not safe."

Animosity flashes on the thin cheeks of the chief. He holds no love for the Sioux, whom he fought alongside the Crow. But these old enmities mean little now.

"The Crow are our brothers," an older warrior asserts.

White Bird shakes his head. His eyes, unblinking, hold Duncan's. "You haven't said everything they counsel, the nimíipuu who stay with you."

He knows his people well. "They're divided," Duncan admits. Beneath the chief's stern look he cannot completely lie. "My mother, her mother Margaret, the Chief Trader my father—all argue for the northern way. Only Eagle from the Light disagrees."

"Some Pend d'Oreille say the same," another man says.

"But their chief won't let us cross their place."

"What of Charlo?" Duncan asks.

"The Salish betray us." Looking Glass speaks with a hiss. "They stood against us at the soldier fort."

"We've always been friendly to the people in Montana." Bird Alighting looks at each face. "They need not fear us. We said so tonight when they passed."

"But they can't be trusted." It's out of his mouth before Duncan knows it. He looks with all his heart at White Bird. "They always lie when it suits their purpose. You know this. The way isn't safe."

White Bird nods. Red Owl purses his lips. Neither Joseph nor the Frog speak.

"My heart says the north," White Bird says. "When things calm, we can come back."

"You would run? Like a woman? You, whose people began this?" Looking Glass's voice is scathing. "I didn't want this fight any more than Joseph. It was your people who started this. And now you'd run and hide."

There's a murmur of agreement, and Duncan feels sweat start to gather on his back.

"How many have already died?" Red Owl stands, lips like a gash in his pale face. "We can't take the old ones or children much farther. Already they're weak and crying." He shakes his head. "I, too, am for the road north."

"The way is short," Duncan says. "I can lead you there in four or five days." Please, please, he thinks. Hear my mother—hear me, you chiefs.

Looking Glass stands, his voice harsh. "I've brought us this far, and now you would run!" He makes a disgusted sound. "We'll hunt and eat, there's no reason for fear."

"What does Joseph say?" White Bird asks quietly. All eyes turn to the young chief. He looks at each in turn. "Either way is the same," he says. "I have nothing left in any case." How crushed he appears. Everyone turns back to Looking Glass and White Bird. For a long, tense moment there is only silence.

White Bird sighs. "I'm an old man. I can't lead all these people. I'd take them north, to the Old Woman's Land. But I'm not chief of this whole camp, just one man." He looks hard at Looking Glass. "If you're determined, I won't speak against you. You've led us well, you're still the chief."

"I believe in the pledges of our friends. Our allies have said we are welcome." Looking Glass eyes Duncan. "Our cousin says the same." With a twist to his gut, Duncan realizes Eagle from the Light has sent his own message too, through some devious means, exhorting them to join their allies on the plains.

"I fear it's a bad way," Red Owl says. "But I'll follow you south."

"So be it then." White Bird lifts the gray wing back up to cover his mouth.

CHAPTER 11

Editorial

The movement of the Nez Perces last Saturday was one of the most brilliant strategically of modern warfare. It was, of all others, the move that nobody expected them to make. Its audacity was stunning. It will ever stand as a monument to the bravery of that people that they moved with their horses and women and little ones through an open country that was swarming with armed men.

These Indians would undoubtedly like to make their peace with the government by some conditional surrender that shall grant them immunity for what is past; but they will fight to extermination before they will give up their murderers to be hung. They must be conquered and a condition of their surrender must be that they are to return to their reservation and never more go on a buffalo hunt. Our security demands this.

—WEEKLY MISSOULIAN
August 3, 1877

BEFORE DAWN CATHERINE suddenly awakes. She feels her mother's force, her silent call. She leaves her husband's sleeping body for the starlight. Margaret stands among the pines beyond her lodge, her white hair glowing. When she turns her face is wet. "I saw them killed. I saw the flaming riders." Her voice is hoarse. Her dream is still within her, pinned by her ferocious will.

Her daughter makes no sound to break the spell, although the warmth inside her drains right to the ground. Her mother strains to see each detail, every bird and blade of grass in this horrific scene that came to her in sleep. *I knew*, thinks Catherine, startled.

"Their land no longer speaks to them; they left it far behind." Margaret sags and Catherine sees the dream has gone. They're only women—mothers, daughters, sisters, aunts, and cousins—hearts contracting. Her mother's face is filled with anguish. Her daughter wipes her cheeks. Why did they go? What foolish pride was yours, young Looking Glass?

When morning comes she'll tell the men. It will change nothing. What's dreamt is done. By now their people have moved far away. They hear no news except the scratchings of the white men—and now this. She'll send Duncan to learn more, she thinks—then stops herself. He tried; how hard he tries. Yet they had failed. She doesn't understand how all their strength and courage can be nothing more than mist. The Bostons have such crushing, evil power over even her and Angus, all their children, though they never did a thing to harm them. Her mother dozes, head tipped slightly forward, and Catherine holds her like a newborn. Her eldest boy is dead; her eldest girl is gone into that other world. Even Duncan they would tear apart, destroy.

How pinched he was when he returned to check on Quil-see. She longed to rock him as she did when he was young. He's enemy to either side; he never will be either. His tall proud shoulders slumped. He kept away from Angus like an injured dog. The agent kicked him out, he told her. Her son was trading without some paper that he had to have. Fight back, she told her boy. But he just shook his head. "The fight is endless, and I'm tired."

Gladly she'd take this pain from him. But she must watch her children and her people suffer. They're surrounded and pursued, denied the right to live and breathe the air of their own land. "And I was even born here." He spoke with a pained puzzlement, the way he always had, the boy who tried so hard to understand.

She walks her mother slowly back to her lodge. She'll bring Angus, she whispers. Duncan she'll leave to sleep a few moments more with his wife, their unborn child.

· In her pride she believed they could hold onto their birthright through sheer strength and stubbornness. She thought with cunning and resistance they'd survive. Not just her mother's people but her own, the tribe of many histories and colors that enlivened all these valleys long before the Bostons came. But she was wrong. It seems to her that they were only little figures at the edge of a vast sea, the birds all flown, the water rising without mercy.

▨

RONAN WAS TRULY sorry; it was out of his hands. The previous agent had set it all in motion. Only Indians can trade—or white men with a license—on a reservation. He doesn't use the word "half-breed," but Duncan understands. It would be different if he were adopted into the confederated tribes of the Flathead, the agent said.

Duncan chews on it all as he returns alone to the Jocko. To the whites all Indians are the same, whether Sioux or Cherokee or Pend d'Oreille—except when they are not. Then he's a half or quarter Nez Perce and isn't welcome anymore. He'll keep his head down, figure it out while awaiting the birth of this child. But even this he won't be allowed: the agency's in too much of an uproar.

Ronan is just saddling up when he arrives. The agent hails him at the same moment Arlee appears, looking grim. It pained Duncan to see his grandmother so upset this morning, but he doesn't put much stock in prophecy. A dream is just a dream, is how he feels. But now Arlee's talking at him rapid-fire about a whole lot of soldiers marching down the Bitterroot and his insides twist.

"Truly?" He turns to Ronan.

"A whole company out of Fort Shaw." Ronan gives him a sympathetic look. "Probably pick up some volunteers as they head south."

This is what hits him hardest. Not the soldiers so much as the ordinary folks. It's the regular settlers, farmers and blacksmiths and merchant volunteers in their ragtag militias, armed with rifles and malice, who always seem to shoot first. Just like at Clear Creek. Not one of them willing to even share this land with Indians, including—perhaps especially—Duncan himself.

CHAPTER 12

A Bloody Battle
—The Hostiles Overtaken and Attacked in the Big Hole
—Gibbon Makes a Desperate But Unequal Fight
—Capt. Logan and Lieut. Bradley Killed

TO GOVERNOR POTTS: BIG HOLE, AUGUST 9

Had a hard fight with the Nez Perces, killing a number and losing a number of officers and men. We need a doctor and everything. Send us such relief as you can.

John Gibbon, Col. Commanding.

THE LATEST.

Deer Lodge, August 11–9 a.m. W. H. Edwards has just arrived from Big Hole, bringing accounts of a terrible battle between Gibbon's command and the Nez Perces in the Big Hole, August 9th. Gibbon's command, consisting of 182 men and 17 officers—133 regulars and 32 citizen volunteers—crossed over from Ross Hole to near Big Hole on Wednesday. Starting at 11 o'clock the same night, they moved down the troops, except a few left with the gun and transportation six miles above, close to the Indian camp, which was made on the Big Hole, about three miles below where the Bitter Root and Bannock trails cross.

At daylight in the morning the fight opened by the volunteers firing on and killing an Indian going after horses. The charge was then made on the camp, and hard fighting occurred for the two next hours, during which time a large number of men and Indians were killed. The soldiers then charged on the lodges, but were repulsed in the attempt.

The Indians then attempted to cut them off from a high wooded point, but the soldiers charged and driving the Indian advance from it held it, and at once fortified. The fighting continued here all day and was still progressing fitfully when the courier left at 11. The fighting was desperate on both sides, the full force of the Indians being in the fight. . . .

The messenger says he thinks 100 Indians were killed, and that nearly half the command, including citizens, were killed or wounded. Gen. Gibbon has sent for medicines, surgeons, supplies etc. Dr. Mitchell will leave today with an escort.

It is one of the hardest Indian fights on record, and Gibbon's command made a most gallant and desperate fight against overwhelming numbers.

—*HELENA DAILY HERALD*
August 11, 1877

HER HUSBAND THINKS she's entirely mad. It's possible—but if so, it's the clearest madness. There's no one else to tend the dead. The rest are dispersed or too terrified to show their faces. Kitalah isn't. She has no fear of these settlers, these vermin with forked tongues who watched the nimíipuu move peacefully through their villages, took their money in exchange for goods, but did not hesitate to join the troops that fired upon them as they slept.

If only Looking Glass had listened. Riding south with her son she knows he feels responsible. If only he could have convinced them. But her cousin is proud, she tells Duncan, even arrogant. Now they'll see the price of that pride. The Salish whisper of the nimíipuu's slow travel, their leisurely pace, as if they felt invincible. The war was behind them, or so they thought. But it's as Angus has always said: the laws of the Americans reach across every line they draw.

He tried to insist on accompanying her, of course. But she refused. Only the people can tend to their own dead. She took her son instead. She turned her back on her husband's anger, knowing it was really fear for her safety. It would have wounded him to know that she couldn't abide the thought of more white skin on that battlefield, however well-intentioned. She can't look at a white now without seeing violent death, the bullets and bayonets that have taken over her mind and filled it with gruesome imaginings. Her son, too, feels this rage. She's always been able to feel what he feels. In any case, he wears it openly on his face.

They ride down the wagon road through the valley of the Bitterroot, stopping only to relieve themselves and drink and eat and sleep. She hasn't been this way in a long time. The rolling country has filled up with little homesteads, villages every ten miles or so like beads on a string. Duncan speaks with some of the Salish as they pass, but she doesn't. They offered no help to her people. Angus says they had no choice if they were to keep peace in their own land. But it's hard to forgive, knowing so many have died. No one knows exactly how many; the Boston newspapers always lie.

Even now, weeks later, no one really knows where White Bird and Joseph and the rest have gone. They get snips of news like drifting leaves: the Nez Perce passed through the Smoky Ground; they took some hostages; they rustled some of Howard's mules. Duncan scours the papers but they're out of date, and for all they know, her people are all dead or dispersed, or—she prays to her Creator now—safe at last above the medicine line.

They stop at the medicine tree, a tall yellow pine on a slope to the west that is sacred to the Salish. A buffalo horn protrudes from the scaly bark some twenty feet up; it's hung with charms. Margaret has given Duncan a medicine bundle to affix to one of its branches; he slips it on a rope and throws. Once, twice, the third time it catches. He grins, for the first time since they left Post Creek. "Three is a good number." She nods, then feels the dread spread through her. How many bodies will they find? The newspapers called it a great victory for General Gibbon, even though thirty of his men were killed and forty wounded. All they said about "Joseph's warriors" is that they numbered three or four hundred, but everyone knows they were fewer—two hundred fifty at most, protecting hundreds of women and children and elders.

They begin to loosen as the valley narrows and they begin the climb. It was difficult, riding past all those watchful eyes. In the last hamlet Duncan went into the store. They'd agreed to keep their business to themselves. Only at that last stop did he buy them two heavy shovels. These slap the horses' rumps, making a whacking sound as they take the last part of the trail across the great divide—which no eye can miss now, trampled as it is from the soldiers' wagons.

"Stampede," her son says with a bitter twist to his mouth. She lifts the reins, leaning forward, urging the horse up and up and up. There are so many ridges to cross, and she can only think how hard it must have been for the people with their babies and old ones, their covers and household goods. Suddenly she's incredibly proud. They're magnificent, her people.

"Imagine," she says when they stop to rest. "How encumbered they climbed this."

Duncan nods, looking around. "They must not have known they were followed."

Then it's back, the feeling of horror and outrage. The only thing they know for sure—because the papers have all said the same—is that the soldiers crept up on the sleeping camp at first light and started shooting. They attacked while everyone was asleep, firing into their lodges.

Each remembers that kind of horror. Catherine is covering her ears against the screams as white trappers pick the people off. She still sees women bobbing in the stream. Duncan is racing Archie to the woods above the creek as bullets strike the earth. The innards of both begin to knot as they drop down from the summit. They know more or less what they'll find.

But even so the bile rises, and they have to turn away when they cross the stream and part the low thicket of willows. Everywhere before them are corpses, unearthed, gnawed and torn, dragged and scattered across the churned earth. Coyotes and wolves and grizzlies have been here, digging and feeding, fighting over the remains. But they're not the only animals who disturbed these dead. Catherine lets out a howl as she crouches over the large body of a man, his face no more than a skull streaked brownish red, caked with shreds of hard, dried flesh. His belly has been opened and the entrails half pulled out. She points at the head and Duncan sees a narrow strip of hair above the hollow of the ear, but nothing else.

"Enemies," she hisses, and he sees his mother as she must have been in some entirely different life. "Animals," she keeps on hissing. Later they'll learn Howard's scouts were Bannocks and the army didn't stop them from scalping and defiling the nimíipuu dead. But this isn't the worst of it.

She walks, zigzagging between the shreds of hide and canvas, the charred and broken lodge poles, stepping carefully. There's no sense to it. The people would have buried their loved ones wrapped in blankets. Quickly, shallowly, no doubt, as they ran to save themselves. Someone else came after and moved the bodies, reburied them hastily. But these graves, too, have been peeled open, mauled.

She covers her mouth with her hand and bends forward, searching. Perhaps by some scrap of cloth, some still-taut skin, she'll know which of her kin lies dead here in the bowl of the Big Hole. Where her own life, such as it is, began. She begins to shake as she stumbles across this charnel ground, remembering her marriage, her uncle's blue-marked lodge, while her eyes take in only muck and charcoal and bones. She searches for White Bird's family, his wife; for the sons of Bird Alighting; for her own second cousin, the daughter of Looking Glass. Nothing human is left to help her. Off to the side of the main camp she comes upon the bodies of two women and an infant; the baby's head has been smashed in. In the moon since they were killed their skin has blistered and popped and there's almost no flesh left, between the maggots and the wild animals.

Duncan stands frozen, leaning wordless on the shovel. He's never seen such brutality. She gestures to him and he crosses to where she squats. She starts to sing, low and halting. Their spirits can't rest until their bodies are returned into their mother earth. She sends him back to the horses to unload the cloth. She knew they'd need cloth. Since the battle other hands have also pawed these bones, stealing the blankets in which they were wound, the rings and bracelets and tokens sent with them to the spirit world.

Together they release the bodies from whatever dirt still holds them. Some are partly exposed, others fully; one corpse sits half-upright. She hears her son cry suddenly and sees him fall on his knees; he's weeping when she goes to him. He looks at her with incomprehension; he hides his face in his elbow. "About Asleep," he chokes out, and she holds him as he cries and cries. After a time he stands and takes the shovel and begins to slice it brutally into the earth. He digs the graves deeper than before, though they both know the animals will return. Still, there's not much flesh left on these poor departed souls. They lay each one they find intact or can reassemble onto a stretch of cloth and wind it and set it gently in the trough. She crumbles tobacco over them, whispering the prayers her mother taught her.

Duncan stands at a remove; he's never followed these traditions. It angers her suddenly—she's surprised by the heat she feels. Whose children are these then, Angus's or hers? To whom do they truly belong? They can't be both, for their souls will be at war forever. She looks at her taciturn son, willing him to sing and say the prayers, but he only moves silently behind her, lifting each body when she's done.

The children are the hardest. They are concentrated near the center of the camp, where the lodges were thickest, the shooting seemingly most indiscriminate. Their flesh the tenderest, perhaps—it's the obvious conclusion, for here the ground is even more churned, a midden of black mud and flaxen grass and the pinkish white of limbs that protrude, most of them stripped but not all. Many animals have been here. She hears Duncan make a sound and turns to see him retching. Gently, ever so gently, they start to work, trying to put these young ones back together. A few mothers are strewn among them. One clutches the empty air; Kitalah prays this means her infant has survived. On these bones they glimpse the aftermath of grievous wounds: wrist separated from arm, rib cracked by a bullet, skull dented or crushed, and as they work, she finds herself weeping, an endless, silently running fountain that anoints her cheeks, her hands, these bones. These innocents, these lambs. Duncan is on his knees beside her, a muscle in his cheek throbbing. "Animals," he rasps, and doesn't mean the creatures with which they share this earth. "They should be court-martialed." She doesn't know what he means but can sense the depth of his revulsion. Suddenly he thrusts out his hand. "Ki-nic-nic." His mouth is tighter than she's ever seen it. He looks not like the hart but the wolf, eyes glittering. She gives the dried leaves to him and intones the prayers as they roll each small bundle, scattering the brown flakes within and without.

Over and over they do this until at last they're done. She's sung it eighty-seven times. With each song her strength has ebbed more and more and now she's entirely spent. Yet gazing at her son, she finds that the opposite has occurred. Each burial has tightened him; each has made his bones, eyes, sinews tauter. So that when she looks at him finally with a nod of exhaustion and he helps her to her feet, she feels that he has turned entirely to stone.

Honorable Hiram Knowles
Missoula

Flathead Reservation
7 October 1877

Dear Judge Knowles

Who would have thought that little band of Indians would make their way through the Territory so peacefully, and to such misfortune. I have only just bid farewell to my son and his mother, who needs must witness Gibbon's foul handiwork. This senseless slaughter confers no honor, only shame, upon our race. It is the old drift: the strong oppresses the weak and Power is always Power right or wrong.

I see the Sisters of Charity out to meet the US wounded and care for them after the Big Hole battle ("Vale of the Squirrel" is the Indian name for it). It is good that God will not, cannot trust all His work to either woman or man. When I see their care for the soldiers of Big Uncle Sam who is rich as he is silly and noble and then I also see a little woman away in the grass lying and moaning in her blood with her murdered infant tightened to her bosom, the red woman, ancient mother of America. Yes, there under the omniscient Eye alone she was passing away but no Sisters of Charity went near her Oh No. Out, Out, Out on our bastard Christianity.

You may have heard much of Col. Wright during the Yakama business, but you can be certain his victory was misleading and built on false grounds. Col Wright only killed in his two battles three Indians. The public do not know that he put his prisoners to death and thereby swelled the roll of the killed. The chiefs after their combat under a flag of truce went in to make a peace and the leading warriors who of their own accord followed them to do the same were all retained for the gallows, and the roll of 17 killed and 45 wounded went on all big and false to Washington.

The treachery there and in other recent instances of the US Army prevented Joseph and Looking Glass and White Bird from making an end of the war at Lolo's fork with the authorities there. I thought of going up *to see you and Gov Potts to see if a solid peace could not be effected with that fine tribe of Indians, but as I could not answer or conceive what might be done to them afterwards, I remained at home. Treachery as usual after peace is the only thing they dreaded.*

Well, goodbye my Lord and commend me as most sincerely yours,

A. McDonald

CHAPTER 13

Defeat and Capture
Of the Nez Perces
Miles Strikes the Final Blow

FORT SHAW, MONTANA, Oct. 6—General Miles surprised
the Nez Perces in camp near the Bear Paw Mountains, on the
30th of September, killing seventeen, including Looking Glass,
Joseph's brother, and three other Chiefs, and wounding forty.
He also captured six hundred ponies. He has the Indians now
closely invested in ravines. General Miles' loss in killed are
Capt. Hale and Lieut. Biddle, 7th Cavalry and 22 men; Wounded, Capt. Mayhew, Capt. Godfrey, 7th Cavalry; Lieuts. Baird and
Romeyn, 5th Infantry and 40 men. None of the officers wounded are dangerously so. Miles says these Indians fight more
desperately than any he ever saw.

  (Signed.) JOHN GIBBON, Col. 7th Infantry
               —*THE NEW NORTH-WEST, Deer Lodge, M.T.*
                             Friday, October 12, 1877

We clip the following from the New York *Sun*:
General Howard, in his final report of the Nez Perces campaign,
says that on the surrender at Snake Creek, "a few Indians,
including White Bird, crept out through the lines during the
night." Since that report was written we have had a more ex-
plicit statement from an undoubted source. Major Walsh writes
to Col. McLeod, commanding the Northwest Mounted Police
of Canada, that, while he was at Sitting Bull's camp, a party of
Nez Perces came in from the Snake Creek battlefield; "I awaited
their arrival, and found the party to consist of fifty men, forty

women, and a large number of children, besides about three hundred horses."

—*BENTON RECORD*
November 19, 1877

▙▚

QUIL-SEE AND he have made a beautiful baby girl. When she arrives with the first snow Duncan feels a pain inside, then heat, a drilling at the shell that formed around him at Big Hole. He loves this infant from a place so deep he never knew it was even there. And still when he hears her chirrup and looks at her solemn black eyes, the funny fountain of soft spiky hair, he sees the bones beneath, the fragile skull so easily broken. And he's afraid of both the world and of himself. Quil-see says he's possessed of the spirits of the soldier dead, and he thinks she must be right. He feels the prying of their finger bones against his chest.

They named her Mary and his father beamed. "The Queen of Scots," he said, and Quil-see gave him her reproving look. "The Queen of Heaven," she replied. All four grandparents were present for the ceremony, in body if not in spirit. Since their return his mother, too, was changed, anger and sorrow eating her from inside. Duncan told his father to give her time; he himself took her tea and sat. Neither spoke, but even so he sensed his presence comforted her somehow.

He and Baird are wintering above the line at the Kootenay mines. He had to get away. He needs to make some money shipping up supplies, he told his wife, if he can't trade at Jocko. Quil-see wasn't fooled. He's a fugitive, that's all—not just from the law but from his own life. At the height of that summer madness he didn't arm a soul—but then the autumn came, and he couldn't sit by and see them starve. He sold them cartridges and skipped across the line like every other bootlegger and renegade. Here in the new Dominion of Canada they are almost neighbors, he and Sitting Bull and White Bird—flown with his kin from that final disaster. They almost made it—all of them—to safety. They were only forty miles from the medicine line when the army caught them; only a few score escaped.

Robert and he are just waiting for the blizzards to stop so they can head home. They sleep in a sad excuse for a cabin rented from the lady who runs the saloon. Wind whistles through the cracks and Duncan wishes he were snug in a fur-lined lodge. He's happiest alone, away from the clamor and stripping of the land. He roams whenever the wind lets up enough, shooting and skinning, packing home meat for them both. Even so Baird is none too pleased to see him return in his skins and furs.

"You're going to get us both killed, dressed like a buck," he said just once when they were first snowbound in this slimy mining town.

"Don't call me that," Duncan snapped back. "You of all people should know better."

Bucks, squaws, papooses. Savages. Breeds. He'll wear as much buckskin as he damn well pleases. Nothing so-called civilization ever devised is half as good in the woods. He moves like the deer, barely rustling. Tim-mina-ilpilp. Red Hart. Quil-see stitched these expressly for him.

"I'm just saying plenty shoot first and look later," Robert said, looking chastened.

He felt bad then; Baird and Angus are the only whites he still half-way trusts. "All they have to do is use their eyes," he said as gently as he could. He looks as crazed as any miner in this godforsaken place, his mustache and beard grown bushy and wild. They were meant to be up and back from the mines in three weeks but the snow caught them just after Christmas. Robert feels bad about skipping out on Mary Ronan: she hired him to tutor her kids. So when the weather relents a bit they make a run for it.

Angus always says moving is the best medicine. Better than physicians and tinctures he means. But it's also Indian medicine, Duncan thinks. For the first time he understands that it's in his blood—his Indian blood. He never saw it that way before. Now as they head south toward the States, he perceives himself as a single beast in that continuous migration begun eons before. Plowing through drifts, swimming water so cold it nearly bursts the heart, pulling deadfall to make saving fire. East and west and back again in an eternal return: to the buffalo, the salmon, the camas, the summer and wintering grounds.

He can't stop thinking about Glencoe, either. When they returned from Big Hole he asked Angus to tell him the whole story again. How the English king sent the Campbells to punish the McDonalds; how they ate and drank in their crofts for nearly a week before rising to slaughter them all. The only meaning Duncan can extract from it is the randomness of survival. He thinks of his brother John: there's no reason he died and Duncan survived. Yes, he's more careful. But that's no different than being in the wrong lodge on a hot August morning, or the wrong hut on the banks of the Coe two hundred years ago.

Survival is not freedom. It's not. It's endurance, nothing more. Chief Joseph surrendered and his people are imprisoned now, those who didn't die en route, in some terrible hot place to the south. Duncan thinks of the Highlands of Scotland before Angus fled, the people cowed, evicted, spurned. Better, his son thinks—as he knows White Bird thinks, and Sitting Bull, and countless other chiefs—to go extinct, just like the bison.

Just before he and his mother went down to that boneyard, he read of the proud procession of the generals of the US Army. At the time it struck him as ironic: while his mother's people were fleeing eastward, Sherman, the Civil War hero, and Sheridan were each making their way westward through that same wild and beautiful land. How the papers enthused about their excursions: Sherman's tour of the wondrous new National Park called Yellowstone; Sheridan's appreciation of the vast grasslands of the Bighorn and Gallatin Valley. Only now does Duncan see that these two movements were of course related: the Natives fleeing for their lives, the soldiers surveying their newly vacant real estate. It won't end until they're all wiped away.

The whole next spring he comes and goes. Across the Marias Pass, back to the Kootenays; he cuts a new trail through the glaciers, carves his name in a tree above a lake. When he's home in the Mission Valley he helps Angus with the branding. The one thing he can't stand is being idle, he allows.

"Just like me," his father says, and laughs.

"Not exactly." Duncan looks at his progenitor, a little stooped now, but still strong.

"Now, then. You're a McDonald."

"Not completely."

His father sighs and nods and doesn't answer. One time when words fail him, Duncan thinks, wishing he could tell Christina. She'd laugh and understand.

They survey the herd, the fields of barley and timothy hay, the well-proportioned house, and it seems to Duncan that his father always had a leg up on the Native people, for all his love of their free way of life. His skin is white; he trusts the world. While down by the agency the lodges of destitute people tell a different tale. There are no farms, no tools, no schools that they'd been forced to trade their land for. Their crops have failed again; the buffalo are gone. In their place on the wide open plain, Red Horn told him—shocked, still disbelieving—piles of skulls and bones as tall as the sky.

SHE SHOULD BE digging her garden. It's spring, after all. Maggie and Tom do it for her, treating her carefully, as if she might break. She feels forever changed. Her cousin Eagle from the Light has also suddenly grown old, air collapsing from him like Angus's skin bag. They're just three old people as mute as posts now, Catherine thinks. Margaret, her mother, is in a different plane, one foot on the ladder, while they remain below. Resentful and forced to salvage something from the dirt besides these bones.

And still Angus writes and writes. His words spin through the air and she thinks they're like butterflies, pretty but useless, until her cousin comes to her and tells her they're more like bees. He and Angus have a plan. He'll die resisting, if need be, her husband says, in whatever poor way he can. Angus reads her the words of Eagle from the Light in their own language—which he'll turn into English for Agent Ronan, who will send them to General Howard, and eventually the Great Father in Washington. This is her cousin's desire.

> "I lost all my children, all my brothers, all my women in the war. It wasn't my fault that my children and my tribe were killed and made prisoners in the war. I was opposed to war, and because I opposed it in the councils of my nation, I was compelled to leave my tribe and come here and ask permission of you to live among the Flatheads until peace came.
>
> Now I will speak as clearly as after the darkness of night—so clear will be my words.

I speak from the earth and from Heaven, because both the Indians and the white people are made strong or weak from Him above.

I know that all the Nez Perce that are now prisoners in the South, among whom are some of my children and relations, are very sad because a great many are already dead, and the rest are fast dying in a climate they are not used to. So I beg of you, Great Father of the white people in Washington, to give them back to me.

We are now at midday—the sun in the heavens is very bright. It's by the law of that brightness that I ask you to give me back my people. I am sorry that they may not go back to Idaho, but they can live in the good air at the Flathead Reservation, while all will die if they are kept in the warm air of the South.

I am Chief as well as you, and when war is over we should agree that brave men and women and children should not die if it can be helped. That is the reason I say again, Give me back my children! I speak for Chief Joseph and his fellow prisoners. I was Chief of those Indians before Joseph was, and left my people because I believed in peace.

Catherine listens but isn't convinced. It will take more than words. Those treaties too were made of words, but the words were lies. She sends her prayers instead to Joseph's people in the hot and deadly place, to her own clan with White Bird across the medicine line. There must be some other way to fight she can't yet discern.

IF HE COULD do it all again, could he have found a better way? He's written letters by the score, the latest from Eagle from the Light to the President. Already Angus knows how they'll answer. Ronan opposes resettling the remnants of that band upon this reservation; Howard and the President are mere formalities. Angus was naïve, a fool. The Company should have fought to hold the northern bank of the Columbia; the Nez Perce should have fought when they still stood a chance, as his friend said— twenty, thirty years ago. Now they're overrun, obliterated, like the chieftains of the Highland clans. Catherine doesn't think he understands her horror and pain, and it's true it is removed in time, his ancient slaughter from her fresher one. But all the same their peoples' hearts have always beat the same wild tune. He thinks of going up to see Christina; she could always lift his spirits. To do so would be selfish though. They need him here, for what he's worth. Not just Catherine, but Duncan.

All his boys are out on the range one day in late May when a letter comes addressed to Angus from Deer Lodge. He opens it and reads its contents. He reads it again and sits down on his porch. He smokes and thinks. When the sun is setting, he calls to his eldest son as he passes from the barn to his own lodge.

"Countryman, lend me your ear." He pats the bench and smiles.

Duncan is sweaty and tired.

"I have news."

His son puts a boot up on the steps. He's a fine-looking man, silhouetted like a knife against the bright orange light. "Good or bad?"

"You be the judge." Angus pulls it out. "It's from the editor of the *New North-West*. He asks if I'll write him something about the Nez Perce war."

Duncan puts his hat back on. "Good luck."

"The thing is," Angus stands. "I don't see why I should do it."

His son is dressed like a cowboy in thick chaps and dusty black hat; he strokes his mustache but says nothing. He was always like this, Angus thinks: a boy—now a man—who listened before shooting off his mouth.

"I used to think I knew about the world. In certain ways I guess I did. But not enough. Not by a long shot." He looks him in the eyes. "I should have seen it coming, but I failed."

Duncan's alert now, listening to every word.

"And then I thought—the man to do this isn't me, but you."

His son is startled; it's not what he expects. Has he been such an overbearing presence? his father wonders. So full of his own faith, his own importance?

"I don't know about that." Duncan makes a face. "I don't spend my waking hours in writing like you do."

"He wants to know the causes of it—and the consequences." Angus pulls the letter out and reads: "He wants, quote, the real story from the Nez Perce standpoint, with as full particulars as possible."

Duncan puts his hand out and Angus watches him as he reads the thing in full.

"It's a chance. To get it down in black and white."

His son is half shaking his head, half smiling. "Well, I'll be damned."

"I'll stake you the trip across the line," says Angus. This is his role now, he suddenly realizes: support and supply. Even White Bird and Joseph concerned themselves with the families, staying with the women and children at the back while the battle chiefs, Looking Glass and Lean Elk, rode ahead. He puts a hand on Duncan's shoulder and his son doesn't shake him off.

"Well." Duncan looks out across the land. "Think he'll pay me too?"

"Mercenary." Angus grins and watches him walk away, his body straighter, or so it seems, if his old eyes don't trick him.

Duncan, for his part, walks to the creek and back, a fizzing inside that makes him want to laugh. How strange life is. He's not a newsman—far, far from it. And yet he's meant to be one now. He sees himself in pin-stripes with a notebook and a little pen, and then he truly laughs out loud. He finds his mother in her garden sitting on an upturned crate, looking at the new green shoots. At last, he thinks, here's something I can give her.

"It'sa," he says. "Mama, listen."

She hears a new note in his voice and turns. "What is it?"

"I'll go to see White Bird."

She rises so briskly he's amazed. "You what?" Her hand snakes out to grasp his arm.

"They want to know what happened, how it happened. The soyapo newspaper. One of them, at least, thinks the nimíipuu should be heard."

"You'll see them—learn who lived." Her face is transfigured.

He nods. "And maybe find a way they can come home."

There's a shine now in her eyes he hasn't seen for a long, long time.

"We never chose war. They pushed us into it." Her voice rings out. "You tell them that. That it was their fault and not ours."

"Yes." He hesitates, but only for a moment. "They asked Father to do it, but he said it wasn't his to do."

She reaches for his arm and tucks it into hers and they begin to walk toward the house. "My mother will say it's as she foretold." Her smile is sly. "When she married us for the sake of the tribe." She looks at him piercingly. "We were married, you know, at Big Hole."

A chill runs through him. "I didn't know."

"Even so you feel your duty—to work to help the people." It's right so, she thinks. *For this I brought you here.*

He'll go north and she'll stay and look after her first grandchild. She'll go to the church with Quil-see and hear that music like the mountain air. Perhaps she'll light their candles too for all the souls that have been lost, while Duncan carries the flame to her people. Her heart swells with pleasure.

"I'll be like Tah-see." He says it teasingly. "Trapped but ever-living, roaring up to scatter all our enemies." It's one of their oldest stories—how they came upon horns that stuck out of the ice on the Salmon River and tried to hack them off—until that ancient beast lurched back to life and drowned them all.

"So many generations past." His mother nods. She reaches and yanks his forehead to hers, like her mother does, and he says, "Ow!"

"But one boy lived, when Tah-see roared," she whispers in his ear. "And now his spirit lives in you."

CHAPTER 14

The Nez Perces
THE HISTORY OF THEIR TROUBLES
AND THE CAMPAIGN OF 1877

By DUNCAN McDONALD

*The writer, a relative of Looking Glass and White Bird, has entered
into arrangements with the New North-West to prepare a series
of papers giving the Nez Perces version of their troubles and their
remarkable campaign. It is a condition of the publication that the
views shall be related from their standpoint. The author has been for
some time collecting data from prominent actors in the great drama,
and the time yet required to elicit incidents of the campaign will be
occupied in preliminary narrative.*

. . . With the steadily increasing pressure and unredressed
crimes of the white men in their country and with the presence
of [General] Howard to remove them from their long-loved
homes—homes of which they never relinquished title even
were they disposed to leave them, and with their Speaker seized
at the point of the bayonet for representing these truths . . . the
Nez Perces determined to revenge their long pent grievances in
the terrible way they did. In Indian laws an armed man putting
his hand on man is punishable with death. When these Indians,
before the time I was born, were in their prime it was death for
one Indian to strike another, as it was also for adultery, or in
defense of any seizure of property from its proper owner.

NOMADIC LIFE

Having made these few most serious observations, I have a little to say on the cry against nomad life. It is wrong for you to think my people are bad because they lead a nomadic life. Where is there a more nomadic tribe than the Flatheads? Yet in the day of need you cried to them for help, and they helped you as far as human nature could do, although they love you fully as little as the Nez Perces. Every Indian's country is his rancho where he has fixed fisheries and little humble huts and fields and marsh ground for his roots and cereals and higher bowers for his fruits. There are left with them a few brood horses or cows in charge of the aged or laborers and the adventurous ones go to secure more comfort and game and trade, as your ships go to the seas for oils and to Canton . . . for teas and silks. And withal, egress and return wear off grievances, local animosities are assuaged and happier life is secured. Were it not for the trips "to Buffalo" it is probable that the Nez Perces war had been of earlier date and a much bloodier one. The great war chiefs of the West, Aeneas, Jutraikan, and others, never went to Buffalo nor one in a hundred of their people, and I learn that the monsters of New York and Paris and London never ran buffalo at all. The white man may shift the causes as he pleases flattering his one-sided, crucifying, and crucified Christianity, but the design, the determination, the fang, the aspiration, the continent are in his own head.

HOSTILE RELIGIONS

Again, we see it advocated through the public papers to open the reservations. A most fallacious suggestion. If a farmer has his rails, the reservation lines are the Indian's fence. What we do want is ampler reservations and true knowledge and thrift and expansion of our little inventive powers; material aid given for material wealth and a great country taken from us; true sympathy and cheer instilled and just freedom to go and come as you would have yourself. But the mere story that a snake spoke to a woman somewhere; that a medicine man went up a mountain somewhere . . . that a married maid had a child in a stable; that he took all the people from hell . . . these old sayings are of little avail to the Red man. He has many such pages himself. But I am not going to startle you with a recital of them at present.

THE NEZ PERCES' RESOLVE

Coming to our own times . . . and to stern reality, you may like to hear the last words of the Nez Perces when their resolve had been taken and the burning expressions on their brains hung smothered on their lips. They said: "It is thus done. This is our dust. Here is our home. The white man takes it from us. Who took it shall not keep it. He will enter the earth with us. Those who come after them will take it and will not be disturbed."

—*THE NEW NORTH-WEST, Deer Lodge, M.T.*
June 7, 1878

JUST NORTH OF Helena his horse shies at a diamondback and throws him against a wall of rock. While she's slicing her hooves at the snake, Duncan draws his revolver and turns it into belt skin. Then he feels his ribs and tries not to gasp at each painful breath. Prone in the heat he wonders what type of man would send him on so strange a mission. He touches his vest pocket; the letter with its impressive wax seal is still there. James H. Mills of the *New North-West* wears several hats, like most of these new men: printer, miner, editor, territorial secretary. His interest in the Nez Perce is a mystery—and a miracle.

When Duncan is set upon at Milk River by a little band of Blackfeet and Gros Ventres, he wonders why he thought it a good idea to come all this way dressed like a soyapo. There's nowhere to go when they whirl around him brandishing guns, and he has to shout, signing to them to back the hell off, wincing as he twists to smack two youngsters lunging at his saddlebags. "Government business," he snarls at the head man, and they fall back.

It's a contingent of American soldiers that really gets his dander up though—blue tunics appearing like an inkblot on the land. He's only twenty miles from the border when he runs into them heading south.

The nimíipuu were almost this close when the army swooped, and White Bird and his people ran. Well, let these bastards try to stop him. He pastes a smile on his face and raises one hand as they draw near. The man in charge doesn't hide his suspicion. Out comes the letter, the waxen seal, the newspaper cuttings as well, to prove he's who he claims to be. Before leaving he interviewed his grandmother and Eagle from the Light and wrote some preliminary stories setting out the history of it all. Here's his name in capital letters at the top. It makes him feel both proud and horribly naked. It's a risk these days to call attention to yourself: the country is still too sore, seething with vigilantes and roadmen, and now, soldiers.

This captain, meanwhile, eyes his clippings like they're forged.

"Heading to Fort Walsh," Duncan repeats, as they shift in their saddles. "On the trail of some Nez Perce," casually he adds.

The commander squints. "Funny. Just took a couple of those redskins up."

"Across the line?"

The officer nods, with a mean little smile. "Looks like you might be too late." He's large and blond with a big mustache like Custer. Duncan is more than glad now of his white shirt, hat, and tie. "Word is they want to surrender, that's why we took those captives up."

"Is that so." Duncan keeps his face blank. He doesn't know, he says; he's only just come up from Helena. Privately he plans to learn what he can at the Canadian fort then head east to where White Bird is supposedly camped with Sitting Bull. He holds his hand out for the clippings and touches a finger to the brim of his hat. "So long, then," he says and reins his way past. He feels their eyes on his back, but they let him go. He could get to like this feeling, he thinks with a little spurt of joy: free agent, beholden to no one, running around gathering information. At least this way no one can claim he's a spy for either side.

He breathes easier once he passes the stone cairn marking the boundary. Fort Walsh is just another forty miles. He'll state his business to the North-West Mounted Police, for his own protection. The British still run things here; Canada is still Grandmother's Country, though the Hudson's Bay Company is no longer in charge. Still, there's something looser, friendlier, about Her Majesty's constables than the Yanks. Half of them, of course, are Scots.

What are the odds, he asks himself when he spies the tracks. Four sets of hoofprints by a stream flowing out of the hills to his left, just a couple of miles before Fort Walsh. These prints are headed east; he sees a pile of dung still steaming. Three captives, the soldiers said. He plunges across the creek into a wood and smells the sweat of horses ahead. Only when they break from the tree line can he see them. Then he just laughs to himself, trying to figure out how to get their attention without getting shot. He cups his hands and shouts, "God Save the Queen!"

The Mountie turns like a shot, the three captives too. He'd better get used to having rifles pointed at him, Duncan thinks as he saunters out from beneath the trees.

Then the Mountie's grinning and slapping his impossibly white trousers, kicking his shiny black boots. "What the devil. McDonald." He kicks his bay close and grabs Duncan's bridle. "A friend," he tosses back to the three warriors, hunched uneasily on their big army horses.

"Ta'c halaxp," Duncan says. *Good afternoon.* They look at him as if he's a ghost. The largest is a handsome man he thinks he might have seen at the Lolo council.

"What in blazes brings you here?" The Mountie is a colonel Duncan met last year while packing goods to the mines.

"Might ask you the same." He pulls out his paper proof. "Meet the correspondent of the *New North-West*, here to track down the notorious White Bird and his band."

"Well, I'll be damned." Colonel Irvine has a thin, off-kilter face, one eye lower than the other. "That's just where I'm taking these gentlemen."

NEVER DID HE imagine he'd wind up translating American demands to the refugee Nez Perce. But his arrival is convenient. Irvine starts by asking if he'll help him get a message to White Bird. That chief isn't with Sitting Bull, the Mountie says; he's hunting to the north with the rest of Crazy Horse's band.

"You heard, of course." Irvine speaks quietly as they jog along. Crazy Horse, the greatest of Lakota warriors, was killed in prison after the Sioux were finally whipped.

"Indian prisoners frequently die in American jails." Duncan doesn't try to hide his disgust. They glance at the constable's charges. They, too, are prisoners—at Fort Leavenworth, where they've been held since surrendering with Chief Joseph. When they halt for the night Duncan sits beside them at the fire. He asks them their names and is shocked when the big man answers "Yellow Bull."

"The father of Red Moccasin Tops?" One of the three youths who started the war, along with Walitze, nephew of Eagle from the Light.

"I was."

There's a look of such pain on his face Duncan quails. Why should he pry? Expose their pain, just for the entertainment of the whites? "I'm sorry," he mutters.

"He was killed in battle." Yellow Bull stares fixedly at the fire. "At the place of the ground squirrels."

Duncan has seen their bodies, maybe even handled them, in the churned mud of the Big Hole. He takes a ragged breath. They can't have died for nothing; their lives and deaths must be of some account. He must do what he's here to do: collect each name, each story, as well as he is able. He touches this father's shoulder. "We'll remember them all."

The prisoners tell him the only thing they know is that they're to tell White Bird how Joseph fares. One is from Joseph's band, the other followed Looking Glass.

"I, too, am of his clan," Duncan says.

"He was killed at the very last moment," the man says. "The last to be shot."

Duncan sees again the proud face, the thin gray eyes. Such waste, such a futile, terrible chase.

When they ride into the hunting camp, he's struck immediately by how the people react. There are shouts of astonishment at the sight of the three captives, then immediate shrinking and fear at the officer who leads them in his bright red tunic. Duncan has never seen such frightened people. Even here, under the relative protection of the Lakotas, the nimíipuu are poised for attack, for flight, he thinks; entirely shattered.

White Bird rises, frowning, when they step in. He's greatly changed. He is bowed now, his mouth set in a bar of utter weariness.

"Uncle," Duncan says, but Irvine has already started speaking. "Tell him we're honored to see him and bring him some friends."

Duncan signs the words. Even before he finishes, he feels the air stirring at his back. Within instants several men, then more and more slip in to surround the chief until they're crammed elbow to elbow and there's scarcely room to breathe.

"You won't take me to prison," White Bird says, and Irvine shoots a look at Duncan. "No, no, not at all. We come as friends. The British policeman has no fight with you." The spit dries in Duncan's throat. Every face is grim: slashed and badly healed and hard with all the horrors of the war. "We're here on business."

"What business?" White Bird's voice remains hard.

"Something to discuss." Duncan glances at Irvine. "We've ridden far, but not so far as Joseph's friends. We should make them welcome first." Irvine nods and reaches for the saddlebag he hauled inside. The men bristle, hands on their carbines, and Duncan signs: "But first a smoke." When he moves toward the chief to greet him properly his path is immediately barred. White Bird pushes the protective arms away. "Maybe my cousin brings news," he says.

"Everything I know, I'll tell."

The policeman offers the twisted roll to the chief and the tension begins to ease.

"Who invited all these people?" White Bird lifts his face toward the smoke hole, his voice amused. "You're taking all my air." He flaps a hand and they melt out as swiftly as they arrived.

"SO, WE'RE EXILES in Grandmother's country after all," the chief says to him late that night, when everyone else has gone. "The way to the north would have been the better way."

They nod grimly at one another. There's nothing else to say.

Neither can quite see why this soyapo wants to know how the Nez Perce war began, and how it ended, and everything in between. It's strange, White Bird says. Duncan agrees. But it's a chance to tell the white men what they did, he says.

Irvine's request is more pressing. The Americans have sent these prisoners to try to convince White Bird to surrender. The chief nods and sends Duncan away. It takes another three days of persuasion before he's convinced he won't be arrested if he goes to Fort Walsh to hear what these Yankees have to say. It smells like a trap. He doesn't know who suggested he's ready to surrender—he's not.

Duncan is familiar with the rules of council. Even so he doesn't like the slowness of this back and forth. Irvine entreats; Duncan signs his increasingly frustrated words. The message isn't Duncan's, yet it issues from his hands and mouth. It only takes one man to mistake messenger for message, if the Bostons prove the liars they have always been. And then the messenger is dead.

It's lucky, in the end, that the Americans have their own translator at Fort Walsh. Within an hour of the meeting's start Duncan grasps their tactics: lies shaped as promises—and when these fail, plain bullying and threats. The Canadians don't want the Nez Perce in their country any more than the Americans do; they have their own Native people to manage. Duncan stands at the back, watching the two sides expound and declaim. White Bird, bent and scarred, turns sometimes to one officer, sometimes the other. In his exile he has somehow managed to salvage his medicine, the gray wing of the eagle; he lifts it now and again to cover his mouth.

How happy he is to know Joseph is alive! His face is illuminated by the truest smile. "I'd like to see him, and back in his own country."

The American is cunning, or thinks he is. "If you here go back to Joseph," he says, "it will be well, you'll go to the same reservation. It may be at your old home, or some other good reservation."

"Joseph was promised that if he surrendered, he'd be taken back to Idaho." White Bird is no longer smiling. "That promise was a lie."

The American starts to speak but White Bird isn't finished. "I was glad when we quit fighting, and here I am with my warriors awaiting news. If the Government sends Joseph back to his home in Idaho, I'll go back at once and make peace."

"But you've already said you wanted to surrender. You sent word to Joseph, that's why these warriors came." The American gestures at the three captives.

"I never said that. I don't know who did." He shrugs. "Of course, my people are tired; they want their homes. If Joseph goes back, we'll join him."

"You either come now or not!" Frustrated, the American officer hammers the table between them. Duncan watches with disgust. Do they really take the nimíipuu for such fools? These warriors successfully eluded the US military over a distance of twelve hundred miles, and still they think of them as dupes? He finds himself thinking of Angus, wondering if this was the way Stevens, too, behaved. If this is how it's been through all the years since Stevens rammed these treaties down their throats—Angus petitioning for reason, respect, restraint? How can you reason with such people? In the end they win by brute and overwhelming force. He is not surprised when at the end of that long session he hears White Bird's voice rise in rage.

"My country is this way!" The chief speaks harshly, flinging his arm toward the west. "Joseph is in the wrong direction. The climate and air are not good where he is." Clearly the captives have reported on their terrible imprisonment, how many scores died of disease and starvation outside Fort Leavenworth, how many more in the brutal conditions of the hot Indian Territory where they've been driven.

"Then I'll send to your camp for others who are ready to return."

"I speak for all my people." The chief looks down on him with derision, then turns and gestures at his men. If only they'd all followed this great leader at that fateful turning in the Bitterroot, thinks Duncan. He accompanies them back to the Sandy Hills in near silence. Only once they arrive does he learn what they planned if he returned without the chief. They would have killed him, says Left Hand, patting him on the shoulder.

His tenure among them is delicate, unclear. He understands that they can never trust a man who's even halfway white. He only feels completely safe when he is seated with the chief. Duncan has a purpose, then, a charge that as the days go by feels ever more important. Those months of fighting and flight, of loss and terror, must not be forgotten. If he can tell their story right, describe the deep injustices that pushed them on the warpath, perhaps Americans will understand the wrongs that they inflicted on these people. Perhaps, he even allows himself to hope, they'll let them go back to their homes.

"Just forty miles." Smoke wreaths the chief's deep-sunk eyes. "Forty more miles and all would have been safe."

The medicine line is as real as anything in the world, the divider between life and death.

Turning in each evening, Duncan feels the same way he felt when he first sat with his grandmother and Eagle from the Light. As if he carried a coal from fire to fire in the long-ago time when flint wasn't known—as if he's charged to keep this flame alive. He inquires after each name and battle, every council, every march. He notes the dead and those remaining. They're but a shadow of the people they set out with. From seven hundred they are now sixty-five warriors and forty-five women, several dozen children. Others have recently slipped away from camp, trying to head home. There may be more with Joseph, but no one really knows.

There's such intensity to the hours Duncan spends with the chief and his closest advisers. Bit by bit he understands it's a ritual of grief and mourning, listing the names and places where their loved ones fell. They relive it in all its horror and sorrow. And Duncan McDonald feels so humbled to have been chosen as their witness. For as long as the people have trod this earth, they've told their stories. The Heart of the Monster, Ant and Coyote, their many hunts and battles. If there are still campfires when this is done, the valiant flight of the Nez Perce will be the tale they tell next, for centuries to come.

On the morning he is to leave, White Bird summons him to the edge of the camp and puts his fingers to his mouth and whistles. A tall gray horse looks up, gallops down the hill, and puts his nose in White Bird's palm. This brave creature took him through each battle, the chief says— all those months, those many hundred miles. He also runs well after buffalo if there are any left. He puts the lead in Duncan's hands.

"It is too great a gift." Tears well in Duncan's eyes. How can he not think of Chief Victor and Angus? He understands his old man so much better now.

"To speed my words." The old chief claps him on the back. "The war is done; my people stand for peace. We only want to go back home."

CHAPTER 15

HE RIDES SOUTH through the parched grasses on the great gray horse, the boundary line stretching invisibly to either side. When he passes the stone cairn he thinks of the Royal Engineers, wondering if this too was the way the Scots and English marked their warring kingdoms. Ahead, the plains stretch massive underneath an even bigger sky and he half fancies he can see the whole vast continent, the endless sweep of it from east to west. And, too, the way the white men came in their recorded time to sweep away the people who had been there all those eons without number, pushing wave on wave before them as if sweeping with some giant broom. Where are the Iroquois, the Cherokee, the Shawnee, and the Cheyenne now? And here before him on this very plain, how brutal were their scythes in his own time, these scythes of pure destruction cutting grasses that stood taller than a man and then the people. What of Baker's massacre, Little Bighorn, Sitting Bull, and Crazy Horse; of Eagle Robe and Looking Glass, Big Hole, and the final battle at Bear's Paw? So many warriors crushed—yet not entirely gone.

He didn't ask for it, but it has fallen to him nonetheless to tell their story. What a story, how that valiant people fled, eluding soldiers four long months across the Rocky Mountains of the west, and then at last to fall. He thinks of the great chief John Ross—half Cherokee, half Scots— forced to drive his people from their land. He thinks of his own father Angus. Once he had weight in this world, but no more. Yet was he really impotent? Were any of them? Was it truly futile to resist? Duncan knows how hard it is to blunt that scythe; now he has seen it for himself. But they are stubborn, Indians and Scots—like sage and heather clinging to the rocks. In this tenacity and thirst for justice lies their hope. All they can do is tell it over and over, until the world has ears to hear.

The stories are in his saddlebags; the heat is ferocious. There hasn't been a drop of water for two days. A muddy hole appears, barely enough for two horses much less a man. Duncan sucks the mud; it keeps him going. By the time they hit the ranches north of Helena, he's imagining things. He pictures a farm girl with a bucket of fresh milk but then he sees a shotgun aimed between his eyes and pushes on. He'll be safer in a town—Helena is a big town by now, all full of itself and ready to pitch itself as state capital if this territory ever gets that far. In the center by the courthouse, a pump. He ruins his hat filling it to let the horses slurp, but the gratitude in their eyes is worth it. And it's cool, too, when he puts it back on.

He sees no brown faces and decides to push on. He intended to head to Deer Lodge, but the horses are played out. He'll stop in Missoula instead and send a dispatch. On his way out of Helena he picks up the latest edition of the *New North-West*. It's dated Friday July 26th; his dispatch should be inside. The pleasant feeling freezes. Here, next to his own item, headlined "White Bird Does Not Wish to Surrender," is a dispatch from Peter Ronan to Governor Potts describing the reaction to "murders committed by a band of Nez Perce coming from the North."

Duncan's throat is still so parched he can hardly swallow.

> . . . Nez Perces who came from the North by the way of the north fork of Sun river, murdering as they came along two men at the Dearborn, in Lewis and Clarke county; two men at Deep creek, Bear gulch, Deer Lodge county, and four or five men at the head of Rock creek, in Missoula county, all of which murders were committed in the direct Nez Perces trail from the North to Idaho Territory, known as the Elk City trail.

"When did these murders occur?" he asks the merchant, who looks at him with suspicion.

"Where you been? It's been in the papers a week or more." The merchant circles back behind the counter where he doubtless keeps a pistol.

Duncan sighs and folds the page back, jabbing his finger at his name. "Just like it says. Up in Canada, for the *New North-West*."

The man peers down at the paper then looks back up, studying Duncan, whose hair is long and greasy, like his mustache. A week's stubble cannot obscure the hazelnut color of his skin.

"Don't look much like a McDonald," the fellow finally says, turning his back and moving deeper inside his store.

▰

THE ONLY PATH to the hotel desk is through the saloon, buzzing with the men of Missoula County washing down their Sunday rectitude. No doubt Duncan stinks; he wishes he'd washed off upstream. He nods at old man Worden, Judge Knowles, some farmers who grow barley in the Jocko. They nod back, stiff about the necks and eyes, and he perceives the air around him charged. He pushes through the sense of something hostile toward the brass keys hanging by the desk. As he's signing for the room, he feels a body close behind him.

"Well, if it isn't the great defender of the red man," comes the low, snide voice of the editor of the *Weekly Missoulian*.

He looks down at the smarmy newsman. "You're just jealous Mills got me first."

"I wouldn't print a word of it." Aggression rises off Barbour like a musk. "So busy defending them you can't see what a mockery they make of you. Or else you love them so you'll whitewash murder too. Only Mills would peddle such crap."

The venom takes him momentarily aback. "I don't defend murderers. If you mean these renegades that killed the miners—they ought to get what's coming to them." He reaches his hand for the key. "They're not part of White Bird's band."

"So you claim. But no one really knows."

"Did they catch them?"

Barbour's smile is sour. "On the Clearwater. They got five." His eyes narrow as he glances around. "But you'd know, wouldn't you? How many more of these killers are on their way." Duncan steps away and the newsman follows him into the hallway. "People are saying a breed showed them the way."

"Yes. A fellow called Henry. Ran off with Joseph's daughter and some others. Henry Tabe-bow."

"That's not the name they're saying." Barbour's eye glint in the dimness. "That's not the name I'm hearing on every lip."

349

HE SPENDS THE rest of the day on the lumpy hotel bed, smoking and thinking and writing his dispatch. Hearing noise in the hall he looks out and asks the chambermaid to fetch some food. When the sun finally sets, it's late; he waits to hear the piling of stools and slamming of doors before splashing water on his face and creeping down the stairs. In the stable he checks on his horses, untying his gelding and leading it around the back. He'll be damned if they drive him out with their malicious gossip. He'll ride out, head high, in the fullness of day on White Bird's gray charger, having put his dispatch on the coach himself. Still, it's prudent to take precautions.

In Shacktown he pokes in and out of huts until he finds a likely candidate, a hungry nephew of Red Horn's. "Ride this horse to your uncle, tell him I sent you." The boy's eyes are wide. Duncan puts the reins in his hand, along with two coins. "If I don't show up by noon, he better come looking. Got that? You tell him that." The kid nods vigorously. "Good." He speaks to the horse then, chucking him under the chin. "Home, fella, get home to Sin-ye-le-min."

The morning dawns hot and brilliant, a perfect clear day in late July. His eyes are holes in a blanket and his throat is raw. Methodically he brushes down his trousers and vest, smoothes the wrinkles from his white dress shirt. Maybe he'll even wear a tie. He fishes it out along with his razor, scraping his cussed face as smooth as he can. There's no mirror but he thinks he makes a decent approximation of a Western pioneer as he shoulders his pack and heads down.

The drop for the mail coach is at Bonner and Hammond's. Trust that bastard Andy Hammond to have gotten his name above the door. They haven't spoken for more than a year. Apparently, Andy now styles himself a lumber baron, though here he is waiting on customers.

"Look what the cat dragged in," Duncan says by way of greeting. Hammond has fleshed out considerably; prosperity hangs off him like lard.

"You could always take your business elsewhere."

"Would if I could." He sets down the envelope. "But you seem to have cornered the mail coach as well."

Hammond's smile is ugly. "Can't think of anything I enjoy more than taking your money, Mack."

He'll never forget how Hammond just hung outside his store doing nothing when he and Maggie were attacked. All along Duncan has only been half a man to these people.

"I know what you and your friends are saying." Duncan pins him with all the force in his eyes. "You're a cowardly piece of shit, as you always were."

Hammond sneers. "I'm not saying anything. I'm just listening. None of us likes what we hear. Squaw man. Indian lover. Goddamn accessory to murder."

"See it gets on the 10 o'clock coach," is all he tosses back as he goes out the door.

Even so he's more alert than he has ever been as he swings up on the gray warhorse for the final leg home. Under Chief White Bird this animal has seen things he hopes he never will. His mind is full of the gore and horror of that desperate flight, his notes with camping spots and marches, raids and battles and captives taken. But even as his brain churns, his every sense is attuned to the hills and dusty gullies, the clumps of thirsty cottonwoods that might shield one or more attackers.

He turns north into the Coriacan defilé, sweeping his eyes from side to side, his rifle resting on the pommel. When the alders and pines close in around him, he stops and listens for a long while to the song of the birds and rustling of the creatures of the ground, then moves on. The steady clop of hooves is the only noise until suddenly a branch cracks and leaves rustle to the right, and he's instantly crouched with a bead on the spot before he even knows he's swung down. Sweat pours from his hat and he feels his heart hammer waiting for the shot, imagining bodies swarming at him from all directions. The underbrush parts just long enough for a snout to emerge and sniff, muzzle gleaming—then crash away through the woods, equally terrified at this unexpected encounter.

He laughs a little at himself and relaxes a bit. Another five miles to the agency; he's almost there. At the big rock that forces the trail in a loop around it before dropping to the stream, he finally breathes freely. And this is when they strike. A lasso catches him, expertly, from somewhere high; he barely hears its evil whine as it lashes through the air and drops over his shoulders, tightening almost instantly, sliding up toward his neck. He twists and gets a few shots off, but these go wild, it seems, or maybe one clips, and this only makes them madder. He can see their dark shirts, white faces, too blurred to know for sure, as he's hauled and spun through the air and lands hard, on his left arm, pulled and scraped along the earth until his sight is cut off by a burlap sack jerked over his head.

"Running off to your squaws, Mack? Not so fast." He writhes in pain from a boot to his side. It gets him on the old bruised bone and he cries out.

"No blubbering, now," another says and then his head explodes, bashed by a boot or a rifle butt. He feels the skin split, tastes the salt of blood escaping from his forehead.

"For Christ's sake," he tries to shout. He can't tell if he even makes a sound. "Get your goddamn hands off, I haven't done a thing to you."

"That's what you think," says the first voice, and he's kicked again, the rope tightening so he nearly strangles, his hand rising instinctively to get between the rope and his skin. But they seize it roughly and bind both arms behind his back and he knows now that he must not move, he must not do anything but wait and think and breathe as shallowly as he can. He can't see a bloody thing.

"That's your trouble, breed, you think you're just like us. When you're nothing—you're scum, you're squaw shit."

"All high and mighty while your precious redskins rampage, thieving and killing."

He strains to recognize their voices but can't. It could be any of them, any one of those white men he bought from, greeted, shopped alongside. He knows he's dead, then.

"I didn't have a thing to do with those murders." He tries to speak as clearly as he can with the blood in his mouth. "It wasn't anything to do with me."

"Like hell. Goddamn Injun lover showed them how to sneak through here."

"I didn't." As if Indians needed anyone to lead them, he is still capable of thinking. "I'm as sore as you at those killers."

"Sure you are." He hears a match flare. "We got a special tree for breeds. Eh, Mack?" It's the taunting vicious one. "One up by the fork, pretty view and all." They guffaw.

"Naw," says another. "Not while it's light. Let's find one closer."

352

They start dragging him off the trail; he feels the scratch of oak leaves and wonders suddenly what's happened to his horse. He can't remember hearing hoofbeats; he'll be sick if they shot it. After a hundred yards or so they drop him like a sack and he hears the muffled sounds of a stick tapping, testing maybe the strength of certain branches. One must be a crack cowhand to lasso like that, he's thinking and praying with a thin and withering hope that somehow his message reached Red Horn. They're still arguing when he feels a sudden chill, and senses through the rough mesh that it's growing dark.

It cannot possibly be night already. He hears muttering as they come back.

"Creeping Christ, what the hell?"

"Shut up. Grab his arms." They pull him roughly to sitting and the first one, holding his arms like a doll's says, "Jesus, will you look at that?"

"What on earth?" another says.

"Don't any of you sonofabitches read? That's all they've been talking about for weeks, the goddamned eclipse."

"Convenient," another laughs as they manhandle him up a rise. Duncan makes himself as heavy as possible, scrabbling in his mind for a way out. If only he could see. It's getting even colder—darker too. Maybe when it's totally dark he can somehow twist away. A small irrational boyish wish comes to his heart. He has always wanted to see an eclipse of the sun.

Beyond his scratchy cowl the air grows dimmer and colder as he's hauled across rough ground, then roots. Out of that gathering darkness comes a bellowing voice he has never loved more.

"Get your mitts off him." Baird. "Get 'em off, or these Indians will blow 'em off."

Silence then and heavy sour breathing in his ears.

"You heard me. Ten warriors have you in their sights. They'd love to shoot your stinking faces off." Duncan hears a slight rustling that might, indeed, be braves melting from the trees.

A cold hard barrel is shoved hard against his skull. "Another step and it's his head that goes."

"He's not the one you want," Baird continues evenly.

One barks an evil laugh. "He's good enough to hang, the meddlesome prick."

Then there's a sharp crack and he hears a howl of pain just above him, the gun slipping from his neck, and he rolls, covering his head as best he can with his bound arms. Bullets are screaming all around him, pattering into the ground, hitting flesh. He hears bodies fall and whoops and galloping and then nothing for the longest instant of his life. Until the bag is lifted gently off his head, and he looks up into the face of Baird and, just behind him, Quil-see—and behind them both, an enormous black hole punched out of the dark gray sky.

Instinctively he shields his eyes. "Quil-see," he breathes, and she's wiping blood from his face with her sleeve.

When he looks again the black hole is encircled by a flaming crown and the woods and grasses and leaves have all turned platinum, drained of color, each blade and branch a brittle outline, tintype sharp. Everything is charred—alien, black, and freezing cold. It feels as if the world has died—or else he has. His heart is wrung with horror.

This is how the white man kills the earth: this is their annihilation of the living world.

"Red Hart," he hears and turns his head to sparks of brilliant pain, and as he looks, he sees his wife's face lightening, regaining color as the dark disc slips and moves with incredible speed across the sky.

"My sun, my moon," he whispers. Her tears are hot on his cheeks. How badly is he wounded? He tries to reach up, but his arms won't move. Baird sits him gently up and cuts the cords that bind him. The air warms as the light strengthens, and he understands that it was just the moon greeting the sun in her passing. He looks around in wonder. Two of his captors lie dead in the dust. The others have fled south, pursued by the warriors. Mutely he gestures at White Bird's horse, patiently waiting by a tree.

"You found him," he whispers.

"He found us."

Red Horn returns then, along with three young Pend d'Oreille, smiling and slapping each other's hands. He kneels and parts Duncan's hair, probing the gash.

"Hard head," he grins. It was Quil-see who saved him, he adds: his wife who flung the rock that spun the gun away. She smiles, but her eyes are worried. They get him up on the gray horse, Red Horn holding him like a bundle against his chest, Quil-see and Baird flanking them, and he wants to say something about how times have changed but nothing comes and all goes black.

▰

WHEN HE AWAKES, he's at home at Post Creek and they're all clustered around his bed. He's surrounded: mother and father and sister and brothers and wife and baby child. His head is a bandaged gourd, but he is alive. His parents sit to one side, faces somber, hands heavy on his limbs beneath the blankets. He tries to smile at the two of them: together, then apart, then together again, as always. How improbable their life. They were always in exile, fighting for their place in this world. Whereas this is his place: this land is his flesh, his blood.

Catherine holds baby Mary on one side of the bed while her son's wife sits on the other, stroking Duncan's face. This son of hers will survive; this grandchild will be the first of many, the continuation of the world as it was made before. They will come in waves, like the sea, across the generations. This baby has her mother Margaret's eyes.

Duncan waggles a hand at his child and looks at his father. He'll have to keep banging on endlessly too, like Angus. He wants to tell him that at last he understands. There's nothing else that they can do but keep on telling it, until the soyapo themselves transform.

Angus prays for them all in his heathen way. The Native people were the ones who were Here Before Christ, of course—long before. And will still be here, long after the passion for Christ has faded away. Eclipsed like the sun, he thinks—but only for a time, until the darkness slides away, the light regains its rightful place.

I'm still here. Duncan smiles at his wife. *We're right here*, she seems to answer, squeezing his hand as he closes his eyes.

Acknowledgments and Sources

THIS NOVEL IS based on the true story of Angus McDonald, the brother of my great-great-great-grandfather Duncan McDonald. It is drawn from McDonald family records and letters, accounts of the Nez Perce war, treaties between the United States and Native American tribes, and nineteenth-century newspaper accounts. In creating the fictional tale of one family caught in the crossfire of westward colonial expansion, I have altered some dates and situations. Any mistakes are my own.

Before listing sources, I wish to acknowledge the tremendous friendship and support extended to me by my distant cousins on the Flathead Indian Reservation in Montana. Without the encouragement and advice of tribal and clan elders, this tale of a Scots Indian family could not have been written. I wish to thank particularly the direct descendants of Angus and Catherine for their kindness and help: Dr. Joe McDonald and the late Sherrie McDonald; Wyman and Thelma McDonald; Dr. Luana Ross; Julie Cajune; Ellen Swaney; Maggie Goode; and Eric Wilson. I was further assisted by members of the Fort Connah Restoration Society; Robert Bigart, historian at Salish Kootenai College; the late David "Chalk" Courchane; and the staffs of the Mansfield Library at the University of Montana, Montana Historical Society, and University of Washington Library. In Scotland I was delighted to discuss the McDonald legacy with Dr. James Hunter, renowned historian of the Highlands whose *Scottish Highlanders, Indian Peoples: Thirty Generations of a Montana Family* (1996)—a close study of our Montana McDonalds—was essential to this project. I am also grateful for detailed family research conducted by my brother, Dr. Stuart Christie, and my English cousins Ann and Andrew Reed.

Heartfelt thanks to the Lucas Artists Residency Program of the Montalvo Arts Center in Saratoga, California, for a writers' residency at which much of this novel was written, and my stellar agents Simon Trewin and Dan Mandel. My family—those who are gone and those who remain to

tend the future, including my brothers, nieces, husband, and children—
has constantly inspired me to celebrate this shared history.

I am indebted to the Nez Perce Tribal Executive Committee and the
Séliš-Qlispé Culture Committee for granting me formal approval to pursue
this project. In researching the nimíipuu story of Catherine Baptiste, I was
first pointed toward her cousin Eagle from the Light by Josiah Pinkham
of the Nez Perce. Allen Pinkham Sr., his father and a former tribal chair-
man, reviewed the manuscript and suggested improvements. I also relied
on many authoritative histories of the nimíipuu, including: *Noon Nee-Me-
Poo (We, the Nez Perces): Culture and History of the Nez Perces* by Allen P.
Slickpoo Sr. (1973); *Nez Percé Texts* by Archie Phinney (1934); *Hear Me, My
Chiefs!: Nez Perce Legends and History* (1984) and *Yellow Wolf: His Own Story*
(1940) by Lucullus McWhorter; *The Nez Perce Indians and the Opening of the
Northwest* by Alvin M. Josephy Jr. (1987); *Nez Perce Summer, 1877: The US
Army and the Nee-Me-Poo Crisis* (1977) and *Beyond Bear Paw: The Nez Perce
Indians in Canada* (2010) by Jerome A. Green; *Chief Joseph & the Flight of the
Nez Perce: The Untold Story of an American Tragedy* by Kent Nerburn (2005);
and *Nez Perce Women in Transition, 1877–1990* by Caroline James (1996).

For descriptions of mixed-race families in the fur trade, I dived into
the records and history of the Hudson's Bay Company in Manitoba,
as well as more recent scholarship, including *Traders' Tales: Narratives
of Cultural Encounters in the Columbia Plateau, 1807–1846* by Elizabeth
Vibert (1997); *Strangers in Blood: Fur Trade Company Families in Indian
Country* by Jennifer S. H. Brown; *Many Tender Ties* by Sylvia Van Kirk
(1980); *Empires, Nations and Families: A New History of the American
West, 1800–1860* by Anne F. Hyde (2012); and "Fort Colvile's Fur Trade
Families and the Dynamics of Race in the Pacific Northwest" by Jean
Barman and Bruce M. Watson, in *Pacific Northwest Quarterly* (1990).

Nearly all the historical events depicted in this novel occurred as described. For purposes of the story, I occasionally placed characters at
events where they may not have actually been. Where there is evidence for
Catherine, Angus, or Duncan's actions in the story, I have noted it below.

BOOK 1: PRO PELLE CUTEM: A SKIN FOR A SKIN

Catherine Baptiste dictated the story of her trapping trip down the Colorado River to her husband Angus. An excerpt was printed as "An Indi-

an Girl's Story of a Trading Expedition to the Southwest about 1841" in *Sources of Northwest History*, State University of Montana, 1930; a full transcript was made by Steve Anderson, author of "Angus McDonald of the Great Divide." Catherine specifically described the markings and song of the little bird she saw on that trip; for this reason I imagined it as her *wyakin*, her guardian animal spirit. Her biography is based on family genealogical research. Her mother, Margaret de Naie, was the daughter of a chief and a great-aunt of Looking Glass the younger, according to notes written by Angus; Catherine herself was a cousin of Eagle from the Light, according to their daughter Christina ("The Daughter of Angus MacDonald," by Christina MacDonald McKenzie Williams, *Washington Historical Quarterly*, 1922). Duncan McDonald indicated in articles for the *New North-West* that he was a relative of both White Bird and Looking Glass the Younger.

Angus McDonald wrote copiously in his HBC ledgers, one of which is preserved in the Mansfield Library. He wrote stories of buffalo and cougar hunts, experiences on the trail, and poems in high romantic style. In retirement he wrote a reminiscence titled "A Few Items of the West," published posthumously in the *Washington Historical Quarterly* in 1917. His career in the HBC is amply documented, as is that of his great-uncle Archibald McDonald. The story of poaching that precipitated Angus's 1838 flight from the Highlands came down through three separate branches of our family, descended from both Angus and his brother Duncan, my own direct ancestor. Angus and Catherine were in fact married four times: Their grandson Joseph McDonald reported a first marriage by "tribal custom," which I imagined in the summer before their arrival at Fort Hall, presided over by Catherine's uncle Apash Wyakaikt (Flint Necklace), a signatory to the 1855 Nez Perce treaty with the US government. The second marriage by Richard Grant is documented by their daughter Christina; the two subsequent Jesuit marriages are proven by mission records.

At Fort Hall, Grant and McDonald welcomed numerous emigrants on the Oregon Trail. Angus even drew them a map showing the way to the Cascades. Joe Meek and other mountain men wintered nearby, according to Hunter. Angus was famous for playing his bagpipes at any opportunity; his set survived for another two generations at the family home near Fort Connah.

The original name of the Clearwater village of Looking Glass near present-day Kooskia, Idaho, was "Clean Water": Kaix-kaix-Koose in nimíipuuimt, the Nez Perce language, according to an online discussion by Otis Halfmoon. Che Wana (Big River) is the name some Columbia Plateau people use for the Columbia River, according to McWhorter. The Heart of the Monster earthen cone stands today on the north shore of the Clearwater between Kamiah, Idaho, and Kooskia; the story is related in many places, including a Salish version told by Duncan McDonald.

Few are aware of the role of the Hudson's Bay Company in ransoming the captives taken during the Whitman massacre of 1847. I placed Angus at the scene due to his friendship with Joe Meek, whose daughter Helen was captured and died of measles following the attack. The actual timeline and location of events differs slightly from that presented here. A full account of the negotiations leading to the surrender are in *Peter Skene Ogden and the Hudson's Bay Company* by Gloria Griffen Kline (1974).

Angus and Father Ravalli had a lifelong friendship; the activities of the Jesuits in the Pacific Northwest are detailed in *The Jesuits and the Indian Wars of the Northwest* by Robert Burns, SJ (1967).

BOOK 2: BOSTONS

Isaac Stevens and George McClellan stayed at Fort Colvile for several days in October 1853. Angus related the visit in "A Few Items of the West," while McClellan and Stevens both mentioned the Scots trader's hospitality in journals and memoirs.

Catherine's full sister Kyuka, sometimes called "Elizabeth the Witch," was a renowned medicine woman who called down weather and could locate buffalo on behalf of the hunters. See *I Will Be Meat for My Salish: The Montana Writers Project and the Buffalo of Flat Head Reservation* by Bon Whealdon (2002). She is buried at Fort Connah. "East Country Boy" is a traditional Nez Perce story. *Yox K'aló* (alternatively spelled *waco qalo*) means "That's all" and is the traditional ending for most tales. All nimíipuu words are taken from indigenouspeople.net/nezperce, compiled by Glenn Welker, or www.nimipuutimt.org.

My characterization of Chief Factor James Douglas is rather critical, as Angus's view of his superior might have been during the Yakama war (though the two men were close friends later in life). Douglas resigned his commission as Chief Factor for the Hudson's Bay Company in 1858, upon his appointment as the first Governor of the Crown Colony of British Columbia.

Chief Eagle from the Light was initially the main Nez Perce spokesman at the Council of Walla Walla between the northwest tribes and Isaac Stevens in early June 1855, until the belated arrival of Chief Flint Necklace (Looking Glass the Elder). Angus McDonald was not in attendance, but I have imagined the report his wife's cousin might have given him on the margins of the council. These are based on speeches of Native participants at the treaty council, as related in *Hear Me, My Chiefs, Lewis and Clark through Indian Eyes: Nine Indian Writers on the Legacy of the Expedition* (2007) and *The Nez Perce Indians and the Opening of the Northwest* (1997), both by Alvin M. Josephy Jr. Eagle from the Light eventually signed the treaty, but many others did not; the resulting split in the Nez Perce tribe was bitter and has left a rift that still exists today.

HBC clerk Edward Huggins reported the colorful arrival of Angus McDonald with his fur brigade from Fort Colvile to Fort Nisqually in 1854, republished much later in the HBC's *The Beaver* magazine. According to Huggins, Angus ran afoul of the Yakama warrior Qualchen on a return journey, either that summer or a year or two later. The news report raising suspicions of HBC collusion with the Natives appeared in the Olympia newspaper in 1857, at the height of the Yakama war. Chief Kamiakin's demand for guns in exchange for horses was described by Angus in "A Few Items of the West." Kamiakin's defeat and the guarded response of the other buffalo hunting tribes to his catastrophe are described on historylink.org.

A full history of the events of February 13, 1692, is in *Glencoe: The Story of the Massacre* by John Prebble (1968). Angus McDonald and his siblings trace their ancestry directly through their grandmother Margaret McDonald of the Glencoe McDonalds to her grandfather, John, who escaped the slaughter as a boy of twelve.

The Corps of Royal Engineers took a series of photographs known as the Northwest Boundary Survey Photographs between 1857 and 1861, and during 1860–1861 established their winter camp forty miles north of Fort Colvile on the Pend d'Oreille River. The engineers photographed

Angus McDonald, daughter Christina, and baby son Alexander, along with Catherine's half-brother, "Red Ox" Bigknife.

The discovery of gold at both Colvile and Connah is described by Angus in "A Few Items of the West." The gold discovery on the Clearwater at Orofino in 1860 and the subsequent Thief Treaty of 1863 are detailed in "Hear Me, My Chiefs!" and in "The Nez Perce Indians and the Opening of the Northwest." In the wake of this huge gold rush, a faction of the tribe signed the 1863 treaty that reduced the Nez Perce Reservation to one-tenth its original size.

According to Duncan, his elder brother John died of blood poisoning from a knife cut.

An account of the final negotiations between the United States and the Hudson's Bay Company is contained in the "British and American Joint Commission on the Hudson's Bay and Puget Sound Agricultural Companies Claims," Victoria, Vancouver Island, August 1, 1865, with commentary by Angus McDonald in his "A Few Items of the West."

BOOK 3: THE SHINING MOUNTAINS

All newspaper excerpts are taken from published accounts in a variety of Montana newspapers from the 1870s, found online at www.chroniclingamerica.loc.gov and in the Montana Historical Society in Helena.

Duncan McDonald's life is documented in a 2016 volume by Robert Bigart and Joseph McDonald, *Duncan McDonald: Flathead Indian Reservation Leader and Cultural Broker, 1849–1937*, published by Salish Kootenai College Press. More personal information was derived from a series of letters he wrote to Lucullus McWhorter in the late 1920s, and his own eloquent writing in the Nez Perce war articles he published between 1878 and 1879 in the *New North-West* newspaper of Deer Lodge, Montana. His sense of his own identity is clear from a remark he made in 1928 to McWhorter: "I'm in the same box as Kaiser Wilhelm II," who had a British mother and a German father. The Germans, Duncan wrote, "cursed him that he is too much of pro British because his mother was British and the British hate him that he was too much of a German. . . . This is my predicament."

I consulted many sources and family members to understand the history of the Bitterroot Salish, Kootenai, and Pend d'Oreille (Qlispé) on the Flathead Reservation. They include *I Will Be Meat for My Salish*; *Challenge to Survive: History of the Salish Tribes of the Flathead Reservation* by the Tribal History Project, Salish Kootenai College (2008); *Getting Good Crops: Economic and Diplomatic Survival Strategies of the Montana Bitterroot Salish Indians, 1870–1891* by Robert Bigart (2010); *To Be Women and Salish: The Biographies of Sack Woman, Iorena Burgess, Agnes Vandeburg, & Oshanee Kenmille* by Jennifer Finley and Sarah Bennett, Salish Kootenai College (2013); *"Honoring Native Women's Voices,"* Tribal History Project, Salish Kootenai College (2006); *A Historical Sketch of the Flathead Indian Nation: Ye Olden Days* by Major Peter Ronan (1890); and *The Surrounded* by Darcy McNickle (1978).

Robert McGregor Baird was a teacher, clerk, and prospector later hired to instruct the Ronan children. James Mills, editor and publisher of the *New North-West*, "was told to give the job" of reporting on the Nez Perce in Canada to Duncan McDonald, according to a letter Duncan wrote to McWhorter. Angus may have suggested this: he wrote to Judge Knowles in August 1878 that the job "required more time and means than he [Angus] had." Accordingly, the first installments were written "initially by Duncan and then prepared somewhat by Baird and Gregg" (Omar Gregg, a printer at St. Ignatius mission).

I took the liberty of inventing a failed romance with a white schoolteacher, partly based on *Montana Memories: The Life of Emma McGee in the Rocky Mountain West* by Ida Patterson (2012). Family records show that Duncan McDonald married Louise "Quil-see" (or Quil-soo-ee) Red Sleep Schumtah in traditional fashion around 1873; they were wed in a Catholic ceremony on May 6, 1875, the same day their daughter Mary was born. They were married for fifty-six years and survived the loss of both children, Mary at age four of measles and John Colvile "Col," at age twenty of unknown causes. Duncan was close lifelong friends with a Pend d'Oreille man named Joseph Que-que-sah, also known as Joe Redhorn, after whom I modeled the fictional character of Red Horn.

The historical role of Nez Perce Chief Eagle from the Light (Tipyehlene Kaupu) is ambiguous and reflects the difficult choices facing every Native leader in this period. Angus refers to him in an 1878 letter to Knowles ("a close relative of my wife and most eloquent savage"). At times this chief advocated war against whites; at others he attempted to calm the situation through reason and compromise. Beyond his speech at the 1855 treaty council with Isaac Stevens, several documentary traces of his life survive, including in a history of the Weiser Indians. His appeal to the government after the Nez Perce war was transcribed by Peter Ronan in his autobiography *In Ye Olden Times*.

Attempts to remove Duncan McDonald from trading on the reservation began during the tenure of Agent Charles Medary, who in February 1877 wrote to the Commissioner of Indian Affairs requesting permission to remove "troublemakers" who were Colvile and Nez Perce Indians, especially Duncan and Angus McDonald. His successor, Peter Ronan, also wrote to his superiors requesting clarification of Duncan's status, as he was not then adopted into the confederated Flathead tribes, though he and the rest of the family would be later. See *A Great Many of Us Have Good Farms: Agent Peter Ronan Reports on the Flathead Reservation, 1877–1887* by Robert Bigart (2014). That fateful July of 1877, Duncan was severely criticized for selling four thousand rounds of ammunition to the tribes. See James Hunter, *Scottish Highlanders, Indian Peoples: Thirty Generations of a Montana Family* (1997).

Chief Victor of the Bitterroot Salish bequeathed his favorite war horse to Angus McDonald; it was delivered by Victor's widow Agnes after his death, according to 1870 newspaper reports. The roundup of the last wild mustangs on what was then called Wild Horse Island in Flathead Lake (Broad Water) occurred around 1870, according to a story Duncan told in 1887.

Fort Connah officially closed in summer 1872, according to *Fort Connah: A Page in Montana's History* by Jeanne O'Neill and Riga Winthrop (2002). "Alouette" was a traditional French voyageur rowing song. For a complete history of Fort Connah, see www.fortconnah.org.

Conflict over allowing Native Americans to hunt across their ancestral grounds, as expressly guaranteed in the 1855 treaties, only sharpened after Custer's 1876 defeat at the Little Bighorn. At different times the Army limited their arms to antiquated muskets and/or required them to travel under Army escort. See "Going to Buffalo," William E. Farr, *Montana: The Magazine of Western History* (2003). Grass fires set by Native peoples for wildland management were also a source of conflict with settlers, according to Ronan's letters and news reports from the 1870s.

It's clear the McDonalds at Fort Connah/Post Creek played some role in the fateful decision of the Nez Perce to go south rather than north after emerging from the Lolo Pass. Camille Williams, a Nez Perce historian, told McWhorter that Angus "sent Duncan to the Nez Perce camp" to try to convince the tribe to go north to Canada rather than south and east to their allies among the Crow tribe. Margaret de Naie allegedly argued for the southern route to the plains; Eagle from the Light's advice remains unclear. According to Williams, he told Looking Glass to go south, while Hunter believes he advocated for the northern route. For his part, Duncan claimed he did not attend the council, saying he was told of it by Left Hand, the brother of Eagle from the Light. Some, however, suspect he did indeed meet with the Nez Perce as depicted in this novel, at the Bitterroot Valley spot now designated as the Looking Glass State Recreation Area.

Jack (T .J.—Telesphore Jacques) DeMers was a French Canadian merchant, cattleman, and hauler married to a Pend d'Oreille woman whose establishment formed the heart of Frenchtown. This entrepreneur wielded considerable power in early Missoula and the Mission Valley. Though charming and friendly, he was one of Duncan's chief rivals for trade on the reservation.

I drew on many accounts of the battle of Big Hole and its aftermath, including exhibits at the battlefield site, part of the Nez Perce National Historical Park, *Battle of Big Hole: The Story of the Landmark Battle of the 1877 Nez Perce War* by Aubrey L. Haines and Calvin Haines (2006), and the annual commemorative ceremony of the Nez Perce tribe. Contemporary news accounts mention the scalping of fallen nimíipuu by General Howard's Bannock scouts; in 1928 letters to McWhorter, Duncan describes the mauling of the graves by animals, an account confirmed by a Methodist minister passing the battlefield that autumn, cited in the account of the war by General O. O. Howard: *In Pursuit of the Nez Perces: The Nez Perce War of 1877*, edited by Linwood Laughy (1993).

Duncan partially recounted his trip to Canada to interview Chief White Bird to McWhorter. His role as interpreter for Colonel Irvine of the North-West Mounted Police and the US Army representative is taken from Duncan's dispatches in the *New North-West* and more significantly from *Beyond Bear's Paw: The Nez Perce Indiana in Canada* by Jerome Greene (2010). Both cite White Bird's gift to Duncan of his warhorse, a touching detail that recalls Chief Victor's gift of his warhorse to Duncan's father. The murder of multiple miners by Nez Perce Indians returning home to Idaho from exile in Canada was reported thoroughly by all the newspapers of the day.

Angus made a cryptic remark in an August 1878 letter to Knowles about "that malicious report" made to Ronan against Duncan; this report "was hawked by a clique of low villains whose greatest pleasure would be to see Duncan McDonald out of the way. No doubt the root of that tree is in Frenchtown and having its branches on the Jocko it would do anything to ruin him."

There was, in fact, a total eclipse of the sun visible across all of Montana on July 29, 1878.

After the fleeing Nez Perce evaded the US Army across nearly twelve hundred miles of present-day Idaho, Wyoming, and Montana, Chief Joseph surrendered on behalf of his band at the Battle of Bear Paw just forty miles south of the international border, referred to by Native peoples as the "medicine line." He was never allowed to resettle in his homeland of the Wallowa Valley, which today lies in the state of Oregon. Chief Looking Glass was the last person killed in that battle; Chief White Bird escaped to Canada with members of his band and was killed some years later there. Former Chief Eagle from the Light remained on the Flathead Reservation alongside the McDonald clan, petitioning the US government for the resettlement of his people in Montana. This request was never granted. At least one hundred Nez Perce men, women, and children were killed during the 1877 war.

Angus and Catherine McDonald lived long and fruitful lives and are buried in the family cemetery at Fort Connah. Their many descendants are members of the Confederated Salish and Kootenai tribes in Montana and the Nez Perce tribe in Idaho. Duncan McDonald had a successful career as a hotelier, trader, rancher, orchardist, entrepreneur, and tribal spokesman, though he lost most of his money in the stock market crash of 1929. He died at the age of eighty-eight and is buried alongside his wife Louise "Quil-see" Schumtah in St. Ignatius.

Fort Connah today is the oldest surviving structure in the state of Montana. It still stands proudly in the magnificent valley of Sin-ye-le-min, beneath the Shining Mountains, as a living monument to this multicultural period in American history